'So,' she said ust want
something
prepared t
Derbyshir

'I do,' he said

Something in his sultry tone kick-st
feelings Livvy had repressed for longer than
she cared to remember, and for a split second
she allowed herself to imagine what it would
feel like to be the object of desire to a man like
Saladin Al Mektala. Would those flinty eyes
soften before he kissed you? Would a woman
feel *helpless* if she was being held in arms as
obviously powerful as his?

She swallowed, surprised by the path her
thoughts had taken, and justifying their
erotic trajectory by reminding herself that he
was being deliberately provocative. He had
made that statement in such a way—as if he
was seeking to shock her—that she would
have defied *any* woman not to have started
entertaining fantasies about him.

The Bond of Billionaires

Super-rich and super-sexy, the ruthless Russian and the sensuous Sheikh are about to meet their match!

Claimed for Makarov's Baby

Erin is about to get married, purely for convenience, when ruthless Russian billionaire Dimitri Makarov barges in! He's the father of her child, and he's come to stop the wedding and claim his son and heir— but what are his plans for Erin?

The Sheikh's Christmas Conquest

When horse 'whisperer' Olivia Miller is summoned by Sheikh Saladin Al Mektala to help him with a distressed mare she is forced to turn the imperious offer down. Now the enigmatic Sheikh has turned up on her doorstep and he's changed tactic: he'll help her—if she spends Christmas with him at his desert palace!

THE SHEIKH'S CHRISTMAS CONQUEST

BY
SHARON KENDRICK

Published in Great Britain 2015
by Mills & Boon, an imprint of Harlequin (UK) Limited,
Eton House, 18-24 Paradise Road, Richmond, Surrey, TW9 1SR

© 2015 Sharon Kendrick

ISBN: 978-0-263-25085-5

Sharon Kendrick once won a national writing competition by describing her ideal date: being flown to an exotic island by a gorgeous and powerful man. Little did she realise that she'd just wandered into her dream job! Today she writes for Mills & Boon, featuring often stubborn but always *to-die-for* heroes and the women who bring them to their knees. She believes that the best books are those you never want to end. Just like life…

Visit the Author Profile page at millsandboon.co.uk for more titles.

To the amazing Anni MacDonald-Hall—
who taught me SO MUCH about horses.

Sheikh Saladin Al Mektala is very grateful
for her expertise!

CHAPTER ONE

LIVVY WAS HANGING mistletoe when the doorbell rang. Expensive, mocking mistletoe tied with ribbon the colour of blood. The sudden sound startled her because the heavy snow had made the world silent and she wasn't expecting anyone until Christmas Eve.

Go away, whoever you are, she thought as several white berries bounced onto the floor like miniature ping-pong balls. But the doorbell rang again—for much longer this time—because whoever was outside had decided to jam their thumb against the buzzer.

Livvy wished the unwanted caller would vanish, because there was still so much to do before the guests arrived, and the snowfall meant that Stella, her part-time help, hadn't turned up. But you couldn't run a successful business and behave like a prima donna—even if it was only four days before Christmas and you didn't have any room vacancies. She climbed down the ladder with a feeling of irritation that died the instant she opened the door.

She was unprepared for the man who stood on her doorstep. A stranger, yet not quite a stranger—although it took a moment for her to place him. He was famous in the horse-racing world she'd once inhabited. Some might say infamous. He was certainly unforgettable with eyes like gleaming jet and rich olive skin that showcased his hawklike features. His hard body spoke of exercise and discipline, and he was the kind of man who would make you take a second glance and then maybe a third.

But it wasn't just his appearance or his undeniable charisma that made Livvy blink her eyes in disbelief— it was his lofty status. Because it wasn't just any man who stood there surveying her so unsmilingly—it was Saladin Al Mektala, the king of Jazratan. A real-life desert sheikh standing on *her* doorstep.

She wondered if there was some sort of protocol for greeting one of the world's wealthiest men, especially when they also happened to be royal. Once upon a time she might have been intimidated by his reputation and his presence—but not anymore. She'd had to do a lot of growing up these past few years and her experiences had made her strong. These days she lived an independent life she was proud of—even if currently it felt as if she was clinging on to that independence by her fingernails.

'Didn't anyone ever tell you,' she said, tipping her head to one side, 'that it's polite to wait for someone to answer the first ring, rather than deafening them with a repeated summons?'

Saladin raised his eyebrows, unable to hide his surprise at her feisty response. It was an untraditional greeting to receive, even here in England where the demands of protocol were less rigid than in his homeland. But even so. His royal presence was usually enough to guarantee total deference, and although he sometimes complained to his advisors that people were never *normal* around him, he missed deference when it wasn't there.

He narrowed his eyes and studied her. 'Do you know who I am?'

She laughed. She actually laughed—her shiny ponytail swaying from side to side, like the tail of a chestnut horse.

'I thought that was the kind of question B-list celebrities asked when they were trying to get into the latest seedy nightclub,' she said.

Saladin felt a flicker of annoyance and something else. Something that was a little harder to define. He had been warned that she was difficult. That she could be prickly and stubborn—but these were qualities that were usually melted away by the sheer force of his personality and his position in society. And, not to put too fine a point on it, by his impact on the opposite sex, who usually melted like ice in the desert whenever he was around. His instinct was to bite back a withering response to put her in her place, but Livvy Miller had something he badly wanted so that he was forced to adopt a reasonable tone, something that didn't come easily to him. 'It was a genuine question,' he said. 'I am Saladin Al Mektala.'

'I know who you are.'

'And my office have been trying to contact you.' He paused. 'Repeatedly.'

She smiled, but Saladin noted that the smile did not reach her eyes.

'I know that, too,' she said. 'In fact, they've been bombarding me with emails and phone calls for the past week. I've barely been able to switch on my computer

without a new message from palace@jazratan.com
pinging into my inbox.'

'Yet you chose to ignore them?'

'That is my prerogative, surely?' She leaned on the
doorjamb, her unusual eyes shaded by their forest of
lashes. 'I gave them the same answer every time. I told
them I wasn't interested. If they were unable to accept
that, then surely the fault lies with them. My position
hasn't changed.'

Saladin could barely disguise his growing irritation.
'But you don't know what it is they were asking of you.'

'Something to do with a horse. And that was enough
for me.'

She drew herself up to her full height but he still
towered over her. He found himself thinking that he
could probably lift her up with one hand. When he'd
heard about her ability to soothe huge and very tem-
peramental horses, he'd never imagined she could be
so…petite.

'Because I don't have anything to do with horses
anymore,' she finished gravely.

Dragging his gaze from her slender frame to eyes
that were the colour of honey, he fixed her with a ques-
tioning look. 'Why not?'

She gave a little clicking sound of irritation, but
not before he had seen something dark in her eyes. A
flash of something uncomfortable that he stored away
for future reference.

'That's really none of your business,' she said, tilting
her chin in a gesture of defiance. 'I don't have to offer
any kind of explanation for my decisions, particularly
to people who turn up unannounced on my doorstep
at one of the busiest times of the year.'

Saladin felt the first flicker of heat. And of challenge. He was not used to resistance, or defiance. In his world, whatever he wanted was his. A click of his fingers or a cool glance was usually enough to guarantee him whatever he desired. Certainly, this kind of opposition was largely unknown to him, and certainly when it came from a woman, because women enjoyed submitting to his will—not opposing it. His response was one of renewed determination, which was quickly followed by the first sweet shimmer of sexual arousal and that surprised him. Because although Olivia Miller was reputed to have a magical touch when it came to horses, she certainly hadn't applied the same fairy dust to her appearance.

Saladin's lips curled. She was one of those women who the English called tomboys—and he didn't approve, for weren't women supposed to look like women? Her hair was pale brown, touched by red—a colour named after the great Italian painter Titian and a colour rare enough to be admired—but it was tied back in a functional ponytail, and her freckled face was completely bare of artifice. Why, even her jeans failed to do the only commendable thing that jeans were capable of—they were loose around her bottom instead of clinging to it like syrup. Which made the undeniable stir of lust he was feeling difficult to understand. Because why on earth should he be attracted to someone who sublimated her femininity as much as possible?

He narrowed his eyes. 'Are you aware that your attitude could be termed as insolence?' he questioned softly. 'And that it is unwise to answer the king of Jazratan in such a way?'

Again, that defiant tilt of the chin. He wondered if

she was aware that such a positioning of her face made her look as if she were inviting him to kiss her.

'I wasn't intending to be insolent,' she said, although the message in her eyes told him otherwise. 'I was simply stating a fact. What I chose to do with my life has nothing to do with you. I owe you no explanation. I am not one of your royal subjects.'

'No, you are not, but you might at least grant me the courtesy of hearing what I have to say,' he bit out. 'Or does the word *hospitality* mean nothing to you? Are you aware that I have travelled many miles in the most inclement weather in order to meet you?'

Livvy eyed the remaining bunches of mistletoe still waiting to be hung and thought about all the other things that needed to be done before her guests arrived. She wanted to make more cake to fill the house with sweet smells, and there were fires to make up in all the bedrooms. Her to-do list was as long as her arm and this handsome and vaguely intimidating stranger was hindering her. 'You could have chosen a more convenient time than just before Christmas,' she said.

'And when would have been a more *convenient* time?' he retorted. 'When you have consistently refused to be pinned down?'

'Most people would have taken the hint and cut their losses.'

'I am a king. I don't do *hints*' came his stony response.

Livvy hesitated. His behaviour confirmed everything she'd ever heard about him. He had been known for his arrogance on the racing circuit—seemingly with good reason—and she was so tempted to tell him to go. But she *was* running a business—even if it was currently a struggling business—and if she angered Saladin Al Mektala any more than he was already clearly angered, he might just spread a malicious word or two around the place. She could imagine it would be easy for someone like him to drip a little more poison onto her already damaged reputation. And adverse publicity could be death if you worked in the hospitality industry.

Behind him, she could see the falling snow, which had been coming down in bucketloads since before breakfast. Fat flakes were tumbling past like a never-ending slide show. Lawns that earlier had been merely spattered with the stuff now sported a thick white mantle—as if someone had been layering on cotton wool while she hadn't been looking. If it carried on like this, the lanes would soon be impassable and she'd never get rid of him. And she wanted to get rid of him. She didn't like him dominating her doorway and ex-uding all that *testosterone* and making her think about stuff she hadn't thought about in a long time. *She didn't like the way he made her feel.*

Farther up the drive stood a black four-wheel drive and she wondered if anyone was sitting shivering in-side.

'What about your bodyguards—are they in the car?' Her gaze swept around the wintry garden. 'Hiding in the bushes, perhaps—or waiting to jump from a tree?'

'I don't have any bodyguards with me.'

So they were all alone.

Livvy's anxiety increased. Something about his powerful body and brooding features was making her skin prickle with a weird kind of foreboding—and an even more alarming sense of anticipation. For the first time she found herself wishing that she had a dog who would bark at him, rather than a soppy feline mop called Peppa, who was currently stretched out in front of the fire in the drawing room, purring happily.

But she wasn't going to allow this man to intimidate her. And if she wasn't intimidated, then it followed that she shouldn't keep avoiding a meeting with him. Maybe this was the only way he would understand that she meant what she said. If she kept repeating that she wasn't interested in whatever he was offering, then surely he would have no choice other than to believe her. And to leave her alone.

'You'd better come in,' she said as an icy gust brought a flurry of snow into the hall. 'I can give you thirty minutes but no longer. I'm expecting guests for Christmas and I have a lot to do before they arrive.'

She saw his faintly triumphant smile as he stepped inside and noticed how the elegant proportions of the airy entrance hall seemed to shrink once she had closed the front door on the snowy afternoon. There was something so intensely *masculine* about him, she thought reluctantly. Something that was both exciting and dangerous—and she forced herself to take a deep breath in an attempt to slow the sudden galloping of her heart. *Act as if he's a guest*, she told herself. *Put on your best, bright smile and switch on your professional hospitality mode.*

'Why don't you come into the drawing room?' she suggested politely. 'There's a fire there.'

He nodded and she saw his narrowed gaze take in the high ceilings and the elaborate wooden staircase as he followed her across the hallway. 'This is a beautiful old house,' he observed, a note of approval deepening his voice.

'Thank you,' she said, automatically slipping into

her role as guide. 'Parts of it date back to the twelfth century. They certainly don't build them like this anymore—perhaps that's a good thing, considering the amount of maintenance that's needed.' The building's history was one of the reasons why people travelled to this out-of-the-way spot to hire a room. Because the past defined the present and people hungered after the idea of an elegant past. Or at least, they had—until the rise of several nearby boutique hotels had started offering the kind of competition that was seriously affecting her turnover.

But Livvy couldn't deny her thrill of pleasure as the sheikh walked into the drawing room, because she was proud of her old family home, despite the fact that it had started to look a little frayed around the edges.

The big fire was banked with apple logs, which scented the air, and although the huge Christmas tree was still bare there weren't many rooms that could accommodate a tree of that size. At some point later she would have to drag herself up to the dusty attic and haul down the decorations, which had been in the family since the year dot, and go through the ritual of bringing the tree to life. Soon it would be covered in spangles and fairy lights and topped with the ancient little angel she'd once made with her mother. And for a while, Christmas would work its brief and sometimes unbearable magic of merging past and present.

She looked up to find Saladin Al Mektala studying her intently and, once again, a shiver of something inexplicable made her nostalgic sentiments dissolve as she began to study him right back.

He wasn't dressed like a sheikh. There were no flowing robes or billowing headdress to indicate his desert king status. The dark cashmere overcoat that he was removing—without having been invited to—was worn over dark trousers and a charcoal sweater that hugged his honed torso. He looked disturbingly *modern*, she thought—even if the flinty glint of his dark eyes made him seem disturbingly primitive. She watched as he hung the cashmere coat over the back of a chair and saw the gleam of melted snow on his black hair as he stepped a little closer to the fire.

'So,' she said. 'You must want something very badly if you're prepared to travel to the wilds of Derbyshire in order to get it.'

'Oh, but I do,' he said silkily. 'I want you.'

Something in his sultry tone kick-started feelings Livvy had repressed for longer than she cared to re-member and for a split second, she found herself imag-ining what it would feel like to be the object of desire to a man like Saladin Al Mektala. Would those flinty eyes soften before he kissed you? Would a woman feel *helpless* if she was being held in arms as powerful as his?

She swallowed, surprised by the unexpected path her thoughts had taken her down because she didn't fall in lust with total strangers. Actually, she didn't fall in lust at all. She quickly justified her wayward fan-tasy by reminding herself that he was being deliber-ately provocative and had made that statement in such a way—as if he was *seeking* to shock her. 'You'll have to be a little more specific than that,' she said crisply. 'What do you want me to do?'

His face changed as the provocation left it and she saw a shadow pass over the hawklike features. 'I have a sick horse,' he said, his voice tightening. 'A badly injured stallion. My favourite.'

His distress affected her—how could it fail to do so? But Livvy hardened her heart to his problems, because didn't she have enough of her own? 'I'm sorry to hear that,' she said. 'But as a king of considerable wealth, no doubt you have the best veterinary surgeons at your disposal. I'm sure they'll be able to work out some plan of action for your injured horse.'

'They say not.'

'Really?' Linking her fingers together, she looked up at him. 'What exactly is the problem?'

'A suspensory ligament,' he said, 'which has torn away from the bone.'

Livvy winced. 'That's bad.'

'I know it's bad,' he gritted out. 'Why the hell do you think I'm here?'

She decided to ignore his rudeness. 'There are revolutionary new treatments out there today,' she said placatingly. 'You can inject stem cells, or you could try shockwave treatment. I've heard that's very good.'

'You think I haven't already tried everything? That I haven't flown out every equine expert to examine him?' he demanded. 'And yet everything has failed. The finest specialists in the world have pronounced themselves at a loss.' There was a pause as he swallowed and his voice became dark and distorted as he spoke. 'They have told me there is no hope.'

For a moment, Livvy felt a deep sense of pity because she knew how powerful the bond between a man and his horse could be—especially a man whose exalted position meant that he could probably put more trust in animals than in humans. But she also knew that sometimes you had to accept things as they were and not as you wanted them to be. That you couldn't defeat nature, no matter how much you tried. And that all the money in the world would make no difference to the outcome.

She saw the steely glint in his dark eyes as he looked at her and recognised it as the look of someone who wasn't intending to give up. Was this what being a king did to a man—made you believe you could shape the world to your own wishes? She sighed. 'Like I said, I'm very sorry to hear that. But if you've been told there's no hope, then I don't know how you expect me to help.'

'Yes, you do, Livvy,' he said forcefully. 'You know you do.'

His fervent words challenged her nearly as much as his sudden use of his name.

'No. I don't.' She shook her head. 'I don't have anything to do with horses anymore. I haven't done for years. That part of my life is over, and if anyone has told you anything different, then they're wrong. I'm sorry.'

There was a pause. 'May I sit down?'

His words startled her as he indicated one of the faded brocade chairs that sat beside the blazing fire—and his sudden change of tactic took her by surprise. And not just surprise. Because if she was being honest, wasn't there something awfully flattering about a sheikh asking if he could prolong his stay and sit down? Briefly, she wondered if he would let her use his endorsement on her website. 'The Sheikh of Jazratan loves to relax in front of the old-fashioned fire.' She met the cold glitter of his eyes. Probably not.

'If you want,' she said as she turned on one of the

lamps so that the fading afternoon was lit with something other than firelight.

But her heart began to race as he sat down—because it seemed disturbingly intimate to see his muscular body unfold into a chair that suddenly looked insubstantial, and for those endlessly long legs to stretch out in front of him. He looked like a panther who had taken an uncharacteristic moment of relaxation, who had wandered in from the wild into a domestic domain, but all the time you were aware that beneath the sheathed paws lay deadly claws. Was that why her cat suddenly opened its eyes and hissed at him, before jumping up and stalking from the room with her tail held high? Too late she realised she should have said no. She should have made him realise she meant what she said before ejecting him into the snowy afternoon before the light faded.

'So,' she said, with a quick glance at her watch. 'Like I said, I have things I need to do, so maybe you could just cut to the chase?'

'An ironic choice of words in the circumstances,' he commented drily. 'Or perhaps deliberate? Either way, it is unlikely that my stallion will race again, even though he has won nearly every major prize in the racing calendar. In fact, he is in so much pain that the vets have told me that it is cruel to let him continue like this and…' His voice tailed off.

'And?'

He leaned his head back against the chair and his eyes narrowed—dark shards that glinted in the firelight. 'And you have a gift with horses, Livvy,' he said softly. 'A rare gift. You can heal them.'

'Who told you that?

'My trainer. He described to me a woman who was the best horsewoman he'd ever seen. He said that she was as light as a feather but strong as an ox—but that her real skill lay in her interaction with the animal. He said that the angriest horse in the stables would grow calm whenever she grew close. He said he'd seen her do stuff with horses that defied logic, and astounded all the horse vets.' His voice deepened as his dark eyes grew watchful. 'And that they used to call you the horse whisperer.'

It was a long time since Livvy had heard the phrase that had once followed her around like mud on a rainy day at the stables. A phrase that carried its own kind of mystique and made people believe she was some kind of witch. And she wasn't. She was just an ordinary person who wanted to be left to get on with her life.

She bent to pick up a log so that her face was hidden, and by the time she straightened up she had composed herself enough to face his inquisitive stare and to answer him in a steady voice.

'That's all hocus-pocus,' she said. 'Nothing but an old wives' tale and people believing what they want to believe. I just got lucky, that's all. The law of probability says that the horses I helped "heal" would have got better on their own anyway.'

'But I know that sometimes nature can contradict the laws of probability,' he contradicted softly. 'Didn't one of your most famous poets say something on those lines?'

'I don't read poetry,' she said flatly.

'Maybe you should.'

Her smile was tight. 'Just like I don't take advice from strangers.'

His eyes glittered. 'Then, come and work for me and we'll be strangers no longer.'

With a jerky movement she threw another log onto the grate and it sparked into life with a whoosh of flames. Had he deliberately decided to use charm—knowing how effective it could be on someone who was awkward around men? She knew about his reputation but, even if she hadn't, you needed only to look at him to realise that he could have a woman eating out of his hand as easily as you could get a stroppy horse to munch on a sugar cube.

'Look,' she said, trying to sound less abrasive, because he was probably one of those men who responded best to a woman when she was cooing at him. 'I'm sorry I can't help you, but I haven't got a magic wand I can wave to make your horse better. And although I'm obviously flattered that you should have thought of me, I'm just not interested in your offer.'

Saladin felt a flicker of frustration. She didn't sound flattered at all. What was the matter with her? Didn't she realise that accepting this job would carry a huge financial reward—not to mention the kudos of being employed by the royal house of Al Mektala?

He had done his research. He knew that this ancient house she'd inherited was written up in all the guidebooks as somewhere worth visiting and that she ran it as some kind of bed and breakfast business. But the place was going to rack and ruin—anyone could see that. Old houses like this drank money as greedily as the desert sands soaked up water, and it was clear to him that she didn't have a lot of cash to splash about. The brocade chair on which he sat had a spring that was sticking into his buttocks, and the walls beside the fireplace could have done with a coat of paint. His eyes narrowed. Couldn't she see he was offering her the opportunity to earn the kind of sum that would enable her to give the place a complete facelift?

And what about her, with her tomboy clothes and freckled face? She had turned her back on the riding world that had once been her life. She had hidden herself away in the middle of nowhere, serving up cooked breakfasts to the random punters who came to stay. What kind of a life was that for a woman who was nearly thirty? In his own country, a woman was married with at least two children by the age of twenty-five, because it was the custom to marry young. He thought of Alya and a spear of pain lanced through his heart. He remembered dreams crushed and the heavy sense of blame, and he cursed the nature of his thoughts and pushed them away as he looked into Olivia Miller's stubborn face.

'You might not have a magic wand, but I would like you to try. What is it that you say? Nothing ventured, nothing gained. And I think you will discover that the financial rewards I'm offering will be beyond your wildest dreams.' He tilted the corners of his mouth in a brief smile. 'And surely you don't want to look a gift horse in the mouth?'

She didn't respond to his attempt at humour, she just continued to stare at him, only now there was a distinct flicker of annoyance in her amber eyes. Saladin felt another rush of sexual attraction, because women didn't often glare at him like that and he was finding her truculence a surprising turn-on. Because no woman had ever refused him anything.

'How many ways do I have to say no before you'll believe I mean it?' she said.

'And how long will it take you to realise that I am a very persistent man who is used to getting what I want?'

'Persist away—you won't change my mind.'

And suddenly Saladin did what he'd told himself he was only going to do as a last resort, which he seemed now to have reached. He leaned back, his eyes not leaving her face. 'So is this how you are intending to spend the rest of your life, Livvy?' he questioned softly. 'Hiding yourself away in the middle of nowhere and neglecting a talent that few possess—and all because some man once left you standing at the altar?'

CHAPTER TWO

AT FIRST LIVVY didn't react to Saladin's cruel taunt because not reacting was something she was good at. One of the things she'd taught herself to do when the man she'd been due to marry had decided not to bother turning up. She'd learned not to show what she was feeling. Not to give the watching world any idea what was going on inside her head, or her heart. But the sheikh's words hurt. Even now, they hurt. Even though it was a long time since anybody had been crass enough to remind her that she had once been *jilted*. That she had stood at the altar wearing a stupid white dress and an eager smile, which had faded as the minutes had ticked by and the silence had grown into hushed and increasingly urgent whispers as it had dawned on the waiting congregation that the groom wasn't going to show.

She looked at the man sitting there with firelight illuminating his hawklike face and in that moment she actually *hated* him. How dare he bring up something so painful just so he could get what *he* wanted? Didn't he care about hurting people's feelings and trampling all over them—or was he simply a master of manipulation? Didn't he realise that such a public humiliation had dealt her self-confidence a blow from which it had taken a long time to recover? And maybe it had never completely recovered. It had still been powerful enough to make her want to leave her old life behind and start a new one. To leave the horses she'd once adored and to view all subsequent advances from men with suspicion.

She would like to take a run at him and *shake* him. To batter her fists against that hard, broad chest and tell him that he was an uncaring beast. But she suspected her rage would be wasted on such a powerful man, and mightn't he regard such a strong response as some petty kind of victory?

'My abandoned marriage has nothing to do with my reasons for not wanting to work for you,' she said, with a coolness she'd cultivated to cope with all the questions she'd had to deal with afterwards. And she'd needed it. She remembered the badly disguised glee in the voices of the women—those wafer-thin blondes who couldn't understand why Rupert de Vries had proposed to someone as unremarkable as her in the first place. *He didn't say why? You mean you honestly had no idea?* No. She'd honestly had no idea. What woman would ever subject herself to that kind of public ridicule if she'd had any inkling the groom was going to do a runner?

She glared into Saladin's glittering dark eyes. 'Though the fact that you even asked the question is another mark against you.'

His dark brows knitted together. 'What are you talking about?'

'I'm talking about the fact that you've obviously been delving into my private life, which isn't making me feel very favourable towards you. No person likes to feel they're being spied on, and you're not doing a very good job of selling yourself as a prospective employer.'

'I don't usually have to sell myself,' he replied, with a coolness that matched hers. 'And surely you can understand why I always investigate people I'm planning to employ.'

'When are you going to accept that you won't be employing me?'

He opened his mouth and then shut it, turning to look around the room, his gaze coming to rest on the faded velvet curtains, as if he'd only just noticed that the sun had bleached them and that moths had been attacking some of the lining.

Had he noticed?

'So is your bed and breakfast business thriving?' he questioned casually.

It was quite clear what he was getting at and suddenly Livvy wanted to prove him wrong. So just *show him*, she thought—though it didn't occur to her until afterwards that she wasn't obliged to show him anything. She wondered if it was pride that made her want to elevate her image from jilted bride to that of budding entrepreneur, even though it wasn't exactly true.

'Indeed it is. It's been a very popular destination,' she said. 'Historic houses like this have a wide appeal to the general public and people can't get enough of them. Speaking of which…' Pointedly, she looked at her watch. 'Your half hour is almost up.'

'But it must be hard work?' he persisted.

She met the mocking question in his black eyes. 'Of course it is. Cooking up to eight different breakfasts to order and making up beds with clean linen most days is not for the faint-hearted. But I've never been afraid of hard work. You don't get anything for nothing in this life.' She paused, her smile growing tight. 'Although I suppose someone like you might be the exception to the rule.'

Not showing any sign of moving, he surveyed her steadily. 'And why might that be?'

'Well, you're a sheikh, aren't you?' she said. 'You're one of the richest men in the world. You own a string of prizewinning racehorses and a palace—for all I know, you might own hundreds of palaces. You have your own plane, I imagine.'

'And?'

'And you've probably never had to lift a finger to acquire the kind of wealth you take for granted. You've probably had everything handed to you on a plate.'

There was silence as Saladin felt a flicker of exasperation. It was an accusation levelled at most people born to royal status, but never usually voiced in his presence because usually people didn't dare. Yes, he was unimaginably rich—but did she think that he had grown up in a bubble? That he'd never had to fight for his country and his people? That he'd never known heartbreak, or stared into the dark abyss of real loss? Once again, Alya's beautiful and perfect face swam into his memory, but he pushed it aside as he met the Englishwoman's quizzical gaze.

'Materially I do not deny that I have plenty,' he said. 'But what about you? You're not exactly on the breadline, are you, Livvy? This place is hardly your average house. You, too, have known privilege.'

Livvy wished he would move away from her, because his presence was making her feel distinctly uncomfortable. As if her plaid shirt had suddenly become too small and her breasts were straining against the tightening buttons. As if those watchful eyes could somehow see through her clothes to the plain and functional underwear that lay beneath.

'It's a rare Georgian house,' she agreed, her fingers playing with the top button of her shirt. 'And I'm lucky to live here. It's been in my family for many years.'

'But the maintenance costs must be high,' he mused.

'Astronomical,' she agreed. 'Which is why I open the house to paying guests.'

He was glancing up at the ceiling now. Had he noticed the ugly damp stain then, or did the firelight successfully hide it? His gaze was lowered and redirected to her face, where once again it seemed to burn its way over her skin.

'So how's business, Livvy—generally?'

Her smile was bland. 'Business is good.'

'Your guests don't mind the fact that the paint is peeling, or that the plaster is crumbling on that far wall?'

'I doubt it. People come looking for history, not pristine paintwork—you can find that almost anywhere in some of the cheaper hotel chains.'

'You know, I could offer you a lot of money,' he observed, after a moment or two. 'Enough to pay for the kind of work this place is crying out for. I could throw in a little extra if you like—so that you could afford the holiday you look as if you need.'

Livvy stiffened. Was he implying that she looked washed out? Almost without her thinking, her fingers crept up to her hairline to brush away a stray strand that must have escaped from her ponytail. It was true she hadn't had a holiday in ages. And it was also true that her debts continued to grow, no matter how many new bookings she took. Sometimes she felt like Canute trying to turn back the tide, and now she couldn't remember how Canute had actually coped. Had he just admitted defeat and given up?

She wished Saladin would stop looking at her like that—his black eyes capturing her in their dark and hypnotic spotlight. She wasn't a vain woman by any definition of the word, but she would have taken a bit more trouble with her appearance if she'd known that a desert sheikh was going to come calling. Suddenly her scalp felt itchy and her face hot, and her shirt still felt as if it had shrunk in the wash.

'Is that your answer to everything?' she questioned. 'To write a cheque and to hell with anything else?'

He shrugged. 'Why wouldn't it be—when I have the capability to do exactly that, and money talks louder than anything else?'

'You cynic,' she breathed.

'I'm not denying that.' He gave a soft laugh. 'Or maybe you're just naive. Money talks, Livvy—it talks louder than anything else. It's about the only thing in life you can rely on—which is why you should do yourself a favour and come with me to Jazratan. My stable complex is the finest in the world and it would be interesting for you to see it.'

He smiled at her, but Livvy sensed it was a calculating smile. As if he had only produced it because it would add a touch of lightness to conversation that wasn't going the way he intended.

'Come and work with my horse and I'll give you whatever you want, within reason,' he continued. 'And if you cure Burkaan—if you ensure that a gun will not be held to his head while I am forced to stare into his trusting and bewildered eyes as the life bleeds out of him, you will walk away knowing that you need never worry about money again.'

The heartfelt bit about the horse got to her much more than the financial incentive he was offering. In fact, she hated the mercenary progression of his words. As if everything had a price—even people. As if you could wear them down just by increasing the amount of money on the table. Maybe in his world, that was what happened.

But despite her determination not to be tempted, she *was* tempted. For a minute she allowed herself to think what she could do with the money. Where would she even start? By tackling the ancient wiring in some of the bedrooms, or sorting out the antiquated boiler that badly needed replacing? She thought about the icy corridors upstairs and the lack of insulation in the roof. Most of the heat was pumped into the guest bed-rooms, leaving her own windows coated with a thin layer of ice each morning. She shivered. It had been a bitter winter and they were still only a third of the way through it, and she was getting fed up with having to wear thick socks to bed at night.

'I can't,' she said. 'I have guests who are due to spend the holidays here who are arriving in a couple of days. I can't just cancel their Christmas and New Year when they've spent months looking forward to it. You'll just have to find someone else.'

Saladin's mouth tightened, but still he wasn't done. Didn't she realise that he would get what he wanted in the end, no matter how he had to go about it? That if it came to a battle of wills, he would win. Spurred on by the almost imperceptible note of hesitation he'd heard in her voice, he got up from his chair and walked over to the window. It was almost dark, but the heavy clouds had already leached the sky of all colour and all you could see was snow. It had highlighted all the leafless trees with ghostly white fingers. It had blanketed his parked car so that all that was visible was a snowy mound.

His eyes narrowed as fat flakes swirled down, transformed into tumbling gold feathers by the light streaming from the window. He ran through the possibilities of what he should do next, knowing his choices were limited. He could go and get his car started before the snow came down any harder. He could drive off and come back again tomorrow. Give her time to think about his offer and realise that she would be a fool to reject it. Or he could have his people deal with it, using rather more ruthless back-room tactics.

He turned back to see her unsmiling face and he was irritated by his inability to get through to her. Logic told him to leave, yet for some reason he was reluctant to do so, even though she had started walking towards the door, making it clear that she expected him to trail after her. A woman who wanted him gone? Unbelievable! When had any woman ever turned him away?

He followed her out into the wood-lined corridor, which was lit by lamps on either side, realising that she was close enough to touch. And bizarrely, he thought about kissing her. About claiming those stubborn and unpainted lips with his own and waiting to see how long it would take before she was breathlessly agreeing to anything he asked of her.

But his choices were suddenly taken away from him by a dramatic intervention as the lights went out and the corridor was plunged into darkness. From just ahead of him, he heard Livvy gasp and then he felt the softness of her body as she stumbled back against him.

CHAPTER THREE

As THE CORRIDOR was plunged into darkness, Saladin's hands automatically reached out to steady the stumbling Livvy. At least, that was what he told himself. He thought afterwards that if she'd been a man he wouldn't have let his hands linger on her for quite so long, nor his fingers to grip her slender body quite so tightly. But Livvy Miller was a woman—and it had been a long time since he had touched a woman. It had recently been the anniversary of Alya's death and he always shied away from intimacy on either side of that grim date, when pain and loss and regret overwhelmed him. Because to do so felt like a betrayal of his wife's memory—a mechanical act that seemed like a pale version of the real thing. With other women it was just sex—something a man needed in order to function properly. A basic appetite to be fed—and nothing more. But with Alya it had been different. Something that had captured his heart as well as his body.

But maybe for now a body would do...

He felt himself tense with that first, sweet contact—that first touch that set your hormones firing, whether you wanted them to or not. He could feel Livvy's heart beating hard as his hands curved around her ribcage.

The soapy scent that perfumed her skin was both innocent and beguiling, and the tension inside him increased. He found himself wishing he could magic away their clothing and seek relief from the sudden unbearable aching deep inside him. An anonymous coupling in this darkened corridor would be perfect for his needs. It might even have the added benefit of making the stubborn Englishwoman reconsider his offer, because a sexually satisfied woman automatically became a compliant woman.

For a moment he felt her relax against him and he sensed her welcoming softness—as if a split second more would be all the time he needed for her to open up to him. But then she pulled away. Actually, she *snatched* herself away. In the darkness he could hear her struggling to control her breathing and, although he couldn't see the expression on her face, he could hear the panic in her voice.

'What's happened?' she gasped.

It interested him that she'd chosen to ignore that brief but undeniable embrace. He wondered what she would say if he answered truthfully. *I am big enough to explode and I want to put myself inside you and spill my seed.* In his fantasy he knew exactly what he would like her response to be. She would nod and then tear at his clothing with impatient fingers while he dealt swiftly with hers. No need even to undress. Access was all that was required. He would press her up against that wood panelling, and then slide his fingers between her legs while he freed himself. He would kiss her until she was begging him for more, and then he would guide himself to where she was wet and ready, and push deep inside her. It would be quick and it would be meaningless, but he doubted there would be any objections from her.

She was flicking a light switch on and off, but nothing was happening. 'What's happened?' she repeated, only now her voice sounded accusatory.

With a monumental effort he severed his erotic fantasy and let it drift away, concentrating instead on the dense darkness that surrounded them, but his mouth was so dry and his groin so hard that it was several seconds before he was able to answer her question.

'There's been a power cut,' he said.

'I know that,' she howled illogically. 'But how did it happen?'

'I have no idea,' he answered steadily. 'And the how isn't important. We have to deal with it. Do you have your own emergency generator?'

'Are you insane?' Her panicked question came shooting at him through the darkness. 'Of course I don't!'

'Well, then,' he said impatiently. 'Where do you keep your candles?'

Livvy couldn't think straight. He might as well have asked her where the planet Jupiter was in the night sky. Because the sudden loss of light and heating were eclipsed by the realisation that she had been on the brink of losing control. She'd nearly gone to pieces in his arms, because his touch had felt dangerous. And inviting. It had only been the briefest of embraces, but it had been mind-blowing. She hadn't imagined feeling the unmistakable power of his arousal pressing firmly against her. And the amazing thing was that it hadn't shocked her. On the contrary—she'd wanted him to carry on holding her like that. Hadn't she been tempted to turn around and stretch up on tiptoe, to see whether he would kiss her as she sensed he had wanted to? And then to carry on kissing her.

'Candles?' he prompted impatiently.

She swallowed. 'They're…in the kitchen,' she said. 'I'll get them.'

'I'll come with you.'

'You don't think I'm capable of finding my way around my own house?'

'It's dark,' he ground out. 'And we're sticking to-gether.'

Saladin caught hold of her wrist and closed his fingers over it, thinking that if only he had been ac-companied by his usual bodyguards and envoys, then someone would now be attempting to fix whatever the problem was.

But he had undertaken this journey alone—instinct telling him that he would have a better chance of success with the Englishwoman without all the dazzle of royal life that inevitably accompanied him. Because some people were intimidated by all the trap-pings that surrounded a royal sheikh—and, in truth, he liked to shrug off those trappings whenever possible.

When travelling in Europe or the United States, he sometimes got his envoy Zane to act as a decoy sheikh. The two men were remarkably similar in ap-pearance and they had long ago discovered that one powerful robed figure wearing a headdress in the back of a speeding car was interchangeable with another, to all but the most perceptive eye.

In Jazratan he sometimes took solo trips deep into the heart of the desert. At other times he had been known to dress as a merchant and to blend into the thronging crowds of the marketplace in the capital city of Janubwardi. It gave him a certain kick to listen to what his people were saying about him when they thought they were free to do so. His advisors didn't like it, but that was tough. He refused to be treated with kid gloves, especially here in England—a country he knew well. And he knew that the dangers in life were the ones where obvious risk was involved, but the ones that hit you totally out of the blue...

He could feel her pulse slamming wildly beneath his fingers.

'Let me go,' she whispered.

'No. You're not going anywhere,' he snapped. 'Stick close to me—I'm going first. And be careful.'

'I don't need you to tell me to be careful. Don't you have a phone? We could use it as a torch instead of stumbling around in the dark.'

'It's in my car,' he said as they edged along a corridor that seemed less dense now that his eyes had started to accustom themselves to the lack of light. 'Where's yours?'

'In my bedroom.'

'Handy,' he said sarcastically.

'I wasn't expecting to be marooned in the darkness with a total stranger.'

'Spare me the melodrama, Livvy. And let's just concentrate on getting there without falling over.'

Cautiously, they moved along the ancient passage. The flagged floors echoed as she led him down a narrow flight of stairs, into a large windowless kitchen that was as dark as pitch. She wriggled her hand free and felt her way towards a cupboard, where he could hear her scrabbling around—before uttering a little cry of triumph as she located the candles. He found himself admiring her efficiency, but noticed that her fingers were trembling as she struck a match and her pale face was illuminated as the flame grew steady.

Wordlessly, he took the matches from her and lit several more candles while she melted wax and positioned them carefully in tarnished silver holders. The room grew lighter and the flames cast out strange shadows that flickered over the walls. He could see the results of what must have been a pretty intensive baking session, because on the table were plates of biscuits and a platter of those sweet things the English always ate at Christmastime. He frowned as he tried to remember what they were called. Mince pies, that was it.

'What do you think has happened?' she questioned.

He shrugged. 'A power line down? It can sometimes happen if there's a significant weight of snow.'

'But it can't!' She looked around, a touch of desperation in her voice. 'I've still got so much to do before my guests arrive.'

He sent her a wry look. 'Looks as though it's going to have to wait.'

A sudden silence fell and he noticed that her hand was trembling even more now.

'Hadn't you better go, before the snow gets much worse?' she said, in a casual tone that didn't quite come off. 'There must be someone waiting for you. Someone who's wondering where you are.'

Incredulously, he stared at her. 'And leave you here, on your own? Without electricity?' He walked over to one of the old-fashioned radiators and laid the flat of his hand on it. 'Or heating.'

'I'm perfectly capable of managing on my own,' she said stubbornly.

'I don't care,' he said. 'I'm not going anywhere. What kind of man would walk out and leave a woman to fend for herself in conditions like these?'

'So you're staying in order to ease your own conscience?'

There was a pause, and when he spoke his voice had a bitter note to it. 'Something like that.'

Livvy's heart thundered as she tried to work out what to do next. 'Don't panic' should have been top of her list, while the second should be to stop allowing Saladin to take control. Maybe where he came from, men dealt with emergencies while the women just hung around looking decorative. Well, perhaps it might do him good to realise that she didn't need a man to fix things for her. She didn't need a man for anything. She'd learned to change a fuse and fix a leaking tap. She'd managed alone for long enough and that was the way she liked it.

She walked over to the phone, which hung on a neat cradle on the wall, but was greeted with nothing but an empty silence as she placed it against her ear.

'Dead?' he questioned.

'Completely.' She replaced it and looked at him but, despite her best intentions, she *was* starting to panic. Had she, in the rush to buy the tree and hang the mistletoe and bake the mince pies, remembered to charge her cell phone? 'I'll go upstairs and get my phone.'

'I'll come with you.'

'Were you born to be bossy?'

'I think I was. Why, does it bother you?'

'Yes.'

'Tough,' he said as he picked up a candle.

But as they left the kitchen Saladin realised that for the first time in a long time he was feeling *exhilarated*. Nobody had a clue where he was. He was marooned in the middle of the snowy English countryside with a feisty redhead he suspected would be his before the night was over. And suddenly his conscience and his troubled memories were forgotten as he followed her up the large staircase leading from the arched reception hall, where the high ceilings flickered with long shadows cast from their candles. They reached her bedroom and Saladin drew in a deep breath as she pushed open the door and turned to him, a studiedly casual note in her voice.

'You can wait here, if you like.'

'Like a pupil standing outside the headmaster's study?' he drawled. 'No. I don't like. Don't worry, Livvy—I won't be judging you if your room's a mess and I think I'm sophisticated enough to resist the temptation to throw you down on the bed, if that's what you're worried about.'

'Oh, come in, if you insist,' she said crossly.

But it was with a feeling of pride that she opened the door and walked through, with Saladin not far behind her. The curtains were not yet drawn and the reflected light from the snow outside meant that the room looked almost radiant with a pure and ghostly light. On a table beside the bed stood a bowl of hyacinths, which scented the cold air. Antique pieces of furniture glowed softly in the candlelight. It was a place of peace and calm—her haven—and one of many reasons why she clung to this house and all the memories it contained.

She walked over to the window seat and found her phone, dejectedly staring down at its black screen.

'It's dead,' she said. 'I was sending photo messages to a school friend when the snow started and then they delivered the Christmas tree…' Her words tailed off. 'You'll have to go out to the car and get yours.'

'I will decide if and when I'm going out to the car,' he snapped. 'You do *not* issue instructions to a sheikh.'

'I didn't invite you here,' she said, her voice low. 'We're here together under duress and in extremely bizarre circumstances—and I think it's going to make an unbearable situation even worse if you then start pulling rank on me.'

He looked as if he was about to come back at her with a sharp response, but seemed to think better of it—because he nodded. 'Very well. I will go to the car and get my phone.'

He left the room abruptly, and as she heard him going downstairs she felt slightly spooked—a feeling that was only increased when the front door slammed. Everything seemed unnaturally quiet without him— all she could hear was the loud tick of the grandfather clock as it echoed through the house. She stared out of the window to see the sheikh's shadowy figure making its way towards a car that was now completely covered in white. The snow was still falling, and she found herself thinking that at least he'd had the sense to retrieve his cashmere coat and put it on before going outside.

She could see him brushing a thick layer of snow away from the door, which he was obviously having difficulty opening. She wondered what would happen next. Would crack teams of Jazratan guards descend in a helicopter from the snowy sky, the way they did in films? Doubtfully, she looked up at the fat flakes that were swirling down as thickly as ever. She didn't know much about planes, but she doubted it would be safe to fly in conditions like this.

Grabbing a sweater from the wardrobe and pulling it on, she went back downstairs to the kitchen and had just put a kettle on the hob when she heard the front door slam, followed by the sound of echoing footsteps. She looked up to see Saladin standing framed in the kitchen doorway and hated the instant rush of relief—and something else—that flooded through her. What was the something else? she wondered. The reassurance of having someone so unashamedly alpha strutting around the place, despite all her protestations that she was fine on her own? Or was the root cause more fundamental—a case of her body responding to him in away she wasn't used to? A way that *scared* her.

Despite the warm sweater she'd pulled on, she could feel the puckering of her breasts as she looked at him.

'Any luck?' she said.

'Some. I've spoken with my people—and the roads are impassable. We won't get any help sent out to us tonight.'

Livvy's hand trembled as she tipped boiling water into the teapot. They were stuck here for the night—just the two of them. So why wasn't she paralysed with a feeling of dread and fear? Why had her heart started pounding with excitement? She swallowed.

'Would you like some tea?'

'Please.' His voice grew curious. 'How have you managed to boil water?'

'Gas hob,' she said, thinking how *domesticated* this

all sounded. And how the words people spoke rarely reflected what was going on inside their heads. She looked into the gleam of his eyes. 'Are you hungry? I'll put some mince pies on a plate,' she said, in the kind of babbling voice people used when they were trying to fill an awkward silence. 'And we can go in and sit by the fire.'

'Here. Let me.' He took the tray from her, aware that this was something he rarely did. People always carried things for *him*. They ran his bath for him and laid out his cool silk robes every morning. For diplomatic meetings, all his paperwork was stacked in symmetrical piles awaiting his attention, even down to the gold pen that was always positioned neatly to the left. He didn't have to deal with the everyday mechanics of normal life, because his life was not normal. Never had been, nor ever could be. Even his response to tragedy could never be like other men's—for he'd been taught that the sheikh must never show emotion, no matter what he was feeling inside. So that when he had wanted to weep bitter tears over Alya's coffin, he had known that the face he'd needed to show to his people must be an implacable face.

His mouth hardened as he carried the tea tray to the room where the bare Christmas tree stood silhouetted against the window and watched as she sank down onto the silky rug. And suddenly the sweet wholesomeness of her made all his dark thoughts melt away.

The bulky sweater she was wearing emphasised her tiny frame and the slender legs that were tucked up neatly beneath her. The firelight had turned her titian ponytail into a stream of flaming red, and all he could think about was how much he wanted to see her naked…

So make it happen, he thought—as the pulse at his groin began to throb with anticipation. *Just make it happen.*

CHAPTER FOUR

'WE HAVE A long evening ahead of us, Livvy. Any idea of how you'd like to fill it?'

Livvy eyed Saladin warily as he drawled out his question, thinking that he was suddenly being almost *too* well behaved, and wondering why. She almost preferred him when he was being bossy and demanding, because that had infuriated her enough to create a natural barrier between them. A barrier behind which she felt safe.

But now?

Now he was being suspiciously compliant. He had drunk the tea she'd given him and eaten an accompanying mince pie—declaring it to be delicious and telling her he intended to take the recipe back for the palace chefs, so that his courtiers and guests could enjoy the English delicacy. He had even dragged a whole pile of logs back from the woodshed and heaped them into the big basket beside the fire.

Despite the thickness of her sweater, a shiver ran down her spine as she watched him. His body was hard and muscular and he moved with the grace of a natural athlete. He handled the logs as if they were no heavier than twigs and somehow made the task look effortless. Livvy was proud of her independence and her insistence on doing the kind of jobs that some of her married school friends turned up their noses at. She never baulked at taking out the rubbish or sweeping the gravel drive. She happily carried logs and weeded the garden whenever she had time, but she couldn't deny that it felt like an unexpected luxury to be waited on like this. To lean back against the cushioned footstool sipping her tea, watching Saladin Al Mektala sort out the fire for her. He made her feel...*pampered*, and he made her feel feminine.

She considered his question.

'We could always play a game,' she suggested.

'Good idea.' His dark eyes assumed the natural glint of the predator. 'I love playing games.'

Nobody had ever accused Livvy of sophistication, but neither was she stupid. She'd worked for a long time in the testosterone-filled industry of horse racing and had been engaged to a very tricky man. She'd learned the hard way how womanising men flirted and used innuendo. And the only way to keep it in check was to ignore it. So she ignored the flare of light that had made the sheikh's eyes gleam like glowing coal and subjected him to a look of cool question. 'Scrabble?' she asked. 'Or cards?'

'Whichever you choose,' he said. 'Although I must warn you now that I shall beat you.'

'Is that supposed to be a challenge I can't resist?'

'Let's see, shall we?'

To Livvy's fury, his arrogant prediction proved correct. He won every game they played and even beat her at Scrabble—something at which she normally excelled.

Trying not to be a bad sport, she dropped the pen onto the score sheet. 'So how come you've managed to beat me at a word game that isn't even in your native tongue?' she said.

'Because when I was a little boy I had an English tutor who taught me that a rich vocabulary was something within the grasp of all men. And I was taught to win. It's what Al Mektala men do. We never like to fail. At anything.'

'So you're always triumphant?'

He turned his head to look at her and Livvy's heart missed a beat as she saw something flickering within the dark blaze of his eyes that didn't look like arrogance. Was she imagining the trace of sorrow she saw there—or the lines around his mouth, which suddenly seemed to have deepened?

'No,' he said harshly. 'A long time ago I failed at something quite spectacularly.'

'At what?'

'Something better left in the past, where it belongs.' His voice grew cold and distant as he threw another log onto the fire, and when he turned back Livvy saw that his features had become shuttered. 'Tell me something about you instead,' he said.

She shrugged. 'There's not very much to tell. I'm twenty-nine and I run a bed and breakfast business from the house in which I was born. My love life you already seem well acquainted with. Anything else you want to know?'

'Yes.' His hawklike features were gilded by the flicker of the firelight as he leaned forward. 'Why did he jilt you?'

She met the searching blaze of his black eyes. 'You really think I'd tell *you*?'

He raised his dark brows. 'Why not? I'm curious. And after the snow clears, you'll never see me again— that is, if you really are determined to turn down my offer of a job. Isn't that what people do in circumstances such as these? They tell each other secrets.'

As she considered his words, Livvy wondered how he saw her. As some sad spinster who'd tucked herself away in the middle of nowhere, far away from the fast-paced world she'd once inhabited? And if that was the case, then wasn't this an ideal opportunity to show him that she *liked* the life she'd chosen—to show him she was completely over Rupert?

But if you're over him—then how come you still shut out men? How come you must be the only twenty-nine-year-old virgin on the planet?

The uncomfortable trajectory of her thoughts made her bold. *So let it go*, she told herself. *Let the past go by setting it free.* 'Do you know Rupert de Vries?' she asked slowly.

'I met him a couple of times—back in the day, as they say.' His mouth twisted. 'I didn't like him.'

'You don't have to say that just to make me feel better.'

'I can assure you that I never say things I don't mean, Livvy.' There was a pause. 'What happened?'

She stared down at the rug, trying to concentrate on the symmetrical shapes that were woven into the silk. She pictured Rupert's face—something she hadn't done for a long time—fine boned and fair and the antithesis of the tawny sheikh in front of her. She remembered how she couldn't believe that the powerful racing figure had taken an interest in *her*, the lowliest of grooms at the time. 'I expect you know that he ran a very successful yard for a time.'

'Until he got greedy,' Saladin said, stretching his legs out in front of him. 'He overextended himself and that was a big mistake. You should always keep something back when you're dealing with horses, no matter how brilliant they are. Because ultimately they are flesh and blood—and flesh and blood is always vulnerable.'

She heard the sudden rawness in his voice and wondered if he was thinking about Burkaan. 'Yes,' she said.

'So how come it got as far as you standing at the altar before he got cold feet?' Black eyes bored into her. 'That's what happened, isn't it? Didn't he talk to you about it beforehand—let you know he was having doubts?'

Livvy shook her head as her mind raced back to that chaotic period. At the time she'd done that thing of trying to salvage her pride by telling everyone with a brisk cheerfulness that it was much better to find out *before* the wedding, rather than after it. That it would have been unbearable if Rupert had decided he wanted out a few years and a few children down the line. But those had been things she'd felt *obliged* to say, so that she wouldn't come over as bitter. The truth was that the rejection had left her feeling hollow…and stupid. Not only had she been completely blind to her fiancé's transgressions, but there had been all the practical considerations, too. Like paying the catering staff who were standing around in their aprons in the deserted marquee almost bursting with excitement at the *drama* of it all. And informing the driver of the limousine firm that they wouldn't be needing a lift to the airport after all. And cancelling the honeymoon, which she'd paid for and for which Rupert had been supposed to settle up with her afterwards. He never had, of course, and the wedding that never was had ended up costing her a lot more than injured pride.

And once the initial humiliation was over and everyone had been paid off, she had made a vow never to talk about it. She'd told herself that if she fed the story it would grow. So she'd cut off people's questions and deliberately changed the subject and dared them to continue to pursue it, and eventually people had got the message.

But now she looked into the gleam of Saladin's eyes and realised that there had been a price to pay for her silence. She suddenly recognised how deeply she had buried the truth and saw that if she continued to keep it hidden away, she risked making herself an eternal victim. The truth was that she was over Rupert and glad she hadn't married him. So why act like someone with a dirty secret—why not get it out into the open and watch it wither and die as it was exposed to the air?

'Because I allowed myself to do what women are so good at doing,' she said slowly. 'I allowed myself to be wooed by a very persuasive man, without stopping to consider why someone like him should be interested in someone like me.'

His eyes narrowed. 'What's that supposed to mean?'

'Oh, come on, Saladin—you haven't held back from being blunt, so why start now? He was known for dating glamorous women and I'm not. The only thing I had to commend me was the fact that my father owned a beautiful house. This house. My mother was dead and my stepmother long gone—and since I don't have any brothers or sisters, I stood to inherit everything. From where Rupert was sitting, it must have looked a very attractive proposition and I think he made the assumption that there was lots of money sitting in a bank account somewhere—the kind of money that could have bailed out his failing business.'

'But there wasn't?'

'At some point there was. Before my stepmother got her hands on it and decided to blow a lot of it on diamonds and plastic surgery and then demand a massive divorce settlement. By the time my father died there was nothing left—not after I'd paid for the nurses who helped care for him in his final years.'

'You didn't think to tell de Vries that?'

Livvy gave a snarl of a laugh as she picked up the poker and gave the fire a vicious stab. 'Most brides labour under the illusion that they're being married for love, not money. It would look a bit pathetic, don't you think, if one were to have a conversation on the lines of, "Look, I've just discovered that I'm broke—but you do still love me, don't you?" And the truth of it was that I didn't realise how little money there was—at least, not until just before the wedding.'

'And then you told him?'

'I told him,' she agreed. She would never forget the look on her prospective groom's face. That leaching of colour that had left him with a curiously waxy complexion and the fleeting look of horror in his eyes. In that illuminating moment Livvy hadn't been able to decide who she was angrier with—Rupert, for his unbelievable shallowness, or herself for having been too blind to see it before. Maybe she just hadn't wanted to see.

'I told him and he didn't like it. I wish he'd told me right then that he'd changed his mind, so that I wouldn't have to go through the whole pantomime of dressing up in a big white frock with my bridesmaids flapping around me in nervous excitement. But obviously that was something he couldn't face doing. So there.' She looked at him defiantly. 'Have you got the whole picture now?'

There was silence for a moment—the firelight flickering over his ebony hair as he studied her. 'Not quite,' he said.

Defensively, she stiffened. 'You want a blow-by-blow account of my subsequent meltdown?'

He shook his head. 'I meant that not everything you said is true.'

His words were softer than before, as if they'd suddenly been brushed with velvet. Or silk. Yet despite their softness, all the time Livvy was aware of the underlying steel underpinning them, and that made him sound even more attractive. Dangerously so.

'Which bit in particular?'

He smiled. 'That you have nothing to commend you other than a house.'

'Oh, really?'

Saladin heard the disbelief in her voice and felt a surge of rage that someone as worthless as de Vries had smashed her confidence and made her hide herself away like this.

'Yes, really.' His gaze drifted over her. 'Would you like me to list your more obvious attributes?'

Splaying her hands over her hips, she struck a pose. 'My old jeans and sweater?'

'Your complexion, for a start, which makes me think

of honey and cream.' His voice dipped. 'And, of course, your freckles.'

Her fingers strayed to her nose. 'I hate my freckles.'

'Of course you do, but in my country they are highly prized. We call them kisses from the sun.'

'Well, that's certainly not what we call them here.' She gave a nervous laugh and then shivered, as if she had only just registered the sudden plummet in temperature. 'It's cold,' she said, rubbing her hands up and down her arms. 'I should go and make us something to eat.'

'I'm not hungry.'

'You must be. I am. Starving, in fact.'

He could hear the lie in her voice as she jumped to her feet and picked up one of the candles, as if she couldn't wait to escape from the sudden intimacy that had sprung up between them.

'I'll come and help you,' he said.

'No.' The word was sharp, before she pulled it back with a smile. 'I'd prefer to do it on my own. Really. You stay here. You look very comfortable.'

He knew why she was trying to put distance between them and that it was a futile exercise. Didn't she realise that her darkened eyes gave her away and her body was betraying all the signs of sexual excitement? He felt the hard beat of anticipation cradling his groin and suddenly the bright beat of sexual excitement burned out everything except the anticipation of pleasure. 'Don't be long,' he said softly.

Livvy felt almost *helpless* as she made her way towards the kitchen through the now distinctly chilly corridors. She couldn't believe she'd just blurted out all that stuff—to Saladin, of all people—and wondered how he'd managed to cut through her defences so effectively. But he had. She had been surprised at his understanding—and then suspicious of it, because it made her feel vulnerable. And she didn't want to feel vulnerable. She didn't want to feel any of the stuff that was raging through her body like wildfire. As if she would die if he didn't touch her. As if her life wouldn't be complete unless she knew what it was like to have Saladin Al Mektala take her in his arms and kiss her.

Because she had made that mistake once before. She'd fallen for a powerful man who was way out of her league—and it was not something she intended repeating.

She set about preparing food she suspected neither of them wanted, putting a plate of newly baked bread onto a tray along with some cheese from the local shop, and adding some rosy apples that she absently polished with a cloth. She wondered if he drank wine but decided against it, making coffee instead. Wine was the last thing either of them needed.

When she returned to the drawing room, he hadn't moved from where he'd been sitting. In fact, his eyes were closed and he was so still that she thought he might have fallen asleep. For a moment she just stood there looking at him, trying to take in the unbelievable scene that lay before her. A real-life king was stretched out in front of *her* fire, his ebony head resting against the faded crimson silk of the brocade chair. He looked powerful and exotic—dominating his surroundings with a brooding sensuality, which shimmered from his powerful frame. His long legs were sprawled out in front of him and the material of his trousers was flattened down over the hard bulge of his thighs. And

all her best intentions melted away because just looking at him made her want him—and it was *wrong* to
want him.

Suddenly he opened his eyes and the crockery on
the tray she was holding began to jangle as her hands
began to tremble. Livvy hoped he hadn't noticed the
rush of blood that was making her cheeks burn, but
she was aware of the glint of amusement in his eyes
as she walked across the room towards the fire. She
waited for him to make some smart comment, but he
said nothing—just watched in silence as she put the
tray down. Her heart was pounding as she sat down
on the rug beside him and tried to behave casually.

'Help yourself,' she said.

'Help yourself?' There was a pause. 'But I am used
to someone serving me, Livvy.'

She heard the mockery in his voice and she turned
her head to catch the provocative gleam in his eyes.
He's flirting with me, she thought. And no way was she
going to flirt back. 'I'm sure you are,' she said crisply.
'But something tells me you are a man who is perfectly
capable of looking after himself.'

Saladin smiled, wondering if she was aware that
her attitude was slowly sealing her fate. If she had
been submissive and eager to please—as women always were—then his desire might now have faded. But
she wasn't being in the least bit submissive. She was
sitting munching her way through an apple, though
she didn't look as if she was particularly enjoying it—
and her body had stiffened with a defiance that he
couldn't resist.

He could feel the sudden beat of anticipation. Apart
from the protected virgins in his homeland who were

expected to remain pure until marriage, he couldn't
think of a single woman in this situation who wouldn't
be coming on to him by now. She was a challenge—in
a world where few challenges remained. Shifting his
position slightly, he tried to alleviate some of the pressure on his rapidly hardening groin.

She had thrown the apple core into the fire and was
holding out her hands in front of the flames again,
spreading her fingers wide. They were *working* hands,
he thought, and something made him lean over and
pour coffee for them both—though she took hers with
a look of surprise she couldn't quite disguise.

He watched as she ate a little bread and cheese, but
he took no food himself and eventually she pushed
her plate away.

'You're not eating,' she said.

'I told you I wasn't hungry.'

She hugged her arms around her knees and looked
at him. 'So now what do we do? More Scrabble? Or
do you want to try calling up your people to see if the
roads are clear?'

'Forget about my people,' he said impatiently, his
gaze straying to the pinpoint tips of her nipples. 'You're
cold.'

Livvy saw the direction of his glance—bold, ap-
praising and unashamed—and felt the instant quicken-
ing of her body in response. Her heart was fluttering
as if it was trying to escape from the confinement of
her ribcage, and she knew exactly what she should
do. She should say goodnight and go upstairs to her
icy bedroom and stay there until the morning brought
snow ploughs, or his private helicopter or *something*
to rescue them from their incarceration.

But she didn't. She stayed exactly where she was, seated on the rug, gazing back at him—as if she had no idea what was going to happen next. Yet despite her lack of experience and the sheer impossibility of the situation, she knew exactly what was about to happen because it was happening right now. Saladin Al Mektala was putting his hand on her shoulder and pulling her close before bending his head to kiss her.

Livvy reeled at that first sweet taste as he began to explore her mouth with the flickering tip of his tongue, and a great wave of desire and emotion swept through her in a stupefying rush. As his arms tightened around her she felt safe. She could taste coffee on his tongue and feel the warmth of his breath as he anchored her head to deepen the kiss and she opened her mouth beneath his seeking lips. His fingertips moved to whisper their way over her neck, but the first touch of his hand to her breast made her freeze as she wondered just what he would expect from her.

She knew exactly what he would expect from her—and it was a million miles away from the reality of what he would actually get. And wouldn't he be horrified if he knew the truth?

'Saladin—' The word came out as a barely intelligible sound as she broke the kiss.

'You're now going to list all the reasons why we shouldn't do this?' he said unsteadily.

'Yes.'

'Starting with what? Lack of desire?' He grazed the pad of his thumb over her bottom lip and it trembled wildly in response. 'I don't think so.'

With an effort she jerked away from him, her words tumbling out of her mouth as she struggled to do the right thing. 'Starting with the fact that you're a sheikh and I'm a commoner and we don't really know each other.'

'Something that can be solved in an instant,' he said unevenly.

'In fact, we don't even seem to *like* one another,' she continued. 'We've done nothing but argue since you arrived.'

'But conflict can make sex so piquant, don't you think?' he murmured. 'Such a blessed relief when all that tension is finally broken.'

Livvy didn't answer. She didn't dare. Would he laugh if he realised the truth? And now he was reaching behind her head to tug the elastic band from her ponytail—and she was letting him. Sitting there perfectly still as her hair spilled down over her shoulders and his eyes narrowed with appreciation.

'You could probably come up with a whole stack of reasons why we shouldn't,' he said. 'But there's one thing that cancels out every one of your objections.'

She knew she shouldn't, but Livvy asked it all the same. 'Which is?'

'Because we want to. Very, very badly. At least, I do. How about you?'

Livvy shut her eyes, afraid that she would be swayed by the desire that burned so blackly from his eyes. *Because we want to.* How simple that sounded to someone who hadn't followed her own desires for so long that she'd forgotten how. But maybe that was because she hadn't ever been tempted before—at least, not like this. After she had behaved so circumspectly with Rupert, his betrayal had come as a complete shock and had made her question her own judgement. She'd been cautious of men—and wary. After she'd packed up her wedding dress and sent it off to raise money for charity, she had felt empty inside—as if there were a space there that could never be filled. She had begun to think there was something wrong with her. That she wasn't like other women.

But now…

Now there was a hot storm of need within her and she felt anything was possible. That the powerful sheikh had all the knowledge required to give her pleasure. And was it such a terrible thing to want pleasure when it had been denied to her for so long?

She tipped her head back to expose her neck to him and instantly he covered it with a path of tiny kisses. Beneath the sweater, she could feel the increasing weight of her breasts and the denim of her jeans scraping against her newly sensitive thighs as sexual hunger began to pulse through her.

'Saladin,' she said again, her voice a throaty invitation as she felt his hand move slowly down her ribcage towards her waist.

'You are very overdressed, *habibi*,' he observed, peeling the sweater over her head with effortless dexterity.

Livvy held her breath with trepidation as he began to unbutton the shirt underneath and she wondered if he would be turned off by her boring white bra, because a man like this would surely be used to fine underwear. But he didn't appear to notice any obvious deficiencies in the lingerie department as he peeled away her shirt—he seemed too intent on bending his dark head to her exposed skin and she shivered again as she felt his tongue slide over her breastbone, leaving a moist trail behind.

'Your body is so tiny,' he said as he edged his fingers beneath the waistband of her jeans. 'I don't think I've ever been with a woman who is so small.'

And that was when reality hit her like an invisible punch to the solar plexus. She was making out with a man she barely knew. A ruthless sheikh who exuded a dark and dangerous sensuality—and she was seconds away from succumbing to him. Heart pounding, she wrenched herself away, grabbing at her scattered clothes and scrambling to her feet as he stared up at her with dazed disbelief.

'What's going on?' he demanded.

She began to button up her shirt with shaking fingers. 'Isn't it obvious? I'm stopping this before it goes any further.'

He raked his fingers through his hair, his expression one of impatience and frustration. 'I thought we'd already had this conversation,' he growled.

'It's an ongoing conversation,' she said, sucking in an unsteady breath. 'On every level, this would be a mistake and it's not going to happen. We're two people from completely different worlds, who won't ever see one another again once the snow melts. It seems you're stuck here until help arrives, but there's nothing we can do about it. We'll just have to make the best of a bad situation. Just so you know—there are seven bedrooms in this house and you're welcome to sleep in any of them.' She glared at him. 'Just stay out of mine.'

CHAPTER FIVE

SALADIN WAS CUPPING her breast again, only this time it was completely bare. His palm was massaging the peaking nipple and Livvy made a mewing little sound of pleasure.

'Please,' she moaned softly. 'Oh, Saladin. Please.'

He didn't answer, but now his hand was circling her belly—slowly and rhythmically—before drifting down towards the soft tangle of curls at her thighs and coming to a tantalising halt. Her throat dried as the molten heat continued to build and she felt her thighs part in silent invitation. *Just do it*, she prayed silently. *Forget all those stupid objections I put in your way. I was stupid and uptight and life is too short. I don't care whether it's right or wrong, I just want you.*

She opened her mouth to call his name again when she heard the loud bang of a door somewhere in the distance and she woke with a start, blinking in horror as she looked around, her heart banging against her ribcage like a frenzied drum. Disorientated and bewildered, she tried to work out what had happened, before the truth hit her. She was in her bedroom at Wightwick Manor with her hand between her legs, about to call

out Saladin's name—and she'd never felt so sexually
excited in her life.

Whipping the duvet away, she was relieved to see
that the other side of the bed was smooth and unslept
in—although her pyjama bottoms were uncharacter-
istically bunched up into a small bundle at the bottom
of the bed. Heart still racing, she grabbed them and
slithered them on, still trying to make sense of the
warm lethargy and pervading sense of arousal that
was threatening to overwhelm her. *So don't let it*, she
told herself fiercely. *Just calm down and try to work
out what's going on.*

Jumping out of bed, she scooted over to the windows
and pulled back the heavy curtains—her heart per-
forming a complicated kind of somersault as she looked
outside. Because there, on the snow-laden lawns, was
her sweetest dream and worst nightmare all rolled into
one. Saladin Al Mektala knee-deep in snow. The man
she'd dreamed about so vividly that she'd woken up
believing he was in bed with her was outside, shovelling snow like a labourer.

He'd managed to find a spade from somewhere and
had cleared the path leading to the front door, although
the rest of the landscape was still banked with white.
More snow must have fallen overnight and the beautiful gardens were unrecognisable—blotted out by a
mantle that was so bright it hurt the eyes. Livvy blinked
against the cold whiteness of the light. And once again,
that sense of unreality washed over her, because it was
beyond *weird* to see the desert-dwelling king standing in the middle of the snowy English countryside.

He must have found himself a pair of the welling-
tons she always kept for the guests in case they wanted

to go walking—because, in her experience, nobody ever brought the correct footwear with them. She wondered why he hadn't put on one of the waterproof jackets, because surely it was insane to be shovelling snow in a cashmere coat that must have cost as much as her monthly heating bill.

She was about to duck away from the window when he looked up, as if her presence had alerted him to the fact he was being watched. He was too far away for her to be able to read his expression correctly—and Livvy told herself she was imagining the glint of mischief in his eyes. Was she? With a small howl of rage, she turned away and headed for the freezing bathroom just along the corridor—only to discover that the lights still weren't working.

After a brief and icy shower, her worried thoughts ran round and round, like a hamster on a wheel. It *had* just been a dream, hadn't it? The aching breasts and heavy pelvis and the hazy memories of him in bed with her all just the legacy of an overworked imagination, weren't they? Probably her subconscious reacting to the way he'd kissed her by the fire.

Pulling on a black sweater over her jeans, she piled up her hair into a topknot, wondering why he'd made a pass at her in the first place. Maybe she looked like someone who was crying out for a little affection. Or maybe he'd just felt sorry for her when she'd told him about Rupert.

He was arrogant and infuriating and dangerous and yet, when she closed her eyes, all she could remember was the sweet seduction of his kiss as he'd pulled her against his hard body.

She ran downstairs and checked the phone but the lines were still down. Which meant…

Meant…

The front door slammed and Saladin walked in, looking as if the wintry wilds of the snowy English countryside were his natural habitat. His golden skin was glowing after the physical exertion of shovelling snow, and Livvy flushed a deep pink as embarrassment coursed through her. Because suddenly all she could think about was her dream and how vivid it had felt. And it *was* a dream, wasn't it?

'Where did you sleep?' she questioned—and wasn't part of her terrified he'd answer 'in your bed'? That he would sardonically inform her that the reason the dreams had been so vivid was because they were real…

'Aren't you supposed to enquire *how* I slept, rather than where?' he questioned coolly, removing a pair of leather gloves and dropping them on a table. 'Isn't that the usual role of the hostess?'

She forced a smile. 'Okay. Let's start again. How did you sleep?'

'For a time I slept the sleep of the just,' he drawled, raking his fingers back through black hair that was damp with melting snow. 'But that was before you woke me up.'

Livvy's throat dried as she stared at him in growing horror. 'I *woke you up*?'

'Indeed you did.' He flicked her a glance from between the dark forest of his lashes. 'You were shouting something in your sleep.'

Her rosy flush was now a distant memory. She could feel all the colour leaching from her face and knew from past experience that her freckles would be standing out as if someone had spattered mud all over her skin. 'What,' she croaked, 'was I shouting?'

There was a split-second pause. 'At first I thought it was my name until I decided I was probably mistaken—given the abrupt way you drew the evening to a conclusion,' he said, his eyes sending out some sort of coded message she couldn't decipher. 'But I thought I'd better get up and investigate anyway.'

Livvy's heart pounded. 'Right,' she said breathlessly.

'So I walked along the corridor to your room, and you shouted it again but this time there could be no mistake, because it was very definitely my name and you were saying it as if you were in some kind of pain. Or something.' His eyes glittered. 'So I turned the door handle and…'

'And?' she squeaked, hating the way he had deliberately paused for dramatic effect.

He glimmered her a smile. 'And I discovered that you'd locked yourself in.'

'So I had,' she remembered, breathing out a shaky sigh of relief.

'Of course—' his eyes narrowed but she couldn't mistake the dangerous glint sparking from their ebony depths '—if there had been any real danger, no door would have kept me out—locked or otherwise. In the circumstances, I can't quite decide whether you were being prudent or paranoid. What did you think was going to happen, Livvy—that I was going to force my way into your room in the middle of the night, all on the strength of one little kiss?'

'Of course not,' she said stiffly, wondering if her words sounded as unconvincing to him as they did to her. What if she *had* left her door unlocked and he'd come running when she'd called out his name? It wasn't beyond the realms of possibility that she would have reached out for him, was it? Grabbed at him and kissed him as hungrily as before. It wouldn't take much of a leap of the imagination to work out what would have happened next…

She wanted to bury her face in her hands, or close her eyes and find that when she opened them he would be gone—taking with him all these confusing thoughts and this gnawing sense of frustration. But that wasn't going to happen, and it was vital she acted as if it was no big deal. As if it had been just *one little kiss*—as he had said so dismissively.

'I certainly didn't mean to disrupt your night,' she said.

'I can live with it,' he said softly. 'Would you like some coffee? There's a pot brewing in the kitchen.'

'You've made coffee?' she questioned.

'Last night you told me to make myself at home. You also made it very clear that you weren't going to wait on me, so it seems I shall have to fend for myself.'

He turned on his heel and began walking towards the kitchen, and Livvy felt obliged to follow him, wondering indignantly how he had managed to assume such a powerful sense of ownership in *her* home.

By daylight and without the mysterious glow of candles, the kitchen seemed a far less threatening environment than it had done last night. Livvy sat down at the table and watched as he poured coffee with the same dexterity as he'd demonstrated when removing her sweater. Oh, God—he'd taken off her sweater. And her shirt. Briefly, she shut her eyes. He would have taken off even more if she hadn't stopped him.

So stop letting him take control. Tell him he's got to stop shovelling snow and making coffee and to concentrate on getting himself out of here as soon as possible. She needed to remember that the response he evoked in her was purely visceral, and it would soon pass. He'd kissed her and made her feel good, and so her body wanted him to do it all over again. It was as simple as that—and it was to be avoided at all costs.

'So did you get through to your people?' she questioned.

Saladin slid the cup towards her. 'I did. On a very bad line and with a low battery, but yes. Sugar?'

'Just milk, thanks.' She took the coffee. 'And they're coming to get you, I presume?'

'Unfortunately, it's not quite that easy,' he said smoothly. 'Several trees are down and some of the lanes are blocked, and all the gritting lorries are needed for the arterial roads.'

Livvy only just avoided choking on her second mouthful of coffee. 'What does that mean?'

Saladin shrugged. He wondered if she realised he could have commandeered a whole fleet of gritting lorries with a click of his fingers—plus a helicopter prepared to swoop down and fly him away to anywhere he chose to go.

But he wasn't planning on leaving. At least, not yet. Not until she'd agreed to accompany him to Jazratan. And he realised there was something else that was making him stay put—and that was a desire for her so intense that he couldn't look at her without his groin aching. 'It means I'm staying here, Livvy,' he said.

Her eyes widened with alarm and with something else—something that was easily recognisable as desire. He could see it in the self-conscious way her body stiffened whenever he approached. He had tasted it in that amazing firelight kiss last night even if— incredibly—she had turned him down afterwards. And it pleased him that her hunger matched his, even if her reluctance to have sex with him astonished him. Did she realise that resisting him was only fuelling his determination to join with her? Why, he could have exploded with frustration and excitement when she'd banished him to his bedroom and barricaded herself into her own room last night. For passion-fuelled seconds he'd actually considered behaving as one of his ancestors would have done and broken down the door—before sanity had prevailed and he had slunk away with a sense of disbelief and a throbbing groin.

'You're staying here?' she echoed as a series of conflicting emotions crossed over her freckled face.

'It would seem so.'

'For how long?'

'Until it's safe to leave.'

'Surely someone like you could call for a helicopter,' she objected. 'I can't believe that the sheikh of Jazratan, with all his power and influence, is stuck in the snow in the English countryside.'

He smiled, because this was something else he wasn't used to. People usually did everything to entice him to stay because they loved the cachet of having a royal in their presence. They didn't stare at him with a mulish expression on their face, not bothering to hide their wish to see him gone. 'Anything is *possible*,' he mused. 'But you wouldn't want me to put one of my pilots at risk, would you, Livvy—just because having me around makes you feel uncomfortable?'

She licked her lips, as if his soft tone had temporarily disarmed her—which was precisely what he intended it to do.

'You don't make me feel uncomfortable.'

Their eyes met.

'Well, then,' he said softly. 'There isn't a problem, is there?'

She glared at him and Saladin felt a heady sense of triumph. Surely she must realise by now that that resistance was futile?

'Just so you know,' she said, glancing up at the wall clock, 'I have things to do and I can't stand around entertaining you all day.'

'If this is what you term as entertainment, I'm happy to pass.'

She slanted him a furious look. 'I have to work on the assumption that the weather is going to clear and that my guests will be arriving on schedule.'

'So let me help you.'

Livvy put down her cup with a clatter. *'How?'*

'Are there logs that need chopping?'

'You chop logs?'

'Yes, I chop logs, Livvy. Or do you think I lie around on silken cushions all day doing nothing?'

'I have no idea. I hadn't given your daily routine a moment's thought.'

Exaggeratedly, he ran his hand slowly down over his biceps. 'You don't get a body like this by just lying around all day.'

'That's the most outrageous boast I've ever heard!'

He smiled. 'So? Logs?'

'A man from the village chops them.' She got up from the table. 'But you can bring some through to the drawing room from the big pile in the storehouse if you like. That would be very helpful. And if you'd like to light the fire, that would also be helpful.'

'And then?'

'Then I'm decorating the Christmas tree.'

She flung the words out like a challenge.

'Ah,' he said. 'Something at which I am a complete novice, which means you can order me round to your heart's content. I'm sure that will give you immense pleasure, won't it, Livvy? You seem to enjoy taking control.'

He watched as she appeared to bite back what she was about to say. She looked as if she wanted to tell him to go to hell.

'I suppose you can hold the ladder for me,' she said, and he almost laughed as she bit out the ungracious response.

Half an hour later he found himself gripping the sides of a ladder while she hauled dusty boxes from the loft and handed them to him. Saladin stared down at different labelled boxes bearing the words *Baubles* and *Tinsel* with the sense of a man entering uncharted territory. He had never decorated a Christmas tree in his life—it wasn't a holiday they celebrated in Jazratan—and unexpectedly he found he was enjoying himself.

From his position at the foot of the stepladder, he was able to study the slender curves of Livvy's body, and from this angle her jeans certainly looked a lot more flattering. Every step up the ladder hugged the denim against the curve of her buttocks and outlined each slender thigh. His gaze travelled up to the back of her neck, which was pale and dusted with a few freckles. He wondered if she had deliberately put her hair into that topknot, knowing he would want to remove the single clip that held it in place. So that it would tumble around her shoulders like a fall of flame, the way it had done last night...

Last night.

He swallowed as she leaned out to attach a sparkly silver ball to the end of a branch, his hands again gripping the sides of the ladder—not quite sure which of them he was keeping steady. He'd lied to her about sleeping well because the truth was that he'd barely slept at all—especially when he'd realised she'd meant what she said, and that she wouldn't be sharing a bed with him. In the silence of his icy room, he'd kept reliving their fireside kiss—thinking how unexpectedly *erotic* it had been. His fierce hunger for her had taken him by surprise—because nobody could deny that she was a very unassuming creature—but just as surprising was her determination to resist him.

At first he'd thought she was joking. Or that she was playing the old, familiar game because women often believed that a man was more likely to commit if they played hard to get. He gave a cynical smile. But if that was her plan then she was wasting her time, because there would be no commitment from him other than the guarantee of pleasure. His mouth hardened and his heart clenched with pain. He had walked that path before and he would not be setting foot on it again.

'Could you hand me that angel, please?'

Angel? Livvy's voice broke into his uncomfortable thoughts and Saladin picked up the figure she was pointing to—a plastic doll wearing a crudely sewn dress. A tiny ring of tinsel wreathed the flaxen hair, and she was holding a foil-covered matchstick, which he assumed was meant to be a wand.

'Homemade?' he ventured wryly, as he held it out towards her.

She hesitated before giving a brief, sad smile. 'I made it with my mum.'

That smile touched something deep inside him and he found himself wanting to kiss her again, but her rapid ascent up the ladder was clearly intended to terminate the conversation, and maybe that was best. *Yes, definitely for the best*, he told himself. Instead, he forced himself to concentrate on the way she brought the bare tree to life by heaping on the glittering baubles and tinsel while the fire crackled and spat. It was one of the most innocent ways he'd ever spent a morning, and Saladin was overcome by an unexpected wave of emotion, because wasn't it captivating to find a woman whose main focus wasn't sex? How long since he'd been in the company of a female who was behaving with restraint and with decorum? Not since Alya, he thought—and a wave of guilt washed over him as he made the comparison.

'Be careful,' he growled as she began to back her way down the ladder.

'I am being careful.'

But suddenly, he was not. He was giving in to what he could no longer resist. He caught hold of her as she made that last step and his hand closed over hers, and to his surprise she didn't pull away from him. She just stared at him as he turned her hand over and raised it slowly to his lips, his tongue snaking out over her palm to slowly lick at the salty flesh.

'Saladin,' she whispered, but he could see that her eyes had darkened.

'Don't talk anymore, because I'm going to kiss you,' he said, his voice deepening with sudden urgency. 'But you already know that, don't you, Livvy? You know that's what I have been longing to do since I got up this morning.'

As a stalling device it was pathetic, but Livvy said it all the same, lifting her gaze to the bare ceiling. 'There's supposed to be mistletoe,' she whispered.

'Damn the mistletoe,' he ground out as his head came down towards hers.

CHAPTER SIX

ONE KISS, LIVVY told herself as Saladin's mouth claimed hers. One kiss and no more. Just like last night—it didn't have to lead anywhere. She could call a halt to it any time she liked.

But deep down she knew she was fooling herself—because this felt *different*. Last night had been all about candlelight and firelight and a sense of other-worldliness that had descended on them as they'd sat around the sparking logs. Restaurants didn't dim the lights for no reason and call it *mood lighting*, did they?

But today…

In the cold clear light of today, in the harsh and blinding reflection of newly fallen snow—there was nothing but rawness and reality. And hunger. Oh, yes. A fierce hunger that had been building all night—even while she slept—and that was being fed by the sweet seduction of Saladin's kiss as he began to explore her mouth. He kissed her softly at first, and then he kissed hard and long and deep—with a warm urgency that was contagious. And she wanted him. She wanted him more than she'd ever wanted anything, because this was like nothing she'd ever experienced before.

Wrapping her fingers around his neck, she kissed

him back and, although he held her very tightly, it was almost as if she were floating free. She felt soft. Boneless. As if every point of her body was a pleasure point. As if every inch of her skin was an erogenous zone. Wherever Saladin touched her she felt on fire. With each kiss he dragged her deeper into the silken web he was weaving. At some point she thought she must have groaned because suddenly he pulled back, sucking in a ragged breath, his eyes as bright as a man with a fever.

'Here?' he questioned succinctly. 'Or upstairs?'

It was a brutal question that killed off some of the romance she'd been feeling, but at least it was *real* and at least there could be no misinterpretation about his intentions. He wasn't dressing it up to be something it wasn't. This was sex, pure and simple. He wasn't *lying* to her, was he?

'Can't decide?' he murmured, and, when she didn't answer, he began to nuzzle her neck.

She tipped her head back while she skated through the possibilities. The bed would be better. She could hide beneath the concealing weight of the duvet, couldn't she? But this wasn't supposed to be about *hiding*. This was about taking control of her own destiny. About taking something she really wanted for once, instead of being influenced by other people's expectations.

She realised he was waiting for an answer, and her heart missed a beat as she stared into the blackness of his eyes. He was the wrong man on so many levels, but did that matter? Doing the *right* thing had never worked out for her, had it? Maybe it was time to run full tilt at glorious fantasy and forget all about reality for once, because this gorgeous man wanted to make love to *her*.

And when some bone-deep instinct warned her that he was capable of inflicting pain—real emotional pain, far worse, she suspected, than any she'd suffered with Rupert—she reminded herself that she was a different person now. She was no longer that innocent bride who looked at the world through rose-tinted glasses. She was independent and she could handle this. So what the hell was she waiting for?

'Here,' she managed from between swollen lips. 'I want to do it here.'

He brought his head down as if to seal her intention with another kiss, but she sensed his growing impatience as he led her over to the fire and pulled her close—close enough for her to feel every sinew of his powerful body. Pulling the pin from her hair, he watched as it tumbled around her shoulders.

'Your hair is like fire,' he murmured, letting silky strands slide through his fingers. 'You should wear it down all the time.'

She opened her mouth to tell him it wouldn't be practical but her words were forgotten as he removed her sweater, his eyebrows shooting upwards as a lacy bra of midnight-blue silk was revealed.

Tiptoeing his fingertip along the delicate edging of lace, he pushed her down onto the silken rug. 'What's this?' he murmured.

'It's…a bra. What does it look like?'

'Nothing like the one you had on last night, that's for sure.' Slowly, he expelled the air from his lungs as he flattened his palm over one peaking mound. 'Did you wear it specially for me?'

Had she? She'd never worn it before. A friend had given her birthday vouchers to an upmarket lingerie shop that didn't know the meaning of words like *sensible* or *refund*. The navy set had been the most practical thing on offer, but up until today it had seemed too delicate for everyday use. There had never been a reason to wear it before, yet something had made her put it on this morning...

'Maybe subconsciously,' she admitted.

He gave a glimmer of a smile. 'A woman only wears underwear like this if she wants a man to take it off. Is that what you want me to do, Livvy? Is that what you've been longing for me to do ever since you got up this morning? To run my fingers over your beautiful pale skin and get you naked?'

She closed her eyes as his hand strayed to the bra's front clasp. She wanted to tell him that his assumption was arrogant, but how could she protest when his fingers had loosened the clip and her breasts were spilling free? The cool air hit her skin and suddenly he was bending his lips to a nipple and he was sucking on it. Nipping at it and grazing his teeth all over the sensitised nub. She gave a little squeal of pleasure and he lifted his head.

'You are very vocal in your approval, *habibi*,' he observed softly. 'Does that feel good?'

Her tongue snaked out to moisten her parched lips. 'So good,' she breathed.

'And this? Does this feel good?'

Against the rug, Livvy writhed with pleasure as his hand moved between her legs, because her body suddenly felt as if was out of her control and words seemed to be beyond her. Did he really need her to tell him that she liked the way he was sucking her nipple? The way his finger was rubbing up and down the stiff seam of her jeans at the very point where she was acutely sensitive. The finger stilled.

'Does it?' he questioned silkily.

Did he want praise? Maybe she was expected to touch *him*. To reach out to where his crotch was straining so formidably against his trousers and to trickle her fingers over his hardness. Livvy's heart began to pound. Her experience of foreplay was limited, because Rupert had known she was a virgin and had wanted to wait until they were married and had said he didn't trust himself to touch her. It wasn't until afterwards that she had discovered the reason why...

Her sex life was something she regarded as an arid area of failure, but instinct told her that Saladin Al Mektala could be the person to change all that. She suspected that what the sheikh didn't know about pleasure wouldn't be worth knowing. Yet surely it would be deceitful to let him make love to her without telling him her secret.

'Does it?' he repeated silkily, and Livvy circled her hips with frustration and guilt.

What if she told him and he rejected her—if he left her shivering and aching with frustration in front of the fire?

She had to tell him.

She stared straight into his black eyes. 'It feels incredible,' she said. 'But maybe you ought to know that I'm—'

'Driving me crazy with desire, that's for sure,' he said, moving over her to silence her words with another breathtaking kiss.

And Livvy let him. That was the shame of it. She just let him. Wrapping her arms around his neck, she kissed him back with a slow, exploratory hunger as he began to slide down the zipper of her jeans.

'Mmm...' was his only comment as he tugged the denim away to reveal the lacy blue knickers that matched her bra, before concentrating his attention on kissing her body. He whispered his lips over her breasts—his breath warm against her skin—before travelling down to her belly. She held her breath as his head travelled downwards until his dark head was positioned between her thighs. For a moment she tensed, but when he licked almost lazily at the moist panel of her panties a spasm of pleasure so intense shot through her that for a moment Livvy was scared she might faint.

Was it the half-broken cry she made in response to that intimacy that made him suddenly stop? Her nails dug hard into his shoulders in protest but he didn't appear to care.

'Don't—' she gasped.

Had he read her mind?

'Don't stop?' He looked up from his decadent position between her thighs, and smiled. 'I have no intention of stopping, but I am hungry to feel my skin next to yours, *habibi*. And while you are almost naked—I am not.'

She didn't want him to move—terrified that any movement would shatter this precarious magic—but she had little choice except to lie there and watch as he stood up and began to strip off. His shirt was silk and so were his boxers and they floated to the ground like fine gossamer. Livvy's mouth dried as his body was revealed. His dark skin glowed like richest gold and the deep shadows cast by the flickering firelight emphasised his physical perfection. A hard and rippling torso, with powerful arms and muscular legs that seemed to go on forever. Narrow hips and rock-hard buttocks. Even the powerful evidence of his arousal wasn't as daunting as it should have been because by now Livvy was alive with a need that had been buried inside her for so long that she felt she would die if he didn't make love to her.

Her heart was pounding as she stared at his erection, but when he reached down into the pocket of his trousers and drew out a condom, she felt a flutter of misgiving. Did he always carry protection with him? Did he take it for granted that there would always be a willing woman lying waiting for him like this? She thought about the women who sometimes used to accompany him to the stables—those models and actresses with their suede boots and miniskirts and real fur. For a moment she wondered how she could possibly compare to those glamorous creatures, until she forced the dark clouds of insecurity from her mind. Maybe there *was* always an accommodating female wherever he went—like a sailor having a woman in every port—but this wasn't about *convention*, was it? She'd done all that stuff and look where it had got her.

She thought about the heartache of the past and the struggle her life had been for so long. She stared over Saladin's shoulder as he slithered her panties off and moved over her. Outside the world was white and still and silent, apart from the distant ticking of a clock. Time was passing, but they were completely alone and this moment would never come again. And she had to seize it—to grab it—and to hell with the consequences.

Yet once before she had blinded herself to the truth. She'd buried her head in the sand and allowed herself to be treated like a fool by the man she'd been engaged to. Was she going to repeat that pattern of behaviour all her life—to run away from what she was afraid to face?

'Saladin,' she whispered as he rubbed his thumb over her clitoris. 'There's something you should know.'

'The only thing I need to know is whether you like… this…'

She closed her eyes. *Like* it? She imagined that even a marble statue would have squirmed beneath his questing finger, but that wasn't the point. The words came out in a bald rush—but what other way was there to say them? 'I'm a virgin.'

His fingers—which had been working rhythmically against her heated flesh—now stilled. He raised his head to look at her, his eyes full of disbelief—but there was something else in their depths, too. Something she didn't recognise. Something dark and tortured. Something that scared her.

'Is this some sort of joke?' he demanded in a strangled kind of voice.

Wondering what had made him look so *bleak*, Livvy shook her head. 'It's no joke,' she said. 'Why would I joke about something like that? It's the truth. I might not be very proud of it—but it's the truth.'

He rolled away from her and she noticed that his erection had diminished. 'How can this be?' he bit out. 'You are nearly thirty years old. You were engaged to be married. I know what Western women are like. They lose their innocence early and they take many lovers!'

His crass generalisations dispelled some of her insecurity and made Livvy start to claw back some dignity—something that wasn't particularly easy when she wasn't wearing any clothes. Did she dare walk over to the sofa where the soft woollen throw she kept for cold winter nights was folded? Too right she did—because staying here completely naked was making her feel even more vulnerable than she already did. On shaky legs she rose to stand, aware of his heated gaze following her as she walked over to get the blanket and brought it back to the fireside. But as she wrapped it around herself and sat at the other end of the rug, she became aware that his erection was back. And how. Hastily averting her eyes, she turned to throw a log into the neglected fire.

'I hate to ruin your prejudices, but not all women conform to the stereotypes you've just described,' she said. 'The law of averages suggests that there will be some older virgins as well as young ones.'

Saladin's mouth thinned with displeasure, thinking that there couldn't have been a more inappropriate moment for her to try to dazzle him with statistics, and he was amazed she should even dare try. He felt the heavy throb of his heart. He had wanted sex. Simple, uncomplicated sex with a willing woman. He didn't want someone with *issues* or *baggage*. He didn't want someone who, with her purity, had stirred up memories he had locked away a long time ago. For he had only ever slept with one virgin before, and that virgin had been his beautiful wife. Pain and guilt clenched at his heart as he stared at her.

'I don't understand,' he said coldly.

'You don't have to. I'm…' And suddenly he saw the uncertainty that flickered across her pale and freckled face. 'I'm sorry if I led you on.'

An unwanted but persistent point of principle made him shake his head. 'We led each other on,' he said heavily. 'But it is true that you have left it a little *late* to drop this particular bombshell.'

Awkwardly, she shrugged. 'Do you want to get dressed?'

Saladin shook his head. What he wanted was to be back where he'd been less than five minutes ago, not stuck in the middle of some damned conversation! 'I don't believe it,' he breathed. 'I thought it was the custom in the West to have sex before marriage—and you were on the very brink of marriage. So what happened?'

'It's difficult to put into words.'

'You don't seem to have had much problem with words so far.'

She shifted uncomfortably beneath his gaze. 'I think I was born in the wrong age,' she said slowly. 'I was a tomboy who loved messing around in the countryside. I climbed trees and used to make dens with the boys from the village. I never had posters of pop stars on my walls like all the other girls in my class. I was more interested in horses—horses were my life. In fact, everything was just like one of those old-fashioned children's stories, until my mum died.'

'That must have been hard,' he said.

She shrugged again and suddenly he thought she looked much younger than nearly thirty.

'Lots of children lose their mothers,' she said. 'But not so many have a father who was left feeling very vulnerable. A rich widower who became perfect marriage fodder for the kind of woman commonly known as a gold-digger.'

'I have some experience of that breed myself,' he observed wryly. 'So what happened?'

She shrugged. 'He fell for a busty blonde with a penchant for diamonds and couture and then he married her. My father was a country gentleman and this house had been in his family for generations, but his new wife preferred luxury travel and sailing in sunny waters on a lavish yacht. She was the kind of woman who would buy an entire new wardrobe before every trip—and we weren't the sort of family who had a lot of ready cash. Most of it was tied up in the house. Would you…?' Again, she licked her lips. 'Would you like a blanket, or something?'

He would like *something*, but he suspected he wasn't going to get it right then. 'Why, is my nakedness bothering you?'

'A little.'

'Just a little?' He let his gaze slide down to his groin before raising his eyes to her flaming cheeks. 'I must be slipping. Very well, bring me a blanket if it makes you feel better.'

He wondered if she was aware that he was being treated to a tantalising glimpse of her bare bottom as she walked over to a second sofa and grabbed another blanket, though he noticed that she averted her gaze again as she thrust it at him before resuming her position at the other end of the rug.

'So what happened?' he questioned, watching as she huddled herself in a cocoon of soft wool. 'Or can I guess? Did she grow bored with marriage to an older man? Did she demand more and more money, until she'd bled him dry?'

Her eyes widened. 'How did you know?'

'Because I know what women are like,' he said. 'And your stepmother was conforming to a pattern that isn't exactly ground-breaking.' His eyes narrowed. 'And ironically, you met your own male version of the gold-digger in de Vries.'

She nodded before staring down at the pattern on the rug as if completely absorbed by it, but when she lifted her face he noted that her expression was calm—as if she had practised very hard to look that way.

'That's right. I can't believe that I didn't see it for myself, my only defence being that I was very young,' she said. 'His stables were in trouble—everyone knew that—but nobody realised quite how bad the problem was. He knew I was an only child and he saw this house and made the assumption we were rolling in money. Which, of course, we weren't. My father was quite an old man by then and he was ill. We had a lot of carers who were coming in and helping me look after him, and they cost an absolute fortune.'

'And I suppose that was also occupying a lot of your time and energy?' he said grimly.

She nodded again. 'He was very frail by then, and Rupert seemed so understanding about it all. He didn't seem to mind when I had to cancel dinner because one of the carers hadn't shown up. And because he was my first real boyfriend, I had nothing to compare him with. I just thought he was being kind. When he said…' She sucked in a deep breath. 'When he said that he wanted to wait until we were married before we had sex, I found that somehow reassuring.'

Saladin nodded. Yes, he could see that. A horse-mad, motherless tomboy whose only role models had been an old man who should have known better and an avaricious stepmother who was out for all she could get. No wonder Livvy hadn't known the rules about relationships, or men, or sex. Nobody had bothered to explain them to her, had they?

'Don't you realise that it reflects badly on him, not you?' he questioned savagely. 'That a man who dumps a woman on her wedding day because she has less money than he thought is not a *real* man. We have a name for that kind of man in Jazratan, but I will not sully your ears with it.'

'But it wasn't just the money. There was something else.' She twisted some of the blanket's tassels between her fingers. 'It turned out that he was sleeping with one of the female grooms and had been for some time, which was why he hadn't tried harder to get into bed with me. Not just any groom, either—but my best friend. And there was me thinking that he was displaying old-fashioned values of chivalry designed to win a woman's heart, not realising that I was being betrayed by the two people I considered closest to me.' She gave a short and bitter laugh. 'What a fool I was.'

'You shouldn't beat yourself up for wanting to believe the best in people,' he said, his voice growing hard. 'Though I hope you've learned your lesson now. It's always better to think the worst. That way you don't get disappointed.'

She stared at him. 'You've been very...' Her voice tailed off.

'Very what?'

'It doesn't matter.'

'I think it does.'

'*Understanding.*' She gave an embarrassed kind of shrug.

'What did you think I was going to do?' he questioned roughly. 'Carry on as if nothing had happened—

kiss away your protests and ignore your obvious reservations? Or maybe you *wanted* me to fulfil the fantasy of the exotic stranger who ravishes the willing but innocent woman. Who takes away the responsibility so you didn't have to make the decision for yourself. Is that what you would have liked? It's a common enough fantasy, especially where desert sheikhs are concerned. Would that have made it easier for you, Livvy?'

She licked her lips. 'I wasn't even going to tell you.'

'No, I gathered that,' he said drily. 'So what changed your mind?'

She shrugged again and the blanket slipped down over her shoulders, before she hauled it back up again. 'I thought it was dishonest not to. I thought you might be one of those men for whom virginity is a big deal.'

Saladin was silent as he considered her words. Was it? Her eyes were wide as she looked at him and he could read the faint anxiety in their depths. He supposed it was. For a man in his position, virginity was an essential requirement of any future queen. But he was not looking for a queen. He had been there, done that. What was it they said in the West? Bought the T-shirt.

His mouth hardened as she held his gaze with those startling amber eyes. Was she seeking reassurance? Holding out for an impossible dream? He felt the hard throb of desire at his groin and shifted his weight. This was a unique situation, but despite his undeniable lust—lust was interchangeable, because there was always another female eager enough to open her legs for him. If it were anyone else, he would get dressed, make a quick phone call and get the hell out of there— no matter how many damned snow ploughs it took.

And that was what he *should* do—he knew that. Because purity was something he always associated with just one woman—and wouldn't it dishonour Alya's memory if he were to take the innocence of another? Every instinct he possessed—except for the sexual instinct—told him to leave now and get away while he still could.

But Livvy Miller still had something he wanted. Something that only she could provide. And maybe he had something *she* wanted, because surely she didn't want to carry on like this. Was now the time for a little adult negotiation? If he fulfilled a need in her— then wouldn't she feel morally obliged to do the same for him?

On her face he could read trepidation warring with desire, and a genuine sense of injustice washed over him. How crazy was it that she had never known the joy of sex? That a woman who was known for her physicality and skill on a horse should have neglected her own body for so long?

He didn't move—he didn't dare—because it was vital he didn't influence her decision, even though he knew that another kiss and she would be melting beneath him. But it had to be *her* decision, not his. His gaze was unwavering as he looked at her.

'So,' he questioned silkily. 'Do you want me to take your virginity, Livvy?'

CHAPTER SEVEN

LIVVY DIDN'T ANSWER straight away. It seemed like
something out of a dream—the powerful sheikh asking if she wanted him to take her virginity, with all the
impartiality of someone enquiring whether she'd like
a spoonful of sugar in her coffee.

As she stared into the provocative gleam of Saladin's black eyes, she thought about everything that had
brought her to this moment. The public shame of being
jilted that had hit her so hard, even though she'd done
her best to hold her head up high afterwards. She'd
walked away from the world of horses without a back-
ward glance and had started a new life.

Out of a sense of loyalty to her father's memory
and a determination that Rupert's rejection wouldn't
destroy her completely, she'd done her best to keep
Wightwick Manor going. On a shoestring budget she'd
worked hard to make her bed and breakfast business a
success. But now she could see that she had neglected
her own needs in the process. She'd put her emotional
life on a back burner, letting her twenties trickle away
beneath the hard work of maintaining an old house like
this. She hadn't done dates or parties or make-up—
she'd spent any spare money on roof tiles, or getting the

windows painted. She hadn't gone off for minibreaks or enjoyed sunny vacations with girlfriends, drinking lurid-coloured cocktails while they were chatted up by waiters. She hadn't even tried to find herself a new boyfriend. She'd told herself she didn't need the potential pain of another relationship.

Yet here she was—naked underneath a blanket while a similarly naked Saladin surveyed her from the other end of the rug. She stared into the dark smoulder of his eyes and wondered how best to respond to his question. She supposed she could say no. Act prim and outraged—and tell him that she wasn't interested in giving her virginity to him, like some kind of medieval sacrifice. He was certainly sophisticated enough to take it on the chin. She doubted he would feel more than a moment of regret, and she would probably be knocked down by the rush of women eager to take her place.

But it wasn't quite that straightforward, because she still wanted him. He'd kissed her passionately and made her feel she was part of something magical. He'd made her feel things she didn't think she was capable of feeling—a powerful passion that had overwhelmed her and a need that had flooded hotly through her veins. He'd set her body on *fire*. She thought about the way he'd touched her—whispering his mouth over each breast in turn, grazing them with his teeth and making her urge him on with writhing hips. She remembered the way his head had slid down between her thighs and something molten and sweet had begun to tug at the very core of her—something that was making refusal seem like a crazy idea. And she knew something else—that she would never get another chance like this.

Desert sheikhs promising untold pleasure didn't come along more than once in a lifetime.

She stared at him.

'Yes,' she said, in a low voice. 'Yes, I want you to take my virginity.'

His face showed no immediate reaction. The hawk-like features displayed no hint of triumph although his lips curved in the briefest of smiles.

'Come here,' he instructed softly.

She wondered briefly why he couldn't come to *her*, but his words were compelling and masterful and Livvy stood up and began to walk towards him, clutching the blanket against her skin like a makeshift dress. She could feel his eyes burning into her—as if that piercing black gaze was capable of scorching through the wool to the body beneath. Her footsteps faltered as she reached him, uncertain about what to do next, but he reached out and slid his thumb over her ankle, massaging briefly against the jut of bone there, before beginning to stroke his way up her calf. Livvy swallowed as pleasure began to ripple over her skin. It seemed such a light, innocuous movement to such an innocent part of the body and yet...yet...

'Saladin,' she whispered.

'Shh.'

The back of her knee was next—a tiny circular movement that must have made her loosen her grip on the blanket because he gave it a single tug and it slid to the ground, leaving her standing naked in front of him. Automatically, her hands flew up to conceal her breasts, before he shook his head.

'Do not cover yourself, Livvy,' he instructed softly. 'Your body is very beautiful. It is small and neat, yet strong and supple. It pleases me very much and I wish to look at it.'

She kept her hands exactly where they were, even though his words were making her nipples peak against her fingers. 'You're making me feel like an object.'

'Not an object,' he demurred, reaching up and pulling her down into his arms, so that her flesh met the comforting warmth of his. He pushed the mussed hair away from her face and used the edge of his thumb to trace the outline of her lips. 'Not even a subject, since I do not rule over you. So stop looking at me with those anxious eyes and relax, because I am going to give you pleasure such as you have never dreamed of.'

'But I don't have a clue what to do,' she whispered.

'And that,' he said unevenly, 'is part of your attraction.'

Only part of it, she wondered dazedly as his mouth came down towards her. What was the other part?

But his kiss was powerful enough to send any last doubts skittering from her mind, and the slow caress of his lips made further deliberations impossible. All she could think about was what he was doing. He was holding her close—so close—making her feel as if every cell in her body were sensitive to each seeking caress.

At first his touch wasn't overtly sexual. The hands that were cupping her face seemed more interested in exploring the thickness of her hair and the outline of her face. And when that innocent exploration made her relax, he started stroking his hands down the sides of her body—until she was moving restlessly against him.

He must have known that her impatience was growing, but he paid no attention to her squirming movements. He just took his time—drawing out the exquisite torture as his fingers slowly acquainted themselves with her skin. Inch by tantalising inch, he touched her. First her breasts and then her ribcage and the undulation of her waist. She held her breath as he turned his attention to her belly and teased her by brushing his fingers farther down to delve inside the soft fuzz of hair. Yet his hawklike features remained impassive even though she could feel the tension building in his powerful body. She could sense his restraint—as if he was battling his own desire in order to feed hers.

'Saladin,' she breathed, looking into his eyes to find herself ensnared by a smoky black gaze.

'Want me?' His thumb brushed against the moist and engorged bud hidden by the soft curls, and she let out a little murmur of assent as she nodded.

'I...I think so.'

'I think so, too,' he said, his voice suddenly growing harsh.

He moved over her, his hardness nudging against her wet heat as she opened her legs for him with an instinct that seemed to come from somewhere deep inside her. She became aware of so many things—his weight and his strength and the subtle scent of sandalwood and salt that clung to his skin.

'Look at me,' he urged softly.

Until he spoke, she hadn't even realised her eyes had closed again. She let the lids flutter open to meet his heated gaze as he made that first thrust deep inside her—a long, slow thrust that made her gasp and instantly he stilled, his eyes narrowing.

'It hurts?'

Breathlessly, she shook her head. 'Not really. It just feels...'

'What?'

'Big.'

Saladin smiled—he couldn't help himself. But her unintentional boost to his masculine ego only increased his hunger—if that was possible—and it was a moment before he could trust himself to move again. Already he felt close to a tipping point that had been reached the moment he had entered her. He could feel her flesh enclosing him as sweetly as an oyster clamped its shell around the glistening pearl. She was so tight. So wet. So...*unexpected*. But he reined back his sudden urgent desire to ride her as fiercely as he would ride one of his horses. Because this was her first time, he reminded himself. This was the touchstone by which she would measure all the men who would follow. And he must make it a good experience—the very best experience— for all kinds of reasons.

So he concentrated on kissing and fondling her. On doing all the things that women liked best and on holding back his own desire. And even though his sexual hunger was at a high that was almost unendurable, it felt exquisite. Maybe because it was the first time in a long time that he had put a woman's needs before his own. Usually he didn't have to, because he prided himself on being able to make a woman orgasm within moments of touching her, but this was different. Virgins were different...

The pain of memory shot through him like a dark streak of lightning and for a moment he screwed his eyes tightly shut, cursing the thoughts that crowded into his mind—and slamming down the barriers before they could take root there.

He drew in a deep breath and began to objectify

what was happening, in order to distract himself. He concentrated on Livvy's reaction rather than his own—watching as her eyes grew dark and her cheeks flushed. He felt the tension in her fingers as they kneaded against his sweat-sheened back. He could feel the urgency in her thighs, which were digging hard against his hips, and the way she instinctively angled her pelvis to encourage him to go deeper. He tipped his head back as she covered his shoulder with a flurry of frantic little kisses that seemed to grow in crescendo as he drove her towards her climax.

He knew when she was about to come. He could sense the change in her body—the unmistakable quiver of expectation and excitement edged with the sense of disbelief that heralded any orgasm. And that was when he kissed her again. Gripped her hips hard as he drove into her. Imprisoned her against his exquisitely aroused length as her back began to arch and he waited for the split second of stillness before she started spasming against his flesh. He thought she called out his name as he gave into his own release, which he could hold back no longer—his own pleasure increased by the sensation of her still quivering helplessly in his arms.

It took him a long time to come down and, unusually, he stayed where he was for a long time—withdrawing only when he felt the returning stir of an erection. He rolled away from her, pulling the discarded blanket over her, unable to resist a glance at her flushed face and the bright, honey-coloured eyes, before her eyelids fluttered sleepily down. But for once he did not want sleep—something his body habitually demanded after sex, which helped emphasise the distance he craved and lessened the chances of being asked pointless questions about the possibility of a long-term relationship.

For once he was wide awake and more alive than he could remember feeling in a long, long time. He wanted to hear what the feisty little redhead had to say about her first experience of sex, although he told himself that his interest was simply academic. He was not looking for praise because he knew how good he was—but he needed her to be satisfied with what had just happened. *He needed to keep her sweet.*

Stroking a slow finger over one flushed breast, he smiled. 'No need to ask whether you enjoyed that.'

His murmured words dissolved the clouds of contentment that had settled on her and, with an effort, Livvy blinked herself awake. Her eyes felt so heavy, it was as if someone had crept in and placed two tiny pebbles on them while she hadn't been looking. She met Saladin's dark gaze. His skin was flushed and his eyes were smoky, yet he sounded more concerned with his own performance rating than with anything else. She told herself that his arrogance didn't matter because nothing had felt this good in a long time—maybe ever—and she'd be a fool not to hold on to it while she could. She felt…warm. Complete. As if she were floating on a pink cloud that she never wanted to get off.

She studied his hawklike features and sensual lips and she wanted him all over again. All she had to do was to lean forward to kiss him, and she had to fight the longing to do just that because something warned her to tread carefully. She needed to remember that the sheikh was unlike other men—and her own track record was hopeless. She didn't want to make a fool

of herself and, more important, she didn't want to give
him the opportunity to reject her. Because hadn't she
vowed that she would never get rejected for a second
time?

She must not make the mistake of falling in love
with him.

What would such a seasoned lover as Saladin normally require in such circumstances? she wondered,
and something told her to play it straight. Just because
her system was flooded with hormones that were making her want to do inappropriate things like stroke his
face and be all *tender*—didn't mean she was going to
listen to them.

'I don't think you'd need me to be wired up to a ma-
chine to register my heart-rate to realise that it was a
very satisfying experience,' she said.

He looked surprised, there was no denying that—
and neither could she deny the little rush of pleasure
that gave her.

'So you don't regret it?'

Livvy chewed on her lip. Did she? She thought about
the vow she had made to herself a long time ago.

'I don't do regrets,' she said quietly. 'Not anymore.'

Saladin's eyes narrowed. It was not the glowing endorsement he had expected, nor the compliancy of a
woman who was eager for more. If he had been on territory he could call his own—a hotel suite, perhaps—
then he might have taken himself off for a long shower
and left her lying there to think about the wisdom of
her words. But he wasn't. He was in *her* house on *her*
rug—and she was still in possession of something he
wanted. He gave a slow smile as he drew a thoughtful
finger down over her breast and felt her shiver. Did she

really think she would be able to deny him now that she had tasted the pleasure he could give her?

'I'm going to make love to you again,' he said.

But instead of being captured by his gaze, she was looking across the room at a radiating blue-white light.

'Your phone's vibrating,' she said.

And her damned *cat* chose that precise moment to stalk into the room and hiss at him.

CHAPTER EIGHT

LIVVY WATCHED AS Saladin walked across the room to answer his phone, not seeming to care that away from the fierce blaze of the fire the unheated room was icy cold on his naked body. Or maybe his careless, almost sauntering journey was deliberate. Perhaps he thought that the sight of him without any clothes would set her heart racing and cast some kind of erotic spell on her. And if that was the case, he was right.

Beside her Peppa gave a plaintive meow, but for once Livvy's stroking of the cat's abundant fur was distracted, because how could she concentrate on anything other than the sight of the magnificent sheikh?

She found herself watching him hungrily in the way that Peppa sometimes watched a beautiful bird as it hopped around the garden. The powerful shafts of his thighs rose to greet the paler globes of buttocks, leading to the narrow taper of his hips and waist. Livvy swallowed. The proud way he held his head and broad line of his shoulders reminded her of a statue she'd once seen in a museum. It seemed impossible that moments before he'd been deep inside her, making her cry out with pleasure.

A man she barely knew—yet one who ironically

knew her more intimately than anyone. She'd told him about still being a virgin and then, very slowly—he had made love to her.

She wrapped the blanket round her as he picked up the vibrating phone and, after clicking the connection, began speaking rapidly in an unknown language she assumed was his native tongue. She noticed that he listened for some—not much—of the time, but mostly he seemed to be barking out commands. She gave a wry smile as she lay back on the rug. She guessed that was what sheikhs did.

Resting her head against her folded arms, she waited—her newfound sense of torpor making her aware of her glowing skin and her sense of satisfaction. And Saladin was responsible for that. For all his arrogance and sense of entitlement, he had proved the most considerate and exciting first lover a woman could wish for.

Lazily, she turned her head and looked out of the window. The snow had stopped falling but there were no signs of a thaw. The landscape looked as pretty as a Christmas card—unreal and somehow impenetrable, as if they were in their own private little bubble and nobody else could get in. Inside, the lack of electricity was beginning to bite and it was starting to get cold. The decorated tree looked strange without the rainbow glow of fairy lights, and despite the blaze of the fire the room had taken a distinct drop in temperature. She dreaded to think how icy it must be upstairs. Some of her euphoria began to leave her as Livvy started to consider the more practical concerns of the power cut. Eight guests were due to arrive the day after tomorrow and she had no electricity!

Her torpor forgotten, she jumped up and grabbed the silky knickers that were lying in a heap on the floor, and had just slithered them on when she felt a light but proprietorial hand on her bottom.

'What do you think you're doing?'

She turned round and steeled herself against the glint of displeasure in Saladin's dark eyes.

'I'm getting dressed.'

'Why?' With possessive intimacy, he trailed his finger down over the silk-covered crack between her buttocks. 'When I want to make love to you again.'

'Because...' Furious at the way her concerns about the electricity should have morphed into concerns about the very different kind of electricity that was sparking from her skin where he touched her, Livvy tried to pull away. 'Because there's no power and my freezer will be defrosting, and the roads might be cleared at any time. And there are eight guests who will be arriving for Christmas who won't have any croissants for breakfast if the freezer defrosts!' She drew in a deep breath. 'And while these might not be the kind of problems that would normally enter your radar, this is the *real world*, Saladin—and it's a world in which I have to live!'

'And how does getting dressed solve anything when your guests aren't due today?'

She met the mocking expression in his eyes. *It stops me from getting too close to you again. It stops me from feeling any more vulnerable than I'm currently feeling.*

Livvy never knew how she would have answered his question because suddenly the electricity came on in a flurry of light and sound. The tree lights blazed into life and three small lamps began to glow. Somewhere in another part of the house a distant radio began playing and Peppa jumped to her feet and gave a growling little purr.

'The power's back on,' he said.

'Yes,' she answered, in a strange flat voice.

And then the landline started to ring—its piercing sound shattering the silence of their haven. Livvy stared at Saladin, aware of a sinking sensation that felt awfully like disappointment. The outside world was about to intrude and, right then, she didn't want it to.

'Better answer it,' he said.

Clad in just her knickers, Livvy scooted across the room to pick up the phone and nodded her head as she listened to the voice on the other end.

'No, no. That's quite all right, Alison,' she said, aware that Saladin was putting a guard in front of the fire. 'Honestly, it really doesn't matter. I quite understand. I would have done exactly the same in your position. Yes. Yes, I hope so. Okay. I will. Yes. Of course. And a merry Christmas to you, too. Goodbye.'

Slowly, she replaced the receiver as Saladin straightened up and suddenly a part of his anatomy was looking like no museum statue *she'd* ever seen, and it was all still so new to her that she didn't know whether it was rude to stare—even though she was finding it very difficult *not* to stare.

'Who was it?' he questioned and Livvy wondered whether she'd imagined that faint note of amusement in his voice, as if he was perfectly aware of her dilemma.

She shrugged. 'My guests. Someone called Alison Clark who was due to arrive with a load of her polo friends. They rang to say that the weather forecast is too dodgy and they're not coming after all. They've decided to spend Christmas at some fancy hotel in London instead.'

'And are you disappointed?' he questioned smoothly.

'I don't know if *disappointed* is the word I'd use,' she said, aware that a long and empty Christmas now loomed ahead of her. And wasn't that one of the reasons why she always stayed open during the holiday? Because being busy meant she didn't have to look at all the things that were missing in her own life. 'It means I won't get paid, of course.'

There was a pause as he glittered her a smile. 'But that is where you are wrong, Livvy,' he said softly. 'Don't you see that fate has played right into our hands? You are now free to take up my offer and return to Jazratan with me. You can forget about niggling domestic duties over the holidays and use your neglected healing powers on my horse, for which I will reward you handsomely.'

The sum he mentioned was so large that for a moment Livvy thought he was joking, and for a moment she was seriously tempted. Yet some stubborn sense of pride made her shake her head. 'That's far too much.'

He raised his eyebrows. 'First time I've ever heard anyone complain about being paid too much.'

'It should be a fair price,' she persisted stubbornly. 'Not one that sounds like winning the national lottery.'

'What is fair is what I am prepared to pay for your services,' he argued. 'If your gift was more widely distributed, then obviously the price would be a lot lower. But it isn't, and what you have is rare, Livvy— we both know that.'

She knew what he was doing. He was manipulating

her and he was doing it very effectively. He was making her an offer too good to refuse and she was scared. Scared to try. Scared of failing. Scared of his reaction if she *did* fail. And scared of so much else besides.

'But what if this so-called *gift* no longer exists?' she said. 'There's no guarantee that my intervention will work. Burkaan may not respond to my treatment, we both know that.'

'Yes, I know that,' he said. 'But at least I will have tried. I will have done all that is in my power to help my horse.'

She wasn't imagining the sudden hollowness in his voice, or the accompanying bleakness in his eyes, and it was that that made up Livvy's mind for her. Yes, Saladin Al Mektala had the kind of unimaginable riches and influence that other people could only dream of, but when it boiled down to it he was just a man who was desperate to save his beloved horse.

'Very well.' She bent down and picked up her bra. 'I'll come to Jazratan with you.'

'Now what are you doing?'

She straightened up. 'I'm getting dressed, of course. There's a lot I have to sort out. I need to organise someone to feed the cat, for a start.'

'I'm sure you do, but there is something of much greater urgency.' His voice had grown silky. 'And don't look at me with those big honey-coloured eyes and pretend you don't know what I'm talking about.'

Taking the bra from her unprotesting fingers, he dropped it to the floor and wrapped his arms around her waist, securing her to the spot, so that he could kiss her. And once he had started kissing her, she was hungry for more. She rose up on tiptoe to curl her hands possessively around his neck and he gave a low laugh of triumph.

But this time he didn't push her to the rug and slowly thrust himself inside her. Instead, he bent and slid his arm underneath her knees, lifting her up so that she was cradled effortlessly in front of his chest.

'Where are you taking me?' she whispered as he headed for the door.

'To bed.'

She looked up at him. 'Why?'

'Are you serious? You know exactly why. Because I want sex with you again, and once on a hard floor is quite enough when there is the promise of a soft mattress.'

'Actually, my mattress happens to be very firm.'

'That's good.' He slid his hand over her bottom and gave it a squeeze. 'I like firm.'

Her cheeks hot with embarrassment and excitement, Livvy turned her face into his chest. He was taking control and she was letting him. *I want sex with you again*, he'd said—in a way that could almost be described as abrupt. There were no euphemisms tripping off his tongue, were there? No tender words of affection to feed her romantic fantasies. *He's being truthful*, she reminded herself. *He's telling it as it is.*

Yet it was difficult to keep fantasy totally at bay when a naked sheikh was in the process of kicking open her bedroom door and depositing her on her bed.

'Now,' he said as he straddled her, his fingers hooking into the soft silk of her knickers.

She thought he was about to slide them down as he'd done before, but the sudden sound of delicate fabric being ripped made her eyes widen in astonishment and, yes, in excitement, too.

'I can't…' Her heart began to hammer against her ribcage. 'I can't believe you just did that.'

'Well, I did—and here's the proof,' he drawled, dangling the tattered fragments from his index finger like a trophy.

'Those are my best knickers,' she protested.

'Were,' he corrected. 'But they were an obstruction to my desire, and I don't do obstruction. Ever. You shouldn't have put them back on, Livvy.'

'That is…outrageous,' she spluttered.

'Perhaps it is,' he agreed unsteadily. 'But you like me being outrageous, don't you, *habibi*? You like the sense that I am now free to do this…' With a light and teasing movement, he began to brush his finger over her searing heat. Back and forth it went in a relentless rhythm so delicious that she almost leaped off the bed.

'Oh,' she breathed.

'And, of course, I shall make sure you have new panties,' he said unsteadily.

She felt his warm breath heating her face as he lowered his lips towards her. 'What, just so that you can rip them off again?' she managed indistinctly.

'Of course. Because I think we're both discovering what we like. You like me being masterful, don't you, my beauty?' His finger was continuing with its insistent, stroking movement. 'Which is very convenient, since being masterful comes very easily to me.'

Livvy was so aroused by this stage that she barely noticed he must have been in possession of another condom all the while he'd been carrying her upstairs, because he was now stroking it on with practised fingers and easing himself inside her, and she gasped—her cry catching in her throat like a crumb. But this time there was nothing but glorious anticipation coursing around her veins like thick, sweet honey as he entered her. Because this time she knew what was coming.

'Oh, Saladin,' she said, the tender words tumbling out of her mouth—driven by her sheer delight in the moment and wanting him to know how special this felt. 'You are...'

But her breathless words died on her lips as she felt him tense inside her, as if she'd wronged him in some way. She looked up to see that his face had become a mask—stony and forbidding.

'Don't say soft words to me, because I don't want to hear them,' he instructed harshly. 'I don't do tenderness, Livvy. Do you understand?'

'S-sure,' she said uncertainly, and closed her eyes so he wouldn't see her hurt and confusion.

But something had changed—although maybe it was just her own perception of what was happening. He seemed like a man on a mission. As if he was intent on demonstrating his sexual superiority—or demonstrating *something*. Why else did he seem to set about showcasing how many times he could have her orgasm? Of having her plead with him not to stop? Over and over again he made love to her in different ways, as if he intended to make up for all the sex she'd missed out on in her twenty-nine years. Or was it all about power? About showing her who was really the boss?

CHAPTER NINE

SALADIN HEARD THE whir of helicopter blades long before the craft entered the immediate airspace of the house. Moving his wrist carefully so as not to wake Livvy, he glanced at his watch and gave a small nod of satisfaction. Exactly on time and exactly as he had instructed.

He glanced over at the head that was lying next to him—Livvy's bright hair spread out over the pillow. Her lips were parted as she breathed and there was a rosy flush on her freckled cheeks. He felt another stir of desire and contemplated moving his fingertip down over one silken thigh as he thought back to the previous night and most of the subsequent day that he'd spent in her bed. They had taken short breaks for food and for a shared and very erotic shower, and at one point they'd even scrambled into their clothes and gone out tramping through the snowy countryside. But for the most part they had been shut in her bedroom, making love so often that he should have been exhausted, when all he felt was a delicious kind of high.

Because Olivia Miller had proved an exciting lover—more exciting than she should have been, given her lack of experience. Her light, strong body had bent beneath his with the suppleness of a young sapling as he'd driven into her over and over again. She had embraced sex with a passion and athleticism that had taken his sometimes jaded breath away. And if at one point she had made the mistake of going all tender on him, it was a mistake she would not be repeating, for he had warned her off starting to care for him—and royal protocol would ensure that the message was slammed home to her. For this was the last time they would lie together like this...

He felt a stir of something else and acknowledged the uncomfortable stab of his conscience, knowing he had manipulated her in a particularly ruthless fashion. He had taken her virginity because it seemed wrong that a relatively young woman should be living such a celibate existence. And because he had wanted her very badly. But there had been another reason why he had made love to her...knowing that a woman rarely refused a man something if he gave her enough pleasure. And it had worked, hadn't it? She would now be accompanying him to his homeland, as he had intended she would all along.

He felt another stab of conscience. His own doubts hadn't stayed around for long, had they? His guilt about taking her virginity and the symbolic betrayal of his wife hadn't lasted beyond that first, sweet thrust.

He felt the returning throb of an erection and wondered if there was time for another swift coupling prior to their flight before deciding against it. She was going to need to wash and brush up before the trip to his homeland, and he was going to have to deal with his advisors and bodyguards who would doubtless be angry about this solo trip, though they would never dare show it. And although they would invariably guess that he had been doing more than taking tea with the fiery-headed horse expert, there was no need to flaunt his affairs openly in front of such a notoriously conservative group of men. And besides, this would be the end of it. His conscience would trouble him no longer, for there would be no sexual relationship once they were in Jazratan. His mouth hardened. He never brought his lovers to his homeland for reasons that were practical and reasons that were painful.

The clatter of the helicopter blades interrupted his introspection and, gently, he shook Livvy awake. Her lashes fluttered open and he could see the momentary confusion that clouded her amber eyes as she looked around and realised she was naked in bed with him.

Much less shy than after their first encounter, she sat up, the duvet tumbling to her waist and highlighting the pert thrust of her breasts, and Saladin cursed the powerful wave of desire that shot through him.

'What's that noise?'

'My helicopter.'

She blinked at him. 'It's *here*?'

'It's about to land.'

'It's dark outside,' she said sleepily.

'That's because we've been in bed most of the day and it's late. You'll need to get showered, changed and packed,' he added. 'Because we have to leave—and as quickly as possible.'

Livvy felt disorientated as she brushed her untidy hair away from her face and wondered why Saladin was suddenly being so cool towards her. Because she'd obeyed his curt instructions to the letter, hadn't she?

She certainly hadn't been in any way tender towards him after he'd warned her off. She'd responded to his lovemaking with nothing more controversial than a newfound passion and enjoyment. She waited for him to touch her again—or to kiss her, or *something*—but he was already picking up his cell phone and tapping out a number, and she told herself not to make a big deal out of it. Because hadn't she been firm in her resolve last night that she wasn't going to do anything stupid like falling in love with him?

Sliding out of bed, she went along the corridor to the shower, grateful that the boiler was working again and there was plenty of hot water. She remembered the shower they'd shared some time after lunch, and her cheeks burned as she tipped shampoo into the palm of her hand and relived the memory of what had happened.

Because despite his emotional detachment, it had been amazing. Every single second of it. Better than she'd ever imagined, even in her wildest dreams. Suddenly she was *glad* that Rupert had never consummated their relationship. Glad that it had been Saladin who had been her first lover, because instinct told her that no other man could make her feel the way the desert sheikh had done.

She tried to envisage someone other than Saladin touching her, but the thought of another man's hands on her body made her stomach clench with distaste. She turned her face towards the hot jets of water, knowing she mustn't read anything into what had just happened, because that would be setting herself up to be a victim. And hadn't she sworn she would never be a victim again? It was sex, that was all. Nothing but sex—

beautiful and empowering, but ultimately meaningless. So why not just enjoy it while she could?

Back in her bedroom, she stuffed her ripped panties into the bin, dressed in jeans and a sweater and then found her old jodhpurs at the back of the wardrobe and began packing a suitcase. Layering in casual clothes and T-shirts plus a couple of smarter dresses, she went over to the bookcase and picked out a couple of long-neglected books. By the time she got downstairs, the helicopter had landed on the back field and Saladin was standing beside the Christmas tree, still talking into his cell phone.

He cut the connection immediately, but his eyes didn't seem particularly warm as he turned to look at her, and he made no attempt to touch her as she walked over to him. There was no lingering kiss acknowledging their shared intimacy. No arm placed casually around her shoulder. Anyone observing them would have assumed that they were simply boss and employee, not two people who, a short time ago, had been writhing around in ecstasy together upstairs.

Boss and employee.

Which was exactly what they were.

'Your hair is still wet,' he observed. 'You'll get cold.'

Trying to ignore his critical stare, Livvy forced a smile. 'I have a woolly hat I can wear.'

'As you wish.' He glanced around. 'Do you need to lock up the house?'

'No, I thought I'd leave the doors open to see if any seasonal burglar fancies taking their chances,' she replied sarcastically. 'Of course I need to lock the house up!'

She wanted him to stop talking to her as if he were a robot and to kiss her again. To convince her that what had happened last night hadn't been some crazy kind of dream that was fading by the second.

But he didn't. He seemed suddenly *distant*. As if he had retreated behind an invisible barrier she couldn't access. Instead of being her cajoling and vital lover, he had effortlessly morphed into his real role of lofty and exalted sheikh.

Like a scene from an adventure movie, she found herself following him across the dark and snowy grass towards the helicopter, beside which stood a couple of burly men who bowed deeply before the sheikh before speaking in a fast and foreign tongue. Briefly, she wondered how Saladin was explaining the presence of a pale-faced woman in a woolly hat who was accompanying him.

With the helicopter lights flickering they flew over the night-time countryside to an airstrip, where a private jet was waiting. Aware of the veiled glances of his advisors, Livvy boarded the sleek plane, whose sides were adorned with the royal crest, startled to discover that she and the sheikh would be sitting separately during the flight.

She wondered if he saw her look of surprise just before one of the stewards ushered her through a door at the rear, to a much smaller section of the plane—though, admittedly, one that contained its own bed. Pulling out her books and music from her holdall, she looked around. Actually, there was a TV screen—and a neat little bathroom offering a tempting display of soaps and perfume. But even so...

Moments later, Saladin came to find her—all quietly

brooding power as he stood in the doorway with his cool black eyes surveying her.

'You are satisfied with your seat, I hope?' he questioned.

She was trying hard not to show she was hurt—but suddenly it wasn't easy to bite back the feelings that were bubbling up inside her. 'I wasn't expecting us to be sitting apart. Not after...' She clamped her lips shut, aware of having said too much. Did expressing vulnerability count as tenderness? she wondered.

He glanced over his shoulder before lowering his voice. 'Not after having had sex with you—is that what you mean?'

'It doesn't matter,' she mumbled.

'It does,' he said, suddenly breaking into an angry torrent of Jazratian, which was directed at the hapless steward who had appeared at the doorway behind him, but who now beat a hasty retreat. 'It matters because I'm afraid this is how things are going to be from now on.'

She stared at him, not quite understanding what he meant until his stony expression told her more clearly than any words could have done. 'You mean—?'

'What happened in England must stay in England, for we cannot be intimate in Jazratan,' he said. 'The laws of my country are very strict on such matters—and it would offend my people deeply if it was discovered that I was having sex with an unmarried woman. Particularly an unmarried foreigner.' He shrugged, as if to take some of the heat from his words. 'For I am the sheikh and you are my employee, Livvy, and from now on we will not be stepping outside the boundaries of those roles.'

It was several moments before Livvy could trust herself to speak, and if the giant plane hadn't already been taxiing down the runway, she honestly thought she might have run up to the steward and demanded they let her out.

But she couldn't. She had agreed to take the job and she was going to have to behave like a professional. And anyway—mightn't this strategy be the best strategy for keeping her emotions protected? If she and Saladin were to be segregated, it would be very difficult to foster any kind of attachment to him. So even though his words hurt, somehow she found the strength to force a careless smile onto her lips.

'Well, that's a relief,' she said.

His black eyes narrowed. 'A relief?'

'Sure. I've got a lot of reading I want to get through before we land. I told you it was a long time since I'd worked with horses.' With a wave of her hand, she gestured towards the books she'd just unpacked. 'So I'd better have a browse through these. Reacquaint myself with the species, even if it's only theoretical—until I get to meet Burkaan. So please don't let me keep you,' she added. 'I'll be perfectly happy here on my own.'

His face was a picture—as if he'd just realised that in effect she was *dismissing* him—yet he could hardly object to her demand for privacy after what he'd just said.

But once he'd gone, and she was left with the opened but unread pages of *Healing Horses Naturally*, Livvy found herself staring out of the window at the black sky as England receded, unable to deny the sudden pain that clenched like a vice around her heart.

He'd made her sound...

Like a cliché.

An unmarried foreign woman he was forbidden to have sex with.

She closed her eyes. He had come to the house determined to employ her, and for a while she had resisted him. Had he looked at her and wondered whether seduction was a price he was prepared to pay in order to guarantee her services? She bit her lip.

Even when she'd told him that she was a virgin—and a twenty-nine-year-old virgin, to boot... A lot of men might have stopped at that point. But not Saladin. Had he guessed that sex would make her eager to do his bidding? Did he realise that she would find it very difficult to refuse to work for him after what had taken place between them?

Damn him.

So stop letting him take control, she thought. *Be grateful that he's shown you are capable of sexual pleasure but also be grateful that he has put this barrier between you, because there is no future with Saladin and there never can be.*

She picked up the cup of jasmine tea that had just been put on the table by a slightly nervous-looking steward.

She was going to have to start being rational. She was here on a life-changing salary to help his horse, and she would do her utmost to accomplish that. The sex she must forget. She *had* to.

She slept for almost six hours and, when she awoke, discovered that the little shower was much better than the one at home. Afterwards she felt a million times better and was just tucking into a bowl of delicious porridge topped with iced mango when the curtain between the two sections of the plane was drawn back, and she looked up to see Saladin standing there.

It was slightly disconcerting that he'd changed from his Western clothes into an outfit more befitting a desert sheikh, because it only seemed to emphasise the vast gulf between them. Gone were the trousers, sweater and cashmere coat, and in their place were flowing robes of pure silk that completely covered him, yet hinted at the hard body beneath. His ebony hair was now hidden by a headdress, held in place by a circlet of knotted scarlet cord—and against the pale material his golden-dark features looked forbidding.

He looked like a fantasy.

Like a stranger.

And that was exactly what he was, Livvy reminded herself grimly.

His eyes fixed on her, he waited, and she was sure he expected her to scramble to her feet, but she simply finished her mouthful of porridge and gave him a faint smile.

'Morning,' she said.

He frowned before slowly inclining his head, as if forcing himself to respond civilly to her casual greeting. 'Good morning. Did you sleep well during the flight?'

'Like a dormouse, as they say in France.' Again, she smiled. 'Did you?'

Saladin felt the pounding of a pulse at his temple, her glib response only adding to his growing annoyance and frustration. No, he had not slept well, for the night had seemed endless. He had tossed and turned and eventually had drawn up one of the blinds to stare out at the jewelled and inky sky as the plane travelled through the night towards Jazratan. It had been a long time since he'd endured such restlessness. Not since...

But the realisation that he was comparing simple sexual frustration to the worst time of his life filled him with an angry guilt. Pushing aside the turmoil of his thoughts, he acknowledged the insolent way in which Livvy Miller was leaning back on her elbows, watching him. Her amber eyes were hooded and her lips gleamed from the mouthful of jasmine tea she had just drunk. How dared she continue to drink and eat in his presence?

He had told her there would be no more intimacy, but he certainly hadn't given her permission to abandon all protocol. Didn't she realise that there was an etiquette that needed to be adhered to whenever he entered the room? You did not greet the king of Jazratan with such blatant carelessness, and this was something she needed to be aware of before she arrived at the palace.

'You are supposed to stand when I enter the room,' he said coolly.

'Am I?' She fixed him with a deliberate look of challenge. 'As I recall, you seemed to prefer it when I was lying down.'

'Livvy!' He glanced behind him as he ground out his protest, feeling the instant rush of heat to his groin. 'You mustn't—'

'Mustn't what?' she interrupted in a low tone. 'Tell it like it is? Well, I'm sorry, Saladin, but I don't intend to be a hypocrite. I accept the intimacy ban you've imposed because, now I've had time to think about it, I can understand it and I think it's a good idea. But if you think I'm going to be sinking to the ground into a curtsy and lowering my eyes demurely whenever you appear, then you are very much mistaken.'

Her passionate insolence wasn't something Saladin was used to, and he was shocked into a momentary silence. He wanted to do a number of things—all of which seemed to contradict themselves. He wanted to kiss her and to simultaneously push her as far away from him as possible. He wanted never to see her again and yet he wanted to feast his eyes on her in a leisurely visual feast. Suddenly he realised that here was one person—one *woman*—who would not be moulded to his will, and with a shock it suddenly dawned on him why that was. *Because he needed her more than she needed him.*

He could not expel her for insubordination—well, he could, but his stallion would only suffer as a result. And even though he was paying way over the odds for an expertise she had warned him herself might not work, he suspected that the money didn't mean as much to her as it might to someone else.

Did it? Or had her initial reluctance to take the job simply been the work of a clever negotiator? Perhaps he should test her out.

'Surely a little civility wouldn't go amiss since I am rewarding you so handsomely for your work.'

'You're *paying* me, Saladin—not *rewarding* me,' she contradicted. 'You were the one who made the over-inflated offer in the first place, so please don't start reneging on it now. And if you want me to show you respect, I'm afraid you will have to earn it.'

'*Earn* it?' he echoed incredulously.

'Yes. Is that such an extraordinary proposition?'

He gave a short laugh. 'It is certainly one that has never been put to me before.'

She stood up then, clenching her hands into two small fists and sucking in an unsteady breath as she looked at him. 'I'm not a complete fool, Saladin,' she hissed. 'I'm fully aware that you seduced me for a purpose. And it worked.'

He looked into the amber eyes that blazed as brightly as her fiery hair. He thought how magnificent she looked when she was berating him, and suddenly he felt a lump rise in his throat. 'Believe me when I tell you this,' he said huskily. 'I seduced you because I wanted you.'

Livvy heard the sudden passion that had deepened his words and something inside her melted. Stupid how she'd almost forgotten what they'd just been arguing about. Stupid how her body was just *craving* for him to touch her.

Did he feel that, too? Was she imagining the slight move he made towards her, when suddenly the plaintive lament of what sounded like *bagpipes* broke into her thoughts and shattered the tense atmosphere. Disorientated, she met Saladin's gaze and it was as if the noise had brought him to his senses, too, because he stiffened and stepped away from her, and in his eyes flared something cold and bleak.

'What the hell is that?' she whispered.

Her question seemed to shake him out of his sombre reverie, though it took a moment before his eyes cleared and he answered. 'A hangover from my great-grandfather's holidays at your own royal family's Scottish residence,' he said. 'He was very impressed by the bagpipes that were used to wake everyone in the morning. After that he decided that they would become a permanent feature of Jazratian life. Thus a returning sheikh is always greeted on his arrival by the unmistakable sound of Scotland.'

'It's certainly very novel.'

'You will find much about my country that surprises you, Livvy,' he replied. 'In a moment I will leave the aircraft and one of the stewards will indicate when it is appropriate for you to do the same. There will be transport waiting to take you to my palace.'

She screwed up her eyes as she looked at him. 'So I won't even be travelling with you?'

He shook his head. 'No. My homecoming is always greeted with a certain amount of celebration. There will be crowds lining the route, and it would not sit well with my people were I to return to the palace in the company of a foreign female, no matter how skilled she might be in her particular field.'

'Right,' she said.

'You will be given your own very comfortable suite of rooms. Once you have settled in, I will send one of my advisors to take you to the stable complex, so that you can meet the vets and the grooms, and get to work on Burkaan straight away. You will, however, take meals with me.'

Without waiting for a response, he turned and walked away with a swish of his silken robes. And if Livvy felt momentarily frustrated by his sudden indifference, that wasn't what was currently occupying her thoughts. It was the way he had looked during those few moments when she'd thought he was going to reach out and touch her.

Because when the smoky passion had cleared from

his eyes, it had left behind a flicker of something haunting. The trace of an emotion that she wouldn't necessarily have associated with a man like Saladin.

Something that looked awfully like guilt.

CHAPTER TEN

LIVVY STOOD BENEATH the bright Jazratian sunshine and looked around her with a sense of awe and a slight sense of feeling displaced—as if she couldn't quite believe she was here in Saladin's homeland, and that it was Christmas Eve.

The Al Mektala stable complex was lavish, and no expense had been spared in providing for the needs and comfort of over a hundred horses. She'd read about places like this, in those long-ago days when an equestrian magazine had never been far from her hand—but had never imagined herself actually working in one.

Fine sand paddocks were edged with lines of palm trees, which provided welcome shade, but plenty of areas had been laid to grass and it was curiously restful—if a little bizarre—to see large patches of green set against the harsh backdrop of the desert landscape. There were plush air-conditioned boxes for the horses and even a dappled and cool pool in which they could swim. Grooms, physiotherapists and jockeys— all clad in the distinctive Al Mektala livery of indigo and silver—swarmed around the place as efficiently as ants working in harmony together.

After arriving at the palace Livvy had been shown

to a large suite of rooms, where she'd changed into jodhpurs and a shirt and then followed the servant who had been dispatched to take her to the stables. She hadn't been expecting to find Saladin waiting for her—and she certainly wasn't expecting to see him similarly attired in riding clothes, his fingers curving rather distractingly around a riding whip.

She had to force her thoughts away from how lusciously the jodhpurs were clinging to his narrow hips and hugging the powerful shafts of his long legs. It was difficult not to let her gaze linger on the way his billowing silk shirt gave definition to the rock-like torso beneath, making him resemble the kind of buccaneering hero you might find on some Sunday-night TV drama. She told herself that she wasn't going to remember the way he had held her when he'd been making love to her, or the way it had felt to have him deep inside her. She wasn't going to think about how good it had felt to be kissed by him—or the way she'd cried out as she had reached her climax, over and over again. She was here to see if she could help his horse—and that was the *only* reason she was here.

But it was hard to stand so close to him and to resist the desire to reach out and touch him, even though she was doing her best to keep her smile cool and professional.

'So what do you think of my stables, Livvy?'

She smiled. 'As you predicted—it's very interesting to see what you've done in such an extreme climate. And it's all very impressive—just as I would have expected,' she observed as she glanced around. 'Perhaps I could see Burkaan now?'

Once again Saladin felt that inexplicable conflict

within him. He was irritated by her lack of desire to make small talk with him—yet couldn't help but admire her cool professionalism. Just as he was irritated with himself for having almost reached out to her on the plane, when temptation had wrapped itself around his skin like a silken snare. But he had stopped himself just in time, and that was a good thing, although it hadn't felt particularly easy at the time. Because he'd forced himself to remember that he was back in Jazratan where expectations were different and where the memory of Alya was at its strongest. Here, his role was rigidly defined, and casual sex with foreigners simply was not on the agenda. He needed to put that delicious interlude out of his mind and to see whether or not she could live up to her reputation.

Raising his hand, he indicated to the waiting groom that his horse should be brought outside, and he felt his heart quicken in anticipation, as if hoping that some miracle had happened while he'd been away and that Burkaan would come trotting out into the yard with his former vitality.

But the reality shocked and saddened him. The sight of his beloved stallion being led from his stable, looking like a shadow of his former self, made Saladin's heart clench painfully in his chest. The magnificent racehorse's frame seemed even more diminished, and his normally glossy black coat looked lacklustre and dull. The stallion was usually happy, but he was not happy now. Saladin could almost read the anguish and the pain in his eyes as he bared his teeth at his master.

'Don't go near him yet,' he warned Livvy. 'He's been very vicious. Few people can get close to him. Even me.'

But to his annoyance and a concern he couldn't quite hide, she completely ignored his words, moving so quietly towards the horse that she could have been a ghost as she held out her hand in a gesture of peace.

'It's okay,' she said to the animal, in the softest, most musical voice he had ever heard. 'I'm not going to hurt you. It's okay, Burkaan. It's going to be fine.'

Burkaan was more used to being spoken to in Jazratian, and even before his accident had been known for his intolerance of strangers, but Saladin watched in amazement as Livvy moved closer to the powerful animal. There was a split second when he expected the horse to lash out at her and braced himself in readiness to snatch the stubborn woman out of harm's way. But the moment did not come. Instead, she slowly reached out and began to stroke his neck. And Burkaan let her!

'It's all right,' she was crooning quietly. 'I've come to help you. Do you know that, Burkaan? Do you?'

The horse gave a little whinny, and Saladin felt his throat constrict with something that felt uncomfortably like hope. But he knew better than anyone that misplaced hope was the most painful emotion of all, and he drove it from his heart with a ruthlessness he'd learned a long time ago. Just because the horse was prepared to allow the Englishwoman to approach and to touch him didn't mean a thing.

'I wonder, could you ask the groom to walk him around the yard a little?' she said. 'Just so I can see how badly he's injured?'

Saladin nodded and spoke to the groom, and the stricken stallion was led forward and began to hobble around the yard.

'You will note that he has injured his—'

'His near foreleg,' Livvy interrupted crisply, her gaze following the horse as it slowly made its way to the other side of the yard. 'Yes, I can see that. He's clearly in a lot of pain and he's hopping to try to compensate. Okay. I've seen everything I need to see. Please ask the groom to bring him back now, and put him in his box.'

Feeling like her tame linguist, Saladin relayed her instructions to the groom, and once Burkaan had been led back into his box, Livvy turned to face him. He thought her smile looked forced, and he wondered if she was aware that the bright Jazratian sunshine was making her hair look like liquid fire. And, oh, how he would love to feel the burn of it against his fingers again.

'I'm just going to try a few things out,' she said. 'So I'd prefer it if you and everyone else would leave now.'

Disbelief warred with a grudging admiration as she spoke to him, because Saladin realised that once again she was *dismissing* him. She really *was* fond of taking control, wasn't she? He had never been dominated by a woman before, and he was finding it more exciting than he could ever have anticipated—but he would not tolerate it. No way. Surely she must realise that this was *his* stable and *his* horse, and of course he would wish to observe her. He fixed her with a steady look. 'I'm not going anywhere, Livvy,' he said. 'I want to be here.'

She sucked in a deep breath. 'I'm sorry, but I prefer to work alone.'

'I don't care. I want to be here,' he repeated.

She narrowed her eyes as if trying to weigh up whether there was any point in further argument, before obviously coming to the most sensible conclusion.

'Very well,' she said. 'But I don't want any distractions. You must keep very quiet and not interfere. I want you to stand over there out of the way, to keep very still and not say a word. Do you understand?'

Saladin's mouth thinned into a grim smile as her cool words washed over him. One thing he *did* understand was that nobody else had ever spoken to him like this before, not even Alya—especially not Alya, who had been the most agreeable woman ever made.

Instinct made him want to march over to Livvy and pull rank and ask her who the hell she thought she was talking to. To remind her that he was the sheikh and he would damned well do as he pleased. Yet what alternative did he have but to accede to her demands, when the welfare of his beloved horse was of far greater importance than his own sense of pride and position?

'Yes, Livvy,' he said drily. 'I think I get the general idea.'

Afterwards he would try to work out exactly what she had done to Burkaan, but, apart from a vague impression of her laying her palms on the animal's injured foreleg, her time with the horse seemed to pass in a blur. Maybe it was because for once Saladin got the distinct impression that her words had been true. She really didn't want him there, and would have preferred it if he had gone back to the palace as she'd requested. It was certainly the first time in his life that he had been completely ignored.

Because sheikhs were never ignored and people were always conscious of his presence. No matter how large an official function or social gathering, everyone always knew exactly where he was situated, although they often pretended not to. Nobody ever left a room while he remained in it, and nobody ever turned their back on him.

But none of this seemed relevant as he watched Livvy whispering into Burkaan's ear and running feather-light fingertips over the horse's injured limb and then stroking their way over his back. To his surprise, the stallion seemed to tolerate almost every touch she made—only jerking back his head and showing his teeth on two occasions. Eventually, she straightened up and wiped the palms of her hands down over her jodhpurs, and he could see sweat beading her pale brow.

'I've finished now,' she said. 'I'll see him later. Make sure he gets some rest and is undisturbed until I do.'

He saw her glance at her watch and realised that he had effectively backed himself into a corner. He had told her—quite correctly—that they would be occupying separate sections of the palace. He had told her that their lives would cross only at mealtimes and when she was hands-on with Burkaan. Yet now the thought of that did not please him—on the contrary, it positively *rankled*. He had found it necessary to lay out his boundaries during the flight over, in order to emphasise to her that the sex had meant nothing—and he had been expecting a host of objections from her, or maybe even a petulant sulk. Because women always tried to cling on to him when he rejected them—as reject them he inevitably did.

But Livvy was showing no signs of clinging—or sulking. She had travelled separately to the palace without protest, and, on arriving at her suite of rooms, had apparently made some complimentary comment to one of the servants about the ancient tiled floors and the beauty of the palace gardens. And ironically, he had found himself curiously unsettled by her apparent acceptance of the situation in which she now found herself.

'We have plenty of time before lunch,' he said. 'Perhaps you would care to ride with me?'

For a moment, Livvy felt temptation wash over her as his suggestion brought back echoes of a life she had left far behind. She thought of being in the saddle again and the feeling of having all that impressive horse power beneath her. She thought of the warm, desert breeze against her skin and the incomparable sense of freedom that riding always gave her, but, resolutely, she shook her head. 'I don't ride anymore.'

'Why not?'

She met the question in his narrowed eyes. 'Because riding demands time and commitment and money— and I've been too busy running my business to have any of those things.'

'But you have time now,' he pointed out coolly. 'And money isn't a consideration.'

'It's out of the question,' she said. 'I'm completely out of practice.'

There was a pause. 'And maybe you're scared of getting back on a horse after so long away?'

His unexpected insight caught her off guard. Was that why she answered him so truthfully?

'Maybe a little,' she agreed. But it wasn't fear of the horse that frightened her. It was the thought of re-entering a world that had brought her pain and that now seemed so long ago it might have happened to another person.

'Then, why not get back in the saddle?' His voice

deepened. 'Kill your fear by confronting it. Don't they say that the more you practise, the better you get?'

And suddenly there was an undeniable sexual innuendo whispering in the air around them and whipping up an unspoken need inside her. She could feel sudden tension heating her skin, and the tips of her breasts had grown suddenly sensitive. She could feel it in the way her lips parted, as if silently inviting him to kiss them—and, oh, how she wanted him to kiss her.

Livvy stared at Saladin as she tried to dampen down the rising tide of desire. To remind herself of the way he'd treated her since she had agreed to treat his horse. He had kept her away from him during the flight and ordered separate journeys to the palace, where she had been allocated quarters in the staff section. She didn't have a problem with that—because she *was* staff. What she *did* have a problem with was his assumption that he could treat her like some kind of plaything. Act icy one minute and then flirt with her the next. Well, he had better learn that it didn't work like that. She didn't dare let it.

'I don't want it to come back,' she said.

'Why not?'

She glanced down at the tips of her riding boots, which were covered in fine dust, before lifting her gaze to meet the jet-dark gleam of his eyes. 'Because when I split with Rupert I walked away from riding. I bolted—and I shut the stable door behind me. I left my job, realising that I had no appetite to face the knowing looks and the knowledge that he'd been sleeping with my best friend.'

'You could have found different stables.'

'I could. But horse riding is a very small world,

and gossip always follows you around. I wanted to be known as more than the woman who'd been involved in a spicy scandal. I wanted a clean break and that's what I got. The old Livvy has gone and so has the world she lived in. I'm not looking to recapture something from the past—I'm here because I'm trying to take care of my future. So if you've finished with the interrogation, I'd like someone to show me back to my room because this palace is so big, I don't trust myself not to get lost.'

With a thoughtful look, he inclined his head. 'Certainly. I will show you to your suite myself.'

'There's really no need. A servant will do.'

'My servants don't speak English.'

'I'm quite happy to forego conversation.'

'I will show you to your room, Livvy,' he said, with silky insistence. 'And please don't oppose me just for the sake of it, or you will discover how quickly my tolerance limit can be reached.'

His reprimand was stern and maybe it was justified, but as Livvy fell into step beside him she realised that even *opposing* him was making her feel things she didn't want to feel. Desire was throbbing through her body and making her want to squirm with frustration. It was all she could do not to reach out and touch him—to whisper her fingers possessively over his riding shirt and feel the hard torso beneath. Was it because he'd been her only lover that she was feeling this way? Was she building it up in her head because he'd taken her virginity so that what had happened seemed powerful and significant?

Yet maybe that wasn't so surprising when sex with Saladin had seemed so *easy*. It had happened so naturally. It had felt as if she'd been waiting all her life for the desert sheikh to make love to her. As if she hadn't been complete until he had completed her.

And wasn't that the way it was supposed to feel?

Blocking out the disturbing thoughts that were threatening to overwhelm her, she focused her attention on the splendour of her surroundings instead. The temperature dropped as they passed through the shaded portico into the main palace, where the polished floors were deliciously cool and smooth.

They crossed a courtyard and, on the far side, Livvy saw a shining silver bower, festooned with tumbling roses of scarlet and orange and pink. Glittering brightly in the midday sun, it was topped with an intricate silver structure of filigree metal flowers and leaves and Livvy's footsteps came to a halt. 'Wow,' she said slowly. 'What is that place?'

By her side Saladin stiffened as he followed the direction of her eyes. 'That is the Faddi gate, leading to the palace rose garden,' he said abruptly.

'Oh, it's beautiful. Could we go that way?'

But suddenly he seemed to be having difficulty controlling his emotions and Livvy looked up to see a tiny nerve working frantically at his temple and that his mouth had hardened with an expression she couldn't quite fathom. He shook his head.

'The gardeners are working there,' he said abruptly. 'And they do not like to be observed. Come, I will take you a different way.'

He remained tense for a minute or two, but as they walked towards her rooms he began to recount some of the history of Jazratan and of the palace itself. And somehow the change of subject was enough to make him relax—and Livvy relaxed, too, so that after a while she found herself engrossed in the things he was telling her. He talked about battles that had been fought and won by his ancestors, of sheikhs whose lifeblood had seeped like rust onto the desert sands. He told her about the brave mount who had led one particular victorious battle—a forerunner to his own, beloved Burkaan.

She realised then why his horse was so important to him, and it had nothing to do with money, or even a close bond that transcended his royal status. Because Burkaan was a link between the past and the future. If the stallion was put out to stud, then his illustrious line would continue. And continuity was the lifeblood of a ruling monarch.

He's so different from you, Livvy thought. *So don't ever make the mistake of thinking it could be any other way than this.*

They had just reached her door when Saladin suddenly reached out to wrap his fingers around her wrist, and the unexpected gesture shocked Livvy into stillness. She wondered if he could feel the sudden hammering of her pulse. He must do. It sounded so thunderous to her own ears she was surprised it hadn't brought the servants running.

'Thank you for what you did today,' he said.

'I did very little.'

'On the contrary. You calmed a horse who has been nothing but vicious since his accident. It was the first time I've seen a fleeting moment of peace in his eyes.'

And Livvy found herself looking into *his* eyes, helplessly snared by their ebony light. She'd seen many emotions in them since that snowy afternoon when he had first walked into her life. She'd seen them harden with irritation and determination. She'd seen them soften with desire and lust. And she'd seen them cloud over with something that had looked very like sorrow as they had stared at the Faddi gate leading to the rose garden. Did Saladin have his own dark demons raging within him? she wondered.

Reluctantly, she pulled her hand away from his—even though deep down she wanted to curl her fingers into his palm, like a cat settling down for the evening. But that way lay danger. He'd already set out the boundaries and, even though her body wanted to push at those boundaries, she recognised that distance from Saladin made perfect sense.

'You really must excuse me,' she said, bringing a note of formality into her voice. 'I need to call England to check that Peppa is okay and that the snow hasn't caused any lasting damage.' She smiled. 'I'll see you at lunch—presumably you will send someone to collect me?'

And with that, she walked into her suite, quietly closing the door—not caring that he was still standing there looking darkly displeased by her dismissal. Not caring about anything other than a need to put some distance between them before she did something crazy like fling herself against that hard and virile body and beg him to make love to her again.

CHAPTER ELEVEN

IT WASN'T AS easy as he had thought it would be.

It wasn't easy at all.

With an impatient flick of his hand, Saladin waved the servant away and lowered his body into the deep tub of steaming water. How was it possible to feel exhausted when you had only just risen from your bed? Could it have anything to do with the fact that he'd spent yet another sleepless night frustratedly recalling that erotic fireside encounter when the innocent Livvy Miller had cried out her passion in his arms?

Maybe he'd been naive to think it would be easy to adhere to his self-imposed sex ban when she was living here at the palace. When thoughts of her kept drifting into his mind at the most inconvenient times—usually without warning or provocation. Sometimes he found himself sitting through meetings of state and thinking about her pale skin and fiery hair. About the way he had cupped her narrow hips and driven into that slender body. He would sit uncomfortably with a massive erection hidden by his flowing robes, and wonder why he had insisted that she remain totally off limits.

Because he could not trash his sacred memories of

the past by indulging in a casual fling, especially here in the palace.

For a while he lay in the cooling water and thought about the long days that had passed since Livvy's arrival. The Englishwoman had settled in well—better than he could ever have anticipated. She had worked diligently with Burkaan four times a day and, although she grudgingly permitted his presence at these sessions, she had made it clear that she expected total silence from him—and he had found himself complying!

At other times he had barely seen her. She hadn't seemed to mind missing any of the holiday celebrations she would have enjoyed back in England. He'd heard from the servants that she spent much of her time reading on the shaded terraces outside her suite. And it infuriated him to realise that it would be completely inappropriate to disturb her there, even though he was master of all he surveyed. He felt as if he was caught in a trap of his own making. Sometimes he caught a glimpse of her as she made her way out to the sprawling expanse of the palace gardens and watched as she peered through the Faddi gate. And wondered why it was no longer Alya's face he could see in his mind, but the face of the freckly Englishwoman.

Because she was off limits?

Because she wasn't coming on to him? That was something else he found it hard to get his head round. There had been no coy glances or lingering looks. She hadn't been flaunting her body in close-fitting clothes to torment him with memories of what lay beneath. No, she had acted with an admirable—if infuriating—decorum.

Only at mealtimes were the wretched rules relaxed—

and then he found himself eager to talk to her. He quizzed her about his horse's progress and gradually, once she had lost some of the new guarded expression she seemed to assume around him, she began to open up a little more. It was a unique situation, he realised, for rarely did he have the opportunity—or inclination—to get to know a woman. Women were there for his sexual pleasure, and once he had taken his fill he walked away. But with Livvy, there was no opportunity for sexual pleasure. And not only was he unable to walk away—bizarrely he found he didn't want to. This pale and stubborn Englishwoman was intriguing him more than he had expected to be intrigued.

She told him about getting on her first horse at the age of three, and her mother's love of riding. Of her own increasing skill on horseback and the way the two of them used to gallop across the dewy fields around Wightwick Manor. She spoke of frosty landscapes washed pink with the light from the rising sun. She told him about the first time she realised that she could understand horses in a way that most people couldn't and the 'awesome feeling of responsibility' it had given her. She described the day she'd brought home her first rosette, aged six, and then her first shiny silver trophy a year later.

It was after one such recollection after lunch one day that he heard her voice falter and Saladin found himself leaning back in his chair to study her.

'You must miss it,' he said. 'Riding.'

She gave a little shrug. 'Sometimes.'

'So what can I do to tempt you back into the saddle?'

'You can stop trying—I'm not interested.'

'Aren't you?'

She put down her golden goblet with a thud. 'No.'

And suddenly Saladin wanted to break all his own rules. He wanted to forget that he was a king and a widower and to behave like any other man. To seek pleasure and comfort when it was available. To try to rid himself of some of this obsession he had for the titian-haired Englishwoman. Because soon there would be no reason for her to remain. Burkaan was improving daily—everyone had commented on the fact. Soon she would be headed back to England and he would never see her again. Because deep down he suspected that, unlike other lovers, Livvy would not be interested in a brief relationship back in England, simply to burn their passion away. He suspected that she would disapprove of such a cold-blooded suggestion.

So couldn't it burn itself out here and now? Wasn't he the king of all he surveyed, who could change the unspoken rules of his land, just as long as he wasn't blatant about it?

'Ride with me today, Livvy,' he said suddenly. 'For mercy's sake—what harm can it do?'

Livvy looked at him, acknowledging the suddenly urgent note in his voice. She wanted to refuse. To tell him that it felt too poignant, too intimate, too…too *everything*. And yet…yet…

She looked into the gleam of his black eyes. The temptation was strong and her thoughts made it even stronger. What harm could one little ride do, on one of the sheikh's magnificent horses, as she had been longing to do for weeks? To be alone with the desert king—far away from the watchful eyes of the palace servants. 'I'll ride with you later,' she said. 'After Burkaan's final session of the day.'

The state of excitement inside her for the next few hours was disproportionate to the short ride that he'd undoubtedly scheduled. At least, that was what Livvy told herself. But no matter how much she tried to minimise the impact of some time alone with Saladin away from the palace, nothing could get rid of the fizz of excitement in her blood.

Her heart was pounding as she swung herself up into the saddle with Saladin watching her closely, his hand on the reins.

'Okay?' he questioned.

She nodded as she felt the first ripple of the animal's power beneath her. 'Okay,' she echoed softly.

The beautiful chestnut mare he'd given her was placid, and, with Saladin mounting a much bigger roan stallion, they trotted out of the stable complex side by side onto the hard desert sands. The rhythmic pounding of the horses' hooves was both soothing and exhilarating as they began to canter. The sun was low and the sky was an inverted bowl of deepest blue as Livvy breathed in the warm air. She felt...*alive*. The most alive she'd felt since...

Since Saladin had made love to her.

She turned to look at him, thinking that he resembled a figure from a fantasy tale. No jodhpurs today—instead, his white headdress billowed behind him and his silken robes clung to the hard contours of his body as he rode alongside her.

'How do you know your way around?' she questioned. 'Aren't you afraid of getting lost?'

He gave a brief smile. 'I grew up in this land,' he said. 'And it is as familiar to me as my own skin.'

'Really?' She thought using his skin as a comparison

probably wasn't the best idea, under the circumstances—but she kept her expression neutral. 'In what way?'

He shrugged as he slowed his horse down. 'You see nothing but sand, but I see ridges and undulations on the surface where the winds have blown—and I can read the wind by sight and sound as others can read music. I know where there are underground rivers and lakes, where vegetation can thrive and provide shelter. And I always make sure I'm carrying adequate supplies of water and a compass—as well as a cell phone.' He flicked her another brief smile. 'Would you like me to take you to an oasis?'

She thought at first that he must be joking, because it sounded so *corny*. She half remembered some pop song her mother used to love. Something about midnight at an oasis. Livvy gripped the reins a little tighter as she met the gleaming question in his black eyes and suddenly she wondered what the hell was making her hesitate. When else in her life was she ever going to get the opportunity to see an oasis?

'I'd love to,' she said.

'Then, come,' he urged, and when he saw the look of hesitation on her face he gave a quick smile. *'Come.'* Pressing his knees into his horse's flanks, he set off at a gallop and after a moment's hesitation Livvy started after him.

It came back within seconds—that raw exhilaration and sheer *joy*. She'd forgotten the speed and sense of power you got when you were riding a horse at full pelt, and any lingering reservations were melted away as she galloped after the sheikh.

Over hard and undulating sands they rode—with nothing but the heavy sound of hooves pounding. They rode until Saladin slowed down the pace so that they could mount a steep incline, and Livvy's breath died in her throat when she saw what was on the other side. For there was an unexpectedly wide gleam of water surrounded by grasses and a line of lush palm trees that provided acres of shade.

'Oh, wow,' she said softly. 'A real oasis.'

'Did you think it was a mirage?' he questioned drily.

The truthful answer would have been yes, because nothing felt quite real as Livvy's horse followed Saladin's down to the desert lake, and she jumped down to lead her mount towards the water. She could hear the strange squawking of a bird in one of the palm trees and the glugging splash as the two thirsty animals drank. Saladin gestured for her to tether her horse in the shade next to his, while he drew out a canister of water and offered it to her.

Rarely had any drink ever tasted as delicious as this, and Livvy gulped it down with gratitude and a strange sense of being at peace with herself. She was standing beneath the shade of a palm tree and Saladin was taking the container from her suddenly boneless fingers and drinking from it himself. And she wondered how sharing water with a man could seem so ridiculously *intimate*. Because they had shared so much more than this? She watched the swallowing movement of his neck and suddenly her mouth felt dry again—even though she'd just drunk about half a litre.

He didn't say a word as he put the empty container back and then took her by the hand, leading her towards the cool canopy provided by the palm trees—and she didn't ask him where he was taking her or what he was about to do when he got there, because she knew.

It was obvious from the sudden tension in the fingers that were firmly laced around her own. The way in which her heart had suddenly started to race in response. He came to a halt when their faces were shadowed by the cool fronds above their heads, and her face was grave as he removed the wide-brimmed hat from her head and placed it on the ground.

'Saladin,' she said breathlessly as he framed her face in the palms of his hands.

His voice was quiet, but insistent. 'I'm going to kiss you.'

'But you said—'

'I said that we couldn't have sex in the palace, but we aren't in the palace now. Are we?'

She shook her head, wishing he'd made it sound a little less *anatomical*, wishing he'd responded with a few romantic words in what was a very romantic setting. But maybe she would have to make do with this—along with the realisation that at least he wasn't making mirages of his own. He wasn't wooing her with empty promises—he was telling it the way it was. And anyway by then he was kissing her and all her objections were forgotten as she opened her lips beneath his, because hadn't she been missing this, more than she would have ever thought possible?

His hands were hot and urgent as they raked through her hair and over her body, and her own were equally hungry as they explored the hardness of his magnificent physique. Impatiently, he slithered off her jodhpurs and shirt before peeling off his own silken robes, and Livvy gasped to discover that he was completely naked beneath.

'It is another characteristic we share with the Scots,'

he murmured as he spread the robes onto the sand to make a silky bed for them. 'Who I believe wear nothing beneath their kilts?'

But Livvy didn't answer because by then she felt as if she were in the middle of a dream—the most amazing dream of her life—as he laid her down. His eyes were unreadable as he moved over her and made his first thrust, and she gasped out his name as he entered her.

'It's good?'

She bit her lip and moaned. 'It's terrible.'

He laughed, but then his voice changed to a note she'd never heard before as he began to move inside her. 'Oh, Livvy.'

She didn't answer. There were things she'd like to have known and questions that maybe she should have asked. But she didn't. She couldn't. She was powerless to do anything other than respond to the feel of Saladin deep inside her. Because by then she had started to come, and there wasn't a thing she could do to stop it.

They rode back after night had fallen, even though Livvy had initially been fearful of crossing the dark desert on horseback. But Saladin had run the tip of his tongue along the edge of her lips, and she had felt him smile as he answered her question.

'I told you that I know this desert as well as my own body,' he said softly. 'Don't you realise that there's a great big celestial map overhead?'

That had been the point when she'd looked up at the stars that she'd been too distracted to notice before. The brightest stars she'd ever seen—silver bright against the indigo backdrop of the sky. And there was the moon rising in splendour—a bright, gleaming curve above the palm trees where they'd spent the past two hours making love. Livvy felt a lump rise in her throat. It was like a fairy tale, she thought.

Except that it wasn't a fairy tale. It was nothing but a brief interlude, and Saladin had already warned her that real life would soon intrude.

He had pulled her against him after they'd dressed and brushed away stray grains of sand from their clothing. He had tilted up her chin so that she was caught in the dark gleam of his eyes and, in that moment, she'd felt very close to falling in love with him.

But his black eyes had been empty. The barrier was back, she realised, with a sinking heart.

'You know that when we return—'

'I'm to act as though nothing's happened.'

His eyes glittered in the starlight. 'How did you know that's what I was going to say?'

'Wasn't it?'

He seemed surprised by her calm response. Was that why he provided an explanation she hadn't asked for?

'This cannot happen within the walls of the palace,' he said. 'It would place you at a disadvantage were people to find out that we were having some sort of relationship.'

'Sweet of you to be concerned about my reputation, Saladin. Are you sure it isn't your own you're worried about?'

'I don't think you understand,' he said, his voice growing cool. 'It will impede your work if there is any suggestion that we are intimate. I will not have any negative fallout because we've just had sex.'

'Because soon I'll be gone and it will all be forgotten?' she questioned lightly.

There was a pause.

'Precisely,' he said.

His honesty should have pleased her, but right then Livvy could have done without it. She wanted him to tell her soft things. Tender things. She wanted the man who had made love to her so beautifully, not this cold-eyed stranger who had taken his place and was swinging his powerful body up onto his horse. But it was a timely wake-up call, she reminded herself. Just because something *felt* like magic—didn't mean it was. She mustn't ask the impossible of a man who had not promised her anything he was incapable of delivering. She must approach this…*affair* like any other woman of her age—with enjoyment and enthusiasm and a lack of expectation. She mustn't start to care for him more than was wise, but take what was on offer and not look beyond that.

She could choose to stay or to run away—and it seemed that she had chosen to stay.

The palace gleamed like a citadel in the distance as they rode in silence towards it. They brought the horses in and handed them over to two grooms, before entering the marbled splendour of Saladin's home. A servant appeared and the sheikh spoke to him in rapid Jazratian, before walking her to the door of her suite.

The corridor was empty, and she could feel the whisper of the warm, scented air that drifted in from the nearby courtyard.

'Sleep well,' he said, and with the briefest of smiles he was gone, leaving her staring at the swish of his silken robes and wondering if she'd dreamed the whole thing.

Livvy went into her suite and slipped into a robe, once she'd showered the desert dust from her body. Afterwards, a female servant knocked on the door with a tray containing iced pomegranate juice, along with a plate of sweet cake and juicy segments of peeled fruit—but although Livvy drank, she had little appetite.

She went to stare out at the night sky, thinking about what lay ahead—knowing that the X-ray that Burkaan had undergone yesterday had shown the 'miracle' to have happened. The stallion was responding to the gift she was terrified she'd lost, and soon her skills would be redundant. No longer would she have those proud and hawklike features to gaze on during mealtimes. There would be no more passionate interludes like the one she had experienced in the desert today. She would become the ordinary person she'd been before the sheikh had awoken her. And he had awoken her in so many ways—she must never forget that. He had introduced her to sex and helped her overcome her reservations about getting on a horse. He had injected colour into a world that seemed to have become monochrome. He'd made her feel vital—and desirable. He'd made her feel that she *mattered*.

And the thought of never seeing him again was like having a knife rammed straight into the centre of her heart.

As she got into bed she found herself wondering why he hadn't married—why some beautiful royal bride hadn't been found for such an eligible man, despite his occasionally irascible nature. Perhaps he was contented with his single status. Perhaps the demands of running a country were enough to satisfy him, or he might just be one of those men who didn't want marriage. She knew he'd had countless liaisons with gorgeous models and actresses, but even so it was confusing. Surely such an autocratic man longed for an heir to carry on his blood-line? She found herself wondering why he had become so emotional the first time she'd seen the Faddi gate, but she hadn't dared bring up the subject again, and none of the servants spoke enough English for her to ask.

She got into bed and the excitement of the day must have caught up on her because very quickly she fell asleep. She thought she must be dreaming when she felt the bed dip and a rough, muscular thigh slide over hers. Heart pounding, she turned over and reached out to find a naked Saladin in bed beside her, his hard body washed silver by the moonlight flooding in from the unshuttered windows.

Her lips swollen with sleep, she stumbled out the words—half-afraid that speaking would break the spell and make him disappear. She wanted him so badly, and yet wasn't there a part of herself that despised her eagerness to have him touch her again? 'Saladin,' she whispered.

'The very same.'

'What are you doing here?'

'No ideas?' he mocked as he reached out to curve his hand over her breast. 'Such a shocking lack of imagi-nation, Livvy.'

And he bent his head to kiss her.

She started to speak but he shook his head.

'Don't say a word,' he warned softly. 'I feel that you and I have done enough talking to last a lifetime.'

'A lifetime? Well, that isn't something that is ever going to be relevant in our case, is it?'

Saladin heard the unmistakable sadness behind her defiance and wondered if she was hoping for reassurance. Perhaps thinking that because he was about to start making love to her in the palace, there was now the potential for longevity. His mouth hardened. But there wasn't, and hypocrisy and raising false hope would be an insult to a woman like Livvy. He wouldn't whisper sweet words that meant nothing, or tantalise her with glimpses of a future that could never be theirs. Nor would he torture himself with the certainty that this was *wrong*, and that he was tarnishing the memory of all that was honest and true.

Ruthlessly he blocked the voice of duty, which had been a constant sound in his head since he'd been old enough to comprehend its meaning. And concentrated on touching Livvy instead, wondering how her petite body could make him almost incoherent with lust.

The ragged moan he gave as he eased himself inside her sounded unfamiliar. Just as the feeling in his heart was unfamiliar—the sense of growing and explosive joy. He said something fervent in his native tongue and her eyes flew open in question.

'What was that you said?'

'I said that you feel as tight as one of the drums played by the Karsuruum tribe.'

Her pupils dilated still farther as she bit back a smile. 'And is that...?' There was a sudden intake of breath as he thrust deeper inside her. 'Is that supposed to be a compliment?'

'Yes,' he ground out. 'It is.'

He wanted to come immediately but he forced himself to wait. He teased her to a fever pitch—until she was whispering his name in something that sounded like a plea. And still he held back—until he felt her convulsing around him, her soft cries muffled by the pressure of his kiss as he cried out his own ragged pleasure.

Even afterwards, he didn't want to let her go. He didn't move from his position inside her, his palms possessively cupping her buttocks to maintain that sweet contact. He could feel her breath warm against his neck and the pinpoint thrust of her nipples and he thought he could have stayed like that all night.

Eventually she spoke, her voice muffled against his neck.

'I thought we weren't going to do this.'

'This?'

'Making love in the palace. That's what you said.'

'Did I?'

'You know you did.'

'Maybe when I had the chance to think about it, it seemed a little short-sighted.' He stroked her hair. 'It suddenly occurred to me that I have much experience while you have barely any at all. It seemed to make sense that while you are here you should learn from me. We are harming no one provided that we keep our liaison discreet—and I am very good at being discreet, *habibi*.'

She lifted her head and her amber eyes were suddenly serious. 'You mean, I'm to be your pupil? Like a novice rider who comes to the stables and needs to be taught everything about horses?'

'In a way, yes. But you are more to me than that.'

'I am?'

'Indeed you are. You are also a temptation I find myself unable to resist.' He saw the hope that died in her eyes as he took her hand and moved it down between his legs. 'See how you arouse me so instantly, Livvy?'

She looked down. *'Oh,'* she said, but her voice trembled a little.

'Yes, *oh*. Now stroke me,' he instructed softly. 'Whisper the tips of your fingers up and down my length. Like that. Yes. Only lighter. Oh, yes. Just like that.'

He came suddenly, his seed spilling over her fingers, and then he stroked her moist flesh until she was writhing beneath him and he had to muffle the cries of her orgasm with the pressure of his kiss.

And only when her eyelids had grown heavy and her breathing had slowed into the steady rhythm of sleep did Saladin slide from her bed and, after pulling on his robes, slip silently from the room.

CHAPTER TWELVE

BE CAREFUL WHAT you wish for.

Livvy stared up at the ceiling, aware of the minutes that were ticking away, knowing that soon Saladin would rise from her bed and leave her room—like a ghost who had never been there.

She'd told herself that she would be contented with what she had. That making love with Saladin was sublime—and she should make the most of the sexual pleasure they enjoyed, night after night.

But it was not enough—and she didn't know why.

During the day he treated her with a polite neutrality. He ate his meals with her and chatted to her, and came to the stables to watch her working with Burkaan whenever he had space in his schedule. It was hard to believe that this very *formal* sheikh was the same man whose touch always brought her to life in bed, leaving her sighing with pleasure as she snuggled up to him. But once the pleasure had worn off she was increasingly aware that he always kept something back. That there was a darkness at his core that he wouldn't share, something hidden from her and the rest of the world.

It left her feeling incomplete. As if she was getting only half the man. She knew that what they had couldn't last—but she couldn't bear to leave Jazratan without having known her lover as completely as possible. Surely that wasn't too much to ask.

So why act like his tame puppet who just accepted whatever he was prepared to dole out? Surely sexual relationships allowed for all kinds of discovery, other than the purely physical?

She rolled over on the bed and ran her fingertips along the rough rasp of his jawline.

'Saladin?'

There was a pause. 'Mmm?'

'Can I ask you something?'

Beneath the rumpled sheet, Saladin stretched his legs, and as he did so his thigh brushed against the softness of hers. She really did have the most beautiful thighs, he thought as he yawned.

As usual, he had come to her bed once darkness had fallen, driven by a fierce sexual hunger that showed no sign of abating. He knew it was a risk to his reputation—and hers—to persist in his nightly seduction, but it was a risk he was prepared to take. Because he was beginning to realise that the qualities that made her such a consummate horse whisperer were the same qualities that made her such a superb lover. She was intuitive and curious—gentle yet strong. He'd thought that the innocence that had stayed with her until a relatively late stage might have made her cautious, or wary. But he had been wrong. There had been no variation on the act of love that Olivia Miller hadn't embraced with an enthusiasm and sensuality that easily matched his own.

He tried not to react as her fingertips made dancing little movements across his chest, but he could feel the renewed throb of desire at his groin. 'You can ask me anything you wish, *habibi*—although whether or not I choose to answer it is quite another matter.'

Seemingly undeterred, a single fingertip now made a journey upwards to drift along his chin—its progress slow as it scraped against the new growth there.

'Why have you never married?'

The question came out of the blue and hit him like a slap to the face. He stilled and moved away from her. Had he been too quick to commend her? Too eager to think the best of her—his perfect lover—when deep down all she wanted to do was to probe into matters that did not concern her?

'It never ceases to amaze me,' he breathed, 'how you can be in bed with a woman and all she wants to do is talk about other women.'

He felt her stiffen beside him.

'Are you trying to change the subject?'

'What do you think?'

She clicked on a small lamp and stared at him. 'I think you are.'

'Well, then. Take the hint. Don't ask.'

'You're not the only one who doesn't *do* hints.' She tucked a strand of hair behind her ear and kept her gaze fixed steadily on him. 'I'm not asking you because I'm angling for some kind of permanent role in your life. I know what my limitations are. I know this is just sex—'

'*Just* sex?' he echoed, the taunt too much to resist as he reached for her breast.

She pushed his hand away. 'I'm only asking because I'm curious,' she said doggedly. 'Your single status doesn't seem to sit comfortably with a man who adores his country, but who seems to care more about the bloodline of his horse than his own. And I can't work out why that is.'

'Maybe you're not supposed to.'

'But I want to.'

Saladin didn't speak for a moment. This was intrusion, unwanted and unwarranted—a question she had no right to ask. Yet something tugged at him to tell her, and he couldn't work out what that something was. Was it an instinct she possessed—the same instinct that made angry and injured horses respond to her, which perhaps she extended to humans?

He hesitated, feeling the momentary sway of his defences as she surveyed him with that air of quiet stillness and determination. Was this why Burkaan had let her pet him, why his viciousness and pain had been temporarily forgotten in her company—because she exuded an air of healing reassurance, despite her occasional spikiness? He told himself not to confide in her, because keeping his own counsel wasn't just a matter of privacy, it was one of power. The unique and lonely power of a monarch who must always stand apart from other men.

But suddenly the weight of his guilt and his own dark secret felt heavy—too heavy a burden to carry on his own, and for the first time in his life he found himself sharing it.

'Because I have already been married,' he said.

She was shocked; he could tell. For all her bravado in saying this was just about sex, it wasn't that simple. It never was. Not where women were concerned. They always had an agenda; they were conditioned by nature to do so. They always wanted to bond with a man, no matter how much they tried to deny it. He watched as she tried to cultivate just the right blend of nonchalant interest, but he could see that her eyes had darkened.

'Married?' she said unsteadily. 'I had no idea.'

'Why should you? It happened a long time ago, when I was very young—in the days before these wretched twenty-four-hour news channels existed. Those distant days when Jazratan was a country without the world looking over its shoulder.'

'And your…wife?'

He could hear the tentative quiver in her voice. What did she expect him to say—that Alya was locked up in a tower somewhere, or that she was just one of a number of wives he kept hidden away in a harem while he entertained his foreign lover?

'Is dead.'

She didn't respond at first. If she'd come out with some meaningless platitude he probably would have got out of bed and left without saying another word, because nothing angered him more than people trying to trivialise the past. Instead, she just waited—the same way he'd seen her wait when Burkaan angrily stamped his hooves in his box before letting her approach.

'I'm so sorry,' she said at last, her voice washing like cool, clear balm over his skin.

'Yes,' he said flatly.

'She…she had something to do with the Faddi gate and the rose garden, didn't she?' she asked tentatively.

He nodded, but it was a moment before he spoke. 'She was designing it to celebrate our first wedding anniversary, only she never got to see its completion. I had landscape designers finish it, strictly adhering to her plans, but…'

'But you never go in there, do you?' she said, into

the silence that followed his words. 'Nobody does. It's always empty.'

'That's right,' he agreed.

Perhaps it was the fact that she said nothing more that made Saladin start telling her the story, and once he had started the words seemed to come of their own accord—pouring from his lips in a dark torrent. Maybe because it was so long since he'd allowed himself to think about it that he'd almost been able to forget it had ever happened. Except that it had. Oh, it had. He felt remorse pierce at his heart like tiny shards of glass, and following remorse came the guilt—always the guilt.

'Alya was a princess from Shamrastan, and we were betrothed when we were both very young,' he began. 'Our fathers wanted there to be an alliance between two traditionally warring countries and for a new peace to settle on the region.'

'So it was—' she hesitated '—an arranged marriage?'

His eyes narrowed and he felt a familiar impatience begin to bubble up inside him. 'Such an idea is anathema to Western sensibilities, is that what you're thinking, Livvy?' he demanded. 'But such unions are based on much firmer ground than the unrealistic expectations of the romantic love. And it was no hardship to be married to a woman like Alya, for she was kind and wise and my people loved her. She was beautiful, too—like a flower in its first flush. And I let her die,' he finished, the words almost choking him. *'I let her die.'*

She tried to touch him but he shook his head and rolled away from her, turning to stare at the flicker of shadows on the walls—as if it were a betrayal to even look at her while he was speaking of Alya.

'What happened?' she said, from behind him.

He could hear the thunder of his heart as he dragged his mind back to that terrible morning—and, despite his having locked it away in the darkness, the memory seemed as vivid and as painful as ever. 'I had to leave at dawn,' he said heavily. 'For I was due to ride to Qurhah to negotiate with the sultan there, and I wanted to get away before the sun was too high.' He swallowed. 'I could have flown—or even driven—but I wanted to visit some of the nomadic tribes along the way and it is better to take a camel or a horse into these regions, for they are still suspicious of modern transport. I remember Alya waking up just before I left, because she always liked to say goodbye to me. She was screwing up her eyes against the morning light, but we had been awake for some of the night and I thought she was just tired.' His voice cracked. 'So when she complained that her head ached, I told her to go back to sleep and to see how she felt when the maid came to wake her for breakfast.'

'Go on,' she said.

He stared straight ahead. 'I remember she smiled at me and nodded, looking at me with all the trust in the world as I bent over to kiss her. She told me to take care in the desert. And that was the last time I saw her alive.' His words ground down to a painful halt, because even now they were hard to say. 'Because when her maid came to rouse her, she found Alya lying dead.'

'Dead?'

He heard the shock in her voice and he turned over to see that same shock reflected on her face. 'Yes, dead. Cold and lifeless—her beautiful eyes staring sightlessly at the ceiling. Struck down by a subarachnoid haemorrhage at the age of nineteen,' he said, his voice shaking with loss and rage and guilt. 'Lost to us all and let down by the one man who should have saved her.'

'Who?' she questioned. 'Who could have saved her?'

He shook his head incredulously. 'Why, me, of course!'

'And how could you have done that, Saladin? How could you have possibly saved her?'

He clenched his fists together, so that the knuckles turned bone white as they lay against the sheet. 'If I'd thought about *her*, instead of being wrapped up in my own ambition. If I hadn't been so full of triumph about the impending agreement with Qurhah, I might have realised the severity of the situation. I should have delayed my trip and called the doctor, who would have been there by the time she started to vomit copiously. I might have been able to help her, instead of being halfway across the desert when news reached me.'

'You don't know that,' protested Livvy. 'That's pure conjecture.'

'It's fact,' he snapped. 'I could have taken her to hospital.'

'And all the intervention in the world still might not have helped,' she said. 'But you'll never know—because that's just the way life is sometimes. We have to accept that we have no control over it. You have to cherish all the beautiful memories you had with Alya and let go of the bitterness and the blame.'

'Oh, really?' He gave a bitter laugh. 'So suddenly you're an expert on relationships, are you, my little virgin horse whisperer?'

She flinched a little as if she had only just registered the harshness of his words. 'It's always easier to diag-

nose someone else's problems rather than your own,'
she said stiffly. 'And presumably you told me all this
because deep down you wanted my opinion.'

He wasn't sure *why* he had told her. He wondered
what had possessed him to open up and let her see
his dark heart. Was it to warn her off the tenderness
that had started to creep into their nightly lovemaking,
even though he had warned her against such tenderness at the very beginning? And now he regretted his
impetuous disclosure. He wanted to rewind the clock.
To take back his words—and his secrets—so that she
would become just another anonymous woman in his
bed. So what inner demon prompted him to voice his
next question? 'And what is your opinion?'

Livvy sucked in a deep breath, knowing that what
she wanted to say required courage, and she wasn't
sure she had enough within her—not in the face of so
much sudden hostility. Yet wasn't it better to live your
life courageously? To face facts instead of hiding away
from them? Saladin might be a sheikh who ruled this
wealthy land, but in this moment he needed the words
of someone who wasn't prepared to be intimidated by
his position and his power. Who would tell it the way
it was—not the way he wanted to hear it. She drew in
a deep breath. 'You once accused me of allowing the
fact that I'd been jilted to affect my life negatively—
and you were right. But haven't you done exactly the
same with Alya?'

His eyes narrowed. 'What are you talking about?'

She licked her lips. 'Aren't you in danger of using
your wife's death as an excuse to stop you from living properly, in the here and now? She died when you

were newlyweds…' Her voice faltered for a moment as she met the angry glint in his black eyes, but she'd started now. She'd started and she had to finish. 'She was young and beautiful and time hadn't tarnished your perfect relationship in any way—'

'And you're saying it would have done?' he demanded hotly. 'That all relationships are doomed to end in failure or misery? Is that your Western view of marriage?'

'That's not what I'm saying at all. Nobody knows what would have happened,' she said fiercely. 'Because nobody ever does. All I know is that you seem to be letting your unnecessary guilt hold you back.'

'And what if I don't think it's *unnecessary*?' he bit out. 'What if I feel it is the burden I must carry until the end of my days?'

'Then, that's your choice, because nobody can change your mind for you, Saladin. Only you.' She hesitated because this bit was harder. 'Though maybe you prefer it this way. Your lovely wife was cut off in her prime and nobody else is ever going to be able to live up to her, are they? She was perfect in every way, and she always will be because you've put her on a pedestal. And no living woman can ever compare to Alya.'

His eyes narrowed with sudden perception and slowly he nodded his head. 'Ah,' he said tightly. 'Now I understand.'

She was alerted to the dark note that had entered his voice, and her head jerked back. 'Understand what?'

He gave a short laugh. 'Self-regard disguised as advice. Isn't that what you're doing?'

'I'm afraid you've lost me now. I was never very good at riddles.'

His mouth hardened into a cynical line. 'Oh, come on, Livvy. You must know what I'm saying. You seem to have settled very well here in Jazratan. Even my advisors have commented on how well you have fit in. Unobtrusive, modest, yet supremely hard-working—you put to shame our enduring stereotype of the Western woman as a hard-living party animal. Of course, nobody but us knows that our nights have become a feast of sensual delights. And that under cover of darkness you become someone quite different—a creature of pure pleasure.' His black eyes became hooded as he looked at her. 'Perhaps you are reluctant to walk away from all that you have found here. Did you look around at my palace and like what you saw—is that it? Did my pure little virgin see herself as the future queen of Jazratan?'

Livvy stiffened as his words shot through her like tiny arrows. He had taken her well-meaning advice and twisted it, making it sound as if she'd been seeking her own happy-ever-after when all she'd been doing was trying to comfort him. He made her sound grabbing and self-serving and *cheap*.

'You dare to accuse me of something so cynical?' she demanded, hot breath clogging her throat.

'Yes, I dare!' he challenged. 'What's the matter, Livvy—have I touched a raw nerve?'

Pushing her hair away from her hot face, she noticed the tremble of her fingers. 'Actually, I find your arrogance and your assumption breathtaking, if you must know, but at least it's made me see things more clearly.' She drew in a deep breath as she wriggled away from him. 'And I'm going back to England.'

He shook his head. 'No, not yet.'

'It wasn't a suggestion, Saladin—it was a statement. I'm going and there isn't a thing you can do to stop me.'

He reached for her then, his hand moving underneath the sheet to slide around her waist, and Livvy despaired of how instantly her body reacted when he touched her. She bit her lip as he began to stroke her and wished he could carry on stroking her like that until the end of time.

'Look, maybe I shouldn't have said those things.' A note of something like contrition entered his voice as he continued with his seductive caress. 'Maybe I was lashing out because I'd told you so much. More than I've ever told anyone else.'

'It doesn't matter what you say to me now. My mind is made up and I'm going,' she repeated, pushing away his hand. 'Because there's no reason for me to stay. You're obviously suspicious of my motives, and that is your prerogative. But I don't want to be hidden away like a dirty secret anymore. Do you understand?'

His face darkened. 'And what about Burkaan?'

Livvy felt her heart plummet as his reaction confirmed what she already knew—that his racehorse meant more to him than anything. Of course it did. When would she ever learn that she was one of those women who fell for the kind of men who would never love her back?

'Burkaan will be fine,' she said. 'He doesn't need me anymore—we both know that. He's got his appetite back and he's no longer vicious with the grooms. The X-ray results are conclusive.' She paused, suddenly realising how much she was going to miss the feisty black stallion. But not nearly as much as she was going to miss his judgemental master. 'The vet told me this morning how pleased he is with his progress—and he'll continue making good progress, as long as you take it slowly. So don't rush him. A month walking, followed by a month trotting. After that, you can try cantering.'

'Livvy—'

'I mean, obviously there's no guarantee he'll ever race again,' she rushed on, desperate to cut him off before he tried another of those appeals, which this time she might not be able to withstand. 'But you should certainly be able to put him out to stud at some point in the future. And now I think it's best if you leave. No. Please don't try to touch me again, Saladin. It will only complicate things. We both know that.'

She saw the incredulity that had narrowed his dark eyes and wondered if anyone had ever ordered him from their bed before, or tried to oppose his wishes. Probably not. But she needed to do this. She needed to put distance between them and she needed to find an inner strength. Because, despite her furious denial that she was hoping for some kind of future with him, wasn't there a part of her that was doing exactly that? A part that had grown closer to this complex and compelling man and wanted to grow closer still, if only he would let her. A part that badly wanted to love him, as she suspected he needed to be loved.

And she couldn't afford to think that way. Because falling for a desert sheikh who was still in love with his dead wife was asking for trouble.

He sat up in bed, the sheet falling away from him. 'You're really asking me to leave?' he demanded.

'I really am.' She forced a smile. 'Think of it as character-building.'

Saladin felt a fury and a frustration racing through his blood as he stared into her stubborn face. Who the *hell* did she think she was, trying to take control like this? She would leave his employment when *he* was good and ready and not a moment before. Yet she enjoyed taking control, didn't she? She had laid down her rules right from the start—not seeming to realise what kind of man she was dealing with—and had expected him meekly to accept them. Well, maybe it was time she realised that he'd had enough of *her* rules and *her* control.

Yes, he had enjoyed her time here—who wouldn't have done? She had entranced and pleased him on so many levels and cared so beautifully for his beloved stallion. But that was all pretty much academic. Because where could this relationship go? Absolutely nowhere—no matter how much he liked her. And wouldn't her infernal refusal to be sublimated by his power and position irritate him after a while?

'You want to go?' he snapped, getting out of bed and picking up his discarded robe. 'Then, go!'

He saw the brief look of alarm in her eyes that she couldn't quite hide.

'Right,' she said uncertainly.

'I'll arrange transport for you tomorrow. You can leave first thing.'

With a sinking feeling of dread, Livvy watched as he pulled the robe on over his naked body and jammed his headdress into place and then stormed across the room. He didn't slam the door behind him, though he looked as if he would have liked to have done.

And she was left in the empty room with the dread growing heavier inside her and all she could think was, what had she done?

CHAPTER THIRTEEN

IT WAS ICY cold back in England after the seductive warmth of the Jazratian sun. Livvy returned to a stack of unopened mail, a cat determined to ignore her and the realisation that she didn't have a clue what she wanted to do with the rest of her life—except that deep down she knew it no longer involved making beds and cooking breakfasts.

She had left Jazratan with a heavy heart—without even a final kiss from Saladin—knowing she had only herself to blame. She had kicked him out of her bed and told him she was returning to England and he had retaliated by angrily telling her to go ahead. Had she really expected the proud sheikh to mount some sort of campaign to get her to change her mind? She kept telling herself that he'd been offering sex, not security or love. And anyone with half a brain could see it was better to get out now, while her heart was still intact.

Unless it was already too late. Hadn't her heart felt crushed when she'd left Jazratan on Saladin's private jet? When, earlier that same morning, she'd crept along to the stables to rub her cheek against Burkaan's thick mane and the stallion had stamped one of his hooves—almost as if he had shared her grief at parting and had known the reason why salty tears were flowing down her face.

Saladin had been courteous when she'd been granted an audience to say a formal farewell to him—in the throne room, where he was surrounded by his powerful advisors and bodyguards. Had he correctly interpreted the silent plea in her eyes that had asked for a moment alone with him—and simply chosen to ignore it? Or had his mind already been on other things?

Either way, he had given her nothing but a brief handshake and a flicker of a smile, accompanied by a few words of thanks—which had only added to her feelings of misery as one of his staff had presented her with a cheque. And she felt as if she'd sold *herself* somewhere along the way.

But she *hadn't*, she told herself fiercely. She wasn't a victim—not anymore. She'd been sexually awoken by a man who had turned out to be an amazing lover. She had been persuaded back onto a horse and had realised just how much she loved riding, and she must be grateful to him for that. If she had learned anything it was that you couldn't let yourself live in the past and be dominated by it. Not like Saladin and the beautiful young wife he was unable to forget. And that was the irony of it all—that he didn't follow the same advice he'd so eagerly given her. He could dish it out, but he couldn't take it.

And if she now believed herself to be in love with him, well—she would have to wait for it to pass.

At least Stella—her part-time help—had disposed of the Christmas tree, and the decorations had been returned to the loft. The snow was all melted and the holiday was nothing but a distant memory when Livvy arrived home. All that remained were a few stray mistletoe berries, which had rolled underneath a bureau in the hall and somehow escaped being swept up.

Livvy wrote an email to Alison Clark and her friends saying what a shame it was they'd had to cancel their visit and expressing her hope that they'd enjoyed their Christmas in the London hotel. Unenthusiastically, she looked down at the blank pages of her diary. Could she really face trying to drum up more business for the year ahead? To wipe out most of her summer by clearing up after people, when she'd been doing it for so long? All to maintain a house that just didn't feel the same any more. Her inherited home now seemed like nothing but a pile of bricks and mortar, not something she was tied to by blood. She found herself looking around the rooms with a critical eye. It was just a too-big house that needed redecoration and a family to bring it alive, not some aging spinster who rattled around in the rooms.

'So what was it like?' questioned Stella as they were cleaning one of the bedrooms a few days after Livvy had returned from Jazratan.

Livvy gave the bedspread another tug. 'What, specifically?'

Stella shrugged her generous shoulders. 'You know. Living in the desert.'

Livvy puffed out her cheeks and sighed as she straightened up. 'It was…different.' She hesitated, trying to be objective. Trying to forget the man who was the very heart of the place. The man who made her own heart ache whenever she thought about him. 'It was lovely, actually. Really lovely. The palace itself is unbelievable—and so are the gardens. There's a kind of beauty in all that heat and starkness, and the stars are the brightest I've ever seen.'

'And didn't they feed you?' asked Stella critically. 'You've lost weight.'

'Of course they did. It's just that—' Livvy gave a wan smile '—I didn't seem to have a lot of appetite. It was very...hot.'

No, not because it was hot. Because she'd been so obsessed with Saladin that she'd barely been able to think about anything else. She still couldn't and it was driving her crazy. There was her future to decide, and she was busy obsessing about a man with black eyes and a hard body, who had taken her to those bright stars and back.

And she would never see him again.

'Well, there's a pipe leaking in the red bathroom. Better get it seen to before it brings the roof down,' added Stella, with her customary love of domestic drama.

The plumbing problems distracted her for a while, and then Livvy burned off a load of frustration by picking up the leaves that had gathered in a sodden heap by the front door.

It was after lunch, when Peppa had finally decided to forgive Livvy for going away and had started winding her furry body around her legs at every opportunity, that the telephone rang. Stella bustled along the corridor to answer it, her eyes nearly popping out of her head as she listened to the voice at the other end.

'It's him,' she mouthed.

'Who?' Livvy mimed back.

'The *sheikh.*'

With a tight smile Livvy took the phone and carried

it through to her little study, trying to control her suddenly unsteady breathing as she gazed out at the garden where water was dripping from the bare branches of the trees and the grass resembled a sea of mud. As a reflection of the way she felt, it was perfect. *You need to stay calm*, she told herself. *You need to be strong.* For all she knew, Saladin might just be phoning for a chat to check she'd got home safely. This was probably normal for people who'd briefly been lovers. He might even be wanting to ask her advice about Burkaan. Yes, that was probably it. But she could do nothing about the wild thunder of her heart.

'Hello?' she said.

'Livvy?'

'Yes, it's me.' But as the silken caress of his voice washed over her, some of her forced calm began to trickle away and Livvy realised that she wasn't any good at playing games, or pretending to be friends. Not when she wanted to blurt out how much she missed him. Not when she wanted to feel his arms around her, holding her very tight. She heard the ping of an email entering her inbox. 'What can I do for you, Saladin?'

'Which isn't the friendliest greeting I've ever heard,' he observed drily.

'But I thought that's the way you wanted it. Formal and polite. I thought we'd concluded our business together. I thought we'd said everything that needed to be said. That was certainly the impression I got when I left.' She paused. 'Which makes me wonder why you're ringing?'

At the other end of the line, Saladin stared out at the sky. Why *was* he ringing? It was a question he hadn't wanted to confront and one that instinctively he shied away from answering. He wondered if he could per-suade her to return to Jazratan by telling her that his horse was pining for her, which was true.

He suspected not. He sensed that financial induce-ments would no longer sway her, no matter how much more generous he made his offer. Just as he sensed that pride wouldn't allow her to accept something that could only ever be second best. He sighed. He re-alised that, for all her newly awoken sexual liberation, Livvy Miller remained a fiercely traditional woman who would not look kindly on the sort of relationship he usually offered his lovers. And the pain in his heart was very real, wasn't it? The question was how far he was prepared to go to be with her.

'I need to talk to you.'

'Talk away. I'm not stopping you.'

'I'm not having this conversation over the phone.'

'And I'm not offering you an alternative,' she an-swered coolly. 'What do you want, Saladin?'

'To see you.'

'Sorry. No can do.'

'Livvy,' he growled. 'I'm serious.'

'And so am I,' she said. 'You said some pretty tough things to me that last night. You were suspi-cious and hostile and accused me of all kinds of devi-ous motivations—'

'For which I apologised.'

Only because you had to, thought Livvy. *Only be-cause you had to.* 'Yes, you did. So surely we've said everything that needs to be said. It was a fantastic af-fair and I'm sorry it had to end that way—but the point is that it had to end some time.' She cleared her throat. 'How's Burkaan?'

'He's fine. Livvy—'

'Look, I've got to go,' she said desperately as she heard another email ping into her inbox. 'Someone's trying to contact me. Goodbye, Saladin, and…take care of yourself.'

She cut the call before she had the chance to change her mind, or to be lulled by a seductive voice into doing something that would only bring her pain.

After Livvy had put the phone down, she sat down at her desk. She wasn't going to make a fuss about it, she thought, even though her heart was crashing painfully against her ribcage, because the pain would go. It might take time, but it would definitely go. She would answer her emails and carry on as normal and rejoice that she'd had the strength to resist him. Her hand hovered over the mouse and her whole body stiffened as she clicked on the first email and began to read…

An hour must have passed before she realised that she hadn't moved and was sitting in total darkness and that Peppa was mewing plaintively by her feet and Stella had long gone. She ought to do something. She ought to feed the cat and…

And what?

Sit there for the rest of the evening thinking about what a *devious bastard* Saladin really was?

Her eyes skated down the rest of the emails. There were two tentative booking enquiries, plus one of those round-robin jokes that one of her school friends always insisted on sending and that she didn't find remotely funny. And a 'Singles Nite' being offered by the local pub. She screwed her eyes up as she looked at the date. Tonight's date.

Print out this voucher for free entry to the Five Bells 'Singles Nite'. Music, karaoke and so much more!

A sudden new resolution flooded through her as, impetuously, she pressed the print button, fed Peppa and then went upstairs to get ready.

She told herself that she was going to stop acting like a startled hermit and get out there and put every-thing Saladin had taught her into practice. No longer was she going to live like a nun. There was no rea-son why she couldn't have other relationships—in the same way that there was no reason she couldn't have another career. Defiantly, she applied more make-up than usual, fished out a sparkly top to wear with her jeans and piled her hair into an elaborate topknot so that it wouldn't get wrecked by the wind on the way out to the car.

When she drew up outside the pub, she almost turned around to go home because music was blaring out at a deafening pitch. Inside it was crowded, but at least the noise became less loud when a woman started swaying around on a small stage, tunelessly singing about her intention to survive. There were a few people Livvy recognised from the village, but not well enough to sit with—so she bought herself a tomato juice, told herself that she would drink it up and then go. *Baby steps*, she thought. *Baby steps. You've come out on your own and it hasn't killed you. And although it's pretty dire—next time might be better.*

She found a corner seat and sat there smiling as if her life depended on it. She tapped her feet to the music and tried to look as if she was having a good time and eventually a man about her age wandered over, with a half-drunk pint in his hand. He had thick hair and crinkly blue eyes and he asked if he might join her.

But before she could answer, a silky and authoritative answer came from behind him.

'I'm afraid not.'

Livvy didn't need to hear the deeply accented voice to know it was Saladin. She should have realised he'd walked in because the pub had suddenly gone quiet and even the woman doing the karaoke had stopped singing as she stared at him incredulously. But who could blame her? Powerful olive-skinned sheikhs wearing dark cashmere weren't exactly at a premium around these parts.

Livvy put her tomato juice down on the table with shaking fingers as the conversation all around them took on a sudden roar of interest.

'How did you get here?' she demanded, her heart starting to race. 'You're in Jazratan.'

'Obviously, I'm not. I flew in today and came here by helicopter,' he answered.

Her face remained unwelcoming, but she kept it that way. *Why* had he followed her and *why* was he here on *her* territory, when she was just starting out on a long journey to forget him? 'What do you want?'

'There are three things I want,' he said grimly. 'And the first involves having a conversation, which won't be possible with all this noise going on. So can we go outside, Livvy? Please?'

She opened her mouth to say that she didn't want to go anywhere with him, except that was a blatant lie and she suspected he would see right through it. And he was asking in the kind of voice she'd never heard him use before. But even so…

'It's raining,' she objected.

'You can sit in my car.'

'No, Saladin,' she said fiercely. 'You can sit in *my* car, and you can have precisely ten minutes.'

He didn't look overjoyed at the suggestion but he didn't object as he followed her into the blustery and rainy night. Outside an enormous limousine was parked with a burly bodyguard standing beside it, but Livvy marched straight past it towards her own little car, feeling inordinately pleased at the almost helpless shrug that Saladin directed at the guard.

But the moment he removed a sock from the passenger seat—what was *that* doing there?—and got in beside her, she regretted her decision. Because the limousine would have been better than this. It was bigger, for a start, and there wouldn't be this awful sense of the man she most wanted to touch being within touching range…and being completely off limits.

'So what's the second thing?' she questioned, in a voice that sounded miraculously calm. 'How did you know I was here?'

'I had someone watching your house who was instructed to follow you,' he said unapologetically. 'When I arrived, they told me you were still here. It was at that point that a ball of fur hurled itself out of nowhere and decided to start attacking my ankles.' He grimaced. 'Your cat doesn't like me.'

'Probably not. I got her from the rescue centre.' She shot him a defiant look. 'She was ill-treated by a man as a kitten and she's never forgotten it.'

There were plenty of parallels between the woman and the cat, Saladin thought. Livvy had been ill-treated by a man, too, and it had made her wary. And he hadn't exactly done a lot to try to repair her damaged image of the opposite sex, had he? He had treated her as if she was disposable. As if she could be replaced. And wasn't it time he addressed that?

He looked at her in the dim light of the scruffy little car, his gaze taking in an unremarkable raincoat and the fiery hair, which the wind had whipped into untidy strands that were falling around her face. She was wearing too much make-up. He'd never seen her in such bright lipstick before and it didn't suit her, and yet he couldn't ever remember feeling such a raw and urgent sense of desire as he did right now. Was that because she had shown the strength of character to reject him—to walk away from the half-hearted relationship he'd given her? Because by doing that she had earned his respect as well as making him realise that they were equals.

'I miss you, Livvy,' he said softly.

He saw a flicker of surprise in the depths of her eyes before her face resumed that stony expression.

'The *sex*, do you mean?' she questioned sharply. 'Surely you can get that with someone else?'

'Of course I miss the sex,' he bit out. 'And I don't want to *get it* with anyone else. There are other things I miss, too. Talking, for one.'

'I'm sure there are many people who would be only too happy to talk to you, Saladin. People who would hang on to your every word.'

'But that's the whole point. I don't want someone hanging on my every word. I want someone who will give back as good as she gets.'

'*I want* doesn't always get,' she responded, infuriatingly.

'I miss seeing the magic you worked on my horse,' he continued resolutely. *And on me*, he thought. *And on me.* 'I want you to come back to Jazratan with me.'

It was as if that single sentence had changed something. As if she'd removed the stony mask from her freckly face so that he could see the sudden glitter of anger in her amber eyes. 'And how far are you prepared to go to get what you want?' she demanded. 'How many people are you prepared to manipulate just so that Saladin Al Mektala can get his own way?'

His eyes narrowed. 'Excuse me?'

Angrily, she punched her fist on the steering wheel. 'I've just had an email from Alison Clark, who you probably don't even remember. She was the woman who was due to spend Christmas here with her polo friends, before you decided you needed me in Jazratan. The group who miraculously decided not to come at the last minute and to spend their Christmas in a fancy London hotel instead. A trip *financed by you*, as I've just discovered in an email written by the grateful Alison. So what did you do, Saladin—have your *people* track down these guests of mine and offer them something they couldn't resist, just so that you could whisk me away from Derbyshire?'

He met her accusing stare and gave a heavy sigh. 'They seemed perfectly happy with the arrangement.'

'I'm sure they were. All-expenses-paid trips to five-star hotels don't exactly grow on trees! But it was a sneaky thing to do and it was *manipulative*,' she accused. 'It was just you snapping your powerful fingers in order to get your own way, as usual.'

'Or a creative way of getting you to come to Jazratan, because already I was completely intrigued by you?' he retorted.

'You just wanted me to fix your horse!'

'Yes,' he admitted, in a voice that suddenly sounded close to breaking. 'And in the process, you somehow managed to fix me. You found a space in my heart that I didn't even realise was vacant. And you've filled it, Livvy. You've filled it completely.'

'Saladin,' she said shakily. 'Don't—'

'I must.' He reached out then and took one of the hands that was gripping the steering wheel and pressed it between the sensuous warmth of his leather gloves. 'Every word you spoke was true,' he said quietly. 'I was using my early marriage and my guilt as a block to forming a meaningful relationship with someone else. But I've realised that what I have with you transcends anything I have known before. That we have a truly adult relationship and we are equals. Yes, equals,' he affirmed as he saw her open her mouth to object. 'I'm not talking about the trappings of my kingdom, or the division of wealth. We are equals in the ways that matter. Or at least, I hope we are because I love you, Livvy Miller. And I'm hoping that you love me, too.'

His words were so unexpected that for a moment Livvy thought she must have imagined them and she tried to ignore the excited leap of her heart—shaking her head with a defiance that suddenly seemed as necessary to her as breathing. 'You're still in love with your dead wife,' she said.

'I will always love Alya,' he said simply. 'But what I had with her was so different from what I had with you. She was very young and in complete thrall to me. I was her king, not her equal. And you were right. She was taken at a time when she was perfect, and that's what her memory became to me. My single status became a kind of homage to her, as well as being a safety net behind which I could hide. When I spoke so disparagingly about romantic love, it was because I didn't believe in it, but now I do. I didn't think it could ever happen to me, but now it has.' His black eyes burned into her steadily. 'There are many different types of love, but believe me when I tell you that my heart is yours, Livvy. That I have found my equal in you. And that even though your stubbornness and refusal to do exactly as I say sometimes frustrates the hell out of me, I love you passionately and truly and steadfastly.'

And then Livvy *did* believe him, because it was too big an admission for a man like Saladin to make unless he really meant it. The passion that blazed from his eyes was genuine and the conviction that deepened his voice crept over her skin like a warm glow, but still something held her back.

'And I love you, too,' she said. 'Very, very much. But I'm not sure if I'm going to be able to be the kind of lover you need.'

'And what kind of lover is that?' he asked gently.

'I've pretty much decided that I'm going to sell up and use the money you gave me to start my own stables,' she said. 'I don't have a clue where that might be. And you'll want a mistress, I suppose. I thought I wouldn't be able to tolerate that kind of relationship, but now that I've seen you again I'm beginning to have second thoughts.' She shrugged her shoulders. 'But when I start imagining the reality—I don't know if I can see myself being set up in some kind of luxury apartment so that you can come and visit.'

He frowned. 'So that I can come and visit?' he repeated, in a perplexed voice.

'Whenever you're in the country. Isn't this how these things usually work?'

His answering laugh sounded like the low roar of a lion as he gathered her into his arms and tilted her chin very tenderly with the tip of his thumb. 'I was hoping you might return with me to Jazratan, as my queen. I was hoping you would marry me.'

Her cheeks burned as she met his eyes, remembering the accusations he had thrown at her.

'I know,' he said ruefully. 'But maybe I accused you of being matrimonially ambitious because already it was playing on *my* mind. Because I've realised there is no alternative scenario that I am prepared to tolerate.' He drew in a deep breath. 'So will you, Livvy? Will you marry me?'

And suddenly Livvy had run out of reasons to keep telling herself that this couldn't possibly be happening and that there must be a catch somewhere. Because there wasn't—and when it boiled down to it, Saladin's past didn't matter and neither did hers. Because right then he was just a man with so much love in his eyes, which matched the great big feeling that was swelling up inside her heart and making it feel as if it were about to burst with joy.

'Yes, Saladin,' she said, putting her arms around his neck and holding on to him as if she would never let him go. 'I'll marry you tomorrow if you want me to.'

EPILOGUE

THEY MARRIED TWICE. Once in the quiet stone chapel where Livvy's own mother and father had been wed, and once in a lavish ceremony in Jazratan, attended by world leaders and dignitaries—as well as a sizeable hunk of the horse-racing fraternity.

At first it felt weird for Livvy to see her photo plastered all over the papers, with Saladin holding tightly on to her hand, her filmy veil held in place by a crown of diamonds and rubies and her golden dress gleaming like the coat of a palomino horse.

She settled happily in the country she had quickly grown to love, determined to learn to speak the Jazratian language fluently and to see Burkaan winning the famous Oman Cup. And if people ever asked her how she had managed to adapt so comfortably from owning a B & B in Derbyshire to being the queen of Jazratan, she was able to answer quite honestly. She told them that the grandness of her husband's palace never intimidated her, because wherever Saladin was felt like home. He travelled less than before, and everywhere he went he took Livvy with him—for he was eager to show off his new bride to the world.

Livvy started working in the stables, whenever her

royal role permitted it, and quickly earned herself a reputation among the staff of being gifted and reliable and never pulling rank. She liked to go riding with Saladin when the sun had started to sink low and the sting of the heat had left the day. Sometimes they rode to 'their' oasis, where they made love beneath the shade of the palm trees.

After a gentle campaign she persuaded Saladin to have a ceremony declaring the beautiful rose gardens officially open—and invited Alya's parents, along with her two brothers and their wives, as guests of honour. It wasn't the easiest of meetings—not at first, for there were tears in Alya's mother's eyes as she tied a small posy of flowers to one of the intricate silver coils on the Faddi gates. And yes, Livvy saw tears in Saladin's eyes, too. But Alya's parents were persuaded to bring their grandsons to play there at any time, and afterwards they all sat beneath the shade of a tree, drinking jasmine tea and laughing as the two sturdy little boys toddled around among the scented bowers.

It would be several years before Burkaan would triumph in the Oman Cup and many more before he was put out to stud, and a new foal—the image of his father—was born. But Peppa the cat grew grudgingly to accept Saladin's presence in her mistress's life and found herself happily living in the royal palace, enjoying the way that the staff fussed around her. There was a bit of a shock when it was discovered that she had sneaked out and mated with a stray tom who had been seen lurking around the back of the stables—but she proved herself an exemplary mother of five kittens.

Wightwick Manor was never sold. Saladin decided that the house should be kept as a base for them whenever they wanted to escape the desert heat to enjoy a spell in the English countryside.

'And it is important that any children we may have will grow up knowing and loving their mother's inheritance, because your roots are just as important as mine, *habibi*,' he said, tenderly stroking Livvy's head, which was currently resting upon his bare chest. 'Don't you agree?'

Livvy wriggled a little, changing her position so that she could prop herself up onto her elbow and stare into the enticing gleam of her husband's black eyes. She trailed a thoughtful path over his chest with her finger, circling lightly over the hard muscle and bone covered by all that silken skin, and it thrilled her to feel him shiver. She liked making him shiver.

'I agree absolutely,' she said as he began to brush his hand against her inner thigh and now it was *her* turn to shiver. 'And in fact, that brings me very nicely to some news I have for you.'

His hand stilled and she knew he was holding his breath—just as she'd held hers when she'd surreptitiously done the test that morning. They hadn't actively been *trying*, but she knew that Saladin longed for a child of his own, and she'd been wanting to have his baby since the moment he'd slid that wedding ring on her finger.

'I'm pregnant,' she whispered. 'I'm going to have a baby.'

And suddenly he was laughing and kissing her and telling her how much he loved her, all at the same time. And it was only after a little time had passed that she noticed that his hand was no longer making its tantalising journey up her thigh.

She caught hold of his fingers and put them right back where they had started from. 'Don't stop,' she said.

'Is it safe?'

She danced her lips in front of his. 'Perfectly safe.'

And that was how she made him feel, Saladin realised dazedly. Safe. As if he'd found something he hadn't even realised he'd been looking for. As if she were his harbour, his refuge and his joy. As if the whole world suddenly made sense. He cradled her head in the palms of his hands and kissed her as deeply as he knew how. And thanked the heavens for that snowy Christmas night, which had given him the greatest gift of all.

The gift of love.

* * * * *

'I want to spend the night with you.'

'One night,' Rashid said, and she recognised it as a warning. 'That's all I can offer you.'

'Perfect,' Tora said with a smile, because that was all she wanted. One night to forget her scheming, cheating cousin. 'One night is all I want.'

Tomorrow she could pick up the shattered pieces of her promises and work out where she went from here.

His eyes glinted in the street lighting—a flash of victory that came with a spark of heat—and he reached out his fingers to push a wayward tendril of her hair behind her ear. It made her skin tingle.

'My name is Rashid.'

'Tora,' she said, even as she trembled under his touch.

He took her hand and brought it to his mouth, pressing it to his lips. 'Come, Tora…' he said.

Desert Brothers

Bound by duty, undone by passion!

These sheikhs may not be brothers by blood,
but they are united by the code of the desert.

Their power and determination is legendary
and unchallenged—until unexpected encounters
with women strong enough to equal them
threaten their self-control…

Read the two concluding stories in Trish Morey's
exciting quartet of searing passion and sizzling drama!

Captive of Kadar
May 2015

Shackled to the Sheikh
November 2015

SHACKLED
TO THE SHEIKH

BY
TRISH MOREY

Published in Great Britain 2015
by Mills & Boon, an imprint of Harlequin (UK) Limited,
Eton House, 18-24 Paradise Road, Richmond, Surrey, TW9 1SR

© 2015 Trish Morey

ISBN: 978-0-263-25085-5

Printed and bound in Spain
by CPI, Barcelona

Trish Morey always fancied herself a writer—so why she became a chartered accountant is anyone's guess! But once she'd found her true calling there was no turning back. Mother of four budding heroines and wife to one true-life hero, Trish lives in an idyllic region of South Australia. Is it any wonder she believes in happy-ever-afters?

Find her at trishmorey.com or facebook.com/trish.morey.

Books by Trish Morey

Mills & Boon Modern Romance

A Price Worth Paying?
Bartering Her Innocence
The Heir from Nowhere
His Prisoner in Paradise
His Mistress for a Million

The Chatsfield

Tycoon's Temptation

Desert Brothers

Duty and the Beast
The Sheikh's Last Gamble
Captive of Kadar

Bound by his Ring

Secrets of Castillo Del Arco

21st Century Bosses

Fiancée for One Night

Dark-Hearted Desert Men

Forbidden: The Sheikh's Virgin

Visit the Author Profile page
at millsandboon.co.uk for more titles.

To my amazing readers,
with grateful thanks and wishing you love always,
Trish
x

CHAPTER ONE

RASHID AL KHARIM was done with pacing.

He needed something stronger.

He needed to lose himself. To dull the pain of each and every one of today's revelations, if only for a few precious hours.

To forget about a father who hadn't died thirty years back as he'd always believed, but a scant four weeks ago.

And to forget about a tiny child—a sister—who apparently was now his responsibility...

His head full of anger and torment, he let the door of his Sydney hotel suite slam hard behind him as he strode towards the lifts, stabbing the call button with intent, because he knew exactly what he needed right now.

A woman.

CHAPTER TWO

GOD, SHE HATED dingy bars. Outside this one had looked like an escape from her anger and despair, but inside it was dark and noisy and there were far too many leering men who looked way too old to be hanging out in a place where the average age of women was probably somewhere around nineteen. Tora upped the demographic just by being there, she figured, not to mention lowered the average heel height by a matter of inches, but it didn't stop the old guys leering at her just the same.

But the bar was only a few steps from her cousin's office and after an hour remonstrating fruitlessly with him, an hour where nothing—neither her arguments nor her tears—had made a shred of difference, she'd needed to go somewhere where she could drink something strong and fume a while.

One of the old guys across the bar winked at her. Ugh!

She crossed her legs and pulled her skirt down as she ordered another cocktail.

God, she hated bars.

But right now she hated her financial adviser cousin more.

Financial adviser cheating scumbag of a cousin, she revised as she waited for her drink, wondering how long it would be before the damned alcohol was going to kick in so she might stop feeling so angry.

She really needed to forget about the curl of her cousin's

lips when she'd refused to be put off any longer with his excuses and insisted he tell her when she'd be able to access the money she'd been due from her parents' estate.

She needed to forget the pitying look in his cold eyes when he'd finally stopped beating about the bush and told her that it was gone, and that the release she'd signed thinking it was the last formality before receiving a pay-out had actually been a release signing the money over to him—only now there would be no pay-out because he'd 'invested' it all on her behalf, only the investment had turned sour and there was nothing left. Nothing at all left of the two hundred and fifty thousand dollars she'd been counting on. Nothing at all left of the money she'd promised to loan to Sally and Steve.

'You should have read the small print,' he'd said ever so smugly, and she'd never had violent tendencies before but right then she'd really fancied doing someone some serious bodily damage.

'Blood is thicker than water,' her parents had insisted, when they'd chosen their nephew Matthew over the financial planner she'd nominated, the father of a woman she'd known and trusted since primary school. And Tora had shrugged and conceded it was their choice, even if her cousin had been the kind of person who'd rubbed her up the wrong way all her life and never someone she'd choose as a friend, let alone her financial adviser.

For damned fine reason, as it had turned out.

Her cocktail arrived and her fingers curled around the stem of the glass as she studied it.

Now she had to work out a way to tell Sally she wouldn't be getting the promised funds, after assuring her—because Matt had promised—that settlement was all on track and that the funds would be coming any day. She felt ill just thinking about it. They'd been counting on her—counting on this money. She shook her head. She would have to find another way, go back to the banks and try again. *Try harder.*

She lifted the glass to her lips and it was all she could do not to swallow the drink down in a rush, wanting the buzz, hoping for the oblivion it promised.

'Hi there, sweet lips. You look like you needed that. Fancy another?'

She blinked against a sudden flash of strobe and opened her eyes to see one of the leery old guys shouldering his way alongside her at the bar, this one with a decent paunch and a skinny ponytail and with a possessive arm curling its way around the back of her seat. Across the bar his friends were watching and grinning as if this was some kind of spectator sport, and their ponytailed friend might have been right about her needing another drink but not if it meant waking up next to this guy. Suddenly getting a taxi home where there was a half-empty bottle of Riesling in the fridge seemed a far better option than staying here and seeking oblivion amongst this lot. She reached for her bag.

The bar was too noisy. Too dark.

Almost immediately Rashid regretted the impulse that had seen him climb down the stairs to the noisy bar in the basement of the building alongside his hotel.

Because the questions in his mind were still buzzing, and as his eyes skated over a dance floor filled with young women wearing more make-up than clothes he wasn't convinced he was going to find the relief he needed here.

He ground his teeth together, the fingers that had been bound so tightly today already aching to curl once more into fists.

He was wasting his time here. He turned to leave, and that was when he saw the woman sitting by herself at the bar. His eyes narrowed. She was attractive, he guessed, under that bookish exterior, and she sure looked out of place here, standing out in her short-sleeved shirt in a sea of otherwise bare flesh. Too buttoned up with her brown hair pulled back into a tight bun. A glass of milk in a wine bar wouldn't have looked more out of place.

But at least she looked as if she was past puberty. At least she looked like a woman.

He watched her down half her cocktail and scowl into the glass, but not as if she was morose, more as if she was angry. So she was as unimpressed with the world as he was? Perfect. The last thing he needed was someone with stars in their eyes. Maybe they could be angry at the world together.

He was already edging his way through the crowd when a man sidled up to her and slipped his arm around her back.

Rashid suppressed a growl and turned away. He might be angry, but he wasn't about to fight over a woman.

'I'm not actually looking for company,' Tora said to her persistent would-be friend. Sure, someone sympathetic to get the whole sorry cheating-cousin saga off her chest might be therapeutic. Someone to lend her a shoulder and rub her back and say it would all be okay might be nice, but she hadn't come here looking for that and she wasn't about to consider any offers, not if the sympathetic shoulder came packaged like this one.

'Just when we were getting on so well, too,' he said, moving his bulk sideways when he saw her picking up her clutch to block her from getting up from her stool.

'I hadn't noticed,' she said, mentally adding another hate to her growing list—leery men in bars who imagined they were God's gift to women, although, to be honest, that one had always been right up there with seedy bars. 'And now if you wouldn't mind getting out of my way?'

'Come on,' he said, curling his arm closer around her back, and breathing beer fumes all over her. 'What's your rush?'

It was when she turned her head to escape the fumes that she saw him. He moved like a shadow in the dark basement, only the burst of coloured lights betraying his movements in the glint of blue-black hair and the whites of his eyes under the lights. He was tall and looked as if he was searching for someone or something, his eyes scanning the room, and, while heads turned in his wake, so far nobody seemed to be laying claim to him.

Surprising, given the way he couldn't help but be noticed if someone was waiting for him.

Not to mention convenient.

'How's about I get you another drink?' the man offered, slurring his words. 'I'm real friendly.'

Yeah, she thought, if only he were sober and could speak clearly and looked a little more like the man who'd just walked in, she might even be interested.

'I'm meeting someone,' she lied, pushing off her stool but making sure it was her shoulder that brushed past his stomach and not her breasts. Her feet hit the ground and even on her sensible heels, she wobbled. Whoa! Maybe those cocktails weren't such a total loss after all.

'He stood you up, eh?' said the man, still refusing to give up on his quarry. Still refusing to believe her. 'Lucky I'm here to rescue you from sitting on the shelf all night.'

'No,' she said, in case Mr Beer Breath decided to argue the point, 'he just walked in,' and she squeezed her way past him determined to prove it.

Half-heartedly Rashid scanned the room one last time, already knowing that he was wasting his time in this place. He turned to leave—he would find no oblivion here— when someone grabbed his arm.

'At last,' he heard a woman say above the music. 'You're late.'

He was about to say she was mistaken and shrug her off, when her other arm encircled his neck and she drew herself closer. 'Work with me on this,' she said as she pulled his head down to hers.

It was the woman at the bar—that was his first surprise—and the only thing that prevented him from pushing her away. The fact Ms Bookish had turned into Ms Bold and Brazen was the second. But she'd saved the best for last, because her kiss was the biggest and the best surprise of all. She tried to get away after a moment but her lips were soft, her breath was warm, and she tasted of fruit and alcohol, summer and citrus, all over warm, lush woman, and she wasn't going anywhere just yet. He ran his arm down her back, from her shoulder to the sweet curve of her behind, his fingers curling as they squeezed, and she arched into him as she gasped in his mouth.

Yes. This was what he needed.

This was what he'd come looking for.

Maybe coming here tonight hadn't been such a bad idea after all.

'Let's go,' she said, purposefully, if a little shakily, as she pulled away, her eyes shot with surprise as she looked from him over her shoulder to where she'd been sitting. He followed her gaze and saw the men lined up at the bar watching her, saw the slap to the back in consolation to the man who'd been talking to her, and he half wondered what the man had said to her that she seemed so shaken now. Not that Rashid really cared, as he wrapped an arm around her shoulders and cut through the crowd heading for the stairs and the exit, given he'd ended up exactly where he'd wanted.

Tora's heart was thumping so loud, she was sure it was only the thump-thump of the music in the bar that was drowning it out. She must be more affected by the alcohol than she'd realised.

Why else would she have walked up to a complete stranger and kissed him?

Though it wasn't just the alcohol fuelling her bravado, she knew. It was the anger, first for her cheating cousin, secondly for that meat market of a nightclub and a creep of a man who imagined there was any way in the world she'd want to spend even a moment with his beery self. And it hadn't been enough simply to walk away—she'd been wanting to show him she wasn't some sad lonely woman who'd be flattered to have his attention. Well, she'd sure shown him well and good.

But a peck on the lips in greeting was all she'd intended. A signal to the men watching that she wasn't alone. She hadn't expected that man to be so willing to join in her game. Nor had she expected to be sideswiped by a stranger's taste and touch in the process, leaving her dazed and confused. And the way her skin tingled and sparked when their bodies brushed as they walked side by side—well, that was interesting, too.

She willed the itching fingers on the hand she'd wrapped around his waist to be still, but, God, it wasn't easy, not when he felt so hard, so lean. Oh, wow... She needed to get outside and let the night air cool her heated skin. She needed the oxygen so she could think straight. She needed to say thank you to this stranger and get herself a taxi and go home, before she did anything else crazy tonight.

Because tonight was shaping up to be all kinds of crazy and the way this man felt, she wasn't sure she could trust herself.

And then they were out on the street and the nightclub door closed behind them and she never got a chance to say thank you because he was pulling her into the shadows of a nearby doorway and kissing her all over again and she was letting him and suddenly it wasn't the alcohol or her anger that was affecting her—it was one hundred per cent him.

Madness, she thought as his masterful lips coaxed open hers. She should put a stop to this, she thought as his tongue danced with hers. She didn't do things like this. They might be in the shadows but they were on a public street after all. What if Matt saw her on his way home?

And then her anger kicked in and she thought, damn Matt, why would she care what he thought? Let him see. And she pressed herself closer.

A moment later she stopped caring about anything but for the hot mouth trailing kisses up her throat to her mouth, his hands holding her tight to him so they were joined from their knees to their lips and every place in between felt like an erogenous zone.

'Spend the night with me,' he whispered, drawing back to whisper against her ear, his breath fanning her hair, fanning the growing flames inside her in the process, and she almost found herself wishing he'd said nothing but carted her off to his cave so she didn't have to think about being responsible. Crazy. She didn't meet strangers in bars and spend the night with them.

'I don't even know your name.' Her words were breathless, but it was the best she could manage when her mind was shell-shocked and every other part of her body was busy screaming *yes*.

'Does it matter?'

Right now? God, he had a point. He could tell her his name was Jack the Ripper and she'd have trouble caring. But still…

'I should go home,' she managed to say, trying to remember the good girl she always figured she was and the plan she'd had—something about a taxi and a bottle of

Riesling in the fridge and a cheating cousin she wanted to forget about—but she was having trouble remembering the details and wasn't that a revelation?

Wasn't that what tonight was supposed to be all about—forgetting?

He pulled away, letting her go even though the distance between them was scant inches. Even now her body swayed into the vacuum where his had so recently been. 'Is that what you want? To go home?'

She saw the tightness in his shadowed features as if it was physically hurting him to hold himself back, she felt the heat rising from his strong body and she knew what it must be costing him to leave her to decide when the power in his strong limbs told her that he was powerful enough to take whatever he wanted. The concept was strangely thrilling. The perfect stranger. Powerful, potentially dangerous, but giving her the choice.

A choice never so starkly laid out in her mind.

A choice between being responsible and playing it safe and going home and sitting stewing about what she'd missed, or being reckless for once in her life and taking what was on offer—one night with a man whose touch promised to make her forget all the things she'd wanted to forget. One night with a stranger. Her cousin would be horrified, and right now wasn't that good enough reason in itself?

Besides, all her life she'd played it safe, and where had that got her? Nowhere. She'd done nothing wrong and yet she'd lost more today than she'd ever thought possible.

Tonight was no night to play it safe.

'No,' she said, her tongue tasting an unfamiliar boldness on her lips. 'I want to spend the night with you.'

'One night,' he said, and she recognised it as a warning. 'That's all I can offer you.'

'Perfect,' she said with a smile because that was all

she wanted. 'One night is all I want.' Tomorrow she could pick up the shattered pieces of her promises and work out where she went from there.

His eyes glinted in the street lighting, a flash of victory that came with a spark of heat, and he reached out his fingers to push a wayward tendril of her hair behind her ear, making her skin tingle. 'My name is Rashid.'

'Tora,' she said, even as she trembled under his touch.

He took her hand and brought it to his mouth, pressing it to his lips. 'Come, Tora,' he said.

CHAPTER THREE

NICE, SHE REGISTERED vaguely as he swept her through the marble-floored lobby of one of the oldest and classiest hotels in Sydney. Very nice. People dreamed of spending a night at The Velatte—ordinary people, that was. Clearly the man at her side was no ordinary person. But then, she already knew that. No ordinary person had ever set her pulse racing just by his presence. No average garden-variety man had ever set fires under her skin merely with his touch.

And now it was anticipation of a night with this far from ordinary man making the blood spin around her veins and her knees feel weak.

The lift whisked them to a high floor, his arm wound tightly around her, another couple in the lift the only thing that kept him from pulling her into his kiss, if the heated look in his dark eyes she caught in their reflection in the mirrored lift walls was any indication—mirrored panels that also gave her the chance to steal a closer look at the man she'd agreed to spend the night with. The flash of strobe in the darkened bar had shown her a face of all straight lines and planes—the dark slash of brows, the sharp blade of his nose, the angles of his jaw—but now she could see the softer lines of his mouth and the fullness of his bottom lip and the curve of flesh over high cheekbones. The combination worked.

It was then she realised that his eyes weren't black but

the deepest, deepest blue, like the surface of the bottom-less ocean on a perfectly calm day.

He was beautiful, way too beautiful to be by himself, and the good girl in her wondered why he was, while the bad girl in her—the newly found bad girl who drank cock-tails in basement bars and threw herself at random men on a whim—rejoiced. Because right now she was the one here in this lift with him.

He opened the door to his room that turned out to be a suite because it was a sitting room they entered, decorated in modern classics in grey and cream and illuminated with standing lamps, lending the room a subtle golden glow. Oh, no, this man was definitely not ordinary. He was ei-ther loaded, or his employer's accountant was going to have a heart attack when the expense-account bill came in.

'It's huge,' she said, overwhelmed, wondering just who this man she'd met in a nightclub and with whom she'd agreed to a night with actually was.

'I got an upgrade,' he said dismissively, as if that ex-plained a suite fit for a king, as he headed towards a phone. 'Something to drink?'

Her mouth was dry but only because every drop of moisture in her body had been busy heading south ever since he'd asked her to spend the night. 'Anything,' she said, and he ordered champagne for two and put the re-ceiver down, the fingers of one hand already unbutton-ing his shirt.

'The bedroom's through here,' he said as he led the way into a room with furniture in both gloss white and dark timber, with white louvre glass doors opening onto a terrace beyond. A super-king-sized bed with a plump quilted headrest and snowy white bed linen held pride of place against the opposite wall.

'So,' he said as he reefed off his shirt and tossed it onto a chair in the corner, exposing a chest that wouldn't have

looked out of place on her annual firefighters' fundrais-
ing calendar. 'Shower first?'

She stood transfixed, drinking in his masculine perfection, the sheer poetry of tightly packed muscle under
skin, until his hands moved to his belt, and with a jolt she
realised she should be doing something, too, not standing
around ogling him and waiting to be seduced.

This wasn't a seduction after all. Clearly he'd done his
seducing in getting her here. This was more like getting
down to business.

'Oh, right,' she said, her tummy a mass of flutters, the
bad girl inside her overruled by the good girl who was
suddenly aware of how far out of her league she was,
and not just because this man came with serious money.
Here he was, shedding clothes and shoes in a lighted
room more easily than an autumn tree shed its leaves in
the wind and no doubt expecting her to do likewise. She
slid off her shoes, her fingers playing at her buttons as
she remembered what she'd put on this morning, wishing she'd worn something a bit more exciting under her
boring black skirt and shirt than her even more boring
underwear. Not that she had a seduction collection, exactly, but she might have managed to wear something that
at least smacked of lace.

She swallowed as she pulled the shirt free from the
waistband of her skirt and eased it over her shoulders,
feeling more self-conscious by the second as she stood
there in her department-store skirt and regulation bra. 'I
didn't dress for...'

He looked at her, a frown tugging at his brows, as he
shrugged off his trousers, revealing denim-coloured elastic
fitted boxers that fitted his hard-packed body so well, there
were no bulges anywhere—except where there should be.

Oh, my...she thought, her stomach flipping over, her
mouth Sahara dry, and she wondered how long the cham-

pagne would take to arrive. She didn't need the alcohol particularly, but her mouth sure could do with the lubrication.

'I'm not interested in your underwear,' he said as he padded on bare feet towards her, his steps purposeful rather than rushed. He lifted her chin with the tips of his fingers and pressed his lips lightly to hers while his other hand eased the tie from her hair, making her scalp tingle, pulling it free so that her hair tumbled heavily over her shoulders. His fingers skimmed down her throat and to her shoulder, found the strap of her bra and curled a fingertip beneath, before slipping it away down her arm. He pushed the hair back and dipped his head and pressed his lips to her bare shoulder and breath hissed through her teeth. 'I'm interested in what lies beneath.'

She shuddered on a sigh, her breasts achingly tight, as she felt his clever fingers at her back as he slid her bra away. And then her skirt was riding low and lower over her thighs before she realised he'd even unzipped it. 'Very interested,' he said, standing back to take her in, dark storm clouds scudding over the deep ocean blue of his eyes. He touched the pads of his thumbs to her bolt-like nipples and twin spears of sensation shot down deep into her belly, triggering an aching pulse between her thighs. Her groan of need was out before she could haul it back, but he didn't seem to mind as he sucked her into a deep kiss that amplified the sensations.

'What happened to the brazen woman who accosted me in a bar?'

She was a fraud. Tora swallowed. 'She was angry. She was proving a point.'

'Is she still angry?'

'Yes, but now she just wants to forget why.'

'Oh,' he said, his eyes gleaming as he swung her into his arms and headed for the shower. 'I can make you forget.'

* * *

Her stranger was true to his words. Granted, he had steam, a rainforest shower head and slippery gel on his side, but his clever hands and mouth had a way of making her forget everything besides being naked with a man she wanted to bed her with a compulsion and an urgency she'd never felt before—an urgency he didn't seem to mirror.

When he'd turned on the taps and shucked off his underwear, she'd gasped at his size, not with fear, but with anticipation. She wasn't a virgin. She knew how things worked and what generally happened and, if she was totally honest, she'd always wondered what it would be like to make love with a man so well equipped. But then he'd hooked his fingers into the sides of her underwear and pushed them down and she'd imagined that a minute or two of foreplay in the form of soaping each other's skin, and they'd be making love right here in the shower.

Apparently he wasn't in such a rush.

He kissed her again, long and deep, as she clung to his shoulders, while the torrent rained down upon them, his slippery hands in her wet hair, down her throat to cup her breasts before sliding down her sides, the touch of his long fingers relaying the dip of her waist in a way she'd never felt or seen so clearly in her mind's eye before. Every curve his fingers seemed to find, every jut of bone explored on their seemingly leisurely but purposeful way south. It almost felt as if his fingers were mapping her terrain.

She gasped again, into his seeking mouth this time, when one hand cupped her mound. She felt his lips smile around hers before his mouth dipped to her throat, to kiss her shoulder and then worship her breasts on his way down to kneeling before her, his lips traversing her belly, his fingers deep between her thighs and the pulsing flesh that lay within.

Oh, God. She shuddered as he parted her legs, turning her face up into the spray as his fingers opened her to him. Exposed her to him. She thought she knew about sex. She'd thought this would be over in a minute. But she might just as well have known nothing. She felt like a virgin all over again.

She knew nothing at all, but…

Pleasure.

It came upon her in waves as his tongue lapped at her very core, teasing her beyond existence, beyond reason, as all she knew was sensation.

His tongue. The steam. The water cascading over her and his fingers teasing, circling her aching centre.

Right now there was nothing but sensation, and the inexorable build to a place a man had never taken her. A place she'd never believed it possible for a man to take her unassisted. This man was taking her all the way.

She felt his fingers stray closer until they edged inside her. She felt the tug of his mouth on her screaming nub of nerve endings and she felt the surge coming. She bit her lip to stop from crying out but there was no stopping the wave that washed over her and the cry that came all the same as her body broke around him.

He supported her before her knees could give way and she fell, and she felt him there, at her core.

Yes, she thought, because even on her way down from the highs he'd taken her to she still wanted this—wanted him deep inside her—more than anything.

But then, just as she thought she had him, just as her muscles worked to urge him in, he pulled away on a curse and slammed open the shower door.

She blinked as he pulled a towel from a rack and wrapped it around her, swinging her into his arms.

'What's wrong?' she said, still trembling after her high

and back to the virgin she wasn't, fearful she'd done something wrong.

'Nothing,' he said as he deposited her in the centre of the big wide bed before pulling out a drawer, 'that this won't fix.'

He tore the top from the foil packet and rolled the condom down on him and suddenly it made sense and she was glad one of them was still thinking.

'Now,' he said, his face grim as he positioned himself between her legs, 'where were we?'

And the virgin inside her turned wanton as she wrapped her hand around his bucking length and felt his power and his need within her fingers, and placed him at her core. 'Right here.'

His eyes flared with heat as he growled with approval, and her heart skipped a beat as he took her hands and pinned them each side of her head, their fingers intertwined, and then with one long thrust he was inside her and sparks went off behind her eyes.

It was sex, she had to remind herself, just sex, because in that moment it had seemed that the world as she knew it revolved around that moment and that moment only.

He leaned down and kissed her then, so sweetly and reverently that she wondered if he'd felt it, too, this tiny spark of connection that went beyond physical, before he let go her hands and raised himself higher and slowly withdrew. She almost whimpered at the loss, wanting to hold him inside and keep him there, but then he was back, lunging deeper if that were possible, the slide and slap of flesh against flesh bringing with it that tidal flow of sensation, in and out and building each time until their bodies were slick with sweat. There was nowhere left to go, nowhere left to hide, and the next wave surge crashed over her and washed her away.

She clung to him as he went with her, tossed helplessly in the foaming surf of her undoing, gasping for air, not knowing which way was up.

He pressed his lips to her forehead before he slumped beside her. 'Thank you,' she heard him say between his ragged breaths, and she wondered if he could read her mind, for they were the exact same words she wanted to tell him.

He watched her sleep in the yellow-grey light, watched the slow rise of her chest and listened to the soft sigh as she exhaled, all the time wondering at a woman who had turned up exactly when he'd needed her. A woman who had made him forget the shocks of today so well that he'd almost forgotten to use protection.

When had that ever happened before?

Never, that was when.

He shook his head. He was more affected by today's revelations than he'd realised if he could forget something so absolutely fundamental. There could be no other reason for it. Other than the way she'd come apart so furiously that he hadn't wanted to wait, he'd wanted to follow her right then and there.

Propped up on his elbow, he lay alongside her, watching her eyelids flutter from time to time. Her hair splayed wild around her head and against the pillow. Tangled. Elemental. He touched a finger to one of the coils, felt the silk and steel within the shafts of hair and congratulated himself for walking down the stairs into that basement bar.

One night with a stranger had never been so desperately needed and so satisfying.

Almost.

He leaned over, pressed his lips to hers. Her eyelids fluttered open and momentary surprise gave way to a tentative smile. 'Oh, hi,' she said as her smile turned wary. 'Is it time for me to go?'

'No way,' he said as he pulled her into his arms. 'You're not going anywhere just yet.'

CHAPTER FOUR

It was still dark when her phone buzzed, only dull yellow street light filtering up from the street far below sneaking between the gaps in the curtains. Disoriented and aching in unfamiliar places, Tora took a while to work out where she was let alone manage to stumble from the bed and find where she'd left her bag. Groggily she snatched up her mobile and stole a glance over her shoulder. Behind her Rashid lay sprawled on his front, legs and arms askew as he slept. He looked magnificent, like a slumbering god, somehow even managing to make a super-king-sized bed look small.

'Yes,' she whispered, and listened while Sally apologised for calling her on her day off, but it was an emergency and could she come in?

She closed her weary eyes and put a hand to her head, pushing back her hair. How much sleep had she had? Not a lot. Not a good way to go to work, especially not when she had news to tell her friend—bad news—and she'd really wanted more time before breaking it. 'Are you sure there's nobody else?'

But she already knew the answer to that or Sally wouldn't have been calling on the first day off she'd had for two weeks. 'One more thing,' Sally said, once she'd told her she'd be there in an hour. 'Pack a bag and bring your passport. Looks like you might need them.'

'Where am I going?'

'I'm not sure exactly. I'll fill you in on what I do know when you get here.'

Tora slipped her phone away and glanced once more at the man she'd left sleeping on the bed, the man who'd blown her world apart and put it back together again more times than she would have believed possible in just one night. She shouldn't be sorry there wouldn't be one more time, she really shouldn't. No, no regrets. It was a one-night deal and now that night was over. She gathered up her discarded shirt and skirt and abandoned underwear and dressed silently in the bathroom.

Leaving this way was better for both of them. At least this way there was no chance of an awkward goodbye scene. No chance of anyone expecting too much or appearing hopeful or needy.

He seemed like the kind of man who'd be relieved she wasn't going to hang around and argue the point.

She picked up her shoes and spared one last glance towards the bed.

One night with a stranger.

But what a night.

He'd done what he'd promised to do. He'd blotted out the pain and the anger of her cousin's betrayal. He'd taken her from feeling shell-shocked and numb with grief and for a few magical hours he'd transported her away from her hurt and despair to a world filled with unimaginable pleasure.

He'd made her forget.

She let the door snick behind her.

It was going to be a hell of a lot harder to forget him.

He woke with a heavy head from too little sleep and with a dark mood brewing yet still he reached for her. There were things he had to do today, facts he had to face from which there was no escaping—headaches, each and every one of them—but the lawyer and the vizier and the head-aches could wait. There was something he wanted more right now in this drowsy waking time before he had to let the cold, hard light of day hit him, as he knew it soon would. Someone he wanted more.

His searching hand met empty sheets. He rolled over, reaching further, finding nothing but an empty bed and cold sheets and not the warm woman he was looking for. He cracked open an eyelid and found no one.

Now he was wide awake. 'Tora?' he called. But there was no answer, nothing but the soft hum of the air con-ditioner kicking in as the temperature rose with the sun outside.

'Tora,' he repeated, louder this time, on his feet now as he checked the bathroom and the living room. He pulled back the curtains in case she'd decided to take coffee out there so as not to waken him. Morning light poured into the room, and he squinted against the rising sun, but the terrace, like every other part of the suite, was empty.

She was gone, without so much as a word.

She was gone, before he was ready.

Before he was done with her.

He growled, a vein in his temple throbbing while his dark mood grew blacker by the minute.

Until he remembered with a jolt the revelations of yes-terday and his black mood changed direction. He glanced at the clock. He had a meeting to get to.

He'd been angry when the lawyer had told him that he'd arranged it—too blindsided by the lawyer's revelations to think straight, too incensed that someone other than him-self was suddenly pulling the strings of his life—but now he welcomed this meeting with this so-called vizier of Qa-jaran. Maybe he would have the answers to his questions.

Only then, when he was convinced, would he agree to take on this baby sister—no, half-sister—the product of a father who'd abandoned Rashid as a toddler, and a woman he'd taken as his lover.

Only then would he agree to take on guardianship of her, to take responsibility for her now that both her parents were dead, and to fill the void in her life, and wasn't that the richest thing of all?

Because how the hell was he supposed to fill a void in anyone's life when there'd been nobody to fill the void in his?

Thanks for that.

He cast one last glance back towards the rumpled bed as he headed to the shower, the bed that bore the tangled evidence of their lovemaking. How many times they'd come together in the dark night, he couldn't remember, only that every time he'd turned to her she'd been there, seemingly insatiable and growing bolder each time.

No wonder he'd been angry when he'd found her gone.

No wonder he'd felt short-changed.

But one night was what he'd wanted and it was better this way. She'd more than served her purpose. He'd lost himself in her and she'd blotted out the shock and pain for a while, but now he needed a clear head and no distractions. He thought back to the night that was. She'd been one hell of a distraction and he would have been hard pressed to send her on her way. It was better that she'd saved him the effort.

Kareem was not as Rashid had envisaged. He'd imagined someone called a vizier to be a small man, wiry and astute. But the man the lawyer introduced him to in his dark-timbered library was a tall, gentle-looking giant of indeterminate age who could have been anywhere from fifty to eighty. He looked the part of a wise man, perfectly at ease in his sandals and robes amongst a city full of men wearing suits and ties.

Kareem bowed when he was introduced to Rashid, his eyes wide. 'You are indeed your father's son.'

A tremor went down Rashid's spine. 'You knew my father?'

The older man nodded. 'I did, although our dealings have been few and far between of late. I knew you, too, as an infant. It is good to meet you again after all these years.'

The lawyer excused himself then, leaving the two men to talk privately.

'Why have you come?' Rashid asked, taking no time to get to the point. 'Why did you ask for this meeting?'

'Your father's death raises issues of which you should be aware, even if I fear you may find them unpalatable.'

Rashid sighed. He was sick of all the riddles, but he was no closer today to believing that this man they were talking about actually was his father than when the lawyer had dropped that particular bombshell yesterday. 'You're going to have to try harder than that if you want to convince me. My father died when I was just a child.'

'That is what your father wanted you to believe,' the older man said.

'*Wanted* me to believe?'

'I take your point,' the vizier conceded, his big hands raised in surrender. 'It would be more correct to say that he wanted the entire world to believe he was dead. I did not mean to give the impression that he was singling you out.'

Rashid snorted. And that was supposed to be some kind of compensation?

'And my mother?' he snapped before the other man could continue. 'What of her? Is she similarly living out a life of gay abandon somewhere else in the world, having tossed her maternal responsibilities to the winds?'

The vizier shook his head. 'I almost wish I could tell you she was, but sadly no, your mother died while you were in infancy, as you are no doubt aware. I am sorry,' he said. 'I know this must be difficult for you, but there is more. Much more.'

Rashid waved the threat in those words away. 'I already know about this so-called sister, if that's what you're referring to.'

'Atiyah? Yes, she is on her way here now, I believe. But I was not referring to her.'

He frowned. 'Then what? In fact, why are you here? What do you have to do with my father's affairs anyway?'

The older man regarded him levelly, his eyes solemn. 'I know you were brought up,' he said, slowly and purposefully, as if sensing Rashid's discomfiture, 'believing your father to have been a humble tailor, killed in an industrial accident...' He paused, as if to check Rashid was still listening.

He was listening all right, although it was hard to hear with the thumping of his heart. Today he'd expected answers. Instead all he was getting was more of the madness.

'In actual case, your father was neither. Your father was a member of the Royal House of Qajar.' He paused again. 'Do you know much of Qajaran?'

Rashid closed his eyes. He knew the small desert country well enough—his work as a petroleum engineer had taken him there several times. It had a problematic economy, he was aware, like so many countries that he visited, not that he had paid this one much more attention than he paid any of them. He had learned early on in his career that it was better not to get involved in the affairs of state when one was a visiting businessman.

But for Rashid's father to have been a member of the House of Qajar—the father he'd believed to be nothing more than a tailor—then he must have been a member of the royal family...

The wheels of his mind started turning. 'So who was my father?'

'The Emir's nephew...' the vizier paused again '...and his chosen successor over his own son who he judged as being too self-centred and weak.'

His nephew? His chosen successor? 'But if what you say is true...' Rashid ground out the words, still not convinced by the story he was hearing '...why was he living here in Australia? What happened?'

The older man took a sip of his milk and returned it to its coaster, every move measured and calm and at odds with the turmoil Rashid was feeling inside.

'Your father was an accomplished polo player,' the vizier said, 'and while he was overseas competing in one of his polo competitions, the old Emir died suddenly.' He paused on a breath, the silence stretching out to breaking point. 'Some would say too suddenly, and, of course, there was some suggestion at the time that the timing was "convenient", but nothing could ever be proved. By the time your father had arrived home, the Emir's son had announced his ascension to the throne and moved the palace forces squarely behind himself. Your father knew nothing of this and was placed under house arrest the moment he returned to the palace. But your father was popular with the people and questions were inevitably asked about his disappearance—uncomfortable questions when all of Qajaran knew he was the favoured choice for Emir—and so Malik announced he was to be appointed special adviser to the Emir while deciding privately that it would be better to have him out of the way completely.'

'So they exiled him?'

'No. Malik was nowhere near that merciful. The plan was to kill him but make it look like an accident. A helicopter accident en route from the mountain palace to where the ceremony would take place.'

Air hissed through Rashid's teeth.

'Fortunately your father had a supporter in the palace.

My predecessor could not stand back and let such a crime happen. They secreted bodies from the hospital morgue and when the time came, they parachuted to safety and the helicopter duly crashed, its cargo of dead burned beyond recognition, assumed to be the pilot and the true heir to the throne. Clothing from a small child was found in the wreckage, jackals assumed to have made off with the remains.'

Rashid felt chills down his spine. 'A small child,' he repeated. *'Me.'*

The vizier nodded. 'You. The new Emir was leaving nothing to chance. But your father's life came at a cost. To protect the lives of those who had saved him and his son, he had to swear he would never return to Qajaran, and he would live his life as an exile with a false identity. Your names were both changed, your histories altered, but, even so, as a father and son you would have been too recognisable together, and so, in order to keep you safe, he had to cut you free.'

Rashid's hands curled into fists. 'I grew up alone. I grew up thinking my father was dead.''

The vizier was unapologetic. 'You grew up in safety. Had Malik suspected even one hint of your existence, he would have sent out his dogs and had you hunted down.'

Rashid battled to make sense of it all. 'But Malik died, what? Surely it's a year ago by now. Why did my father keep silent then? Why did he not move to claim the throne then if he was still alive?'

The older man shrugged and turned the palms of his hands up to the ceiling. 'Because he had made a solemn promise never to return and he was a man of honour, a man of his word.'

'No, that doesn't cut it. He still could have told *me*! He could have sought me out. Why should I have been denied knowing my father was alive because of a promise he'd made to somebody else years ago?'

'I know.' The vizier exhaled on a sigh. 'Rashid, I am sorry to be the one to tell you this, but your father decided it was better that you never knew of your heritage. I sought him out after Malik died. I begged him to reach out to you—I begged him to let me reach out to you—but he refused. He said it was better that way, that you never knew the truth, that it couldn't hurt you any more than it already had. He made me promise not to contact you while he lived.'

Rashid shook his head, his jaw so tightly set he had to fight to squeeze the words out. 'So he decided to keep me in the dark—about everything. Even the fact my own father was still alive.'

'Don't you think it cost your father—to be cursed with only seeing his son from afar and searching the papers for any hint of where you were and what you were doing? But he was proud of you and all that you achieved.'

'He had a funny way of showing it.'

'He saw all that you achieved by yourself and, wrongly or rightly, he chose to let you remain on that path, unfettered by the responsibility he knew would come if you knew the truth.'

The sensation of scuttling insects started at the base of his neck and worked its way down his spine. He peered at the vizier through suspicious eyes and asked the questions he feared he already knew the answers to. 'What do you mean? What responsibility?'

'Don't you see? You are Qajaran's true and rightful ruler, Rashid. I am asking you to come back to Qajaran with me and claim the throne.'

CHAPTER FIVE

RASHID LAUGHED. He couldn't help but laugh, even though he'd half suspected something similar, but the old man was so fervent and the idea so preposterous. 'You can't be serious!'

'Please forgive me, but I am not in the habit of joking about such matters.'

Rashid got the impression the man was not in the habit of making jokes at all, the complete lack of humour in the vizier's response stopping Rashid's mirth dead. 'But I haven't lived in Qajaran since I was a boy, if what you say is true, because I certainly can't even remember a time when I did. I have visited it briefly two or three times since at the most. There must be someone better, someone more qualified?'

'There has been a power vacuum since Malik's death. A Council of Elders has taken over the basics of governing, but there is no clear direction and no one person to take responsibility. Qajaran needs a strong leader, and there can be no one more fitting than the son of the true successor. In the beginning, I know it is what your father wanted for you, to reclaim your birthright, even though with time he changed his mind and wished for you the freedom that he had found. He had made a life here, after all, and I think the longer he was away from Qajaran, the less connection he felt and the less your father felt he owed his homeland.'

'The father I never knew,' he said, not even trying to prevent the bitterness infusing his voice. 'If indeed he was my father. Why should I take your word that he was?'

The old man nodded. 'I would be concerned if you accepted too quickly the challenge that lies before you. I would think you are attracted to the concept of power, other than the benefit of our peoples.' He slipped a hand into the folds of his robes and pulled something from a pocket. 'Malik sought to destroy all likenesses of your father. This one survived.' He handed it to Rashid.

It was one of those old photo folders that opened like a card, the cardboard crinkled and dog-eared around the border but the picture inside still preserved. A photo of a man dressed dashingly in the Qajarese colours of orange, white and red, sitting proudly astride an Arab polo pony, a mallet casually slung over his shoulder as he posed for the camera.

'My God,' Rashid said, for he recognised his own features in the photograph—his own high cheekbones and forehead and the set of his jaw. The eyes the same dark blue. It could have been him sitting on that horse.

'You see it,' Kareem said. 'There is no denying it.' The old man leaned forward. 'Your country needs you, Rashid. Qajaran is at a crossroads. Thirty years of a ruler who wasted every opportunity unless it benefited him directly, thirty years of frittering the revenues that came from its industries and rich resources on follies and peccadilloes. It is more by good luck than good management that the economy of Qajaran has not been completely ruined. But now it is time to start building. There is a desperate need for strong leadership, education and reform.'

Rashid shook his head. 'Why would the people accept me as leader, when I am supposed to have died in a helicopter crash three decades ago? Why would they believe it is even me?'

'The people have long memories. Malik may have tried to wipe your father from the collective memory of the Qajarese people, but never could he wipe the love of him from their hearts. Truly, you would be welcomed back.'

'When I am supposed to be dead? How does that work?'

'Your body was never found, assumed to be taken by the desert beasts, which means there is doubt. The people of Qajaran are in desperate need of a miracle. The return of you to Qajaran would be that miracle.'

Rashid shook his head. 'This is madness. I am a petroleum engineer. That is my job—that is what I do.'

'But you were born Qajarese. You were born to rule. That is in your blood.'

Rashid stood, his legs too itchy to remain seated any longer, and crossed to a window, watching the traffic and the pedestrians rushing by in the street below. They all had somewhere to go, somewhere to be. Nobody was stopping them and telling them that their lives up till now had been founded on a lie, and that they must become someone they had never in their wildest nightmares thought they would be. Nobody was telling them they had a tiny sister they were now responsible for—let alone a nation full of people for whom they were now responsible.

He shook his head. He didn't do family. The closest he had ever come to having family was his three friends, his desert brothers, Zoltan, Bahir and Kadar, their friendship forged at university in the crucible of shared proximity and initial animosity, all of them outcasts, all of them thrust together as a kind of sick joke—the four had hated each other on sight—only for the joke to backfire when the four became friends and the 'Sheikhs' Caïque', as their rowing four was nicknamed, won every race they ran.

And even though his three desert brothers had found matches and were starting their own broods of children, it didn't mean he had to follow suit.

He had no desire for family. Even less now given he'd learned his father had lived all those years and hadn't bothered to let him know—his own son!

And what was a nation but the worst kind of family, large, potentially unruly and dependent.

He turned suddenly. Faced the man who had brought him this horror. 'Why should I do this? Why should I take this on?'

Kareem nodded. 'I have read widely of you and seen your long list of achievements and your powers of negotiation when dealing with disparate parties. You would come eminently qualified to the task of Emir.'

Rashid shook his head, and the older man held up one broad hand. 'But yes, this is no job application. This goes beyond mere qualifications. Your father was the chosen Emir before circumstances forced him into exile. You are his heir. It is therefore your duty.'

Rashid's blood ran cold. 'My duty? I thought you said I had a choice.'

And Kareem looked hard into his eyes. 'The choice is not mine to give. I am saying you have this duty. Your choice is whether you accept it.'

Duty.

He was not unfamiliar with the concept. His best friends were no strangers to duty. He had seen Zoltan take on the quest for the throne of Al-Jirad. Rashid had done his brotherly duty and had ridden together with him and Bahir and Kadar across the desert to rescue Princess Aisha, and later to snatch her sister, Princess Marina, from the clutches of Mustafa. He had always done his duty.

But never had he imagined that duty would be so life-changing—so unpalatable—for himself. Because if he did this thing, his life would undergo a seismic shift. He would never be truly free again. And if he didn't, he would be failing in his duty.

Duty. Right now the most cursed of four-letter words.

'What I tell you is not easy for a man to absorb or accept,' Kareem said. 'I can only ask that you will come and see the country for yourself. Bring Atiyah, for it is her heritage and birthright too.'

'You want me to willingly turn up on the doorstep of a place that was so happy to see my father and me dead? You expect me to take an infant into that environment?'

'Malik is gone. You have nothing to fear from him or his supporters now. Please, you must come, Rashid. Come and feel the ancient sand of our country between your toes and let it run through your fingers. See the sunrise and sunset over the desert and maybe then you will feel the heart of Qajaran beating in your soul.'

'I'll come,' Rashid said, his head knowing what he had to do, his gut twisting tighter than steel cable in spite of it. 'For now that is all I am promising.'

The vizier nodded. 'For now, it is enough. Let me call the lawyer back in and we will make the arrangements.'

'What can they be doing in there?' Tora said as she gave up pacing the lawyer's waiting room and sat down in the chair alongside her boss. She had to pace because every now and then her lack of sleep would catch up with her and she'd find herself yawning. 'Whatever can be taking so long?' she said, trying not to sound too irate so that she didn't disturb the infant in the capsule alongside. She'd had barely enough time to get home to shower and change and pack her things, before she'd met Sally at Flight Nanny's office and they'd headed off together to pick up the baby from the foster home where she'd been looked after for the last few days, only for them to have been kept sitting and waiting so long that the baby would soon need another feed.

Her boss twisted her watch around her wrist. 'I don't know, but I can't stay much longer. I've got a meeting with Steve's doctors in less than an hour.'

'I'm sure it won't be too long now,' the middle-aged receptionist assured them when Sally asked how long it would be, before disappearing to fetch refreshments.

The baby started fussing then and Tora reached down to soothe her. She was a cherub. With black curls and dark eyes with long sooty lashes and a tiny Cupid's-bow mouth, it was obvious that she'd grow up to be a beauty. But right now she was a tiny vulnerable infant without a mother or a father—or anyone who seemed to care what happened to her.

The baby wasn't about to be placated and became more restless, her little fisted hands protesting, and Tora plucked her out of the capsule to prop against her shoulder so she could rub her back, swaying from side to side in her seat as she did so.

She smiled as she cuddled the infant close, enjoying the near new baby smell. It was unusual to have such a young infant to take care of. Most of Flight Nanny's charges were small children who needed to be ferried interstate or overseas between divorced parents who were either too busy with their careers to travel with their children, or who simply preferred to avoid any contact with the other party, even if only to hand the children over. Those cases could be sad enough.

But an infant who'd been left orphaned, that was beyond tragic. That was cruel.

'You poor sweetheart,' she said as she rocked the tiny bundle in her arms, her heart breaking a little at the injustice of it all.

Sally shifted in her seat and Tora could feel the tension emanating from her friend and colleague. Something was seriously wrong. 'How is Steve?' she ventured, once the baby had settled a little, scared to ask, even more scared for the answer.

Her boss grimaced and it occurred to Tora that Sally had aged ten years in the last couple of weeks. 'He's struggling. There's a chance they won't be able get his condition stabilised enough for the flight to Germany.' She looked up then and Tora saw the desperation in her eyes, desperation laced with a flash of hope. 'Look, Tora, I didn't want to ask—I really wanted to wait for you to say something— but how did you get on with your cousin last night? Did he give you any idea when the estate might be finalised and that settlement might come through?'

And Tora's heart plunged to the floor. There was damned good reason she hadn't wanted to come to work today and it wasn't just that she'd hardly had any sleep. Without the funds from her parents' estate, she'd have nothing to lend to Sally and Steve, funds they'd been counting on to pay for his medical transport and his treatment overseas. And she'd really wanted some time to explore any other ways of raising the money before she had to come clean on the fact that the promised funds were never going to materialise—not from that particular source. 'Ah,' she said with false brightness, as if she'd only just remembered, 'I wanted to talk to you about that.'

Sally crossed her arms and Tora could see her fingernails clawing into her arms. 'Damn. I knew I shouldn't have asked you that. I don't think I could bear to hear bad news today.'

'Oh, no,' Tora lied, doing her utmost to smile. 'Nothing like that. Just paperwork and more paperwork.' She shrugged. 'You know how it goes with these things. I'm really hoping it gets resolved soon.'

Sally glanced at her watch. 'Well, sorry, but I'm going to have to leave you with some more paperwork if I'm going to make this appointment.' She reached into her satchel and pulled out a folder that she left on the seat behind her as she rose. 'I'm really sorry to leave you like this when we still don't know all the details. Will you be okay to handle everything yourself?'

'Hey, I'll be fine. If you're going to be disappearing offshore soon,' she said, trying to stay positive and not wanting to dwell on how big that 'if' was right now if she couldn't secure the funds to make it happen, 'we're all going to have to get used to doing more paperwork here at home. Don't worry, I'll email you when I know where this baby is going and scan all the documentation for you before we go anywhere. You just worry about you and Steve right now.'

Sally smiled, giving Tora a kiss on the cheek as she bent down to pick up her bag. 'Thanks.' She curled a fingertip under the baby's tiny hand. 'Look after this little poppet, okay?'

'You bet. Now get going. And give my love to Steve.'

Sally was gone by the time the receptionist returned with her iced tea, and Tora's was half drunk when the door to the office opened then, and an older gent with bushy eyebrows and a shock of white hair peeked out. 'Ah, Joan,' he said. 'We're ready for our guests now.' He looked at Tora and the bundle perched over her shoulder.

'I'm sorry,' she said, 'but Sally Barnes couldn't stay.'

'I quite understand,' he said kindly. 'This has all taken rather longer than we expected. Thank you for being so patient, Ms Burgess. Do come in. It's time for the little one to meet her guardian.'

She stood up with the baby in her arms, and the lawyer surprised her by shoving the folder Sally had left under his arm, before picking up both the baby capsule and baby bag.

'Gentlemen,' he said as he shouldered open the door and ushered her into the room, 'here is Atiyah at last, along

with Ms Victoria Burgess, who comes to us highly qualified from Flight Nanny, the number one Australian business that transports unaccompanied children all around
the world. Victoria will be caring for Atiyah and accompanying you both to Qajaran.'

Tora raised her eyebrows as she digested the news. So
that was where she was headed? That would be a first.
She'd been to many ports in Europe and Asia but so far
she'd never had an assignment that took her to the smaller
Middle East states. A tall, gentle-looking man wearing Arabic robes came towards her, a warm smile on his creased
face as he looked benevolently down upon the child in her
arms. He reached a finger to her downy cheek and uttered
something in Arabic that sounded very much like a blessing to Tora. If this man was the tiny Atiyah's guardian,
she was sure she would be in good hands.

'Excuse me,' he said with a bow. 'I will inform the pilot
we will be on standby.' And with a swish of his robes, he
left the room.

'Victoria,' someone else said from a chair in the corner of the room behind her, in a voice as dry and flat as
a desert in summer—a voice she recognised as one that
had vibrated its way into her bones last night with desire but that now set off electric shocks up and down her
spine with fear. 'Most people would shorten that to *Tori*,
wouldn't they?'

Please, God, no, she prayed, but when she looked
around, it was him all right. He rose from his chair then,
the man she'd spent the many dark hours of last night with
naked, the man now looking at her with storm-swept eyes.
Her heart lurched and she clutched the baby in her arms
tighter, just to be sure she didn't drop her.

'I don't know,' she said, trying and not sure she was
succeeding in keeping the tremor from her voice. 'Is it
relevant?'

The lawyer looked strangely at Rashid, questions clear in his eyes. 'Yes,' he said, 'what does it matter? Come, Rashid, and see your sister and your new charge.'

His sister? Surely that didn't mean what she thought it meant? And Tora felt the cold tea in her stomach turn to sludge.

He hadn't been in a rush to get up—he might have agreed to go to Qajaran and take the child with him, but he was in no desperate hurry to meet her. He was glad he'd hung back in his chair now, glad of the time to let incredulity settle into cold, indisputable truth.

Because it was her.

The woman who'd stolen away from his bed like a thief in the night.

The woman he'd never expected to see again.

She looked almost the same as she had last night in the bar, in a beige short-sleeved shirt and hair that he now knew fell heavy like a curtain of silk when pulled out of that damned abomination of a bun, but with black trousers this time, covering legs he could still feel knotted around his back as he drove into her.

She looked almost the same in that bland mouse-like uniform she wore that he knew hid a firebrand underneath.

And it seemed that twenty-four hours of being blind-sided didn't show any signs of letting up yet.

'Rashid?' the lawyer prompted. 'Don't you want to meet your sister?'

Not particularly, he thought, and least of all now when she was being cradled in the arms of a woman he hadn't begun to forget, though he supposed he should look interested enough to take a look.

He rose to his feet. Was it his imagination or did the woman appear to shift backwards? No, he realised, it wasn't his imagination. There was fear in her eyes even though the angle of her chin remained defiant. She was scared of him and trying not to show it. Scared because he knew what the nanny got up to in the night time.

She should be worried.

In spite of himself, he got closer. Close enough that the scent of the woman he'd spent the last night with curled into his senses, threatening to undo the control he was so desperately trying to hang onto. Didn't he have enough to contend with right now—a father who'd removed himself from Rashid's life, only to leave him this tiny legacy, a country that was floundering where he was expected to take up the reins—without a woman who had the power to short his senses and make him forget? He needed his wits about him now, more than ever, not this siren whose body even now seemed to call to him.

He shifted his head back out of range, and concentrated instead on the squirming bundle in her arms. Black hair and chubby arms and a screwed-up face. Definitely a baby. He didn't know a lot about babies, but then he'd never expected to need to.

'Would you like to hold her?' the woman he knew as Tora ventured, her voice tight, as if she was having trouble getting the words out.

It was his turn to take a step back. 'No.'

'She won't break.'

'I said no.' And neither, when he thought about it, did he want this woman holding her, let alone accompanying them to Qajaran. Not that he was about to take the child himself. He turned to the lawyer. 'Is there no one else you could have found for this role?'

The woman blinked up at him, her brown eyes as cold as marble. Too bad. Did she expect him to greet her like a long-lost friend? Not likely.

'Excuse me?' the lawyer asked.

'Someone more suitable to take care of Atiyah. Couldn't you find someone better to take care of my sister?'

'Ms Burgess comes to us highly qualified. She has an exemplary record with Flight Nanny. Would you like to see her credentials?'

'That's not necessary.' He'd already seen her credentials, in glorious satin-skinned detail, and they qualified her for a different type of position entirely from the one she was required for now.

'If you have some kind of problem—' she started.

'Yes, I have "some kind of problem", Ms Burgess. Perhaps we should discuss this in private and I'll spell it out for you?'

The lawyer looked at them nervously. 'If you excuse me, a moment, I'll see how Kareem is going,' and he too was gone.

Rashid took a deep breath as he strode back towards the wall of windows.

'What are you doing here? How did you find me?'

'What? I didn't find you. I was asked by my boss to take this job on. I didn't know you had anything to do with Atiyah.'

'You expect me to believe it's some kind of coincidence?'

'You can believe what you like. I was retained to care for Atiyah on her journey to wherever it is that she is going. Frankly, I'd forgotten all about you already.'

His teeth ground together. Forgotten about him already? In his world, women had always been temporary, but he'd been the one to decide when he'd had enough. He'd been the one to forget, and it grated...

'So you're a qualified child-care worker?'

'That's my primary qualification, yes, though I have diplomas in school-aged education and childhood health care along with some language skills as well.'

'You are forgetting about your *other* skills,' he growled, his lip curling as he looked out of the window, still resentful at a world going on about its business while his life didn't resemble a train that had merely changed direction, his life was on a train that had jumped tracks, and he wasn't sure he liked where it was headed.

'They're hardly relevant,' she said behind him, and around and between her words he could hear the sounds of the baby, staccato bursts of cackles and cries, and then a zipper being undone.

He spun around, angry that she seemed oblivious to the impossibility of the situation, to see her sitting down, the baby in her lap as she dripped milk from a small bottle onto her upturned wrist before putting the bottle to the baby's mouth, looking every part the quintessential mother with child.

That was a laugh. She was no Madonna. It didn't matter what she was wearing or what she was doing, he could still see her naked. He could still remember the way she'd bucked beneath him as she'd come apart in his arms.

'Impossible!' he said, and even the baby was startled, her big eyes open wide, her little hands jerking upwards, fingers splayed. 'This cannot work.'

'Hold it down,' she said, rocking the child in her arms. 'Do you think I like the situation any more than you do?'

'I want another carer.'

'Why?'

Because I don't trust myself with you. 'Because a woman like you is not fit to look after an innocent child.'

She laughed. 'A woman like me? What kind of woman is that, exactly?'

'A woman who goes whoring in the night—picking up men in bars and sleeping with them.'

She smiled up at him and he felt his ire rise. 'But a *man* who goes whoring in the night—picking up women and inviting them back to his hotel room—he is perfectly qualified to be that child's guardian. Is that what you are saying?'

'This is not about me.'

'Clearly not, or there might be a double standard at work, don't you think?'

Frustration tangled in his gut. He hated that she had seen through his arguments but he could hardly tell her the real reason—that he needed more than ever right now to be able to think clearly, without his brain being distracted with replays of last night every time he looked at her. Why couldn't she see that he didn't want her—that this would not work? 'I want somebody else to care for Atiyah!'

'There is nobody else. All Flight Nanny's employees are busy on other assignments.'

'I don't want you coming with us.'

'Do you think for a moment that I want to come? As soon as I realised it was you, I wanted to sink through a hole in the floor. So don't worry, I'm not looking for a re-peat of last night's little adventure. I'm not here because of you. I'm here to take care of the baby, nothing more.'

A brief knock on the door interrupted his words, and Kareem entered with a bow, and there was no way their visitor couldn't have heard her words or misinterpreted the tone in which they were delivered. 'A thousand par-dons for the interruption, but the plane will be ready to leave in two hours.'

And Tora looked up at Rashid. 'So, do you want to tell everyone why you'd prefer to find another carer, or shall I?'

Kareem looked to him expectantly, his placid features betraying only the barest hint of surprise, and Rashid cursed the woman under his breath. But he was out of time and out of options, and, besides, what was the worst that could happen? She'd accompany them to Qajaran and then her role would be complete and she would be on the next flight home and he would be rid of the constant reminders of their night of passion together, rid of the distraction of a woman who had turned an already upside-down world spinning through another three hundred and sixty degrees in the course of one night. He could hardly wait. 'I expected someone older,' he muttered, 'but I suppose this one will just have to do.'

CHAPTER SIX

BLUFF WAS A beautiful thing, when it came off.

Tora got the baby capsule secured and sank into the buttery leather of the limousine and took a deep, calming breath. Because she'd done it, she'd saved the assignment. Sally would have been devastated if she'd lost this contract—and Tora would have found it next to impossible to explain how she'd let it happen. How did one go about explaining that you'd inadvertently slept with the client after meeting them in a bar the night before your assignment? It didn't bear thinking about.

But Rashid had given himself away when he'd asked to speak to her in private. Clearly he wasn't too keen on sharing the details of exactly why he deemed her unsuitable to care for his sister. So sure, she wasn't about to go advertising the way she'd behaved last night, but it seemed she wasn't the only one with a secret to keep.

Was he married? Was that his problem? She hadn't thought to ask last night. One night he'd offered and she'd taken it, no questions asked. And maybe it didn't reflect well on her, but last night had been just about perfect as far as she was concerned, at least until she'd entered that lawyer's office today and found him lying in wait and in judgement.

He'd been a different man last night. Bold. Decisive. He'd been angry, as she had been—and she'd felt it with his every move, his every thrust. Whereas today he seemed to be on the defensive.

What was that about?

Kareem climbed into the front seat beside the driver and turned to her. 'Do you have everything you need, Ms Burgess?'

She nodded. 'Thank you,' she said as she checked the sleeping infant, a tiny milky bubble swirling in the corner of her mouth. 'We're both very comfortable.'

Kareem nodded. 'Then we shall go.'

Tora looked around. 'Where is Rashi—? Where is Ati-yah's guardian?'

'His Excellency is travelling separately. He will meet us at the airport.'

She nodded dumbly and settled back into her seat as the car cruised away. *His Excellency?*

Exactly who had she spent last night with?

He was stuck with her now. At least for the next however many hours it took to fly to Qajaran.

Only a few hours, Rashid reasoned as the driver made his way towards the coast, and then she would be on her way home again. It should be easy, given he'd only known her a few hours, but the way they'd spent them, and the way she'd left so abruptly, was it any wonder that he was still aching for more?

But he didn't want more, he told himself. He didn't need the distraction. He didn't need to be reminded of his want-ing her every time he saw her. He didn't need to know she was close enough to take.

A few hours? God, already they felt too long.

Rashid had the driver stop just before the road turned to the right along the cliff face, and climbed out into the full force of the wind blowing off the Pacific Ocean. In front of them the ocean waves pounded against the rocky cliffs, sending the boiling spray high into the air, while to the left sprawled a cemetery as big as several city blocks, the marble headstones and funerary ornaments marching up the hillside to the silent blare of the angels' trumpets.

It was a wild place, elemental, the blue-skied summer day's temperature turned on its head as the tiny sparkling droplets of sea water drifted down and conspired with the wind to suck your body heat away. He welcomed it as he turned up the collar of his linen jacket.

It was the perfect place to forget about her.

He started walking, gravel crunching underfoot, towards the place the lawyer had marked for him on a map. He didn't need to look at the map again, the paths were wide and the way clear, and before long he could make out the fresh mound of earth that marked the grave where his father and his lover had been laid to rest.

He stood there, at the foot of the grave with its two white markers, feeling hollow inside. He had no flowers. He wasn't here to shed tears. He wasn't even sure why he'd come, only that he'd been compelled to visit, just once before he left this country.

Wasn't sure if he'd come to pay his respects to a father who'd cast him adrift when he was but a child, or to rail against him and demand to know why he'd abandoned him. Sure, he'd heard the lawyer's version of events, and he'd heard Kareem's, but surely he'd had a right to hear it for himself?

Surely he'd had a right to ask whether his father had ever thought of him on his birthday or whether he'd ever felt a hole in his heart where his son should have been?

He stood there, battered by the breeze caused by sea slamming into rock, until in the end Rashid knew there were no answers for him here.

Yet still he stayed a while, a silent sentinel, while the wild wind tugged at his jacket and hair and the spray from the crashing waves on the cliffs behind rained like mist over him, until finally he said in a gravelly voice to a father he couldn't remember, 'I will never understand why you did what you did. And I will never forgive you.'

And then he turned and walked away.

The jet was whisper quiet, piercing the air with the maximum of speed and the minimum of fuss or inconvenience to its passengers. Tora sat wrapped in one of the enormous leather seats, still shell-shocked. She'd travelled business class with a rock star's child once, and that had seemed luxurious after usually being consigned to economy with the children, but this was more than luxurious, this was sumptuous.

Timber-panelled walls with gold trim, plum-coloured leather seats that reclined and spun and laid flat and looked more suited to a lounge room than a plane, and opulent carpets in vermilion on gold on the floor, with enough space in between the seats to swing an entire herd of cats, while fresh frangipani placed discreetly in tiny vials around the cabin walls perfumed the air.

But then, this wasn't business class and it wasn't the only reason for her shell shock. This was the royal jet of Qajaran, and her tiny charge was some kind of princess.

What did that make Rashid?

He sat across the aisle in the row ahead, deep in conversation with Kareem. She could hear their voices every now and then, Kareem's measured and calm tones, interspersed with Rashid's arguments, though she couldn't make out what they were discussing but could see that whatever they were talking about was raising temperatures—Rashid's at least. She could make out his profile—strong lines even down to the lips on a mouth that was now snapping out words. Lips that she knew could give an inordinate amount of pleasure. She squirmed a little in her seat as she watched him, remembering, tingling in places that shouldn't be tingling right now.

God, she was kidding herself if she could forget, but it would be better for everyone if she could put those particular memories aside for however long this assignment took.

And then he turned, and caught her watching him, and she held her breath as a tremor zigzagged down her spine, unable to tear her eyes away as his dark eyes gleamed and pinned her to her seat. Then he said something short to the man beside her before turning away and severing the bonds between them.

Breath whooshed out of her in a rush as she felt his hold on her release. She took a couple of restorative breaths. What was that about?

Why had he looked at her that way, not with anger or resentment exactly, but with eyes that were so cold, hard and calculated?

Beside her, Atiyah gurgled happily in the bassinet strapped to the seat, and she blinked, focusing on what was important here. Not Rashid and his clear preference that she'd disappeared into the past and stayed there when she left his bed this morning, but this tiny baby.

Tora smiled as she leaned over the bassinet. She couldn't help but smile when she looked at Atiyah's face with her big dark eyes and tiny button nose and the pink lips busy making shapes and testing sounds. Likewise, she couldn't help but feel the tug on her heartstrings when she thought about how she'd grow up never knowing her mother or father. It was so unfair. It was wrong.

She should be smiling at two months. She probably would, if she saw her mother's face. For now, she looked up with those big eyes at Tora as if everything was new again, as it must seem to her.

It was so unfair to lose her parents just when the world

was coming into focus and making sense. She needed stability now, and people to love her. Hopefully, once she was in Qajaran with a regular carer, she would remember how to smile.

Maybe Rashid might even take an interest in her by then. He'd shown precious little interest to date, treating her more as a parcel he had to convey rather than as his tiny sister. He just didn't seem interested.

What was with that?

But then, he didn't look like a man who smiled much. He seemed angry about everything.

The baby cooed and closed her eyes and took a deep breath, settling back for another brief nap. Tora reclined her chair a little and sat sideways, almost envying Atiyah's ability to turn off the outside world. She watched her sleep, the low drone of the plane's engines like white noise, and the wide chair so comfortable, and yawned, feeling her own eyelids grow heavier.

'There is just one more issue that is of concern,' Kareem said, after a welcome pause that Rashid had taken to meaning their business was over, 'that must be discussed.'

'Why, when I still haven't agreed to take on the throne?' Kareem had gone through page after page of notes to explain the path to the throne and the coronation that must take place if he did agree, while going on to outline not only the history of the tiny but resource-rich state but the current challenges, both internal and external, that it faced, and right now Rashid's head felt as if it were about to explode.

Surely there couldn't be anything else?

'I am sorry, Excellency, but, now that we are on our way home, there is a question over Atiyah, and her place in the royal family.'

Rashid shook his head. This one at least was a no-brainer. 'She is my father's daughter. She is my sister. What possible question could there be?'

The vizier nodded. 'Both true. However, the fact remains that thirty years ago your father was supposed to have been killed in a helicopter crash. A body was recovered and accepted as his. Questions will be asked if you claim Atiyah is your father's daughter. Uncomfortable questions. The people will want to know where he has been all that time and why he abandoned them to their fate with his cousin while he was enjoying his life with a young mistress the other side of the world...'

'You said he had to promise not to return!'

'He did. But you had problems accepting that truth. Magnify that doubt by the population of Qajaran...' He paused. 'And of course, there are pockets still loyal to the memory of Malik. They will not want to believe this could be true. Is it not better to let history lie so they cannot dispute? Is it not better to let the population continue to believe your father died in that helicopter crash? Your coming home will still be the miracle they need—the child who miraculously survived and was spirited away to safety.'

Rashid's head was pounding. His life was getting more complicated by the minute. 'What does it even matter?' he growled. 'I'm Atiyah's legal guardian, aren't I?'

'Technically, yes.'

'Only "technically"?'

'Guardianship of infants and minors by unmarried men is not recognised under Qajarese law.'

'So? I don't even know if I'm going to be staying all that long.'

'It is an inconvenience, I know, but Atiyah will not be able to share your palace quarters if she is not officially acknowledged as part of your family.'

He sighed, pressing his head back deep into his head

rest. He hadn't asked to be this child's guardian but it was pretty clear that he could not let her be whisked away to God knew where to be looked after for however long this thing took. 'Then what can be done?'

'There is a way.'

'Which is?'

'Adopt Atiyah. Claim her as your own, if only in public.'

Rashid sat back in his seat, his mind reeling. What was happening to him that this proposal sounded half reasonable? Minute by minute he could feel the weight of the responsibility of a tiny desert kingdom pressing down on his shoulders, and he wondered, when it all came down to it, how much choice he really had.

'All right,' he said at last. 'What needs to be done?'

'Oh, it is but a stroke of the pen. I can handle it if you so desire.'

'Fine. Do it, then.'

If he thought that was an end to the matter and he could finally close his eyes and relax, he was sadly mistaken. Kareem was still there, watching him. 'What?' he snapped.

'There is but one *tiny* formality.'

There would be. Rashid rubbed a hand over his jaw. 'And that is?'

'To adopt in Qajaran, one must be married.'

'What? Why the hell didn't you say that before? It's pointless, then.'

'There is no one you have in mind to take for your wife?'

'No! Surely there is another way?'

'There is no other way.'

'Great. And you've only just discovered this now, when we're already on our way to Qajaran?'

Kareem bowed. 'My apologies, Excellency, this is a situation without precedent—I was hoping there would be something in the texts that might provide some comfort on this issue, but no. The texts are clear—only married couples can adopt. Perhaps, if there is no one you can suggest, I might be able to procure a suitable candidate on arrival in Qajaran City?'

'You? Find me a wife?'

'If only as a temporary measure, if it pleases you.' He raised one pen-laden hand as if he were being perfectly reasonable and Rashid only had to see it. 'It would simply be a matter of convenience.'

'And then?'

'And then you can divorce the woman and she can go her own way and you would retain custody of Atiyah. Please be assured when I say that both marriage and divorce in Qajaran are arrangements that require not much more than the stroke of a pen.'

'You said the same about adoption,' Rashid growled, 'and yet it seems needlessly complicated.'

The older man had the grace to smile ruefully as he held up his hands. 'Some strokes of the pen are more straightforward than others, but if you want to protect Atiyah, this is the only way.'

Rashid found it hard to argue the point, put like that, but he had his doubts about Kareem choosing him a bride, for however long or short this marriage was to be. Just because he had never entertained the concept of marriage was no reason to hand over the responsibility of selecting a wife. 'This wife I need—what would she be required to do?'

'She would have to perform as your wife in the public arena. She would have to be by your side during the coronation, if you go through with it, of course. Similarly at any public appearances where a mixed audience is in attendance—'

'And night times, Kareem. What would she be expected to do then?'

And for the first time Kareem looked somewhere ap-

proaching nonplussed. 'A wife populates her husband's
bed at night. What else would you expect of her?'

'Of course,' Rashid said, frowning for added gravitas,
while absolutely determined now that Kareem would have
no part of choosing him a wife. Someone to escort him
to official functions was one thing, but someone to take
to his bed—only he decided who that would be. 'That is
how it should be.'

'So you would like me to arrange a wife?'

'No. That won't be necessary. I've got a better idea.'
One that would show a certain woman that when he said
he did not want her for his sister's carer she should pay
heed, that she was far better off agreeing with him and
vanishing from his life just as silently as she had done
from his bed this morning, or he might just think they
had unfinished business.

A temporary wife to populate his bed could be some
kind of compensation for this whole crazy scenario.

'Perhaps,' Kareem prompted, 'you would care to share
this better idea?'

Rashid suddenly swung his head around and caught
Tora watching him and he smiled.

Because although it seemed the train his life was on
hadn't just changed tracks, it had changed planets, for
the first time in a mad day he felt as if he was back in the
driver's seat.

'I'm going to marry Victoria.'

'Ms Burgess?' Kareem forgot how to be serene and
fairly spluttered. 'When you were so against her caring
for Atiyah?'

'I know,' he said, unable to explain because the reason he was against her coming was the reason that made
her most qualified to be his temporary wife. 'It's perfect.'

CHAPTER SEVEN

'TIRED, MS BURGESS?'

Tora came to with a start to see Rashid leaning down before her, as attentive and seemingly caring as any of the flight attendants as he held what looked like a pot of coffee in one hand and a cup in the other, and it wasn't the coffee she could smell. He hadn't bothered to exchange two words to her since she'd walked out of that lawyer's office in Sydney. Something was definitely up.

'I must have dozed off,' she said warily, sitting up straighter and checking her watch. No, she'd only been asleep a few minutes and one glance towards the bassinet beside her was enough to tell her that Atiyah was still sleeping, her little arms flung back either side of her head.

'Anyone would think you've been working too hard.'

Her eyes snapped back to his. There was a cunning gleam there that had her on alert. 'Anyone except you, you mean.'

'Come, come, Ms Burgess,' he said as he put the coffee down on a small table. 'I brought you coffee.'

She looked around the cabin but it was deserted, the cabin crew all discreetly tucked away wherever it was they waited between being called upon. Even Kareem had disappeared somewhere. 'Yes, I can see. What's with that? Did you sack all the flight attendants or something?'

He smiled as he swivelled the chair in front of her around and sat down, though she sensed danger in the curve of his lips. She tucked her feet under her chair. Even with the room between the seats his long legs ventured way too far into her space for her liking. 'I have something I need to discuss with you, something that might work to our mutual benefit.'

Her eyes shuttered down. Yeah, right. 'I told you I wasn't here for you. I am here for Atiyah, nothing more.'

'You have a suspicious mind.'

'You have a transparent one.'

He shook his head. 'This is not about bedding you.' He hesitated there, and she wondered what had gone unsaid. 'This concerns Atiyah.'

'How?'

He leaned forward. 'For reasons you don't need to know about, I need to adopt Atiyah.'

She looked across at him blankly. 'And how does that concern me?'

'In order to adopt, under some quaint Qajarese law, I must be married.'

She swallowed down on a lurch in her stomach because this could in no way mean what crazy idea ventured first into her mind. 'I repeat,' she said, schooling her voice to level and wishing her heart rate would also take heed, 'how does that concern me?'

'It's not for long, it's just a temporary thing. A mere formality, really, and then in a matter of months we can be divorced.'

There was that lurch again, but this time there was no misreading his words. 'We?'

'Well, you and me.'

She blinked, hoping it covered the jolt to her senses that came with his answer. 'There is no you and me.'

'There doesn't have to be, not in any real sense. All I need is a wife. Someone to play the role of Atiyah's mother temporarily. Kareem tells me the marriage must last twelve months to ensure the adoption satisfies the laws of Qajaran, but that's only if I decide to stay. Otherwise, it might be over within a week.' He smiled, as if he were asking her nothing more than the time of day. 'Like I said, it's just a formality.'

'But a year! There's a chance I have to be married to you for an entire year!'

'If it happens. But you would not need to stay in Qajaran all that time. Once the formalities were over, you could go home.'

She looked at the coffee he had poured for her. She liked coffee, but right now she felt the need for something a whole lot stronger.

She licked her lips. 'Who are you?'

'I told you. My name is Rashid.'

She shook her head. 'No. I met someone called Rashid in a hotel bar. He was just a man. An angry man wanting to let off steam the way men do. But you—' She looked around. 'You fly in a plane with a golden crown for a crest, you have staff that bow and scrape and seem to wait on your every word and call you Excellency. So, Rashid, who are you, that you think it is perfectly reasonable to ask a near stranger to marry you so you can divorce them when it suits?'

His eyes left her face, to wander a scorching trail down her body, lingering on her breasts before venturing lower. He smiled. 'Near stranger?' he questioned, his voice husky around the edges, rasping against her very soul. 'We are hardly strangers.'

She crossed her arms and legs to stop the tingling under her skin, relieved when his gaze once again found her face. 'You don't know me and I sure as hell don't know anything about you.'

'I am not asking the world, merely for a few weeks of your time and then you can go home.'

'I said I wouldn't sleep with you again and I sure as hell won't marry you.'

'Nobody said anything about sleeping with me. You served a purpose last night, but now I'm looking for something else.'

She laughed, not sure whether to be offended or not. It was so mad, she had no other option but to laugh. 'Well, as attractive as you make your proposal sound, that I pretend to be your wife, no thank you.' She glanced at the baby and assured herself she would be all right for a minute or two more, before she pushed herself up to stand. Maybe if she headed for the bathroom, it might put a stop to this ridiculous conversation. But Rashid rose too, stepping sideways and blocking her path. 'Excuse me,' she said. 'I need to use the bathroom.'

'Not yet. You haven't heard what I'm offering in return.'

'I don't need to, to say no. You made it very clear when we were in Sydney that you didn't want me to be here at all. You made it clear that you wanted nothing more to do with me and that's fine, because I don't plan on sticking around any longer than I have to in order to do this job. As soon as I hand this child over to whoever is going to be her carer in Qajaran—because I assume from your lack of interest it won't be you—I'll be heading home.'

His eyes narrowed. 'Come now, Ms Burgess, how can you say no when there is so much on offer?'

'Like what?'

'Like an all-expenses-paid holiday in Qajaran, complete with a bird's-eye view of a possible coronation and all the festivities surrounding it, along with a return flight home in the royal jet.'

A shiver ran down her spine. 'Whose coronation?'

'Mine.'

Ri—ight. So that was it. She did her best not to sway

on her feet. Did her best not to look stunned. 'So you're kind of king-in-waiting, then?'

He nodded. 'You could put it that way. Qajaran is currently without an Emir. Apparently I am next in line to the throne, if I agree to take the role on.'

A kind of king. Well, that was kind of funny when she'd thought he'd looked like a god on the bed only this morning. A demotion almost, and that thought almost brought a smile to her face when there should be none.

She shook her head. 'Sorry, not interested.'

'How much, then?'

'Excuse me?'

'How much would it take? Everyone has their price—name it.'

She shook her head. She must be dreaming. That or she'd woken up on some bizarre television game show. Any minute now and they'd be cutting to a commercial break for disposable nappies or dishwashing liquid. 'I told you, I'm not interested.'

'Name it!'

She sucked in air. She didn't want to do this. She didn't want to spend a moment longer in this man's company than she had to. The night she'd spent with him was too fresh, too raw in her mind, the passions he'd unleashed in her still making her senses hum at his proximity as if his mere presence was enough to switch them on—but then she thought about the amount her cousin had stolen from her and the money she had assured Sally she would find...

He wouldn't say yes, she told herself, there was no way he'd say yes, but if he really wanted a figure—if he really wanted to know how much it would take for her to agree to this crazy plan... 'All right, you asked—two hundred and fifty thousand dollars. That's my price.'

And his eyes might have damned her to hell and back, but he smiled—he actually smiled—and her stomach dropped to the floor like a brick even before he said his next word.

'Done.' He turned and yelled for Kareem. 'Prepare for the ceremony.'

Tora was reeling. 'But—'

'But nothing,' he said, smiling like the cat that had the cream. 'You named your price. I agreed. The deal is done.'

Kareem married them, neatly fitting the ceremony in between Tora feeding Atiyah her bottle and changing the infant's nappy, the bride's gown nothing more than black trousers and a fawn-coloured shirt with smudges of baby milk on the shoulder.

It wasn't a ceremony as such. There was nothing more to it than for the two of them to stand before Kareem in his white robes and with her hand on Rashid's, and for Kareem to utter a few words, before Rashid dropped his hand, jettisoning hers in the process, and saying, 'Right, that's that out of the way. Let's get this adoption signed off, shall we?'

Out of the way? thought Tora, feeling stunned as she returned to her seat and changed Atiyah. So that was it, then. No *You may kiss the bride.* No congratulations or champagne or even a pretence of celebration. She was married to Rashid, according to Qajarese law, and it felt—*hollow.*

Marriage wasn't supposed to feel hollow, she was sure. She'd always imagined getting married would be one of the happiest days of her life, with her father to walk her down the aisle and her mother proudly and no doubt tearfully looking on. Sure, that was before the glider accident that had killed them, but even now she would have liked to think of them somewhere up there looking down on her approvingly on her big day…

She gulped down on that bubble of disappointment before it could become something more.

This was hardly her big day though.

This was a means to an end for her, exactly as it was to him, the opportunity for her to obtain the funds she'd promised Sally, a formality in order for him to adopt Atiyah. After all, it wasn't as if she *wanted* to be married to Rashid, even if he made her feel like no more than an adjunct to the process, like a box that had been ticked or a task on a to-do list that had been crossed off.

He'd dropped her hand as if he couldn't bear to touch her. My God, what a difference, when last night he hadn't been able to stop touching her.

Then again, what had she expected? Last night might as well have been a lifetime ago. Rashid had been a different man—attentive, creative and infinitely attuned to her pleasure—and she'd been someone she didn't even recognise. Impulsive, reckless and brazen in bed. She'd behaved like a wanton.

She dragged in a breath, trying to find calm in a world that was teetering off balance. She'd shocked herself last night at just how shameless she'd been, as if the frustrations of Matt's betrayal and the despair of letting Sally and Steve down had spilled over on an effervescent tidal wave of passion that had washed away her moral values. Last night there'd been no off switch, no holding back. Talk about out of character for a girl who normally wouldn't kiss a guy until at least the second date.

Memories of that night should have been her secret thrill, something to smile privately about and wonder at her bravado and total abandonment. Not something to be constantly reminded of every minute of the day by being confronted with the star performer of her night of the pleasures of the flesh. The last thing she'd wanted was to learn that the man at the centre of her night of nights was Flight Nanny's and her very next client.

No, she wouldn't want her parents around to witness

this. One day she'd marry for real. One day she'd find a man she loved and who loved her more than anything, and they'd be married under a brilliant blue sky and her parents could look down upon her and smile.

One day.

She slipped Atiyah's legs back into her sleep suit and did up the snaps. Think of the money, she told herself. Think of Sally and Steve and the quarter of a million dollars, merely for marrying Rashid for however long it took. Even if nothing else, now she'd have the money to complete this deal, without having to beg from the banks. Now there'd be nothing stopping Sally and Steve heading for Germany and the radical new treatment that might save him. Just as soon as she managed to give Rashid the bank account details for the transfer of the promised funds.

No wonder she felt a little hollowness in her gut.

The pilot came back then, smiling as he advised them personally they would be beginning their descent soon, and to assure them all would be well.

All would be well? She held Atiyah in her arms and softly sang her a favourite nursery rhyme, wanting to cuddle the baby for as long as she could before she'd have to be strapped into her capsule on the seat for landing.

After a night with Rashid and a mad on-paper marriage, she wasn't sure things would ever be well again.

It was done.

Kareem had completed the paperwork on both the marriage and then the adoption in short order.

His faux wife was installed and Atiyah was adopted and for now he could take a deep breath. That was one crisis averted.

His friends would laugh. Rashid married, just as they had warned him. Well, he would let them laugh. It wasn't as though it was a real marriage. It wasn't as though he was in love as Bahir and Kadar had attested to be, and it wasn't that he had to marry and impregnate a wife before he could be crowned Emir, as Zoltan had been required to do by the ancient texts of Al-Jirad when he had married the Princess Aisha.

He grunted. Though if that had been a requirement, he'd already well and truly ticked that box. Memories of last night's passion rolled through him like replays of a movie, except this was a movie in which he'd had a starring role. He'd only needed to touch her hand to be reminded of the satin smoothness of her skin, and to remember the sleek feminine beauty of the curve of her hip, the dip to the gentle round of her belly and all the places above and below that his fingers, and then his lips, had traversed.

He hadn't held her hand a second longer than he'd needed to, and yet the mere touch of her had fired his memories and kindled a need that burned like coals inside him.

There was too much going on in his life without complicating it with a woman that had blown his world apart.

He looked over his shoulder, through the gap in the seats, and saw her holding the child as if she were her own, the baby all dark-eyed innocence staring up at her as she spoke words he could not make out. What was with that? Atiyah was nothing to do with her.

So why did she seem to care so much?

Atiyah was supposed to be his sister, after all, even if the sister he'd never asked for or wanted.

And the wrongness of it all got to him and something inside him snapped.

He got out of his seat, determined to tell her so, but as he drew closer he realised she wasn't talking to the child, she was singing to it, some kind of lullaby, and she was looking down at the baby so intently, she didn't hear his approach.

He didn't interrupt at first—for a moment he couldn't because he was rooted to the spot—because for some reason he recognised the music. The notes were buried, but they were there and they were true, and each note she sang was like a shovel in his gut, exposing more.

'What are you singing?' he growled, when he could wait no longer, because he had to know.

Her singing stopped, and she looked up, suspicious, her eyes wide at finding him so close. 'Just a lullaby. I think it's Persian. Why?' she said, and suspicion turned to concern as she scanned his features. 'Is something wrong?'

He didn't know. All he knew was that there was something churning in his gut that brought him out in a cold sweat and made his skin crawl. How would he know the tune to a lullaby he was sure he'd never heard before?

But the way she was looking at him, as if he were mad, or worse... He looked for something that he could talk about to cover his confusion. His eyes fell on the infant. 'How is she?' he forced out, his mind clamouring to remember why he was here. 'I thought babies were supposed to scream through flights.'

Her doubting eyes told him she knew he hadn't come back to discuss the flying habits of babies. 'She's a good baby. Have you changed your mind? Would you like to hold her a while?'

He looked away, wondering where his anger had gone. He'd been sure he was angry when he'd left his seat, but now he was wondering why.

'Only I get the impression you haven't had a lot to do with babies. Do you have no other brothers or sisters?'

'No.'

'Babies aren't hard to look after,' she said. 'They just need to know they're loved.'

Well, that was the problem right there. How was he supposed to let a child know it was loved when he wasn't entirely sure how that was supposed to work? What did he have to offer? 'Look,' he said, 'I really just came back—to make sure you were comfortable.'

Liar.

She knew it, too, and yet still she attempted a smile. A nervous smile. She snagged her bottom lip between her teeth, before saying, 'Rashid, now that you're here, can I ask you something?'

'What?'

The 'fasten seat belt' sign lit up then and she put the baby back in her capsule, fastening the clasp over her belly and checking the seat belt. When she looked back up, her teeth were scraping over her bottom lip again. 'It's just about the money. I need to have it transferred as soon as possible.'

He breathed out on a sigh as resentment seeped like black ink into his mind, banishing his confusion with something he was entirely more comfortable with. 'The money.' He nodded. Now there was something that made sense. There was something he could understand. 'We haven't been married ten minutes and you can't wait to get your hands on your precious money.'

'Excuse me? You're the one who couldn't wait to land the plane before we were married. I've upheld my end of the bargain.'

'You expect the money now?'

'Well, we're married now, aren't we? So I thought—'

'You thought?' He was happy beyond measure that she'd turned the conversation away from where he felt so challenged and vulnerable and to money, which was solid and real and which he knew. 'You thought you could suddenly start dictating the terms?' Because if she thought that, then maybe it was time to start changing them.

'You're the one who agreed to pay me if I agreed to marry you.'

'Oh, you'll get your money, Ms Burgess. But I have to say, I'm disappointed you put so low a value on your services. I would have paid a million dollars, maybe even two for the pleasure of having you in my marital bed.'

Her face flushed bright red. 'Our deal didn't include me sleeping with you. I told you that wasn't going to happen.'

He was teasing her, of course. He had no intention of touching her again; he was still raw from losing himself too much—and too deeply—but her reaction pleased him inordinately and he was enjoying it. 'But you also told me you wouldn't marry me, and look at us now, happy newly-weds.'

'You can't make me sleep with you. That's unconscionable.'

He leaned down, one hand on the back of her seat, the other toying with a tendril of hair that had come loose from her bun.

'Don't you think it's a bit late to take the moral high ground? Who was it who picked me up in a bar? And after last night I know you're no shy, retiring virgin. Far from it. Why pretend you don't want a repeat of last night as much as I do?'

She swallowed and he tracked the movement in the kick of her chin and in her throat and his fingers let go of her hair to trail a line down the same way.

'I know what you think of me—that I'm cheap and easy.'

'I think you're expensive and easy, as it happens. But I'm willing to pay the price you ask.'

'Go to hell!'

'I have no doubt that's exactly where I'll end up. But don't fret, my charming wife, your reputation—or what's left of it—is safe with me. I have no intention of a repeat of last night's performance.'

CHAPTER EIGHT

QAJARAN CITY ROSE from the golden sands of the desert as if it had sprung from it organically, the buildings fashioned from bricks made of mud, hay and the desert sand itself, so their walls sparkled in places when the light caught on the tiny crystals as they passed, but it was the people that most fascinated Tora.

From the airport the streets were lined with people waving flags and clapping their hands—happy, smiling people. A woman in colourful robes held her young child aloft to better watch them pass, a crumpled old man leaning on walking sticks had tears running down his leathery cheeks but a smile so wide it was obvious they were tears of joy. And it struck her then that this was for Rashid—the man who might soon be their Emir, ruler of Qajaran—the man who was her new husband.

The same man whom she'd spent an illicit night of sex with.

The man who had barely an hour ago assured her there would be no repeat performance.

She trembled, the muscles between her thighs clamping down on a sudden bloom of heat in spite of his assurances. It was crazy, she should be exhausted after a night of little sleep and the drag of international flight halfway around the world, even if it was in the sumptuous surroundings of a private jet, but, looking across at Rashid, never had she felt more alive, never had she felt more aware of her sexuality.

Should she believe him when he said that it wouldn't happen again? Or was it just that she didn't want to?

Oh, God, it would be so much easier if she could simply hate him. He'd railroaded her into this deal, after all. Not without her agreement, but he'd done his best to make her feel small and mercenary even with that.

But…there was still that night between them—that unimaginable night of pleasure—how could she hate a man for that? And there were those moments since then when the blustering faltered and he looked lost and lonely and so achingly sad that she wanted to reach out to him. Because who couldn't love a tiny child? What had gone wrong in his life that he felt that he couldn't?

She wished she could hate him. Then she wouldn't be drawn to him. Then she wouldn't feel this damnable pull.

He'd told her there would be no repeat performance, but, when it came down to it, if he turned to her in the night she doubted whether she'd have the strength to say no to him. When she remembered back to the night they'd spent together and the masterful man he was then and all the ways he had pleasured her, it was hard to imagine why she'd even want to.

She looked out of the window at the people lining the street, all so keen for a glimpse of this man who might rule them, feeling shallow and superficial and hating herself right now. There was history being made here today and, even in her unsubstantial way, she was part of it, yet all she could think about was sex.

Well, that was Rashid's fault, too. That night they'd spent in each other's arms had a lot to answer for.

'Did you arrange this welcome committee?' she heard Rashid ask Kareem, and Tora looked at him, because his voice sounded as tight as his jaw looked, and as uncomfortable as it must feel. And for the first time, she saw Rashid looking like a man who was uncertain with his place in the world, and she was intrigued. He didn't seem like a man who would doubt himself.

'Good news has a way of getting out,' Kareem answered, with a shrug of his white-robed shoulders. 'Even in Qajaran, where the Internet is not as readily accessible as it is in the west. The people have waited a long time to see the Qajarese flag flying on a royal limousine. Your return is welcome.'

'If I am to do this,' Rashid said, 'I am going to need help,' and if Tora wasn't mistaken there was a sheen of sweat on his forehead in this very much air-conditioned car.

Kareem smiled even as he bowed his head, as if Rashid had said exactly what he'd wanted him to. 'I am at your disposal, of course.'

'Thank you,' Rashid acknowledged. 'And I have a friend who had to lead his country unexpectedly. I would like to seek his advice.'

'You refer to Sheikh Zoltan, the King of Al-Jirad.'

'Yes. You know him?'

'But of course. Al-Jirad and Qajaran have been friends since ancient times. He would be most welcome here. It would further cement the bonds between our two countries.'

Rashid seemed to relax then, taking a deep breath and lifting his hand in acknowledgment as they passed the cheering onlookers. He looked the other way and caught Tora watching him as his gaze drifted past hers. His eyes immediately snapped back. 'What?'

'Nothing,' she said, shaking her head, for the first time feeling a little sorry for this man, who appeared to have been thrust into a world not of his making. Nothing she could tell him or that he would want to hear at any rate.

* * *

The limousine slowed as it waited for a set of high metal gates, sculpted to look like twin peacocks, to be opened. 'I have taken the liberty of installing you in the Old Palace,' Kareem said as they started along a long palm-lined driveway. 'Emir Malik built six new palaces during his reign, all of which are more modern, and you are more than welcome to make one of the others your base, but, for your comfort and the sake of tradition, I feel the Old Palace will be more suitable.'

Tora swallowed as she caught glimpses of a building out of her window through the garden of palms and greenery, the curve of a domed roof here, a peep of a decorative window arch there, snippets that held the promise of fantasy.

But of course, they would be heading for a palace. Where else would an Emir live?

And then the palms parted and the car rolled slowly past a fountain that was the size of a small lake, featuring stallions made of gleaming marble and standing tall on their hind legs, their manes alive to an unfelt breeze as they pranced in the tumbling water that sparkled like jewels in the sun.

But while the fountain was spectacular, it was a mere accessory to the palace. Tora took one look and knew she'd left her old world behind and stepped into the pages of a fairy tale. Surely it was the most beautiful building she'd ever seen, with decorative arches and rows of columns and a golden dome adorning the roof, and the whole effect was as romantic as it was impressive.

The limousine rolled to a stop under a colonnaded entrance shaded from the weather and before a flight of stairs where a dozen uniformed men, wearing the colours of the flags she'd seen waved in the streets, stood waiting.

'Welcome home, Excellency, Sheikha,' Kareem said

with a nod as one of the guards stepped forward to open the door.

Sheikha? Tora swallowed as she unfastened Atiyah's capsule and prepared to enter this strange new world. But of course, she supposed, she must be a sheikha if she was married to a sheikh.

And then she caught a glance of Rashid's grimly set jaw. She was married to this man. As good as shackled to the sheikh. *A fairy tale?* And suddenly Tora wasn't so sure.

'If you please, Sheikha Victoria,' Kareem said with a bow as he gestured her to enter, 'this is your suite.'

Tora was reeling. She'd thought the outside of the palace was breathtaking, but then she'd stepped inside into air scented with jasmine and musk and known she was in some kind of fantasy land. Walls were decorated in gilt and mosaic, chairs and tables inlaid with mother of pearl. It was a feast for the eyes, and everywhere she looked another work of art demanded her attention. It was all she could do not to gape.

It was all she could do not to run. Still dressed in her serviceable, travel-weary uniform while everything around her was exotic and beautiful, she had never felt more out of place.

And now Kareem was showing them a suite that would swallow up her entire house in Sydney and still leave enough room to live in, and that was without taking into account the terrace overlooking the pool and garden outside her windows where the now setting sun was bathing everything including a row of mountains far in the distance in a ruby glow. It was utterly magical, and that was only the outside.

The bedroom itself was enormous, hosting a magnificent gilt four-poster bed, and there was a room prepared for Atiyah along with another room for Yousra, a local

girl who'd been assigned to be her nursery maid, and the
main bathroom had a bath that put some of the lap pools
at home to shame.

Her suite. All hers. Which meant that Rashid would be
sleeping elsewhere, and for the first time since arriving
Tora started to relax. If she wanted to avoid Rashid, she
need never leave the safety of her room.

She eyed the four-poster bed longingly. Weary from
both the travel and the emotional roller coaster of the last
however many hours since she'd walked into her cousin's
office, already she imagined herself lost in blissful sleep
amongst the cushions and the pillows. Tomorrow would be
soon enough to chase up the funds Rashid had promised
and let Sally know they were coming. By then she might
be able to sound convincing when she told Sally that her
delay in returning home was caused by nothing more than a
simple request to stay while Atiyah settled in. Not that anyone was likely to believe her if she did tell them the truth.

But that could wait until tomorrow. Once Tora had
bathed and fed Atiyah and seen her comfortable, bed was
the first place she was headed.

'And through this door,' Kareem continued, opening a
door of exquisitely carved timber, 'is Your Excellency's
suite. The rooms are interconnecting, of course.'

'But of course,' said Rashid with a smirk in Tora's direction.

He was teasing her again, she realised. No more than
taunting her. And yet all of a sudden Tora's sprawling
apartment didn't seem anywhere near big enough.

Atiyah cried out, growing restless, and Tora saw her
chance.

'If that is all?' she asked, not interested in venturing
into Rashid's apartments. 'I will take care of Atiyah. She's
had a long day.'

'Cannot Yousra take care of the child for you?' Kareem asked. 'Would you not like to dine together with us?'

While the girl's eyes looked up at her hopefully, Rashid's dark eyes gleamed, his lips turned up in one corner. He knew she was avoiding him and right now she didn't care.

'I will welcome Yousra's assistance, of course,' Tora said, smiling at the girl so as not to offend her, but also because she really would appreciate the help, especially when sleep tugged so hard at her, 'but Atiyah has been through many changes recently, and until she's settled in I'd like to keep some routine in her life. Besides, I'm sure you and Rashid have many matters to discuss that don't require my input.'

'As you wish,' Kareem said with a bow, and Tora was surprised to see what looked like approval in his eyes. 'I will have your meal sent up.' He touched his fingers to Atiyah's brow, uttered a blessing to the child and wished Tora goodnight.

'I'll see you later,' said Rashid.

'Seven in the morning for breakfast?' Tora suggested, refusing to acknowledge the implicit threat in his words. 'That would be perfect. We have some details to discuss also. Goodnight.'

And the flash of his eyes and the flare of his nostrils told her he did not like her dictating when they would meet or being so summarily dismissed. No doubt, he didn't like being reminded about his end of the bargain either. Tough. He had promised, he could pay up. 'Come,' said Tora, turning to Yousra. 'Let's give Atiyah her bath now.'

With a swish of Kareem's robes, she heard him disappear with Rashid through the interconnecting door and Tora could breathe again.

Zoltan was coming. Rashid felt the tight bunching ache in his gut loosen a fraction, but it was fraction enough to be able to breathe more deeply than he had since arriving in Qajaran. He gazed out from his terrace over the gardens surrounding the expansive pool below. Around him the palace slept. Night had fallen fast and now the sky above was a velvet shroud of blue black.

Zoltan would arrive in three days, to be joined by Aisha and the children, and Bahir and Kadar with their own families, the day before the coronation. The last time they had been together had been in Melbourne for Kadar's wedding six months ago. It would be good for the desert brothers to be together again, although once there were just four of them, and now every time they got together there seemed to be more, wives and children swelling their numbers. He shook his head. Such an eventuality would have been unthinkable even a few years ago, one by one his brothers falling into marriage.

He alone was left. He wasn't counting his hastily con-trived marriage to Tora. It wasn't as if she were a real wife. She would be gone in a matter of weeks, even if their mar-riage needed to last a year on paper. In some ways, it was unfortunate that his desert brothers and their wives would meet her at all, for they were bound to make something of this temporary arrangement.

He heard a sound and looked sideways towards where Tora's suite of apartments lay, but the night settled into quiet again, the rustle of the palm fronds on the barely there breeze the only sound.

He sighed. Well, let his brothers make of it what they would. He had much more important things to think about now, like a country full of people who had been offered morsels through years where the Emir had grown rich on its resource revenues. Things needed to change. Less money would be lavished on palaces and fripperies. More money would go to funding schools and hospitals, especially outside the city, where needs went unseen and often ignored when they were.

His grip on the alabaster balustrade of the balcony tightened until his knuckles hurt.

It was easy to see where the inequities and injustices lay, but there was so much to address. Could he fix the problems of the past thirty years of maladministration?

Why was he even considering it?

But then somebody had to do it—share the riches and drag this country into the twenty-first century—and he was next in line to the throne.

His gut screwed tighter all over again. God, what was he even doing here? He was a petroleum engineer by day with a reputation as a playboy by night. Apart from his DNA, what qualifications did he have to equip him to run a country?

He looked around. There was that sound again. The child, he realised. But this time there was more.

She was singing that song again.

Both drawn and repelled in the same instant, he watched as Tora emerged from her suite, the baby clutched in her arms as she sang the soft, soothing words of a lullaby he never knew and yet that somehow tugged at some deep part of him. He melted into the shadows as she swayed in the night air, singing words of comfort and peace, her hair down out of that damned bun, just the way he liked it, while the blue light from the pool below turned her long white nightdress translucent so that it floated like a cloud around her slim legs and tickled the tops of her bare feet.

He swallowed back on a surge of lust as he watched, transfixed.

The breeze toyed with the hem of her nightdress, shifting shadows and whispering promises as she sang of apricots and pigeons and waterfalls, and some of her words were wrong or mispronounced, but it didn't matter because the overall effect was still beautiful.

She was beautiful.

He stood in the shadows with his heart beating too fast at a mystery he didn't understand.

He stood there utterly bewitched.

Bewitched and rock hard.

She finished the song, the last of the sweet notes trailing away on the night air, the baby in her arms asleep. She turned to go back inside the same moment as he emerged from the shadows. She gasped.

'Tora.'

And she took a deep breath and then another. 'You frightened me. What are you doing on my terrace?'

He looked back the way he had come. 'It appears we have adjoining terraces, as well as adjoining suites.'

Her eyes blinked her disappointment before shuttering down. 'Well, goodnight.'

'Tora, wait.'

'Why? Atiyah needs to go back to bed.'

He looked at the child, her face at peace in Tora's arms, oblivious to the electricity charging the air between them. 'She's asleep.'

'Which is where I want to be.'

'Tora.'

'Why are you here?'

'I couldn't sleep.'

'No,' she said, her soft voice tremulous in the velvet night, 'why are you *here*? What do you want?'

A heartbeat later he answered. 'You.' And in that moment, Tora lost all perception of time, all cognizance of space. Because Rashid was standing there in nothing more than thin white sleep pants slung low over his hips that made no secret of his arousal. And his chest was bare and in his eyes she could see torment and right now he looked as if he'd been sculpted in shadow.

And then he drew closer and she could see there was more than torment in his dark eyes—something far more carnal.

She shuddered from the top of her head all the way to the tips of toes that curled on the cool paving stone, seeking to get a grip on a world where she was a stranger.

'Rashid...' But he was already stepping closer, stepping into her space even as she drew back, her arms protecting the baby, leaving her defenceless as his fingers laced through her hair.

'Rashid...'

And then his lips brushed hers and she breathed him in and he tasted warm and musky and male and his taste and scent sent her spinning back to the place she'd been that first night. *So good.* So very good that her body hummed into life as readily as if his lips had flicked a switch.

Oh, God.

She wasn't about to turn it off.

His lips were as soft as the night sky, the sweep of his tongue like a shooting star to her senses, and there was magic in the air all around them.

Instinctively she opened to him—she knew him—and his kiss deepened. Hardened. As he angled his head and pulled her closer.

There was a squawk. A protest from between them. And Tora's attention snapped back to the child in her arms—to where it should have been before she'd been seduced by the shadows. She turned her face away, freeing a hand to push at the hard wall of his naked chest.

'Rashid, stop.'

He blinked, feeling sideswiped all over again. This woman did things to him. She made him forget himself and his determination to lock down his emotions when he was around her. She made him forget everything. He'd been so blindsided by lust that he'd forgotten completely about the child in her arms—his own tiny sister. And he'd known all along that he would be rubbish caring for an infant, and still he felt ashamed.

'Is…is she all right?'

'She's fine,' Tora said, rocking her in her arms. 'No harm done.' Although the quake in her voice told him otherwise. 'Maybe you should go back to your suite.'

He reached out for her. He didn't want to go. 'Tora—' but she spun away.

'Stop it! Don't you care about this baby at all?'

'I adopted her, didn't I?'

'Lucky Atiyah.'

'Look,' he said, shaking his head as he turned it towards the heavens, 'I didn't ask to take on the care of an infant. I don't know the first thing about babies.'

'Well, maybe you should start learning because frankly, Atiyah deserves better. You have a ten-week-old child who has lost her parents and you treat her like something you wished you could shove away in a filing cabinet somewhere and forget about.

'Don't you understand? She's not a thing, Rashid, she's a child. A baby. She needs to be nurtured, not merely tolerated. She needs love and smiles and someone who truly cares about her. Instead, she got stuck with you—sullen, resentful, miserable you—and I can't work out why you have to be that way. Have you forgotten what it's like to be a child?'

His jaw was so tightly clenched, he felt a muscle pop. 'No, as a matter of fact I haven't, but rest assured I don't plan on sending Atiyah to boarding school to be looked after by strangers the first chance I get, so I guess I do know something about bringing up children, even if it's nowhere near your high standards. But thanks anyway, for pointing out my failings so succinctly.' He turned to leave and this time it was her that stopped him.

'Rashid,' she said, concern swirling in her gentle eyes. 'Is that what happened to you? How old were you when they sent you away?'

'It doesn't matter,' he said on a sigh, raking a hand through his hair. 'Other than the fact it makes me the most useless person ever to be appointed guardian of anyone, let alone an infant like Atiyah.' He looked down at the baby, now settled again. 'She deserves better.' He turned his eyes up to Tora's. 'I'm sorry I interrupted you. Good-night,' he said, and he was gone.

Tora stepped breathlessly back into her suite, meeting a distraught-looking Yousra coming the other way. 'Is everything all right? I heard voices,' she said as she caught sight of the child in Tora's arms. 'Oh, no. I should have woken. Did she cry? I am so sorry not to let you sleep.'

'It's okay,' Tora soothed her. 'I would normally be awake at this time and I was only half asleep. You go back to bed.'

And the younger woman bowed. 'If it pleases you, Sheikha.'

'Call me Tora,' she said. 'I am much more comfortable with that.'

'But...?'

'Tora,' she insisted. 'As I call you Yousra. We are both looking after Atiyah after all. We should be friends.'

The young girl smiled uncertainly and bowed some more. 'If you are sure, Sheikha,' and Tora smiled as the young woman withdrew.

Tora settled Atiyah back into her bed and watched her for a while, marvelling at how placid she was in the wake of having had her world turned upside down, a world that at ten weeks she'd only just been getting to grips with.

Tora ran one fingertip across her downy cheek. She was a little sweetheart, no two ways about it.

A sweetheart with a tortured brother. What had happened that he felt so incapable of loving Atiyah? What kind of childhood had he had? Boarding school, and from an early age by the sounds. But why, when his father had only recently died? Why would he have done that?

She crawled back into her bed, and tucked her knees up under her crossed arms, trying not to think about how in Sydney it would be halfway through the afternoon instead halfway through the night, trying not to think about the meeting with Rashid at breakfast that she had asked for and that now seemed so close as the clock edged closer to a Qajarese morning.

Thinking instead of how she could help him overcome whatever failings he thought he had and bond with his tiny sister.

Thinking that she cared because she wanted Atiyah to be happy.

She stretched her legs out and laid her head back in her deep, welcoming pillows. It was nothing to do with the ache she could feel in Rashid's eyes. All she wanted was for Atiyah to be happy.

That was all.

CHAPTER NINE

THE SOFT SKY outside her windows was layered in pink and blue like cotton candy when Tora rose. Atiyah was gurgling and examining her hands and fingers when Tora peeked over the side of her cot.

'Good morning, beautiful,' she said, only to be rewarded by a big, gummy smile that made her heart sing. 'Oh, you sweetheart,' she said, lifting her up as Yousra appeared with a tray of coffee.

'She's awake?' asked the girl.

'Yes, and she's smiling. Look,' and Yousra came closer and tickled her tummy and the baby kicked her little legs and made a sound like a hiccup and both women laughed.

They played with her until it was almost time for Tora's meeting with Rashid. There were preparations being made outside on the terrace—she could hear someone giving instructions as staff set a table for two. Breakfast on the terrace overlooking the pool? That should be pleasant enough, if only it didn't remind her of what had happened on that terrace last night.

She closed her eyes as she twisted her hair into a bun and pinned it to her head, trying to keep her mind on how she was going to get Rashid and Atiyah together and not thinking about that kiss. She really would have to keep her distance, especially when the velvet shadows of the night stroked her soul and dimmed her logic. No more night-time wandering for her. No more assuming she was alone.

And definitely no more kissing. She touched a finger to her lips, wondering how a man who could be so hard and cold could feel so gentle and warm…

She shook her head to banish the thought. Oh, no. She wouldn't go making that mistake again. If she hadn't been holding Atiyah, she didn't know how it might have ended.

Liar. She knew exactly how.

On her back.

Or in the shower.

No! She could not afford to think of that night in Sydney. That was in the past, when they had been nothing more than strangers in the night. Things were different now. She had a job to do and she would show him that he could not just click his fingers to get his way. If she achieved nothing else before she left, she would show him that he could love Atiyah.

She gave her hair and make-up a final check before adding a slick of neutral lip gloss. There, cool and professional on the outside at least, just the way she needed to be for this meeting. She wouldn't let him rattle her today. Besides, she was too happy to be rattled. Because Atiyah had smiled.

Rashid was already seated at the table reading some papers when she approached. The sun was still low enough not to cause them any grief, but there was the promise of heat in the air. He glanced up disapprovingly. 'Haven't you got anything else to wear?'

Tora sighed as she sat down. If she'd thought that his opening up to her a little last night might have made his attitude towards her less adversarial, she was wrong. The walls between them were up again, not that she was about to let him spoil her good mood. 'Good morning to you, too. I trust you slept well.'

He grunted as a waiter appeared, laying a napkin

across her lap and fetching a dish with yoghurt and fruit before enquiring if she'd like tea or coffee. She smiled and asked for coffee, waiting for it to be poured while all the time she was aware of the man opposite simmering where he sat.

'It's a beautiful morning,' she said, when the waiter had departed.

'You can't expect to wear—' he nodded disdainfully in the direction of her clothes, ignoring what she'd said '—*that* every day.'

Tora looked down at her clothes, at her short-sleeved shirt and skirt, both fresh and, as far as she knew it, baby-spew free. 'What's wrong with what I'm wearing?'

'Nothing, if you've got a thing about those boring shirts you probably call a uniform. For the record, I don't.'

'*You're* wearing a shirt.' Although, to be fair, it was one hell of a lot sexier than hers, the white cotton so fine she could see his skin tone and the darker circles of his areolae where the fabric skimmed his chest. *Damn.* She looked away and concentrated on her coffee.

'Couldn't you find something more appropriate?'

'It's a funny thing,' she said with a smile, refusing to be pulled into Rashid's dark cloud of a mood, 'but, for some strange reason, I seem to have left all my resort wear at home. Go figure.' She shrugged. 'Besides I actually like my uniform. It's comfortable, practical and it scares men away—well, it usually scares men away... present company excepted, of course.' Her friend Sally had always joked that she'd worn her uniform as a form of self-defence against unwanted attention, and she wasn't right exactly, but it generally didn't bring Tora too much interest from the opposite sex. 'Men aren't supposed to like bookish-looking women. Come to think of it, did you miss that memo?'

He scowled. 'What's got you so cheerful?'

'You mean aside from seeing you?' she said, smirking as she sipped her coffee, savouring the heady aroma of the spiced brew, before she continued, 'Red letter day. Atiyah smiled this morning. Maybe you should try taking a leaf out of her book some time.'

'She smiled,' he said, frowning a little. 'Is that good?'

'It's better than good, it's great. It's the first smile I've seen her give. You want her to be happy, don't you?'

'Of course,' he said, with as much conviction as if the concept had never occurred to him. And then he nodded and his eyes softened. 'Of course, yes, I want her to be happy.'

'There you go,' she said, feeling that he was not the lost cause he made out and that he would overcome whatever was holding him back from embracing his new role. 'I swear, you won't be able to resist falling in love with her when she smiles at you. I wish I'd brought her now, so you could see for yourself.'

He looked at a loss for what to say next, as if once again he was in unfamiliar territory. 'Anyway,' he said, 'you're supposed to be the wife of the Emir. You can't wear that every day—you'd look ridiculous. Kareem told me last night he'd organised an entire wardrobe of clothes for you.'

'Oh.' Is that what that was about? She'd opened the door to the walk-in wardrobe last night wondering where she could stash her suitcase and found it bursting at the seams with garments. Robes of silk and the finest cottons and in all the colours of the rainbow. And she'd shut the door again because they obviously weren't hers and found another place to leave her case. She picked up her spoon to try her yoghurt.

Rashid glanced at his watch. 'What did you want to talk to me about?'

Right. She put her spoon down again. Clearly this wasn't

a breakfast meeting where one actually expected to eat breakfast. In spite of her good mood, her heart gave a little trip at having to broach the subject again. But there was no point beating about the bush. She pulled a folded paper from her pocket. 'Here are the bank details for you to transfer the funds.'

He took it, checking the details before his eyes flicked back to hers. 'Not your account?'

'It's a trust account for a firm of solicitors.' *Matt's solicitors*, she thought, biting her lip. Damn. She really wanted nothing to do with Matt or his cronies, but it would just have to do for now.

'A trust account?' His eyebrows raised, he cast his eyes over her shirt again. 'You know, you're much more interesting that that uniform lets on. But then, we already knew that.' He put the paper down on his others. 'So, was there anything else?'

'You'll do it?' she said, hardly believing it would be that simple after the grief he'd given her on the plane. 'Today?'

His eyes narrowed, as if they were trying to find a way inside her to gain the answers he wanted, but still he said, 'It will be done today. Was that all?'

'Not quite,' she said. 'There is one more thing. I'd like Internet access. I see it's password protected.'

'You wish to Tweet that you're now sheikha of Qajaran?'

She grimaced. 'Hardly. I need to contact my work and let them know there'll be a delay in me getting home so they can start reallocating assignments.' *And tell Sally the funds are on their way.* But he didn't need to know that.

'I'll have Kareem arrange it. Just be careful what you send from the palace.'

'Of course, I will.'

'Then,' he said, collecting his papers as he rose to his feet, 'if there's nothing more, I'll leave you to it. Enjoy your breakfast.'

* * *

Rashid had indigestion but it had nothing to do with what he'd eaten. He strode through the palace towards the library he'd chosen last night with Kareem for his office, his stomach complaining the entire way. Cursing Tora the entire way.

Because he still had to make the biggest decision of his life and, with her around, he couldn't think straight.

And it didn't seem to matter how much he tried to block her out and tell himself that she was irrelevant, she was there, alternately smiling, needling or offering him sympathy.

He shook his head as he walked down the long passageways. Why had he told her what he had last night? His past was his business, nobody else's. It was not the kind of thing he shared with anyone, let alone a woman he'd picked up in a bar.

But then, that was not all she was. Tora was much more than a casual pick-up.

She was his sister's carer.

And now she was his wife, even if in name only.

And he wanted her despite all his claims and words to the contrary, wanted her like there was no tomorrow. Last night was proof enough of that. He'd been blind with desire and she'd come willingly into his kiss, only stopping when Atiyah had protested.

He'd beaten himself up at the time, thinking he was the one at fault, but when he'd thought about it much later, in the long hours when sleep had eluded him, he'd realised that she'd made no effort to push him away before Atiyah had cried—she'd been as much a participant in that kiss as he had been—which proved to him that he wasn't the only one feeling this way. Feeling this need.

It wasn't just one-sided. There was still unfinished business between them.

So why was he fighting it? What point was there to erecting walls between them, when they seemed so futile and no wall had yet stopped him from wanting her?

Maybe it would be better to deal with the problem head-on, rather than pretending it didn't exist. Sleep with her. Get it out of his system so he could at least think straight.

He needed to think straight.

He paused, his hands on the door to the library.

Then again, maybe he was better off keeping his distance. She was trouble. Madonna, siren and shrew all wrapped up in one irritating package.

He snorted. Yeah, he'd tried leaving her alone and look how far that had got him. But he could hardly just tell her he'd changed his mind about his hands-off policy and expect her to go for it. She'd made it plain she wasn't about to simply fall into bed with him again at a click of his fingers. But what to do?

Fed up with torturing himself over her, he pulled open the doors.

'Excellency,' said Kareem, who was waiting for him inside, already busy at his notes and making his countless plans for Rashid while he waited. 'I trust you slept well.'

'More or less,' he said, not wanting to think about how little he'd slept or any more about the why. 'So what do we have to consider today?'

'Many things,' Kareem confirmed. 'But I know it is all very dry and Sheikh Zoltan will be here soon so I thought perhaps tomorrow we might take a tour of Malik's new palaces, to see if you would prefer to use one of them for your official residence.'

'If you think it's important. How many were there again?'

'Six.'

Good grief. Rashid suppressed a sigh, feeling already weighed down with the volume of the historical and economic texts he had been given to digest. 'Are there not more important matters to consider?'

'Certainly. But if I can use an expression you might well know, Rome wasn't built in a day. You are yet to accept this role, and anyone would be foolish to expect you to conquer it overnight. There are things to be assessed in the kingdom that do not require your poring through old documents or dusty tomes twenty-four hours a day, things that might give you a broader view of the kingdom, before your possible coronation.'

'Fine,' Rashid conceded, pinching the bridge of his nose with his fingers. 'Arrange it.'

Kareem bowed. 'It will be done.'

And suddenly Rashid had a brainwave. 'What about Tora? Could she come, too?'

'Sheikha Victoria?' The vizier shook his head while he deliberated. 'I don't see why not. She would no doubt appreciate seeing some more of our architecture.'

'So long as it won't cause any problems, if people were to see Tora with me, only for her to subsequently disappear?'

Kareem looked unabashed as he weighed the air with his big hands. 'This will not be a problem. In past years, our people are used to seeing our Emir with any one of a number of consorts, and frankly they would be more surprised to think you were unmarried.'

'Excellent,' said Rashid, rubbing his hands together as he found his first smile for the day. Maybe a day out with him would prove to her he was not the sullen, resentful and miserable monster she had painted him. Maybe if they could be friends first, they could be more… 'Now, where were we?'

Tora was enjoying a day of sheer girly fun. It started in the morning, with Yousra giving her a tour of the various gardens of the palace and around the pools and fountains where the lush foliage and flowers and sprays of water combined to turn the air deliciously cool and fragrant while tiny birds darted from bush to bush. It was exotic and different and serene. And after her tense breakfast with Rashid, Tora felt that serenity seep into her bones and she could breathe again.

Just when she thought it couldn't get any better or more beautiful, Yousra showed her to the secret garden, hidden away in a courtyard and thick with trees and palms that gave way to a lily pond where small ducklings paddled. And there tucked away in the centre like a gift-wrapped jewel stood a square pavilion with ivory-coloured columns and red balustrade with a tiled roof and white curtains for walls that billowed gently from on high.

'It's beautiful,' she said, cursing the inadequacy of the description as Yousra smiled, waiting for her reaction. It was like something from a fairy tale that became more so as two peacocks emerged from the foliage and quietly wandered away. Tora was entranced by it all. 'What is it?'

'It is called the Pavilion of Mahabbah and was built by Emir Haalim when his favourite wife died. This was her favourite courtyard, you see. And he had loved her so much he had named her after the Qajarese word for love—*mahabbah*. It is said he filled this pool with his tears. Come,' she said, leading the way. 'I have arranged us to take tea there.'

'So it is the pavilion of love,' Tora said a few minutes later as she sat on one of the low sofas, thinking how appropriate it was, how romantic and how tragic, imagining the Emir standing between the curtains, looking out over the pond and remembering his beloved wife. Beside her on the rug on the floor, Atiyah played under a baby gym, kicking her legs as she swatted at the hanging toys above her with her little hands. 'He must have really loved her.'

Yousra nodded. 'The heart of a Qajarese Emir is worth the hearts of ten men. And it is said the Emir loves ten times truer.'

Tora sipped her tea, not wanting to argue, but not entirely sure that was true for all the Emirs. Malik might have loved ten times as many as other men with his palaces full of harems, and then there was Rashid.

She wanted to believe Rashid had a heart. She hadn't seen much evidence of it so far, but she so wanted it to be there, if only so his sister might grow up surrounded by love rather than indifference. And she wondered again about a man who'd let slip that his own childhood had been lacking. Something dreadful had happened to him, that much was clear, something bound up in a tortured history that had scarred him deeply and, if she wasn't mistaken, was still hurting.

She shouldn't care, she told herself. He was nothing to her but the means to fund a promise she'd made to her best friend. Nothing more to her than that—if she discounted one heated night of the best sex she'd ever had and one stolen kiss last night that she hadn't wanted to end.

She really shouldn't care.

And yet it was hard not to.

The afternoon provided a different kind of entertainment. There were just the three of them, Tora, Yousra and Atiyah, amidst a dressing room overflowing with the most amazing clothes Tora had ever seen.

Yousra sat holding Atiyah on the sofa at the end of the four-poster bed, as Tora turned model and tried on garment after garment to much applause and encouragement in between cups of honey tea and sweets made of nuts and dried figs, apricots and dates. Yousra advised her on which were more suitable for during the day, and which she might consider for night-time events like formal dinners.

How Kareem had pulled this off, Tora wondered as she slipped into another gown, she had no idea. They'd all been on their way to Qajaran when this whole mad marriage scheme had been contrived, so he would have had to have messaged ahead from the plane with his instructions.

Clearly it was a different world when one was connected to royalty.

'That one, yes!' said Yousra, as Tora turned to the young woman wearing a robe of aqua-coloured silk, embroidered around the neckline and the cuffs of the sleeves. 'That colour suits you so well. You look beautiful.'

Tora turned to the mirror and was inclined to agree. But then it was a beautiful gown, whisper-soft against her skin and so cool. 'I like it,' she said, and moved on to the next.

And after she'd exhausted both the contents of the wardrobe and tiny Atiyah, who'd been put down for a nap, Tora couldn't bear to go back to her serviceable skirt and shirt, but returned to the aqua gown that felt so deliciously cool against her skin. Yousra brushed out her hair and made up her eyes, so she had Qajaran eyes, she called them, ringed with kohl, before she hennaed Tora's feet. 'Just a little,' she said, 'for you will have your hands and feet done for the coronation.' Tora returned the favour by painting Yousra's fingernails and toenails and making the younger woman giggle as she tickled her toes.

They were both laughing as they compared the results when there was a knock on the door and Rashid entered.

'Nice to see someone having fun,' he said, his eyes sweeping the room to take in the situation. 'Won't all that noise wake the baby?'

Yousra bowed immediately, her hands clasped demurely in her lap, her painted toes tucked discreetly under her robe, as if she'd been chastised. 'Excuse me,' she said softly.

Tora saw no reason for repentance. She did see an opportunity for bringing Rashid closer towards caring for his sister. 'It's actually a fallacy babies need silence to sleep. They hear plenty of noise while in the womb and it is good for a child to grow up hearing laughter. Come and see for yourself how untroubled she is.'

His eyes raked over her. Confused eyes, as if he didn't know how to respond, so she slipped her hand in his and steered him towards Atiyah's darkened room, pulling aside the netting. Atiyah lay on her back, one hand to the side of her head as she slept. 'You see,' she said with a smile as she looked up at him. 'Sleeping like a baby. Isn't she beautiful?'

He supposed she was, with her black curls framing her face and her eyes a dark line of lashes, her lips pink and perfectly serene. He nodded. 'She is,' and only then, when he went to reach out a hand to see if the skin of her cheek was as smooth as it looked, realised Tora's hand was still in his. 'I take your point,' he said, and squeezed her fingers before he let them go, and touched fingers warmed by Tora's to his sister's cheek. So smooth. So perfect. The baby stirred slightly before sighing back into sleep, and Rashid took his hand away so he didn't disturb her more.

Tora was still smiling and it was all he could do not to pull her into his arms, but no, that was not the way. 'Kareem gave me this for you,' he said, pulling a paper from between the books he carried, and handed her the instructions for accessing the Internet.

'Thank you,' she said.

'And your money has been transferred.'

Tora closed her eyes and clutched the paper to her chest. 'Thank you so much for letting me know.'

She looked beautiful. She'd ditched the drab uniform and that too-tight bun and was wearing a silken robe that didn't cling and yet that turned her into a woman again, the woman he knew was hidden below, with breasts and hips and curves in between, and she'd done something with her eyes so they looked smoky and seductive and now, because of something he'd said, she looked radiant.

He'd been mad to ever imagine he could leave her alone.

'There's more,' he said, and his voice sounded thick even to him. 'Kareem is giving me a tour of the six new palaces tomorrow, and I came to ask you if you would like to accompany me.'

'Me?'

Her eyes had lit up, as if she wanted to say yes, but they were wary. Guarded. She didn't trust him. She had good cause. 'You.'

She looked down at the child. 'And Atiyah?'

'There is no reason to haul her around with us. We will be in and out of cars in the heat of the day. She will be much more comfortable staying here.'

'But—'

'Please, Sheikha, I can look after her.'

Tora looked at Yousra. 'Are you sure? We may be gone a long time by the sounds.'

'It is no trouble. Atiyah is a delight.'

'So, it's settled, then,' Rashid said, feeling better than he had in a long time. 'We will leave after breakfast.'

Tora looked up at him, her accentuated eyes hauntingly beautiful and her lips slightly parted. 'After breakfast, then,' she said as they walked towards the door.

But he turned back before leaving, wanting one more look at her, like this, like a woman dressed in silk and not a buttoned-up nursemaid with a bun. 'I see you found something else to wear.'

'Yes. You were right—Kareem had organised an entire wardrobe of clothes for me. Yousra's been helping me go through them.'

'I like what you're wearing,' he said, nodding at her choice. 'You look beautiful.'

And her lips moved uncertainly, but he didn't hear if she actually said anything, because he was gone.

CHAPTER TEN

THERE WERE SIX of them in all. A white palace, covered in mother of pearl shell that dazzled in the sun. A red palace with red turrets and domes that paid homage to the ruby. A palace with extensive scented gardens and called Yasmin—named after Malik's favourite of the time, they were informed—the Grand Palace that was based on a Venetian row of palazzos complete with canals and gondoliers on demand if required together with vast rooms filled to the brim with Murano glass, and a palace that looked like a double for the palace of Versailles. There was even park-cum-palace called the Fun Palace with a fantasyland theme and an expansive garden full of perfectly maintained and oiled rides that sat eerily empty, just waiting for someone to push a button.

To Tora they seemed like the folly of a boy who'd never grown up, buildings that lacked the elegant good taste of the Old Palace despite the wealth of treasures they contained, buildings that ventured into the territory of ostentatious display of wealth for wealth's sake.

'Why so many?' she asked Rashid as their convoy left the last on the list, the so-called Fun Palace, a rococo confection based on the retreats of the renaissance royals that wouldn't be out of place in the French countryside. 'Who even needs so many palaces?'

'Malik did,' he said, 'because apparently the harem in the Old Palace was nowhere near big enough.'

'So he built six additional palaces to accommodate his women?'

'Apparently he was a man of insatiable tastes. I can't think how else he could have so happily squandered so much money and so many hours when he should have been working for his people.'

'But he had no children?'

'It didn't stop him from trying,' he said drily, and Tora couldn't help but laugh.

'What?'

'You. You sounded almost funny then.'

'I'm sorry. I didn't mean to.'

'I know,' she said with a grin. 'That's what makes it so funny.'

He looked away, feigning umbrage at her laughter, when in fact he was enjoying himself immensely. It was good to get away from the endless papers and the spreadsheets filled with numbers that showed just how badly the economy had been neglected over the last three decades while its treasury had been plundered to pay for the Emir's follies.

It was good to be with her.

Surprisingly good.

He'd imagined this outing would give her the chance to see him in a better light. He hadn't expected to discover he liked her more in return.

She made a pleasant change from Kareem, who he liked and respected but whose conversation was limited to the necessary and delivered without humour.

Needless to say, she was more appealing on the eyes than Kareem, too. Much more. Today she was wearing another of those silky robes, this one coloured in ripples of yellow and orange so she looked like a shimmering sunset as she walked. He'd been right to ask her along. She made the tour a holiday excursion, expressing delight and sometimes horror at the old Emir's excesses, rather than a dry exercise of checking out the inventory.

And suddenly he didn't want it to end. They were on the outskirts of the city, only a sprinkling of buildings amidst the desert sands, and he had an idea. 'Stop the car,' he told the driver, and the vehicles rolled to a halt. Rashid climbed out to talk to Kareem and a few minutes later he was back and their car peeled away from the others and headed towards the desert proper.

'What's happening?' Tora said. 'Where are we going?'

'Seeing we are so close, I thought we should see something of the desert. Apparently there is an oasis not far from here.'

He saw her bite her lip as she glanced at her watch. 'Will it take long? We've been gone hours already and I feel bad leaving Yousra by herself for too long.' And he felt a pang of admiration for this woman who he could see wasn't using Atiyah as an excuse to get away from him, but was genuinely concerned for his sister.

'It won't take long,' he promised.

It was only a few kilometres further on through the desert sands that they found it, an oasis of palm trees, an island of green amidst the golden landscape, almost empty but for a few families picnicking on and paddling in the shores of a pond alive with waterfowl, its fringes thick with water lilies of white and pink.

'It looks idyllic,' she said as the car pulled into the shade of the palms, and they climbed outside. The desert air was hot and dry, but there was a breeze fanning through the greenery and over the water and Tora's *abaya* fluttered in the warm air as she took in the contrast between desert sands and lush greenery.

'Kareem said this was once a resting place for the caravans that traversed the dunes. Now the city has spread closer and it has been retained as a park for the people of Qajaran.'

'It's beautiful.' She turned to him then, her eyes alive and bright. 'Can we paddle, do you think? Only it's been such a long day and my feet are killing me.'

He wasn't sure why she asked when she was already slipping off her sandals and raising the hem of her *abaya* to slip her feet into the water's edge. 'Oh, it's gorgeous,' she called over her shoulder. 'Bliss. You have to try this for yourself.'

He shook his head, even as he laughed. It was crazy. He swam laps for fitness and he'd been a champion rower along with his desert brothers when he'd been at university, but he wasn't sure he'd ever paddled before. And then, because he figured there was no time like the present, he shucked off his loafers and rolled up the bottom of his trousers and joined her.

She was right. The water was cool and clear and the perfect antidote to hot feet tired from traipsing around half a dozen palaces. Tiny fish darted around his ankles while a crane stood on one leg, watching warily from a distance, and Rashid wondered at the pleasure in such a simple occupation. Tora turned around then and pointed to one of the families whose children were laughing in the shallows at their father holding up a baby whose little feet kicked at the water, giggling gleefully as he splashed himself and everyone around him. 'We should bring Atiyah here for a picnic—what do you think?'

And something shifted enough inside him that it almost sounded like a good idea. He would like to, he thought, if this woman came with them. 'Maybe,' he said as he stepped out of the water and sat on the grassy edge, looking up at the mountains in the distance, and thinking...

She came and sat down next to him. 'Thank you for bringing me here,' she said, flapping at the bottom of her wet hem while she studied the henna designs on her feet as they dried in the warm air. 'That was magic. I don't think you're ever too old to paddle.'

Alongside her he made a sound, half snort, half laughter. 'Just as well, really, given that's my first time.'

Her head swung around. 'Seriously? You've never paddled before?'

'Not that I recall.'

'But when you were a kid—you must have gone to the beach or something?'

He shook his head as he looked out over the water, his elbows on his bent knees. 'The school I went to had a pool. It's not like I didn't learn how to swim.'

But he'd never experienced the simple delights of paddling in the shallows? And she thought back to that night on the terrace when he'd told her he wouldn't send Atiyah off to boarding school, and she wondered. 'How old were you when you were sent to school?'

'I don't remember, I just remember always being there.' He shrugged. 'It was a good school, set in leafy Oxford. I can't complain.'

'But so far from home.'

'That was my home.'

'But your parents?'

'My mother died when I was in infancy. I grew up believing my father was also dead.'

A chill went down Tora's spine. Atiyah was his sister so his father had been alive… It was so horrible, she couldn't help but want it to be untrue. 'You've got to be kidding.'

And he turned and looked at her with eyes that were dark empty holes, and she regretted her words even before he spoke. 'Do you really think I'd kid about a thing like that? No, I never knew he'd been alive all that time until I was summoned to a meeting in Sydney to be told that he'd actually been alive for the thirty years I'd believed him dead, only to have been killed in a car crash weeks before. Not only that though, because I was now the proud guardian of his two-month-old child. How would you feel, learning all that?'

Under the heavy weight of his empty eyes, she knew. Gutted. Devastated. *Angry*.

And her breath caught. He'd been angry the night she'd met him. Because that was the day he'd learned the truth? God, he'd had good reason. No wonder he'd been so resentful of Atiyah, charged with the responsibility of a child of a father who'd as good as abandoned him three decades before.

She looked out over the surface of the water and the ripples that sparkled under a hot sun. 'Why would any man do such a thing to his child?'

Rashid swiped at an insect on his legs. 'Apparently he was protecting me,' he said. 'Protecting both of us.' And he told her of his father being chosen as the Emir's successor, the plot to dispose of both father and child and the exile and separation that had followed.

'And he never once contacted you in all that time.'

'No.'

'So you were brought up by strangers?'

He leaned back on his elbows. 'My houseparents were my guardians. A good couple, I suppose, but I never felt I belonged. I was never part of their family, so much as a responsibility.'

It explained so much about the man he was. No wonder he felt so ill-equipped to care for a child. 'What a hard, cold way to grow up.'

'It wasn't so bad, I guess. What they might have lacked in affection, they made up for in instilling discipline. I was the perfect student in the classroom or on the field.'

Discipline, yes. But no love. No warmth. And her heart went out to the little boy who'd grown up alone and now had the unexpected weight of a country on his shoulders. 'Will you stay, do you think? Will you become the new Emir?'

Rashid sighed. 'I'm not sure,' he said, being honest. 'My father chose not to tell me any of this—I think he valued his freedom in the end, and he wasn't about to force me into a role he saw himself having escaped. Either that, or he thought one attempt on my life was enough.'

'Would it be dangerous?'

'Kareem says not. Apparently the longer Malik ruled, the more of a buffoon he became, interested in satisfying only his own appetites. Everyone knows the last three decades have been wasted. The people want change.'

Rashid stared into the middle distance. Why was he telling her all this? But somehow putting it into words helped. Somehow her questions helped. *Would he stay?*

Qajaran needed help, that much he'd learned these last few days, but was he the man who could turn the country's fortunes around? Zoltan would be here tomorrow to advise him, but there would be no need for that if he decided to walk away.

Could he simply walk away?

And once again his eyes were drawn to the line of mountains that lay across the sands, and he thought about the words Kareem had spoken in an office in Sydney what seemed like a lifetime ago, words that had made no sense to him at the time, words that now played in his mind to the drum beats of his heart.

'Where are you going?' she asked as he rose to his feet and walked towards the sands that lay beyond the fringe of green.

'Just something I need to do,' he said, before stepping from the grass and onto the sands, feeling the crunch of the thin surface give way to the timeless hot grains of Qajaran's sands beneath. Anyone watching would think him mad—Tora must certainly think him mad—but his heart was thumping as he walked, feeling the grains work between his toes and scour his soles. And when he'd walked far enough, he stopped and leaned down to pick up a handful of sand and let it run through his fingers while warm desert air filled his lungs and the breeze tugged at his shirt, whispering the secrets of the ages. He turned his head to listen and found his gaze looking across the desert plains, back to where the blue mountains rose in the distance, and, with a juddering bolt of sensation, he saw the colour of his eyes in the distant range and he felt it then—the heart of Qajaran beating in his soul.

And he knew he was part of this place.

He was home.

His skin still tingling with the enormity of the revelation, he turned back towards the oasis. He was staying. He knew that now, and he wanted to tell Tora, to share it with her because somehow he knew she would understand.

He frowned, because there were more people gathered there where he had left her. They bowed as he drew closer, calling blessings upon him and wishing him well, their eyes full of hope, while Tora stood there in their midst, her beautiful face alight with a smile that warmed his newly found soul.

The children were less hesitant than their parents. They ran up to him, wanting to touch his hand, and he knew he didn't deserve this kind of reception, and he didn't know if he would make a good leader, but the people of Qajaran needed a good leader, and he would try.

The price of failure was too high.

Their return to the Old Palace was subdued, Rashid lost in thought as he watched the desert retreat in the face of the city. Kareem would welcome his decision, he knew, and throw himself into executing the plans for the coronation he already had mapped out. And still he wondered if it was the right decision.

'So what will you do with the palaces?' she asked. 'Unless you're planning on establishing your own harems, of course.'

Lord help him. He couldn't imagine having six women, let alone six harems. One woman was more than enough and he didn't have her. Not really. And there was another problem...

He shook his head, because there were no easy answers to anything. 'I'm not sure. But the state can't keep paying for them. Kareem wanted to show me, in case I preferred one of them over the Old Palace.'

'I like the Old Palace,' she said. 'It has history and character. You have to keep that as the kingdom's base, surely?' And then she paused. 'Not that it has anything to do with me, of course.'

'But that still leaves the problem of what to do with the rest. Qajaran already had a Desert Palace and a Mountain Palace before Malik took it into his head to increase the number of palaces by two hundred per cent.'

'Sell them, then.'

'Not possible. They belong to the people of Qajaran. For better or worse, they are part of their heritage. Even if they could be sold, nobody would pay what Malik spent on them. The country would lose a fortune.'

'So you have six white elephants costing a fortune to upkeep?'

'That's the problem.'

'Could they be turned into boutique hotels? So many bedrooms already with en-suites—surely it couldn't be too hard.'

He looked at her. Really looked at her. 'Did someone tell you that? Did Kareem mention it while we were looking around the palaces?' Kareem had mooted it as a possibility with him just yesterday when he was going over the final details for the inspection.

She shrugged and shook her head. 'No. But what else could you do with them? You could hardly turn them all into museums—that would never pull as many tourists from overseas or earn you as much money. But think of the tourists who would flock here, wanting to tick off staying at Qajaran's quirky hotels one by one, or get married alongside a Venetian canal in the desert. And think of the employment that could be generated in servicing busy hotels rather than in maintaining six empty palaces waiting for their next visit from their Emir.'

He rubbed his chin between his thumb and his fingers, the gravel of his whiskers like a rasp against his skin. The tour had taken the better part of the day and he had a five o'clock shadow to show for it. 'Maybe it's possible.' The palaces couldn't be sold, but they could be leased to a luxury hotel chain to manage...

'Yes!' she said, cutting into his thoughts, 'but not the Fun Palace. That one would be different. You should open that one up to the people of Qajaran. The palace can still be a hotel, but the park should be free for all citizens who just want to visit with their families, not to stay in the rooms.'

'And for those that do,' he said, intrigued, 'they would have to fight the crowds to access the rides that others get free?'

'So give them two hours' exclusive use in the evening or morning. I don't know. It's not exactly my line of expertise. I'm just offering a suggestion. And while you'd probably make money if you converted them all to boutique hotels, it would just be a shame if the Qajarese people couldn't enjoy something that is their own heritage, especially when it's already a fun park.'

Not her line of expertise. So why did what she said

make so much sense? Even down to offering the Qajarese people an opportunity to sample the luxury and in-
dulgences they had so unwittingly paid for.

'How did you come to work at Flight Nanny?' he said,
wondering about this woman who looked after babies and
children and who came up with solutions to problems way
outside her apparent field of expertise.

'Simple,' she said. 'Sally and I went through school
together and then university. When she and Steve started
Flight Nanny, I jumped at the opportunity to join them.'

'They sound like good friends.'

'The best. Sally is like my sister. When my parents died,
I was devastated. She kept me going. And then, when I
poured my grief into a love affair with Mr Wrong that
ended spectacularly badly, she was there to pick up the
pieces. I owe her my sanity.'

'What happened,' he asked, 'with this Mr Wrong?'

'It was my fault just as much. I wanted it so much to
work out—I needed to love someone enough to compensate for the loss of my parents and I was too needy, too
demanding. I can see that now, of course. I can see that
when he tried to let me down gently, I wouldn't let him go.'

'So how did it end?'

She gave a wan smile. 'Badly. He announced to the
world that he was dumping me on every social media account he was signed up with, because I was "a bitch, a
total cow and crap in bed". I do believe those were his
exact words. Mind you, they worked.'

'You're not any of those things,' he said, 'for the record.'

She gave a half-smile. 'For the record, I thank you.
And I'd rather you didn't post that anywhere, if it's all the
same to you.'

It was his turn to smile. The guy was a loser—that
much was clear. 'You're better off without him. Anyone who could say those things wasn't worthy of being

a friend, let alone a lover, especially when you were already so low.'

'I know. Sally said the same thing.'

'So why child care?' he asked, changing the subject, because the thought of her with another man was suddenly unpalatable and not something he wanted to dwell on.

She shrugged. 'I don't know exactly. But I always loved babies and little kids—maybe because I was an only child and grew up alone. They always fascinated me. When I found out I could make a living working with them, it seemed a no-brainer.'

He nodded, although he wasn't sure he entirely understood. He'd grown up alone and he'd mostly kept to himself. If he hadn't happened upon his three desert brothers, he'd probably still be wandering the world alone.

'Have dinner with me,' he said on a whim, because he realised they were nearing the Old Palace and soon she would excuse herself and take herself off to her apartments and the care of Atiyah and he was suddenly sick of being alone.

She looked flustered, her lips parting and closing as if searching for and not finding any words.

'Just dinner.'

'Um… I have to check on Yousra and Atiyah. We've been gone a long time.'

'So check.'

'And if Yousra has had enough or is tired?'

'Bring Atiyah to dinner with you,' he said, surprising himself that he meant it. 'Bring her anyway,' he added, if that helped. Anything to postpone the time she would close herself off from him again.

She blinked. 'Why are you suddenly being so reasonable?'

He turned to her, careful not to reach out a hand and

touch her, as he'd been wanting to all day, to touch the molten sunset of her robe, to feel her heat. In the end, he reached out a hand and wrapped it around hers. No pressure, just a hand hold, warm and true. 'Because I've just had the best day I've had in a long time. And I don't want it to end.'

God, he meant it. Tora's skin bloomed all over. From just the touch of his hand. No, from the import of his words and the dark intent of his eyes. He actually meant it.

And it had been a good day. She'd had a personal tour of six amazing palaces and been both dazzled by their brilliance and appalled at their waste, in the company of a man who knew how to push her buttons, be they physical or emotional, and who now was testing out a new one, one that simply said like.

She was intensely aware they'd just entered the palace gates. Aware they'd soon have doors opened and the outside world would intrude and the moment would be gone—as maybe Rashid himself would be, whisked away to put to rights whatever problem besetting the country next needed addressing.

She didn't want the world to intrude. Not just yet.

There would be time enough for the world later.

'Yes,' she said. 'I will have dinner with you.'

'Good,' he said, drawing her hand to his mouth and pressing his lips to the back of it, while his eyes smiled and warmed her in a place she hadn't expected his eyes to warm. Because it wasn't just sex she saw there, she was sure. There was more.

And she welcomed finding more.

The car slowed, even as her heart raced. Dinner with Rashid. Could they really be friends? After today, she wanted to believe it possible.

He was still holding her hand when the car pulled up to the steps. She liked the feel of her hand in his. She liked

the way it made her feel, liked that today their hitherto
stumbling relationship had advanced to another level, one
that involved both trust and respect.

There was someone there waiting for them, standing on
the steps in addition to the guard of honour that seemed to
grace their every entry and exit. Someone tall and broad-
shouldered with deep black hair and he was looking at
their car and smiling.

'Who is that man?' she said, and Rashid looked to
where she was indicating.

'Zoltan!' he said, with a wide smile. A man Rashid was
clearly beyond excited to see from the way he didn't notice when she slipped her hand from his, and Tora figured
the dinner invitation was off.

'Zoltan!' Rashid called as he jumped from the car. 'You're
early.'

Rashid ran up the steps and pulled his friend into a hug.
'I was told you were arriving tomorrow.'

Zoltan laughed. 'I thought I'd surprise you.'

'It is a good surprise. Thank you for coming. You don't
know what this means to me.'

'To me, too. Whoever thought a humble orphan child
turned petroleum and gas billionaire would ever finally
make good?' he joked before turning serious. 'You have
had a rough ride of it lately, I understand.'

Rashid shook his head. 'I am glad you could come.
There is so much to tell you.'

'Tell me over dinner.'

And Rashid suddenly remembered and looked around,
to where the cars of the convoy were spilling their contents, but with Tora nowhere to be seen.

'Tora,' he said. He'd asked her to have dinner with him
and now she was gone and he felt her absence like a sudden hole in a perfect day.

'What did you say?' Zoltan asked, and Rashid once again felt the jolt of pleasure that his brother was here. It was probably for the best that she'd gone, he thought, given the circumstances. At least it saved an awkward introduction. With any luck, Zoltan wouldn't have heard he was married. He'd save that gem for later. There were more important matters to discuss right now.

'So tell me,' he said, turning his back on the hollow feeling in his gut as he led Zoltan into the palace. 'How are Aisha and the family?'

It was for the best, Tora told herself as she made her way back to her suite. He was so excited to see his friend, he would have regretted asking her to have dinner with him the instant he saw him. Besides, dinner would have been pointless. It was all so pointless. She would be going home soon and leaving this world behind. Why establish links that would have to be broken?

Because when it all came down to it, this wasn't about her. This was about ensuring a bond between Rashid and Atiyah, and the signs were heartening.

It was enough.

Yousra was waiting for her in her apartments, singing to Atiyah as she rocked the baby's cradle. She looked so relieved when she saw Tora coming, Tora thought the girl was going to burst into tears.

'How was she?' Tora whispered with a frown, peeking over into the cot expecting to find a sleeping child, only to find two dark eyes that immediately locked onto hers and widened before her face crumpled and she started wailing before Tora could duck out of the way.

'I'm so sorry,' she said to Yousra, scooping the child into her arms. 'I shouldn't have left her.' After all the turmoil she'd already suffered, all the losses, Atiyah had grown used to having Tora around, only for Tora to disappear for hours, and her heart was breaking for the little girl. She should never have agreed to go with Rashid.

And she knew she couldn't afford to think that way. Knew that it was wrong. She couldn't afford to become a fixture in this child's life, and yet already it was happening. She should have returned home as she'd been supposed to. She should have handed Atiyah over and walked away. And she would have, if Rashid hadn't come up with this whole crazy marriage deal.

And now the longer she stayed, the harder it would become because the more attached to her Atiyah would become, and one day soon she'd be leaving for good and Atiyah would be hurt all over again.

She swayed as she pressed her lips to Atiyah's soft curls and felt tears sting her own eyes as Atiyah's tears threatened to rip out her heart. Staying longer was such a double-edged sword. It gave Atiyah security for a little while. But it gave Tora more time to fall in love with a precious dark-eyed child.

She'd never felt this way about one of her charges before. She'd never come so close to feeling what a mother must feel—protective and defensive and determined that she should have only the best of everything, including love. But then, she'd never had such a tiny baby to look after.

If only Rashid had been more accepting of his sister in the start. If only she hadn't felt as if she had to compensate, to give Atiyah the love she should have got from him.

Damn.

CHAPTER ELEVEN

NIGHT FELL FAST, the way it seemed to do here, the daylight hurrying away to make way for the night. Atiyah settled the same way, her bellowing cries becoming snuffles and then sniffs and before long sleep had overtaken her. Tora knew she had to wean herself off Atiyah and take a back-seat role in looking after her, but still she sent Yousra to visit her family and have a night off after her trying day. She'd talk to Rashid tomorrow about getting an extra carer then. He was busy with his friend tonight and, besides, for now she was happy to sit back and relax with the meal they'd had sent up to her and check her emails.

She smiled when she found one from Sally with the subject line I love you!

After she'd read the message, she was sniffing and there were tears in her eyes for the second time tonight. Steve was doing all the right things according to his test results and he was ready to be transferred to Germany. Sally had been able to tell the doctors to get the ball rolling.

They wouldn't waste any time now. If all went well and Steve could hang in there, Sally wrote, he'd be on his way within the next day or so towards the treatment that could save his life. And there were no promises, she said, being brave, but it was the only chance he had and they were staying positive and whatever happened, she owed Tora a debt she could never repay.

Happy news, Tora thought, blinking away the tears. The

very best kind of news. And she was glad of Rashid's deal now, for all the grief it had caused her, and for all the grief it would inevitably cause her when she had to return home.

It would be worth it if the treatment worked.

It would all be worth it.

'So what's she like, this half-sister of yours?' Zoltan asked, plucking grapes from a bunch on a platter. They were seated on low sofas in one of the palace reception rooms that had doors that opened onto the gardens so that the scent of frangipani wafted in.

'I don't really know,' Rashid said. 'She's a baby.' But then he thought about Tora leading him to Atiyah's cradle to look down upon the sleeping infant and felt a pang of pride. 'She's a cute little thing, though.'

'Huh,' said Zoltan. 'That's all you can say? Spoken like a man who hasn't had children yet. Just wait until you have your own. You won't be so vague about the de-tails then. You'll be hanging out for that first smile and that first tooth.'

Rashid snorted. 'Dream on,' he said, because even if he was warming to the child, he wasn't about to go all gooey over her any time soon. Not like Tora at least, who had been so excited about Atiyah smiling.

'That's where you're wrong, brother,' Zoltan said, wav-ing a grape between his thumb and forefinger for empha-sis, 'An Emir needs an heir. So you don't want to wait too long—you're not getting any younger.' He popped the grape between his teeth and crunched down.

Rashid shook his head. Just because he'd had some kind of epiphany out at the oasis today, didn't mean he was looking to ensure there were an heir and a spare any time soon. 'Give me a break, Zoltan. One thing at a time.'

'Not a chance. Now you'll have to find yourself a wife. Last desert brother standing, but not for long. You don't have a choice any more. Your footloose and fancy-free playboy days are toast.'

It was all Rashid could do to stop from blurting the news that in actual fact he *was* married, just to shut his friend up. Because that would be a mistake and there would be no shutting Zoltan up once he learned that particular snippet of information. What was more, he'd be off and running, firing off messages to Bahir and Kadar before they got here, get their wives all excited in the process, and Rashid would never hear the end of it.

No, he had serious stuff to get done before he let that particular cat out of the bag. He didn't want them to know about Tora just yet. He didn't want them making a bigger deal out of it than it was. Let them find out in their own good time—but by then he'd be halfway to sending her home.

Although why that left him suddenly cold, he wasn't entirely sure.

'You make marriage sound such fun,' he said, suddenly grumpy, and not just because he knew for a fact that it wasn't fun and that in his case it was nothing more than the means to an end. 'Anyway,' he said, needing to change the subject, 'I didn't ask you here to talk about my love life. Let's get to work.'

Rashid stood on his terrace, his hands spread wide apart on the balustrade, looking up at the inky sky. Below in the gardens the fountains played and the birds settled in for the night, the world at peace.

While inside him his emotions clashed and raged in a war that had forgotten what peace was. It didn't seem to matter the decision he'd made today, or maybe his emotions clashed because of it.

Duty.

Self-doubt.

Fear.

Duty.

It always came back to duty.

His heart thumped like a drum, a tattoo cursing the ever-present, inescapable duty. His stomach squeezed tight and he inhaled the dark night air in response to the bite of pain. It didn't matter what he'd decided out in the desert today, his first session with Zoltan had given him no comfort. There was so much to do. So much he needed to learn. So many doubts about what was possible to best help this country and its people…

Fear.

He wasn't used to feeling fear.

He had never failed at anything he had put his hand to, but then he had made choices that reflected his desires and wants. He'd decided his path. He'd worked hard and acted on hunches and educated guesses and he'd been successful by taking calculated risks and when those hunches had paid off. But it had always been his choice to do those things and follow that path.

Never before had he been sucked into a bottomless pit from which there was no escaping and where there was no choice.

Duty.

Self-doubt.

Fear.

Together they tangled and churned until his gut felt battered and heaving and one thing emerged victorious from the mayhem, as if that one thing had been lying in wait, ready to step into the void.

Need.

Powerful and insistent, it rose up like a mushroom cloud that reached out to fill every part of him. He turned and looked along the terrace, towards her suite, to where the glow from her lamps spilled into puddles.

Tora.

Talking to her today had been the one thing that had let him make sense of the tangled thoughts in his mind when nothing else had. She had listened and understood. She had shown him the simple fun of paddling.

And he had repaid her by leaving her cold.

And without being aware that he'd made a decision, his feet started walking.

Towards the light.

Towards Tora.

She should be sleeping. She kept telling herself to put the book down, but she was reading a book about Qajaran, about its treasures and its colourful history and the wars and crusades that had touched its shores and crossed its desert borders, and she was fascinated. And being right here, in the Old Palace that had seen so much of what she was reading, brought it all to life.

Just one more chapter, she promised herself as she glanced at the clock and turned the page anyway.

She jumped at the soft rap on the glass, her heart giving a crazy leap in her chest so that she almost didn't hear when the tap came again. She slid from the bed, her feet cool on the marble tiles, and pulled on a robe, because, whoever it was, she wasn't going to be caught on the terrace in just her nightgown again.

'Tora,' she heard, and she didn't know whether to be worried or relieved when she recognised Rashid's voice. 'Are you awake?'

The door to the terrace was open to let in the breeze, but she stayed her side of the filmy curtain, just inside the room, an invisible barrier between them. 'What do you want?'

He shook his head as if he didn't know why he was here, standing outside her door in the middle of the night. 'I don't… No, nothing. I wanted to apologise for how things worked out tonight. For leaving you in the lurch when Zoltan arrived.'

'It's okay. I understand. Your friend would be wanting to catch up with you.'

He nodded. 'And,' he said, his lips pulling to one side as he struggled with the words, his eyes troubled, 'I just wanted to see you.'

Her heart tripped and her breath caught in her throat. Her mind told her it meant nothing—but her heart…her heart wanted to believe the words he had said, just a little. 'I had a good day today, thank you.'

'Good. I didn't have a chance to thank you. For your thoughts. I will speak to Kareem tomorrow.'

And she remembered that she'd wanted to talk to Rashid, too, about changing the arrangements for Atiyah, so that she wouldn't grow too fond of her, but that could wait, because right now the night air wore a velvet glove that stroked her skin, bringing with it the scent of him, warm and musky, masculine and spicy, much like Qajaran itself.

And she remembered another night, and her head on his shoulder, drinking in that scent, thinking it would never get old, that she would never get enough of it.

'What's it like,' he said suddenly into the silence, 'when a baby smiles?'

She blinked at the question, wondering where it had come from when this was a man for whom babies didn't seem to register. 'It's like sunshine in a hug,' she said. 'It's like the world lights up and wraps you in love.'

He nodded, but his eyes looked as conflicted as ever, as if he was warring with himself, and she wondered what he'd made of what she'd said or what he'd expected to hear. 'Good. I would like to see that. I won't keep you any longer.' He turned to leave, but he looked so tortured, this man who had the weight of Qajaran on his shoulders, that she couldn't bear him to go like that, so she touched his forearm.

'Rashid?'

He looked down at her hand as if it were a foreign object. 'Yes?'

She pulled herself up, and pressed her lips to his fevered skin, a kiss that was tender and sweet, a kiss designed to soothe rather than inflame. 'Thank you, for coming by,' she said, before letting go and drawing back into the relative safety of her suite. 'Goodnight.'

He was still too keyed up to sleep. Rashid lingered on the terrace under the soft dark sky lit with its sliver of moon and sprinkle of stars and breathed deeply of the night air, air that came scented with frangipani and the blossom of lemon and lime, the ache in his belly subsided for now, the factions raging inside him finding an uneasy truce.

Only the need remained undiminished.

Need for a woman who gentled away his fears merely by her presence and her own evocative perfume and the press of her lips gentle on his cheek. Need for a woman it had taken every ounce of his self-control not to pull her to him and forcibly satisfy.

The need—and something else he couldn't quite put his finger on.

He went to sleep dreaming of Tora and her honeyed voice that played in his mind over and over, so that he woke with it still in his head.

He asked Kareem when they met over breakfast if he knew it, a lullaby about oranges and apricots and fat pigeons. 'It seems familiar but I cannot work out where I have heard it before.'

Kareem regarded him solemnly, his eyes a little sad. 'You would have heard it, of course. It is a classic Persian lullaby, very popular, very beautiful. It is a song your mother used to sing to you when you were just a baby.'

Sensation skittered down his spine like spiders' legs. 'But my mother died when I was just a few months old. Surely I couldn't remember that?'

The older man shrugged. 'Perhaps your father sang it after she was gone. Who can say? But it is something left to you from your parents—a link to your past—something to be treasured.'

He sat back in his chair with his hand to his head. Treasured? For the life of him he couldn't picture himself with his father, let alone imagine his father singing him a lullaby. He might have believed it once, but not now. It didn't fit with a man who had hidden himself from his son for thirty years.

Kareem smiled sadly. 'He loved you, Rashid. I know that it is hard for you to believe, but, for better or for worse, he did what he had to do. As you, his son, have to do.'

Rashid sighed.

His father loved him? Why did he have such a hard time believing it?

'So when can I meet her?' Zoltan asked after a heavy morning going through protocols and affairs of state with Rashid and Kareem and the Council of Elders.

Rashid's first thought was of Tora. Her kiss had haunted him last night, as he had lain on his bed waiting for sleep to claim him, her kiss and the feel of her smooth fingers on his arm and her wide cognac eyes.

'Why do you want to meet her?'

'Well, she is your sister, isn't she? You don't have to keep her locked away in a cupboard somewhere. You do let her see the light of day sometimes, don't you?'

'Oh, Atiyah,' he said, struck by Zoltan's words, because once again Tora had said something similar.

'Who did you think I meant?' asked Zoltan, and his friend looked at him as if he thought he was losing it in the desert heat.

Maybe he was. He blinked. 'I'll send for her,' he said easily, because it was a good idea, because it meant he would see Tora again, and after last night's sweet encounter he yearned to.

But when Atiyah arrived, it was not Tora's arms that bore her but Yousra's instead, and he felt a piercing stab of disappointment.

'Oh, Rashid,' Zoltan said, 'what a beauty,' and he surprised the other man by taking the baby and holding her in front of him to look at her properly. Atiyah's dark eyes were wide and uncertain, the bottom lip of her little Cupid's-bow mouth ready to start quivering. But before it could, he had the child tucked into his arms and was sitting down on the sofa again, and Rashid blinked at the ease with which he handled the child. To him she was too small, too full of traps for the unwary. 'You are going to have your work cut out for you when she becomes a young woman.'

Was he? Something else to look forward to. Wonderful.

The baby started fussing and squirming but Zoltan remained unfazed and uncovered her tiny toes and stroked the bottom of her feet with his middle finger. Tiny feet, thought Rashid, looking on, struck by life in miniature.

'Are you ticklish, little one?' Zoltan said, and Atiyah's little legs started pumping, chuckles now interspersed with her complaints. For a while it looked as if Zoltan had the baby's measure, but soon her face became redder and more screwed up and the chuckles gave way to her cries.

'Whoa,' said Zoltan, admitting defeat as her cries became bellows. 'I think it's time you went to your big brother, little one.'

And before he could say no, his tiny sister had been deposited into his hands. He stared down at the squawking bundle in his lap, wondering at the weight and her energy and the power of her lungs.

His sister.

His blood.

Who looked nothing like she had when she'd been sleeping.

And his gut churned anew as he tried unsuccessfully to quieten her.

There was no quietening her. The baby screamed and no wonder. Because what did he have to offer her? He knew nothing of what a baby would need. He had no experience—nothing but the shred of a lullaby...

'Yousra!' he snapped to the young woman who was watching helplessly on. 'Take Atiyah. There is somewhere I have to be.'

Zoltan frowned as Yousra took the child. 'Don't we have the next meeting with the council coming up shortly?'

'I won't be long.'

Tora's blood spiked with heat when she saw the name pop into her inbox. She had half a mind to delete the message straight away but the subject header stalled her—Good news.

What would he think would be good news to her— unless he'd had a change of fortunes or mind and somehow managed to recover her funds? She opened the message.

Dear Cousin Vicky
An opportunity's just come up to make some quick money, so obviously I thought of you!

I'm expecting some funds to come in and meanwhile they're promised elsewhere. I need half a million dollars fast, just to tide me over, and wondered if you might mort-gage your flat for a couple of weeks to help me out? It's

only temporary until those funds come in, and the good
news is I'll be able to pay you a one-hundred-thousand-
dollar fee guaranteed.

Let me know ASAP.

Your cousin

Matt

PS Like your folks used to say, blood is thicker than water
after all!

Good news? Tora stared incredulously at the screen.
Her cousin must think her stupid. First he screwed her
out of her inheritance and then he wanted her home? Pigs
might fly. And as for blood being thicker than water—
after the way he'd betrayed the trust of her parents and of
her, he was no family to her at all.

She was about to hit the delete button and send the message to the trash where it belonged. 'ASAP' be damned—
let him wait for an answer that would never come.

And then she had a better idea. Much better.

So she hit Reply and changed the subject header to Better News! and started typing.

Dear Matt...

She added kisses at the end and then deleted them. No
point laying it on too thick. She'd just hit Send with a satisfying click when another message pinged into her inbox.
This time she was eager to open it.

We're on our way! Sally wrote. Next stop, Germany!

Yes! She fired off a quick 'good luck' reply and this
time added plenty of kisses before she sent it off with a
sigh. At least that was going right.

'Tora,' she heard Rashid bellowing from somewhere
inside her suite. 'Tora!' He appeared at the doorway to
the terrace. 'What are you doing out here?'

'You couldn't just knock like a normal person?' she said drily, wondering where the fire was.

'Why didn't you bring Atiyah when I asked for her?'

'Because you summoned Atiyah, not me. And Yousra is perfectly capable of delivering a child for your inspection. She did bring you Atiyah?'

'Yes, but that's not the point. You should have brought her.'

'Why?'

'Because you're her nanny. She's your responsibility.'

'No, Rashid. She's *your* responsibility, but you like to pass it off to me and that's a bad thing.'

'Why?'

'Because she's becoming dependent on me. She's bonding. Yesterday when I came home from our day out, Yousra was exhausted from trying to settle her.'

'She started screaming when Yousra brought her down.'

They heard her coming, still crying as Yousra entered the apartments. 'I'm sorry, Sheikha,' the young woman said as Tora went to meet her, taking the child and hugging her to her chest.

'It's okay,' Tora said, to both the baby and Yousra as Atiyah grabbed her hair in her tiny hands and her tears soaked her gown. 'It's okay.' Tora sent Yousra off to fetch some warm milk as the baby snuffled into her, her cries slowly abating.

'You see,' she said, speaking softly to Rashid as she swayed. 'I had to send her with Yousra as she's become too attached to me. You need to get more carers or take care of her yourself.'

He looked taken aback. 'But if she feels safe with you—'

'I'm leaving, Rashid. Going home as soon as our marriage can be dissolved. Or had you forgotten?'

He shook his head. 'So stay longer if Atiyah needs you. Do you need to go back straight away?'

'Stay for how long? And then what? She grows even more dependent on me. How is that going to work? That's no kind of solution.'

'How much would it take to make you change your mind?'

She sighed as Yousra returned with the milk. 'You know, Rashid, there are some things in the world that money can't fix.'

'Then show me how to do that,' he growled as Tora sat down to feed Atiyah. 'Show me how to hold her so she doesn't cry.'

Tora blinked up at him. 'Do you really mean it?'

'Of course, I mean it. She is my sister. How do you think it makes me look if I do not know how to hold her?'

And Tora looked down at the infant, still snuffling, her eyes red-rimmed and puffy from crying. She could say no now, to save Atiyah any more distress, but that would be fair to neither of them. So instead she waited until the baby was a little more relaxed, her eyelids fluttering closed as she drank. 'Then sit down and I'll pass her over to you and maybe she won't notice.'

Neither of them really believed that, but Rashid did as she suggested and Tora gently passed the baby over. Atiyah instantly jolted into awareness, her eyes wide open, her feeding stopped as she worked out what had changed in her world. 'It's okay, Atiyah, you're safe,' Tora crooned, even as she tried to show him how better to cradle the infant by relaxing and softening his arms.

Atiyah wasn't convinced and in the end they both conceded defeat, letting Tora take her back.

'I can't stay,' he said. 'I have to go.'

Tora nodded, rocking the child in her arms a little as

Atiyah resumed feeding, keeping her eyes open this time for any more tricks. 'I know,' she said. 'It will get easier, I promise,' and she couldn't help smiling as he left, because Rashid had tried.

Tora's words stayed with him as he made his way back through the palace to the meeting on foreign policy with a heavy heart made heavier by the fact that nothing seemed to work with Atiyah, even when he wanted it to. He'd tried. By God, he'd tried to do all the things Tora had told him, to relax and yet hold her securely so that she'd felt safe, to sway her gently without jerking, to comfort her.

'There are some things in the world that money can't fix.' Didn't he know it? She was preaching to the converted there. There was no amount of money he could throw at the predicament he was in and make it go away.

But surely her case was different. Why did she have to go? If she really cared about Atiyah and didn't want to upset her, surely she could agree to stay a bit longer. She didn't have to rush off. At least to give him enough time to get used to his new responsibilities.

Besides, he was intrigued by her, this woman who could be temptress, Madonna, businesswoman and even comforter. As she'd comforted him last night when he'd gone to her room with her quiet words and her sympathetic eyes.

And he didn't want her to go.

Not yet.

'Ah,' said Kareem coming out of the meeting room he was just heading into. 'We have been waiting for you to begin.'

And Rashid knew what she'd said was right. No amount of money in the world could help him now.

Tora and Yousra were sitting in the Pavilion of Mahabbah the next morning where it was still deliciously cool alongside the lake, a soft breeze stirring the curtains. Atiyah lay on a rug on her stomach on the floor attempting mini push-ups on her chubby arms. Tora was keeping out of her line of sight, but every now and then the baby would look around until she found her before resuming her exercises, assuring herself that, yes, Tora was still there. She was so alert and way too knowing for such a small bundle, Tora thought, and she was just about to disappear for a walk around the garden to see if she might forget, even for a little while, when they heard the voices, young and older.

Through the gossamer curtains Tora could see the three women, two striking dark-haired beauties and one blonde and equally stunning, heading towards the pavilion with a clutch of children in tow.

'It looks like we have visitors,' she said to Yousra. 'Do you know who they are?'

'No,' the other woman said, watching their progress. 'I've never seen them before.'

Tora forgot about hiding and scooped up Atiyah from the floor, the child gumming at her fist as the women hovered at the door. 'We're sorry to intrude, but we were told we'd find Atiyah here. We couldn't wait to meet her.'

'This is Atiyah,' said Tora, holding the baby in her lap.

'Oh, she's gorgeous,' said the first, coming closer. 'You must excuse us. We've been so excited since we heard the news that Rashid had a baby sister. We're the wives of Rashid's desert brothers—his good friends—and we've arrived for the coronation. I'm Aisha, wife to Zoltan, who has been here advising Rashid, and this is my sister Marina, wife to Bahir, and Amber, wife to Kadar. And these,' she said, gesturing to the active group around her, 'are our children.'

'It's lovely to meet you,' said Tora, introducing herself, feeling a little overwhelmed but delighted too that Atiyah would have more distractions over the coming days.

There were three toddlers and two children a little older, a girl and a boy. Other children would be the best entertainment of all. Already she was watching them eagerly, smiling when they came to say hello to her, kicking her little legs with delight.

'One more baby for the desert brothers tribe,' laughed the second dark-haired woman called Marina who was kneeling down and holding Atiyah's hands. 'And now the children have an aunty. Hello, little Atiyah,' she said with a broad smile, earning one back from the infant.

'You're Australian,' said the blonde woman called Amber, who settled herself down on the sofa next to Tora, a sizeable bump under her dress. 'Me, too. Where are you from?'

'Sydney,' Tora said.

'I'm from Melbourne.'

'And now you live—somewhere around here?'

'Kadar and I live mostly in Istanbul. We were married six months ago.' She smiled. 'It's kind of a long story.' She patted her stomach and her smile widened. 'We're expecting our own first baby in a few months. But how did you end up here, looking after Atiyah?'

It was Tora's turn to smile. 'That's kind of a long story, too. But I'm only here temporarily. I'll be going home soon.'

'Oh,' said Aisha, exchanging glances with the other women, 'for a moment I thought—I was hoping…'

'We were all hoping,' her sister said. 'As soon as we saw you, we were hoping. Rashid needs a good woman, and we thought, maybe he has found one at last.'

'He's the only desert brother left,' added Amber, 'and now he will need a woman by his side, more than ever.'

Tora said nothing, just bounced Atiyah on her knee, silently cursing this stupid marriage and the position it put her in, because it wasn't her place to say anything. Just then the peacocks put in an appearance and distracted everyone and the conversation changed direction and Tora could breathe again and enjoy being in the company of other women.

They drank honey tea and laughed and talked of their children and their husbands. They were bright and beautiful like butterflies in the garden and Tora found herself wishing she could be one of them, but that would mean marrying Rashid for real.

'Forgive me for interrupting,' Kareem said, appearing at the doorway to the pavilion with a gracious bow, 'but His Excellency would like to see you privately, Sheikha Victoria.'

Aisha's ears pricked up first. 'Sheikha?'

'I thought that's what he said,' Marina said.

Amber was staring at her strangely. 'But wouldn't that mean...?'

Tora shook her head, excusing herself as she swept past them, her face ablaze with heat. 'It's not what you think...'

'I've been thinking,' said Rashid a few minutes later, rubbing his chin as he paced the Persian rug in his big study, 'now that my friends are here with their wives and families, we need to be careful about them getting the wrong idea about us.'

He paced the other way. 'I know my friends and they'll blow it out of all proportion so I've decided it's best if I ask Kareem to be careful how he addresses you and I tell them that you're simply filling in for the role of my consort for the coronation. I think it's better that they don't know about the marriage at all.'

He suddenly stopped pacing and looked up at her, his eyes panicked. 'What do you think?'

Tora swallowed as she stood there, her fingers tangling as she selected her words carefully. 'I think it might actually be a bit late for that.'

CHAPTER TWELVE

'WHAT?' ZOLTAN'S HEAD swivelled from Aisha to Rashid when the women joined them before lunch. 'You're already married? You sly dog! And you made out like it was the furthest thing from your mind.'

'But it is!'

'So how does that work when you're already married?'

'Because it's not a real marriage!'

'I want to know how come you didn't invite your best friends?' demanded Bahir.

'Yeah,' Kadar said. 'We invited you to our weddings.'

'Right, you really want to know why I didn't invite you to my fake marriage? Maybe it's because Kareem married us in the plane on the way over here. Sorry, but when you're flying at forty thousand feet it makes it a bit awkward to get the wedding invitations out.'

'But when we were talking before, you acted as if you weren't married at all,' said Zoltan. 'Like anything like that happening was years away.'

'Did any of you guys hear me? It's not a real marriage!' He gave a long sigh. He'd known this would happen. He'd damn well known it. 'Look, I had to marry someone, in order to adopt Atiyah.'

'Why did you have to adopt Atiyah?' asked Marina. 'She's your sister, isn't she?'

'Yes, but our father was supposed to have died in a helicopter crash thirty years ago and the people believe that and— Oh, what the hell does it matter why? Kareem said she had to be adopted and in order to do that, I had to be married. End of story.'

'Hardly!' snorted Bahir. 'We're just getting to the good stuff. So this woman volunteered to marry you to get you out of a tight spot, did she?'

'Tora,' said Aisha. 'Her name is Tora. I like her.'

'Me, too,' said her sister. 'And she's gorgeous.'

'She's Australian,' chimed in Amber with a grin. 'What's not to love?'

'Agreed,' said Kadar, giving his wife a squeeze as he kissed her cheek. 'This Tora must be some kind of a masochist to volunteer to marry you. What was in it for her?'

'What do you mean, what was in it for her?'

'What, she did it out of the goodness of her heart?'

'I bet it wasn't for his bedside manner.'

'Maybe it was,' suggested Kadar.

'Okay, okay,' said Rashid, who'd had enough, holding up one hand to silence his friends. 'So there may have been a financial inducement involved. We made a deal. So what?'

'Alas, poor Rashid,' Zoltan said with his hand over his heart. 'Unloved and unwanted, left on the shelf, the only one of the desert brothers who actually had to resort to paying a woman to get her to marry him.'

'Give me a break,' growled Rashid. 'Don't you guys make out you wrote the guidebook on romance—we all know that's a lie.'

'But none of us had to break out the chequebook.'

Aisha looked around. 'Why isn't Tora here? You did invite her to have lunch with us, didn't you?'

He rolled his eyes.

'You didn't!' said Marina, eyes wide with accusation. 'Don't tell me you treat her like the hired help?'

'She *is* the hired help.' But that wasn't true either, he

had to concede. She was more than that. Much more. He just didn't know what to do about it. 'Anyway, I did invite her to lunch and she declined—said she didn't want to get in the way of a desert-brothers-and-their-families reunion. Is that good enough for you?'

Nobody else thought so, which was why one minute later he was on his way to insist Tora join them for lunch.

Tora turned off her tablet still smiling. Sally had emailed with the news that Steve was installed at the clinic and that treatment had commenced and to keep her fingers and toes crossed.

Good news. She sent up a silent prayer. At least something was going right at last.

'Excuse me, Tora,' Yousra said. 'His Excellency is here to see you.'

Tora braced herself. She'd known there'd be a fallout from his friends discovering about the marriage, although for the life of her she couldn't believe how he had ever thought he'd manage to keep them from finding out.

She expected anger. What she didn't expect was him insisting she join him and his desert brothers and their wives for lunch.

'Are you sure?' she said. 'It won't give them the wrong idea?'

'They've already got the wrong idea. How about we prove them wrong and show them there's nothing going on? Besides,' he added, 'it seems you're a hit with the women. They threatened that if I failed to bring you back, then they would come and bodily drag you to lunch themselves.'

She laughed. 'In that case, how can I refuse?'

'Did you want to bring Atiyah?'

Tora shook her head. 'Yousra will have no problem. Atiyah had so much fun with the children this morning, she'll probably sleep for a week. I think the children coming is the best thing that could have happened.'

'Speaking of Atiyah,' he said as they walked down the passageway, past fabulous treasures, brightly coloured urns and dishes set in recesses in the walls, 'have you thought any more about staying on? At least until you can give me some more lessons in handling her.'

Tora sucked in a lungful of air. She hadn't for a moment believed he'd been serious when he'd suggested it and no, she hadn't given it any more thought. She couldn't stay longer and he couldn't expect her to. It wasn't fair on Atiyah and it certainly wasn't fair on her.

As it was, she was struggling to remember all the reasons she shouldn't care about Rashid. She was only a temporary fixture but the longer she was here, the more she liked him. And she didn't want to feel that way, not when it would make it harder to forget him when she was gone.

Not when it would be easier to resist him...

'Rashid—'

'No,' he said, stopping her just shy of the doors beyond which his friends waited, 'don't say anything now. Take your time to think about it. I do want the best for Atiyah, even if it doesn't seem like it. I'm learning, Tora, what she needs. Maybe too slowly for your liking, but I am determined to do right by her.'

He took her hand then, wrapping it between his own, warming her skin as his eyes were warm and tugging on her heart.

'Just promise me you'll think about it. I know it's asking a lot but I won't expect you to stay for nothing. We can work something out.

'What I want now is for Atiyah to feel secure, and she feels secure with you. So will you think about it? Will you think about what it would take to make you stay—even just a little longer?'

Tora looked up at this man, who once she thought was hard and unflinching, arrogant and overbearing, but who she knew to be trying his best.

'I'll think about it,' she promised, although she knew that whatever it would take to make her stay was nothing to how much it would ultimately cost.

'Finally,' came the cry from inside when Rashid opened the door. 'We were about to send out a posse.'

'Welcome, Tora, come and join us,' said another. 'At last, some adult company for you. It will make a nice change from Rashid, I am sure.'

Tora smiled and looked at Rashid, who was scowling. 'My desert brothers,' he said, introducing the three men, 'whom I love with my life. Apart from the times I want to kill them, that is.'

Coronation day dawned pink and clear and just about perfect, he supposed, if you didn't have a spiked cannonball rolling around in your gut.

Rashid rose early, knowing there was no putting it off, watching the layers of the early-morning sky peel away from where he took coffee on his terrace, pink giving way to blue, just as peace would give way to madness.

The day would be long—interminable at times, no doubt—a breakfast with foreign dignitaries and officials and then a long tortuous motorcade through the city to show off their new Emir before a public feast in Qajaran City's biggest square. Then while the official party headed to the formal coronation ceremony, the gates of the Fun Palace would be thrown open to the public, the ceremony relayed on big screens, before a state dinner for six hundred, all topped off with cannon fire and fireworks.

He was exhausted already.

Exhausted and still more than a little daunted.

His cup rattled against his saucer when he went to pick it up and he lifted his trembling hand to inspect it.

God, what was wrong with him? He had studied the books. He had read the histories and pored over enough economic papers and reports to sink a ship, he had listened to the advice of Kareem and Zoltan and the Council of Elders, and still he wondered what he was doing here.

Duty.

There came a knock at the door and Kareem entered with two assistants bearing the robes he would wear today. 'Excellency, it is time to prepare.'

He was dressed and taking his last few breaths as a free man when he heard the soft knock, but it wasn't Kareem this time. It came from the connecting door to Tora's apartments, the door he had never opened although temptation in the shape of a seductress lay just the other side. The door opened and a soft voice called his name, a voice that, to his fevered mind, sounded as cool as a waterfall. And then she entered, and for a moment he forgot the pain and the fever and the damnable tremble in his hands, because he had never seen anyone more beautiful.

She was dressed in a golden robe, exquisitely embroidered, with gold trim similar to his own, and with long sweeping cuffs on the sleeves and a gossamer-thin silk shawl over her hair that framed her face and floated like a cloud as she moved. She looked like something out of a medieval fantasy.

His next fantasy.

'Rashid,' she said, and her eyes opened wide as they took in the sight of him dressed in his unfamiliar robes, the first time she had seen him dressed this way. She blinked and seemed to gather herself. 'I just wanted to wish you well today,' she said, 'before it all gets crazy.'

As they both knew it would.

He nodded, because his jaw set too tight to talk and the spiked cannonball in his gut rolled and stuck its spikes in his innards, and he had to take himself to the window to ease the pressure.

For her gesture, her simple act of kindness, had almost brought him undone.

She understood a lot for a woman who wouldn't be here if he hadn't needed to adopt Atiyah and coerced her into a convenient marriage. Because she had become so much more than simply a convenient wife. Her suggestion of opening the Fun Palace to the public had led to its inclusion in the proceedings today, an inclusion he had been informed had been met by the people with huge anticipation and great excitement. He was sharing some of the riches of the state and it was he who was being lauded for it.

She understood a lot more than he had given her credit for.

She would be gone soon.

And his breath caught, as the pointed barbs of that cannonball stuck their points into his raw and wounded flesh anew.

Tora had never seen Rashid in robes—had never imagined that a man who was so at home and looked so good in western clothes could own a look so traditional and yet he did. His snowy white robes and the tunic beneath were lined with gold trim, his headpiece bound with a band of black that would be replaced with a band of gold, in the final step of the ceremony that would make him Emir.

Tall and broad-shouldered, his skin looking as if it had been burnished by the sun against so much white, he looked magnificent, as if he had been born of the desert sands—born to rule—and yet Tora could see the battle going on behind his features, could see the slight tremble in his hands that he was at pains to disguise, and she ached for him.

'You have no need to be afraid,' she said softly.

'What?' He turned sharply.

'You have no reason to fear.'

'Is that what you think? That I'm afraid?' But his voice lacked the conviction of his words and he knew it by the way he dropped his head and turned away again.

'You're strong,' she said behind him. 'You're intelligent and just and a good man, and you want to do the best for the people of Qajaran. They are lucky to have you.'

He heaved in air, and his words, when they came, might have been blasted raw by the desert sands and the hot wind. 'I was not brought up for this.'

'But it's in your blood. Your father—'

'How is finding you're suddenly responsible for the welfare and futures of millions of people in your blood?'

'You can do this, Rashid,' she said, more sternly than she'd planned. 'You would not be here if you did not believe that. Nobody who knows you, nobody here in this palace does not believe that.'

'How can you—someone who I have known for the tiniest fraction of my life—say that?'

'Because I have seen how hard you work. I have seen that a weaker man would walk away and that a greedy man would stay even if the task was beyond him. You are not like that. You can do this, and you will prevail and you will be a good Emir.'

Kareem interrupted them with a knock on the door. 'Excellency, Sheikha, if you are ready?'

She glanced at him one more time before nodding and saying she would check on Yousra and Atiyah, and had turned to go when he caught her hand before she could disappear. 'Thank you for those words. They mean more than you know.' He squeezed her hand tightly in his before he let her go. 'I just hope you are right.'

She smiled up at him in a way that warmed him from the inside out in a way the sun had never done. 'I know I am,' she said, and her words and her warmth gave him the courage to believe it.

It was exhausting but it was exciting, too. Tora sat alongside Rashid on a sofa under the shade of a tent that had been set up on a dais before a huge square that was full of the longest tables she had ever seen. They had breakfasted with the foreign dignitaries at the palace and now it was the turn of the people to meet their soon-to-be Emir before they returned to the palace for the coronation proper. Bright banners in the Qajarese colours fluttered in the air, competing with the cheerful holiday colours worn by the women and even some of the men. There was a party atmosphere as the feasting got under way, musicians and dancers providing the entertainment, and the sound of laughter was everywhere.

And not even the knowledge that theirs was a marriage of convenience, and that soon she would be heading home and no longer the sheikha, could not diminish her delight in being part of the proceedings. For now, legally at least, she was the sheikha and she would do the best job she could, even if her stomach was a mass of butterflies. But this wasn't about her, it was about Rashid, and the coronation of a new Emir, and it was a once-in-a-lifetime experience and she was going to lap up every single moment of it.

And then a young girl climbed from her seat and approached the dais, in her hands a posy of flowers, her eyes wide and a little in awe as she stood waiting at the steps. Kareem leaned low over Tora's shoulder. 'She has flowers to welcome the new sheikha, if you so wish.'

'For me?' Today was supposed to be all about Rashid,

she had thought. But still she smiled and held out her hand
to urge her up and the little girl smiled back and climbed
the stairs and bowed before handing over the flowers and
uttering something in Qajarese.

'What did she say?'

Kareem leaned low again. 'She wished you many sons
and daughters.'

'Oh,' Tora said, suddenly embarrassed, before adding
thank you in Qajarese, one of the few words that she'd
learned, feeling guilty because now she wasn't just observing the proceedings; she was a participant in them.

There were more children after that, and more blessings
and more flowers, until their table was transformed into a
sea of flowers, and Tora smiled at all comers, girl or boy,
and their faces lit up when she thanked them.

She glanced across at Rashid at one stage and felt a
sizzle down her spine when she found him watching her,
his gaze thoughtful and filled with something that almost
looked like respect.

Rashid watched her accept another bunch of flowers,
touching her fingers to the child's face as she thanked
her, and the girl skipped back to where her family were sitting, almost luminescent with delight. Tora was a stranger
to this pomp and ceremony as much as he was, an ob-
server caught up in a world not her own, but you wouldn't
know it.

She was a natural with the children just as she was a
constant for him, always at his side, looking calm and serene and so beautiful that his heart ached. And it was hot
and there were hours to go before they could escape, and
she so easily could have resented having to take part in
the ceremony at all when she was no real wife of his, but
she made it look easy.

She made him think anything was possible.

He could do much worse for a wife.

And later, when they were back at the palace during the coronation, when Kareem removed his black headband and lifted the gold *igal* to replace it, it was her words from this morning that he remembered. *'You're strong... You will be a good Emir.'*

Kareem then uttered the ancient words to install him and placed the crown on his head and it was done. He was the Emir.

Cheers and applause broke out across the banquet room, the loudest coming from the quarter where his desert brothers and their families were sitting, and he smiled as he let go a breath he hadn't realised he'd been holding.

He turned to her and saw the moisture there in her eyes—*the tears she'd shed for him*—and he was moved beyond measure.

But before he could tell her, before he could thank her for this morning's words and for her quiet strength today, first there was another feast, another party complete with cannon fire and fireworks, a display above the palace that was echoed all over the city and in the tiny desert and mountain villages of Qajaran.

It was after midnight by the time the festivities wound down. Yousra had taken Atiyah back to her bed hours ago—a day of formalities interspersed with playing with the children had worn her out—and now Rashid walked silently beside Tora towards their suites.

And it seemed to Tora that the very air around them was shimmering, there had been so much energy generated by the celebrations of today, energy that now turned the air electric as they moved, into currents charged by every swish of robe against robe, every slap of leather against the marble floor a metronome, beating out the time she had left.

And all she knew was she didn't want this night to end. She didn't want this feeling to end—this feeling of being at peace with Rashid, of being part of his life…an important part…if only for a day. She wanted to preserve the magic of this moment and hold it precious to her for ever.

For soon her time in Qajaran would be over. Soon she would be back in Sydney in her black skirt and buttoned-up shirt and there would be no more robes of silk to slide against her skin, no more frangipani on the air.

No more Rashid.

Her heart grew tight in her chest.

He was nothing to her really. A roll in the hay and then a quick buck—a deal made with the devil—with plenty of grief along the way. He was nothing to her—and yet her heart had swelled in her chest when he was crowned, she'd been so very proud.

Nothing to her?

And her heart tripped over itself in its rush to tell her she was a liar.

All too soon, it seemed, they were at the door that led to her apartments and she turned and looked up at him, so handsome in his robes, his features a play of dark and shadow against the stark white, the gold *igal* on his head gleaming in the low light. 'Thank you for seeing me to my rooms.'

He shook his head. 'It is you who deserves thanking, Tora. What you said to me this morning…' He trailed off, searching for the words, and she put a finger to his lips.

'I didn't say anything you didn't already know. Maybe you just needed to hear them.'

He caught her hand and pressed it hard against his mouth. 'You are a remarkable woman, Tora.'

'No, Rashid.'

'Yes, you know it's true. From the moment you arrived, you have impressed everyone you have met.

'Today, you were the star of the show, charming everyone from the tiniest child to the most important dignitary. I know our hasty marriage was foisted upon you and unwanted, but you have been one of the highlights of my return to Qajaran.'

'We had a deal, Rashid, remember? I got something out of it, too. The money—it helped a friend of mine out at a tough time.'

'It was nothing compared to all you've done. I owe you, Tora. I don't know how I can possibly repay you.'

And she knew that the moment was now, that if she wanted this night to continue she would have to be the one to make it so.

She looked up at him, at his dark eyes and his beautiful tortured features, and knew that when she left she would be leaving a part of herself right here in Qajaran.

Her heart.

'Make love with me, Rashid.'

CHAPTER THIRTEEN

THE GROWL RUMBLED up from low in his throat. But then words wouldn't come close to how he was feeling right now. He swept her into his arms and pressed his lips to hers before he carried her through to his suite where he scattered coloured cushions in all directions with one hand before he laid her reverentially in the centre of his bed.

There was no rushing as there had been that first night together. No stripping of clothes separately before they came together. This time Rashid undressed her as if he were opening a gift, taking his time to expose each part of her skin, worshipping it with his lips and his mouth—the hennaed patterns of her hands and feet, the insides of her elbows and the backs of her knees—until she was quivering with desire and need before he'd even slipped her golden *abaya* over her head.

Breath hissed through his teeth when he looked down on her. 'You're beautiful,' he told her with his words and with his adoring eyes, and warmth bloomed inside her. She felt beautiful when he looked at her that way.

He shed his robes and turned from desert ruler into her ruler. Tonight she was his kingdom and his most loyal subject. Tonight she was his queen. Tonight she was his, utterly and completely, and he gave her everything in return.

They made slow, sweet love, long into the night. Making love, she thought, not sex this time, for that tiny seed of a connection had grown into something more, something richer and more powerful.

Love.

And the thought simultaneously terrified and thrilled her, but tonight it seemed so right. She loved him.

And when he followed her into ecstasy and she heard him cry out her name on his lips, she knew he must love her, too, even just a little.

He pulled her close and kissed her and it didn't matter that he was sleeping like the dead less than a minute later. In just one night, he'd given her more than she could have ever wished for.

'I love you,' she whispered, testing the words, touching his lips with hers, before she snuggled closer and closed her eyes, still smiling.

There was a noise from beyond the interconnecting door. A cry. *Atiyah.* Tora listened in the dark, waiting, and a few seconds later came another cry, more insistent this time. Tora strained to hear Yousra's footfall on the tiled floor but heard nothing and Atiyah was working herself up to full throttle now.

Beside her Rashid slept on. He would be exhausted after the strain of the coronation and the physical excesses that followed. She should leave it to Yousra but she didn't want Rashid to be woken, so she rose from the bed, pulling on Rashid's oversized robe, and slipping into her suite.

She scooped Atiyah from her cot and held her to her chest. 'What's wrong, little one? What's the matter?'

Yousra appeared looking ill with dark shadows under her eyes and Tora sent her straight back to bed. Rashid would have to find another carer to share the load now.

Tora checked the baby's nappy and made sure there was nothing pressing in her clothes or bedding. A nightmare,

she guessed, just something that spooked her in her sleep.
The baby whimpered and snuffled against her chest and
she massaged her back and started singing the lullaby she
liked to sing to Atiyah. Eventually the little fingers of the
fist holding on so tightly to her robe finally relaxed as she
drifted back to sleep.

'Where did you learn that song?'

She started and turned, the baby still in her arms, to
find him standing there, a towel lashed low on his hips.
'You're awake.'

'That song,' he said. 'It's beautiful. How do you know
it?'

'I learnt it at the child-care centre where I worked.
We had children whose families came from all over the
world and we tried to learn songs from most of the major
languages, even though we were never quite sure of the
words.'

'Did you know it was Persian?'

She looked up at him. 'I knew it was Middle Eeastern.
Why do you ask?'

'Because I've heard it before. Apparently my mother
used to sing it to me. And maybe my father, too. I'd forgotten it until I heard you singing it to Atiyah, that first
night on the plane.'

She stilled at his side, her heart going out to him. She
couldn't begin to imagine how it must feel—the pain on
discovering your parent had been alive all those years
you'd thought him dead. The betrayal and the hurt would
be almost too much to bear.

'Your father must have loved you a lot,' she said.

He sniffed. 'How do you figure that?'

'Because he left you Atiyah,' she said, trying to find
some way of soothing his pain. 'I read that her name means
gift. He left you questions without answers, I know, but
he left you Atiyah, and the gift of joy and love as well, if

you will only see it. He must have loved you to have entrusted her in your care.'

He blinked and reached out a hand to touch Atiyah's curls.

She watched his hand, saw the moment man connected with sleeping child, saw wonder on his face in the low lamp light, and felt a rush of joy. Baby steps, she thought, it would take one baby step at a time. But in time, she knew, he would learn to love Atiyah as he should.

She kissed the baby on the head and tucked her back into her cradle. 'Come,' she said to Rashid, and led him back to bed.

'It's strange,' he said, thinking in the dark, amazed at her wisdom. 'I feel like I know you, and yet I know nothing about you.'

She shrugged in his arms. 'There's not a lot to tell. I grew up in Sydney and became a child-care worker. And then, like I told you before, when my friend Sally and her husband opened the business, I joined Flight Nanny. End of story really.'

'What about family? Pets? Favourite colour?'

'Orange,' she said, with a smile. 'No pets. I'm away from home too much.'

'How did your parents die?'

'It was a glider crash, three years ago now. Dad was piloting when they collided with another glider and lost a wing. They were too close to the ground to have time to parachute out.'

He pulled her close, pressed his lips to her forehead. 'It must have been hard to lose them both together.'

'Yeah, and there are days when it's still hard. But overall, it gets easier with time. I was lucky enough to have them both until I was in my twenties. And I know it sounds a cliché, but it makes me feel better knowing they died doing something they both loved. Dad used to say you can never be freer than in the sky. I like to think of them soaring somewhere in the sky together.'

He squeezed her shoulders. 'Did you have any other family to help you, then?'

'I have a sprinkling of cousins but they're mostly all interstate so I hardly ever see them. Oh, except for one who lives in Sydney. But we're—well, we're not close.'

'Why's that?'

'Matt let me down badly over something.' Absently she ran her fingers through the coarse hair of his chest. 'I'm finished with him now. Sally's more family than any of them, really.'

'I'd be lost without my brothers, too. But then, they're not real brothers. Maybe that's what makes them special to us.'

'Maybe.' She squirmed and rolled over, as if the topic made her too uncomfortable. 'You know, can we talk about something else?'

'I've got a better idea,' he said, liking the way her bottom wiggled so provocatively against him and feeling his body react accordingly. 'Maybe we should *do* something else.'

'Oh,' she said, when she caught on. 'I like the way you think.'

'And I like the way you do this…' He pulled her astride him and handed her a condom, liking, too, the way eyes widened appreciatively as she realised how aroused he already was and took him in hand. He cupped one breast and ran a palm up her thigh while her fingers worked their magic on him as slowly she rolled the condom down his hard length. She gasped when his thumb grazed her inner lips.

'Oh, my,' she said, her job complete, but not her enjoyment as his fingers explored her slick folds. 'You do make it hard for a girl to concentrate on a task.'

'Maybe,' he said as he lifted her hips over him and positioned himself at her core, 'this might make it easier?'

And he pulled her all the long way down on him until he was seated deep inside her and she was stretched up like a cat, her back arched, all curves and sleekness above him such that he could not resist running his hand up over her smooth, firm flesh.

'Oh, yes,' she said on a sigh as her muscles let him go enough to lift herself from him until she was at his very tip, 'I think I can concentrate on this,' before she lost herself as she plunged down on him again.

'Stay here in Qajaran,' he said in between breaths as he brushed her hair from her face as they lay side by side waiting for their heart rates to return to normal. 'There is no need to go home yet.'

'Atiyah is settling,' she said, relishing the tickle of his fingers on her skin. 'She is becoming more used to Yousra and her new surroundings. Find her another carer and you will not need me soon.'

'I'm not asking you to stay for Atiyah's sake,' he said. 'I'm asking you for mine.'

And like one of the bursts of fireworks she'd witnessed against tonight's sky, hope bloomed bright and beautiful in her chest.

Could it mean that he was feeling something for her, as she felt for him? Was it possible that this crazy marriage could turn out to have a fairy-tale ending after all?

'I have my work…' she said, because a crazy idea still had to be met with a rational mind and she would be leaving Sally in the lurch at the worst possible time.

'I wouldn't expect you to drop everything and walk away empty-handed.'

'It's not about money.'

'No, but money can make problems easier to sort out,'

he said, and she thought about the money that had got Sally and Steve to treatment in Germany.

'I guess that's true.'

'We'll work something out,' he said, kissing her brow.

'I haven't said I'll stay yet.'

'You haven't said you won't.'

Rashid left Tora in his bed with a smile on his face. It was perfect. She was perfect. When he'd agreed to come to Qajaran, doubt had been foremost in his mind. Need he do this, could he do this? And he'd decided to stay, and a lot of it was all down to Tora being here, right beside him all the way. When he'd been consumed by doubt, she'd been the one who'd convinced him he could be the leader Qajaran needed.

And the thought that she was leaving filled him with dread. He didn't want her gone. He wanted her to stay. More than that, when it all came down to it, he *needed* her to stay.

It was a strange feeling, this need. He'd never needed anyone in his life before, and if there was one thing his father's sudden and short-lived blip back into his life had reinforced in him, it was that he didn't need anyone else. That he was right to rely on his own devices and his desert brothers.

He knew for a fact his desert brothers would never betray him.

He'd never needed anybody else.

Until Tora.

His heart beat a little faster in his chest as he remembered how she'd looked when he'd left her. Sleep and sex tousled, her hair in wild disarray, and with a smile just for him, a smile that lit up his world.

He smiled to himself, even as he headed to work. Like the day of the ceremony, today had been declared a public holiday for everyone. Everyone, that was, who didn't happen to be the Emir or his Grand Vizier who both had work to do. He would make time later to see off Bahir and Kadar and their wives and children, who were heading off to Istanbul together. Zoltan would join him for some final talks this afternoon, before he and Aisha and the twins returned to Al-Jirad.

His thoughts returned to Tora and how he might get her to stay. The people would be happy, they clearly loved her as their sheikha, and so would his desert brothers and their wives. But he would be happier than all of them, because he wanted and needed her right there by his side.

His footsteps faltered on the marble tiles as a thunderbolt jagged through him.

Was this what his brothers always talked about, when they had found a woman to share their lives with? Was this what love felt like? Was Tora the one?

He shook his head, simultaneously baffled and in awe.

He'd never looked for love. He'd never expected to find it.

Still in a state of wonderment, he entered his office and found the unfaltering Kareem already there waiting for him.

'So, Kareem,' he said, feeling more light-hearted than he had in a long time, 'what do we have on the menu today?'

Kareem didn't seem to share his good mood. Instead he looked more troubled than Rashid had ever seen him, and older than his years, and for a moment Rashid wondered if the endurance test of the coronation had worn him out. 'Sire,' he said at length, 'I have news which may concern you.'

Rashid doubted it. Right now it would take a volcano to suddenly appear in the desert to concern him, and then only after it erupted. 'What is it?'

'A message was sent through the palace server. I did not wish to bring it to your attention yesterday. It's from Sheikha Victoria to her cousin, a man called Matthew Burgess.'

Rashid remembered her talking about her cousins and how she didn't have anything to do with one in particular—he was sure that one was called Matthew.

'That doesn't sound right. Was it definitely her cousin?'

Kareem looked tense. 'A search proved it to be true.'

He told himself that it could still be innocent, that she might just have been informing him where to contact her, although why would Kareem consider that noteworthy?

'And do I really need to read a private email from Tora to her cousin?'

'I think perhaps you should.'

And a chill descended his spine as he took the letter from his vizier's hands.

Dear Matt

Don't think twice about the quarter of a million—it's a drop in the ocean to me right now. I'm just sorry you're having a tough time of it.

As it happens, I won't need to mortgage my home to help you out—we'll never have to mortgage anything ever again!—as I've stumbled on the mother lode: a rich petroleum billionaire who has royal connections. I know! The dollar signs in my eyes lit up too! I am confident I will be able to send you at least half a million dollars in one or two days.

Hang in there and keep watching that trust account— and keep listening for the ka-ching!

It's coming!

Your cousin

Victoria

PS Yes, blood really is thicker than water.

Rashid's blood ran so thick and cold it was practically curdling in his veins. A rich petroleum billionaire who has royal connections. The dollar signs in my eyes lit up too!

Something new and fragile threatened to crumble inside him then, his faith in her wanting to shatter into tiny pieces to scatter on the desert winds.

'You see, Excellency,' said Kareem, 'why I thought you might be interested in reading the contents.'

He could see all right, but no, this was Tora they were talking about. 'It cannot be true.' No way could it be true. This could not be Tora writing this. And even if it was... He flicked the paper in his hand. 'Surely this is some kind of joke?'

'I am sorry, sire, we thought the same, but there is more. It seems this Matthew Burgess and a solicitor colleague are both being investigated by the financial authorities for misappropriation of client funds.'

'There must be a misunderstanding, then. If this is the cousin Tora told me about, she doesn't have anything to do with him.'

Kareem bowed his head.

'What?' demanded Rashid.

'I wish I could say there had been some kind of mistake, but the solicitor's account at the heart of the fraud case—it is the same account the sheikha had us transfer the quarter of a million dollars to.' He paused. 'And there is evidence that the sheikha had repeated visits and phone calls to her cousin's office in Sydney before she came to Qajaran.'

'But she told me that she has nothing to do with the cousin who lives in Sydney. Is there another cousin?'

Kareem bowed again. 'I am sorry, sire. There is only the one.'

And Rashid's fragile new world splintered around him, leaving him shell-shocked and raw again, just as he'd been when he'd learned of his father's three-decade deception.

But Tora's deception cut still deeper, because she'd played him for a fool.

'It's not about money,' she'd told him, after sending this message to her cousin.

It wasn't about money?

Liar.

'So her cousin is a crook,' said Rashid tightly. 'Which is no doubt why she needed the quarter of a million dollars so urgently, and another half million besides, so she could try to bail him out.'

'So it would seem, sire.'

And Rashid closed his eyes and turned his head to the ceiling. He had to hand it to her—all that talk that money couldn't fix things. All that holding out on him while all the time comforting him, reassuring him, making herself indispensable to him. All the while making out that she cared for Atiyah when it appeared now that all she had been concerned about had been riches.

His riches.

Betrayal wrapped its poisoned arms about him. There was a reason he didn't get close to anyone. There was a reason he preferred to wander this world alone.

'Kareem, as soon as the desert brothers and their wives have left today, I want you to remove Atiyah from Tora's suite and place a guard on her door. From then on until she leaves here, the sheikha is under house arrest.'

Kareem inclined his head. 'It will be done. I am sorry, sire.'

'Why are you sorry?'

'For pressing the urgency of your marriage to adopt Atiyah.'

'God, Kareem, it wasn't your fault I got lumbered with Tora. I chose her. I should have waited for you to find me a proper wife.'

'I did think, for a time, that she would make a good sheikha.'

Rashid ground his teeth together. He'd been thinking along the same lines. More fool him.

Tora took coffee and yoghurt with fruit on the terrace feeling happier than she'd felt for what seemed like ever. She ached in all kinds of places she hadn't known could ache and she didn't mind a bit because every twinge reminded her of why she ached and how she'd earned it, and every memory made her smile anew.

Because she'd spent a night making passionate love with Rashid.

Not sex. *Love.*

It was mad. She'd known Rashid for such a short time, but what she felt for him was special. Love? She didn't know, but she felt the bloom of warmth every time she thought of it. It was a new discovery, shiny and pretty and wondrous, and she wanted to take it out and examine it and hold it close to her heart.

Beside her on a rug under a sun shade Atiyah practised her push-ups, gurgling happily, and all of a sudden flipped herself over. She lay there on her back, looking totally surprised at her different view of the world.

'Oh, you clever girl,' Tora said, clapping her hands at this early milestone, and Atiyah broke into a gummy grin, suddenly delighted with herself.

And Tora couldn't wait to tell Rashid.

Surely this day could not get any more perfect?

CHAPTER FOURTEEN

THE WEATHER HAD turned humid and oppressive, the kind of day that made your clothes stick to your skin and made you want to stay in the cool inside the thick palace walls, and it was late afternoon before the two remaining women had a chance to venture outside to sit and drink tea by the pool in the courtyard before Aisha had to depart.

They had bade goodbye to Marina and Amber and their families earlier in the day and now Tora and Aisha sat in the shade, baby Atiyah lying sleeping in a cradle that Tora set swaying with a gentle push every little while, while Aisha's two-year-old twins ran around chasing each other. Jalil was bigger, and faster on his feet, but Kadija was more agile and would dart away at the last moment, shrieking in delight as her brother lunged for her and snatched only handfuls of air.

'Your children are beautiful,' Tora said, more than a little wistful that they would soon be gone. It had been hard for her to say goodbye to Marina and Amber, who had both hugged her and said they hoped to see her 'next time'. She hoped to see them again, too, but she couldn't afford to imagine herself a permanent place in Rashid's future on the strength of one night and a mere request to stay longer. No matter what this new-found emotion centred at her heart wove into wanting. It was all too new and there were too many unknowns, and what Rashid felt and wanted was the biggest unknown of them all.

Aisha beamed suddenly beside her, unable to suppress a smile. 'Thank you,' she said, putting her hand low over her belly and looking up at Tora with bright shining eyes as she reached across and squeezed Tora's hand with the other. 'I've been waiting to share the news with Zoltan ever since I had it confirmed today, but he and Rashid have been so busy. I told Marina and Amber just before they left, and I know we haven't known each other very long, but I'm bursting with the news and you feel like a friend already.' She took a breather. 'Jalil and Kadija are going to have a little brother or sister.'

'That's wonderful news,' Tora said. 'I'm so honoured that you'd tell me. Congratulations!'

'Thank you.' Aisha hugged her hands in her lap as she watched her twins. 'Zoltan will be so pleased. He thought after me getting pregnant so quickly with the twins that it would happen again just as easily.' Tora saw a glimmer of pain in her eyes and the words she hesitated over, the words she left unsaid. 'Of course, it wasn't that easy at all. But now...' and Aisha smiled again and looked radiant with it '...now he will be so thrilled.'

'You two are so much in love,' Tora said on a sigh. 'You deserve every happiness.'

Aisha nodded, adding a conspiratorial smile. 'Thank you, but, I have to admit, it didn't start out that way.'

'Really? You're both so perfect for each other, I imagined you two falling in love at first sight.'

Aisha laughed. 'That's very funny, given the first time we met I bit him on his hand, although, to be fair, he was wearing a mask so I couldn't see how handsome he was.' She seemed to think about that a second. 'No, actually that would have made no difference, because the second time we met I clawed his face with my nails, though that was after he told me we were to be married. Against my will, as it happened.'

'You were forced to marry Zoltan? That seriously happens?'

She nodded. 'Yes. It happens and I had no choice. I wanted to marry for love but my father said I had to marry Zoltan, or both our kingdoms would be compromised.'

'And so you went through with it.'

'I did. Zoltan wasn't happy though, when I refused to sleep with him on our wedding night.'

Tora was so shocked she laughed. 'You didn't?'

Aisha smiled and shrugged. 'How else could I show my displeasure at being forced into marriage? I did not know this man I was expected to fall into bed with. He was a stranger to me and I wanted a love match.'

'What happened?'

'He showed me he was a good man and I could not help but fall in love with him.'

Tora shook her head. 'Nobody would ever guess you two started out like that.'

'Don't think I'm the only one—Marina and Amber had no easy path to love either. You see, there is something you must understand about these four men, Zoltan and Bahir, Kadar and Rashid—they are like brothers, only their bond is stronger, and duty is everything to them. They may not like it, they may strain against their fate, but ultimately they know what they must do.

'But they are so focused on their duty they don't take easily to the concept of love. None of them had an easy upbringing, and they all grew up looking after themselves. They are so used to being in control of their lives and their destinies that love is foreign to them. They are caught unawares how powerful love can be, but when they do fall in love, they fall hard.

'It has been the same for Zoltan, Bahir and most recently Kadar. And now Rashid is one hundred per cent focused on his new role and, in truth, is probably still coming to terms with this change in his life, but you will see, in time, Rashid will come good, too. He will be a good husband to you.'

And Aisha sounded so certain that Tora's uncertainties came brimming to the fore. 'Except this is still a marriage of convenience. As soon as we're divorced, he'll no doubt marry a meek Qajarese woman with the right connections the first chance he gets.'

Aisha shook her head. 'No, this cannot be true. I have seen you two together. I saw you during the coronation where Rashid's eyes followed your every move. We all saw him watching you. I cannot believe he would let you go, now that he's found you.'

Tora tried not to read too much into Aisha's predictions. 'He did ask me last night, to stay longer.'

Aisha smiled. 'You see! It is happening already. Soon he will not be able to imagine living without you. Do you love him?'

And Tora looked away to escape from the other woman's direct question and even more direct gaze. 'I… I'm not sure. How do you know for sure if you love somebody?'

Aisha put a hand over her heart. 'You feel it here, and—' she touched her head '—you know it here and suddenly it consumes you and you need him with every fibre of your being. You know that without him, you can never be complete. And when you make love with the man you love, you are complete.'

Tora let go a breath she'd been holding.

Love.

That was how it had felt to her last night.

'So,' prompted Aisha. 'Is it love?'

'I think it is,' she said, smiling at the flutter in her heart as she admitted it. 'I think I've fallen in love with Rashid.'

'So here you all are.'

Tora spun around at Zoltan's voice, humiliated enough that he must have overheard her words, but no, it was worse than that, because there was Rashid, right beside him, and his eyes were as cold as the slabs of marble that lined the floor. She shivered from their impact as Zoltan leaned down and kissed his wife while the twins shrieked and came running to greet their father.

Tora looked away, busied herself looking anywhere but at Rashid and at those damning eyes.

Why would he be so angry, even if he'd overheard her? How could a few innocent words banish what they'd shared last night?

'Have you had a good day?' Zoltan asked, still leaning over his wife, their faces mere inches apart. That was love right there, thought Tora. Love in abundance.

'The best,' Aisha replied, aiming a conspiratorial smile towards Tora. 'Just wait till I tell you.'

And a glance towards Rashid saw his eyes still locked on her, so cold and hard that she was almost sure she must have imagined last night in her dreams.

And if there was any love between her and Rashid, right now, it was one-sided. He stood in the terrace doorway looking as rigid and unmoving as if he'd been planted there and sent down roots.

'Our plane is ready,' Zoltan told his wife.

'Already we must go?' she said, smiling sadly in Tora's direction. 'It's been so good to be here. So good to meet you.' And she pulled Tora into a hug that felt bittersweet, because whatever her hopes and dreams, given the dark look on Rashid's face, she had an uneasy feeling in her stomach that she would never see Aisha or the other desert wives again.

Tora went to Atiyah's cradle, ready to take her inside, when Rashid suddenly stepped forward in her path. 'No. Leave her. I will take my sister.'

And Tora's gut clenched at the tone in his voice. Something was seriously wrong.

* * *

Aisha and Zoltan and the children were gone and Rashid must have spirited Atiyah off somewhere because she—along with Yousra—hadn't made an appearance since she'd returned to the suite.

But what had she done between this morning and this afternoon to deserve such a cold-shouldering? Other than to be overheard saying that she loved him?

Even if she hadn't intended blurting it out as she had, was that so serious a crime?

She sat down on the sofa and switched on her tablet. Maybe there would be some good news waiting for her, something to lighten this cloud of impending doom that she'd sensed in Rashid's cold eyes.

There was an email from her cousin she groaned at but ignored—no doubt Matt wondering where the money was—because there was one from Sally that demanded her attention—one that had the subject header Prayers needed!

Feeling sick to the stomach, she opened it up and read its contents as the cloud of impending doom circling above her head rained its poison down on her.

Oh, my God—please, God, no!

And the news was so awful, so devastating, that she had to tell someone, had to share this burden. She ran to her door and pulled it open, confused when she found two palace guards waiting outside, blocking her exit. She swept tears from her cheeks as she asked, 'What are you doing here?'

'By order of the Emir,' one proclaimed, 'you must remain where you are. You are now a prisoner of Qajaran.'

CHAPTER FIFTEEN

TORA STOOD IN the centre of her suite, too uptight to sit, too frozen by fear to move. There were guards on the terrace, too, and behind the interconnecting door to Rashid's suite. Guards everywhere, but why? On a day where it was sweltering outside, inside she felt chilled to the core.

Tora clutched at her goosebumped arms, her face still streaked with tears she'd shed in protest and shock at being arrested in a palace halfway around the world from her home.

A palace where nobody would ever find her, even if they knew where to come looking. And the vulnerability of her situation hit her. A lone woman, a long way from home, at the mercy of a man she'd thought she was beginning to understand—beginning to love.

Fool!

But what had she done to deserve being treated this way?

Nothing! She was sure of it.

She sniffed. She would make sure she told Rashid the same too.

A guard marched across the terrace in front of her windows. 'I want to see Rashid!' she called out.

The guard didn't so much as twitch in response, just kept right on marching as if she hadn't spoken.

'I *demand* to see the Emir!'

Tora waited, her heart thumping so loud in her chest, but nothing changed. Nobody was listening.

Nobody cared.

And her grief and pain and confusion coiled together inside her like the smoke from a candle flame that had been extinguished, acrid and swirling, until a new emotion rose out of it.

Fury.

It turned her shock to resolve and her tears to ice, setting her jaw to aching tight and her fingernails clawing into her arms. So the guard wouldn't tell Rashid she wanted to see him. So he wanted to make her wait. Well, let him. Because when he eventually arrived, she would be ready for him.

There was a thunder cloud hanging over him. Dark and threatening, it weighed heavily down upon him, blackening his world and poisoning his mood.

Tora.

He had not expected to be betrayed by her. Maybe at first he would have thought it possible. A woman picked up in a bar who coolly demanded a quarter of a million dollars when asked to name a price—why wouldn't he expect a woman like that to want to take advantage of the situation?

But that would have been at first.

Because since that time she'd worked her way into his life and under his skin. Floating on the air as she seemed to do in her silk robes, displaying an insight into economic and social matters he hadn't expected, telling him that he was strong.

And to top it all off, giving herself to him like a coronation gift, as if she were offering water to a man who'd been in the desert too long.

All the while it seemed she'd been scheming.

All the while waiting.

Well, now she could wait in her apartments. By the time he got to her, she would be a pathetic mess. She would apologise—profusely and with tears—and beg for his forgiveness, but there would be none. He would not fall for her ways again.

Why the hell was he waiting? He would tell her now. He stormed to his feet, upsetting a low table, and his anger went ballistic.

It was high time he told her.

Her door was flung open, and Tora held her breath. Rashid. At last!

He nodded to the guard who pulled the door shut, and then he looked grim-faced to where she stood in the middle of her room, her arms still crossed, her chin still high.

'What the hell is going on?' she demanded.

A dark eyebrow arched as he moved slowly towards her, and she could tell that if he had a shred of remorse for putting her in this situation, she couldn't see it anywhere in his stormy blue eyes. They were empty of anything but cold, hard resentment.

'Why, Sheikha, do you not like your new living arrangements? All this space to yourself, I see, and so much privacy. Who could ask for more? But if you have a complaint, there are stone cells in the floors below the palace, I believe, if these rooms are not to your satisfaction.'

Her chin ratcheted up a notch higher. 'Why am I prisoner here? What have I done?' Her voice broke on the last word and then her strength and resolve gave way. 'Rashid,' she appealed, taking a step closer even though the very air felt like bars between them. 'What is happening?'

He snorted. 'Didn't I tell you to be careful what you sent using the palace Internet? Didn't I warn you?'

He made no sense. She hadn't plastered anything up on social media. She hadn't sent anything she shouldn't.

'But then,' he continued, 'why would you listen to me? Blood *is* thicker than water, after all.'

'What?'

'Oh, come now, Sheikha, surely you can't have forgotten this little gem? *"The dollar signs in my eyes lit up too!"* Or maybe this one will strike a chord: *"keep listening for the ka-ching".*'

And like a sledgehammer it hit her. The email she'd sent to Matt. The nonsense email to get him excited and frothing at the mouth with anticipation.

'You read my emails? How dare you? That was private.'

'What did you think I meant when I warned you? Of course the palace has to monitor communication coming in and out. Did you think your little missive to your cousin would go unnoticed—a cousin you are supposedly finished with now?'

'I *am* finished with him.'

'What, after you sent him the two hundred and fifty thousand dollars, or will that be after the five hundred thousand you have promised him next?'

'What? I didn't send that money to Matt—it went to a solicitor who—' And with a sickening thud, she realised just who she'd sent the funds through—the very solicitor Matt had instructed to draw up the documents complete with the small print she'd been too naive to read and so signed her inheritance over to him. And if Matt was in some kind of financial trouble, then, chances were…

'Let me finish your sentence.' Rashid confirmed it for her. 'It went to a solicitor who is now being investigated, along with your beloved cousin, for misappropriation of funds.'

Tora squeezed her eyes shut, reeling at her naivety, cursing the rush she'd been in that she'd trusted a colleague of Matt's. What if that money, too, had been lost?

But surely Rashid couldn't believe that she'd sent the money to Matt. 'I didn't know about the charges. I didn't know any of that. Matt gave me his solicitor's name because he was dealing with my parents' estate. But the money wasn't for him. That went—'

'Then why did you tell him not to worry about it?'

'No. Listen,' she said, putting out her hands in supplication, 'you're confusing two different things. Matt cheated me out of my inheritance from my parents' estate—that was the two hundred and fifty thousand he was talking about. When he asked for more, I thought I'd send him a taste of his own medicine. What I sent him was rubbish, Rashid, to lure him in and make him think I'd stumbled on a fortune and was going to share it with him. You have to believe me.'

'Two hundred and fifty thousand dollars,' Rashid said, ignoring her explanation, 'which just *happens* to be the same amount of money you asked for and got.'

'Yes, because I had promised it elsewhere and I needed it as quickly as possible.'

'Why? What was so urgent that you were so desperate to get the money then?'

'Because Sally's husband has cancer and they needed the funds to get him to a cancer clinic in Germany. And I'd promised to loan them the money from my inheritance because they'd already mortgaged their house and they'd exhausted every other means. That's where your precious two hundred and fifty thousand dollars went, and Steve's there now lying in that clinic, fighting for his life and close to death and now it looks like everything I've done has been for nothing.'

Her vision blurred and swam and she dropped her face to the floor. She didn't know when she'd started crying, she hadn't been aware of the tears falling, but now there was no stopping the torrent coursing down her face. Because if Steve died, everything would have been for nothing.

The sound of a clap forced her head up. Followed by another. A slow clap coming from Rashid that matched the slow pace of his feet as he drew closer to where she had fallen. 'Bravo, Ms Burgess, that was an award-winning performance. It had pathos, melodrama, even tears. Unfortunately some of us recognise that was all it was—an act. I didn't see you looking too upset last night when you were coming apart in my bed. I didn't see any tears fall then.'

She sniffed. 'Sally wrote this morning with the news.'

'Oh, this morning. How convenient.'

'Steve is dying. It's the truth!'

'I don't think you'd recognise the truth if it slapped you in the face. You climbed aboard that royal jet and ever since then you've been scheming to make it worthwhile to you and your crooked cousin. You played it well. Exceptionally well. One time a siren, another a virgin Madonna, you kept ducking and weaving and spinning your web of lies so well that you almost had me convinced that you were special, that there might even be a future for us beyond this short-term deal.'

His lip curled. 'What a fool I've been.' His cold dark eyes were filled with abhorrence as they raked over her, all but scraping her skin with their intensity. 'And I must be a fool because I thought—I actually thought…' He shook his head. 'A fool. You will stay here in your rooms until it is time to send you home.'

'Rashid,' she begged as he turned to leave, because in his words was a tiny kernel, a glimmer of hope, if she could only prove to him that she was telling the truth. 'Please, I beg of you…'

His feet paused at the door. 'What?'

'There is one thing you should know. One thing you have to believe.'

'Well?'

She licked her lips, her heartbeat frantic as she prepared to lay it on the line and bare herself to him utterly. 'I couldn't do the things you say. I would never betray you. Because... Because, I love you.'

He laughed, the sound cold and jagged as it echoed around her room, until she felt as if her heart had been sliced apart. 'Nice try.'

And then he was gone.

She threw herself down onto her bed and let herself weep in great heaving sobs—because she'd only ever married Rashid to secure the funds for Steve's treatment and, somewhere along the line, she'd fallen in love with a despot in the process, a despot who'd laughed at her when she'd bared her soul to him.

And now Steve was fighting for his life in a German clinic and it had all been so pointless.

It had all been for nothing.

And she hated the man who had done this to her with all her heart.

The man she'd thought she had loved.

She loved him. Talk about desperate. As if he'd believe that. As if she'd thought it would excuse what she'd done.

Atiyah was crying when he returned to his rooms and the black cloud above his head thundered and roared.

'She won't stop,' a tearful Yousra said. 'She wants Tora.'

'Give her to me!' he demanded, and the young woman's eyes opened wide with surprise, but still she handed the bundle over. He juggled the unfamiliar weight, the arms and legs working like little pistons, the face screwed up and red, and he caught a flailing arm with one finger and tucked her in close to his chest as he tried to remember how Tora had told him to try to calm her. 'Atiyah,' he said, trying to stop the storm cloud hanging over him from making him shout over her screams, 'Calm down. Calm down.'

He walked with her one way, he walked back the other, but there was no settling her. 'Atiyah,' he said, 'little sister, you must stop this.' And on impulse, when he could not think of anything else that might help, he started humming the tune, the lullaby he'd heard Tora sing to her, the lullaby that had been dredged up from the depths of his memories. And eventually, somewhere along the line, the notes filtered through to the tiny infant and Atiyah's cries became more brief, staccato bursts between the listening moments, bursts that became hiccups. Until finally she fell silent apart from a low whimpering sound.

'Is she asleep?' Yousra whispered in awe. And he shook his head as he sang that soft lullaby, because, while her face had unscrunched, she was wide awake and staring up at him, a frown knitting her brow as she focused intently on his face, almost as if she recognised him.

He stared back at her, equally fascinated until he came to the end of the song and he smiled, and the little girl wiggled in his arms and smiled right back.

And his world turned on its axis and he knew it would never be the same.

'Like the world lights up and wraps you in love.' Tora had said that.

And yet he should have known that, because that was exactly how he'd felt when Tora had smiled at him. When she'd come apart in his arms. When he'd seen tears in her proud eyes at his coronation.

Those tears... Had she been scheming even then? How could she have known he'd turn to her in that moment? How could she have faked those tears? Tora had been the one who had got him through the coronation. Knowing she was there had been his one constant. Having her in his corner had lent him strength and made him wonder if their relationship could not be more permanent.

She'd made his duty more possible, more bearable, more palatable.

She'd made him wish she could stay by his side for ever.

She'd said she'd never betray him.

She'd said she loved him.

Oh, God, and arresting her was how he repaid her? He'd been so angry, had felt so betrayed, so manipulated, as if he'd been played for a fool from the start.

And the rank, horrible feeling in his gut told him that they had got things very wrong, and that he'd been the fool all along, he hadn't needed anyone to play him.

He had to find the truth—find the story behind the email to her cousin—there had to be proof. He owed her that much. There was an email this morning, she'd said, saying her friend was dying. It would be easy enough to check. Surely there would be something to prove or disprove her story one way or another. 'Yousra,' he said, the child still held close in his arms. 'Get me Kareem.'

An hour later, he had what he needed. A small stack of printed emails. 'Innocuous,' Kareem had labelled them. 'There was no mention of any amount of money.'

And Rashid believed him. Innocuous by themselves, but together with her story they painted a different picture... You're a lifesaver... Next stop, Germany! And the kick to the heart he deserved with the subject header on the email that had come overnight—Prayers needed!—and he knew with an icy cold rush down his spine that she'd been telling the truth.

And he dropped his head into his hands.

What the hell had he done?

And how was he ever to make amends?

CHAPTER SIXTEEN

TORA'S HEAD JERKED up from her pillow when she heard the sound of the door opening. For a moment she hoped it was Rashid so she could tell him exactly what she thought of him. She got out of bed and ran her fingers over her cheeks. Her tears had dried in the heat of her growing anger, but her skin felt tight, as if it were crusted with salt.

But it wasn't Rashid returning, but two young women, smiling shyly and holding baskets. They bid her to sit down and fed her honey tea while they brought out warm towels to wash her face and hands, and a hairbrush to brush her hair. There was even a freshly laundered gown to wear, and Tora didn't know what it meant but it was so blissful to clean the salt from her skin that she went along with it.

'Come with me, Sheikha Victoria,' the guard said, when she was feeling refreshed and human again and the women had vanished.

'What's going on?' she asked. 'Where are you taking me?' But he said nothing, just turned and led the way out.

Only one guard, she thought as she followed him. There had been four outside her doors and now only one—what did that mean?

'Where is the Emir?' she asked, but the man in front of her said nothing as he strode ahead of her through the long corridors and past the accumulated treasures of millennia and out the front doors of the palace and into an inky night.

A car idled quietly, its lights on low beam.

And there was Kareem, standing there, watching her approach. He bowed low, his hand on his chest.

'Sheikha,' he said. 'I have done you a great disservice. Please forgive me.'

And she guessed it was Kareem who had been alerted to her email to Matt and who had then alerted Rashid.

'It doesn't matter, Kareem. It was never meant to be. Can you tell me what is happening?'

'You are leaving,' he said, and, as if to support his words, her suitcase was delivered to the top of the steps. She swallowed.

'Now?' she said, caught between relief and a pang of regret for all she'd leave behind. The soft velvet night sky. Atiyah. Her heart. 'Already?'

'Already. His Excellency insisted.'

'Where is Rashid?'

'Waiting at the plane. He thought you would be happier travelling to the airport without him.'

Coward, she thought, but it was an accusation tinged with sadness. So she was to be seen off the premises like an employee who had been dismissed, her possessions hastily flung together, no chance to say goodbye to those she wished to? There was a lump in her throat the size and shape of a small child. 'You'll give Atiyah a hug for me?' she said, trying to push back on the sting of tears, and Kareem solemnly nodded.

She hauled in a breath, casting a look over her shoulder at the amazing fairy-tale palace that wasn't, before she turned back to Kareem and said with false brightness, 'Then let's go.'

He saw the headlights approach from where he stood at the foot of the stairs and felt sick to the stomach. She was leaving. Well, she'd always been going to leave, she was just leaving a little earlier, that was all.

And how could he not let her go? How could he keep her here as his prisoner and punish her for his own blind stupidity? How could he expect her to forgive him?

The car drew alongside the plane, its engines starting to whine, pulling up so the back door lined up with the red carpet that had been rolled out waiting for it, and Kareem emerged and offered his hand to the other passenger. Rashid swallowed.

Tora.

Looking like a goddess. Wearing the robe of orange and yellow she'd worn that day when they'd toured Malik's palaces. Such a few days ago and yet it seemed like a lifetime, so much had happened, so much had been felt. He saw her thank Kareem as he handed her out and retrieved her suitcase and then she glanced up and her eyes snagged on his. She looked away at her feet, and his heart snapped in two.

Well, what did he expect? It was no more than he deserved. She'd told him she loved him and he'd flung that love back in her face with a few choice insults besides. Call himself an Emir? A ruler of men? He couldn't even rule his own heart and mind. And if he couldn't make them act in consensus, how was he supposed to manage a country?

As he might have, with this woman by his side. He might have believed it was possible.

'Tora,' he said as she drew closer.

She angled her head, her eyes sharp like daggers, even if their edges seemed a little dulled with disappointment. 'Seeing me off the premises, Rashid? Making sure I don't escape with the silverware.' She held her arms out. 'Do you need to frisk me to make sure I haven't run off with any of Qajaran's treasures to pawn when I get home?'

He sucked in air that smelt of aviation fuel. He deserved that. 'I was wrong,' he said. 'And in so many ways, and I know I can never apologise for all the wrongs I have done to you. But please believe me when I say I am truly sorry for the hurt I have done to you.'

Her lips pressed tightly together. 'Well, I guess that's all right, then. So, what about my divorce?'

'You will be notified when it is finalised.'

He saw her hesitate. 'What will become of Atiyah now?'

And it struck him that even in the midst of her own private hell, she was worried about his sister. His sister, for whom Tora had cared more and been more loving. God, he'd been a fool!

'She will be fine. She smiled at me tonight.'

'She did?' And Tora smiled, too, for a moment, until she remembered why she was here. 'Excellent,' she said before her teeth found her lip, and she looked up at the stairs, putting one hand on the rail. 'I'm looking forward to being back in Sydney.'

'Tora,' he said, stopping her from taking that first step just yet, 'once upon a time, you said you loved me. Did you mean it?'

She turned her head to the velvet sky and the wide belt of stars that was more clearly visible now they were out of the city precinct. 'I thought I did. And then I was just so angry with you, that it blocked everything out. I hated you for what you had done and what you had believed of me. After everything we had been through. I was so angry.'

He closed his eyes. 'And now?'

'Now I'm just sad for what could have been.'

And he couldn't let her go without telling her. 'I know it's too late, but I am a fool where love is concerned, but I want you to know that there was love between us. There is love that I feel for you.'

She swallowed back on a sob. So good of him to tell her that now, when he was putting her on a plane to leave. 'Do you call it love to judge someone as guilty before you even ask them for the truth? Do you call it love to treat that person like a criminal? Because if you do, you have a very warped idea of love.'

'Tora, I am so sorry. I didn't want to believe it was true, but you said you had nothing to do with your cousin, and there was evidence you'd spoken to him just recently, and I felt betrayed and deceived and it was like my father all over again, except this time it was you, and that felt a hundred times worse.'

She stared at him. 'My darling cousin stole my inheritance. All the money from my parents' estate. All the money I'd promised Sally and Steve. I'd just come from a meeting with him to tell me the happy news that all the money was gone. Why do you think I was so angry that night in the bar?'

He hung his head. 'God, I'm a fool. I will never make up to you the wrongs I have done you.'

'No,' she said. 'I don't believe you will. Goodbye, Rashid.' And she turned and fled up the stairs into the plane, knowing she had to get into the safety of the cabin before she lost it completely. Knowing she had to escape while she had the chance, while she still had one last shred of dignity intact, even if her heart lay broken into tiny pieces.

Something was wrong. Tora blinked into wakefulness after a tortured sleep. 'We're coming in to land,' the flight attendant said.

'Already?' said Tora, knowing she couldn't possibly have slept for that long.

'Yes,' said the attendant, clearing away cups and plates. 'If you look outside your window, you'll see the lights of Cologne ahead.'

Cologne?

'We're landing in Germany?'

'But of course,' said the attendant. 'Didn't you know?'

* * *

Sally hugged her friend so tight when Tora reached the hospital that she thought she might snap in two but she didn't mind one little bit. 'I couldn't believe it when I heard you were coming. And now you're here!' And she hugged her again.

'How's Steve?' Tora asked, hoping above hope that Sally's happiness wasn't solely down to her arrival.

Sally smiled over clenched teeth, a tentative smile of optimism. 'We thought it was the end—it looked like the end—and the doctors suggested trying something experimental but it was so expensive and I couldn't give them the go ahead, but then some anonymous benefactor contacted the clinic just last night and asked them to pull out all stops.' She shook her head. 'You wouldn't believe the difference in him in just a few hours. It's a miracle,' she said, and fell into her friend's arms again.

Anonymous benefactor?

Tora had a clue she knew exactly who it was and why he'd done it. And a broken heart made its first tentative steps to heal and love again.

She was punch drunk when she wrote the email. High on life and one life in particular, who was looking more human every day as he made a steady recovery. High on the happiness that her friend radiated constantly.

She hit Send and turned off her tablet and sat back on the lounge chair of the tiny flat she shared with Sally, feeling the rapid beating of her heart.

Well, it was out there. Now all she could do was wait.

CHAPTER SEVENTEEN

THERE WAS A glow coming from the courtyard, coming from inside the Pavilion of Mahabbah. And when a smiling Kareem led her inside, she could see why. The pavilion was lit with a thousand candles, their flames flickering and dancing in the night breeze, and for a moment as Kareem disappeared there was just the croak and plop of frogs amongst the lily pads and the haunting cries of the peacocks as she took it all in.

And then there were footsteps, and he was standing there in the doorway, Rashid—her Rashid—his dark features and golden skin standing out in his snowy white robes. So handsome. So darkly beautiful.

'Tora,' he said, blinking as if she were some kind of vision. 'But how—?'

'Kareem helped me.'

'But you came back,' he said, as if he couldn't believe it, his eyes full of wonder as his eyes drank her in.

'How could I not come back?'

'But after everything I did, after all the wrongs I did you.'

'You did some right. You helped Sally and Steve when they had nowhere else to turn to. You did a good thing. Steve's doing well. It's a miracle and we all have you to thank.'

'What else could I do? I had to do something.'

'It was a good thing you did. A generous thing. Thank you.'

'Thank you for coming to tell me that.' He gave a small sigh, a brief smile. He was a man at a loss. 'Did you want to see Atiyah? She's sleeping now, but you can stay a little while?'

'I'd love to see her.'

'That's good.' He looked around as if for Kareem, frowning as he seemed to notice for the first time the candles and the decorations. 'I imagine Kareem's organised a suite for you?'

'Rashid.'

'What?'

'There's another reason I came.'

His eyes grew wide. 'What?'

'When I left here, I wanted to hate you. You made that harder with what you did for Sally and Steve—'

'That doesn't make up for what I did.'

'I know. But while I sat there supporting Sally, I had time to think. And I thought about all the time that I watched you struggle with responsibilities that had been thrust upon you, struggle with the demands and needs of a tiny child you'd never asked for from a father who'd cast you into the world alone, even if to protect you—I thought about all that time, and how I could see you were a good man.'

'I was not good to you.'

'Not then, it's true, but what man would act differently when he'd been subject to the turmoil of your life, when he'd felt betrayed by the most important of people, his own father? How could he trust anyone ever again?'

'I should have trusted you.'

She put a finger to his lips to silence him. 'What's done is done. Can't we draw a line under what happened in the past? Can't we start anew?'

She saw hope swirling in the deep blue depths of his eyes. 'What are you saying?'

'I'm saying that, once upon a time, you hinted that you loved me, at least a little. I'm asking if you still do, and if you would do me the honour of marrying me, for real this time.'

'Marry you?'

'Yes. Because I love you, Rashid, for better or for worse. But I hope it's for ever.'

'Yes!' he cried as he picked her up in his arms and spun her around. 'A thousand times yes. I love you so much, Tora,' Rashid said, his lips hovering over hers. 'You have turned my life from a desert into an oasis. You have given life where there should be none. I owe you everything. And I will love you to my dying day.'

Tora smiled beneath his lips. 'As I will love you, Rashid. Aisha told me you desert brothers don't fall easily, but you fall hard.'

'I never expected to fall in love. I didn't think it was possible. But now I can't imagine a day in my life without you being in it.'

'That's good,' she said, 'because I don't plan on going anywhere without you.'

'You'll never have to, ever again.'

And they made love there that night, in the Pavilion of Mahabbah, the pavilion of love, the first night in all their nights of for ever.

EPILOGUE

THEY WERE MARRIED for the second time in front of the iconic sails of the Sydney Opera House alongside the sparkling waters of the harbour on which pleasure craft made the most of a perfect sunny day. Overlooking it all sat the magnificent backdrop of the Sydney Harbour Bridge.

The bridal procession was strikingly original, a confection of sheer joy, and headed by the combined children of the desert brothers and their wives strewing rose petals and jasmine flowers, the older children holding the hands of the younger ones and guiding them back to the red carpet when they strayed off course or got distracted, to the delight of all the assembled. Behind them came the three stunning matrons of honour wearing gowns in glorious jewel colours, ruby, emerald and sapphire, the Sheikha Aisha and Princess Marina and the blonde, blue-eyed Amber.

And last came Tora, wearing a sleeveless gown of golden silk ruched over her breasts and hips with a sweeping train and with her hair piled high and studded with champagne-coloured pearls and who was walked along the foreshore to meet her groom by the three best men, Zoltan, Bahir and Kadar.

At the very front stood Rashid, waiting as each group made its way to him, waiting impatiently for the moment he would be joined by his glowing bride. Under Qajarese law, he had been a married man for six months, and Tora a married woman. Six months during which the state of Qajaran had grown up, a period full of the necessary aches and pains of change but the benefits were already there, the confidence of the economy picking up, the lacklustre tourism sector finally getting off the ground.

Six months during which he had grown up and changed and become the ruler Qajaran needed, but only, he knew, because this woman had been by his side every step of the way.

Half a year they had been together, but today was the start of their real marriage, he knew. Today what had begun as a hastily arranged marriage of convenience would become a marriage of necessity, a marriage of free choice, a marriage to last until the end of days.

He smiled at the children as they made their way closer, saw Yousra in the throng holding a growing Atiyah in her frothy white dress, a white ribbon tying up her black curls, and he knew life was good.

The three brides of his brothers, their beautiful faces beaming, stepped to his left. How was it possible for his brothers to find such remarkable women, each and every one of them, and yet to leave the pearl of the collection for him? How lucky was he?

She was drawing closer, his brothers cutting in on each other to take turns on her arms. She was laughing at something one of them said and Rashid was struck by her beauty and her joy. She was radiant. She looked up then, and the laughter died on her lips as their eyes locked. He saw the cognac-coloured eyes darken with smouldering need and the smile that she gave just to him and his heart swelled.

And then she was there before him and his three desert brothers lifted her hand to place in his, before, with a slap to his back, they peeled away to stand on his right.

'You look beautiful,' he said softly. 'I love you.'

'As I love you,' she said, unable to stop the two tears of joy that squeezed unbidden from her eyes. 'For ever.'

It was a fairy tale, it occurred to Tora in that moment as she looked up into the dark gaze of the man she loved. A tale of trials and tribulations decorated with palaces and pavilions, peacocks and fountains. A tale of the exotic. And yet a tale of the most basic human needs.

Like life.

She glanced towards her friend Sally where she sat beaming alongside Steve in his wheelchair—Steve, who was growing stronger by the day. Sally blew her a kiss and Tora smiled back, before looking up to the sky and feeling her mother and father soaring in the heights and beaming down upon her on her proudest day. They were here, she knew, and it was good.

Even better when she felt Rashid's lips on her cheek. 'You have made me the happiest man in the world,' he whispered, and she wondered just how much joy it was possible to feel before one exploded with it.

For together they had conquered the tests put before them, had overcome their own fears and confronted their own feelings, and as their reward they had won the greatest prize of all. Had earned the greatest gift of all, for even life itself was worthless without it.

Love.

'Dearly beloved,' the celebrant began then as the gulls wheeled in the sky above and the passing ferry drivers tooted their horns in celebration, 'we are gathered here today for this very special Christmas wedding...'

* * * * *

_ST19